# SHATTERED *Sun*

STONE BAY SERIES

BOOK ONE

USA TODAY BESTSELLING AUTHOR

# PERSEPHONE AUTUMN

BETWEEN WORDS PUBLISHING LLC

# SHATTERED *Sun*

STONE BAY SERIES

BOOK ONE

USA TODAY BESTSELLING AUTHOR

# PERSEPHONE AUTUMN

BETWEEN WORDS PUBLISHING LLC

**Shattered Sun**



ISBN: 978-1-951477-75-2 (Ebook)

ISBN: 978-1-951477-76-9 (Paperback)

ISBN: 978-1-951477-77-6 (Hardcover)

Editor: Ellie McLove | My Brother's Editor

Proofreader: My Brother's Editor

Cover Design: Abigail Davies | Pink Elephant Designs

*This is for all my bookish peeps. The ones that stick with me no matter what. I love you. I'm grateful for you. And I don't know where I'd be without you.*

# BOOKS BY PERSEPHONE AUTUMN

**<u>Lake Lavender Series</u>**

Depths Awakened

One Night Forsaken

Every Thought Taken

**<u>Devotion Series</u>**

Distorted Devotion

Undying Devotion

Beloved Devotion

Darkest Devotion

Sweetest Devotion

**<u>Bay Area Duet Series</u>**

<u>Click Duet</u>

Through the Lens

Time Exposure

<u>Inked Duet</u>

Fine Line

Love Buzz

<u>Insomniac Duet</u>

Restless Night

A Love So Bright

<u>Artist Duet</u>

Blank Canvas

Abstract Passion


<u>Novellas</u>

Reese

Penny


**<u>Stone Bay Series</u>**

Broken Sky—Prequel

Shattered Sun

Fractured Night


**<u>Standalone Romance Novels</u>**

Sweet Tooth

Transcendental


**<u>Poetry Collections</u>**

Ink Veins

Broken Metronome

Slipping From Existence

Poisonous Heart

Beneath Wildflowers


PUBLISHED UNDER P. AUTUMN

**<u>Standalone Non-Romance Novels</u>**

By Dawn

# CONTENTS

# PROLOGUE

## KIRSTEN

*Past—Two Years Ago*

Skylar slides another shot glass in front of me and Delilah, and I groan as I stare down at the clear liquid filled to the rim. A silent promise to make the night fun and the morning hell.

By no means am I a lightweight. I've done my fair share of partying before legally allowed. But I tend to stick with beer, the occasional fruity cocktail, and Long Island Iced Tea. Undiluted hard liquor, though… not really my thing. I learned that lesson the hard way at my first high school party and vowed to never do shots again.

Yet here I am, reaching for the saltshaker and contradicting the one drinking rule I carved in stone.

*One time, Kirsten. For Skylar.*

My best friend owes me after this. Big time. And I'll be sure to remind her tomorrow, when our heads are clear and the world wobbles less.

Making a loose fist, I lift my hand to my mouth and lick the web near my thumb. Salt in my other hand, I shake it over the damp skin a couple times before passing it down the line. Skylar and Delilah mirror the action with a touch more enthusiasm. Their eagerness to liven the evening further is the ass kick I didn't know I needed.

Tonight isn't about me and what *I* want. Tonight is about Skylar and what *she* wants.

No way in hell will I ruin her night.

Skylar lays a lime wedge on a napkin and slides it in my direction, then does the same for Delilah. Lifting her shot glass high, she announces loud enough for half of Dalton's to hear, "Happy twenty-first birthday to the hottest bitch in Stone Bay. Me."

My eyes widen as the bar patrons hoot and holler. Skylar licks the salt from her hand, shoots back the tequila, then brings the lime to her lips and sucks. Meanwhile, Delilah and I sit shell-shocked on our stools. It's not until Skylar elbows us that we take our shots.

Skylar isn't the most outgoing person in public. Hell, the level of peer pressure it took to get her in my favorite little black dress tonight was excruciating. Behind closed doors and in the company of friends and family is where she tends to dominate the room. But her commanding the attention of a bar full of people… she would never do that sober.

And here I thought I was the only drunk one in our group.

*Wrong.*

"I'm tapping out," I tell them, slashing a hand across the front of my throat for emphasis.

"No," Skylar whines.

"Drinks, Sky. I'm tapping out on drinks." I pat her thigh beneath the bar top. "Not with the night. It's too early to go home."

A lazy smile lifts the corners of her mouth as she leans into me and rests her head on my shoulder. "I love you, K. You're the bestest."

"Hey," Delilah complains, her voice a touch playful.

Skylar bolts up and reaches for Delilah. "You're the bestest, too. You know I love you, Dee Dee." She constricts Delilah in a fierce hug. "I can love you and her." A finger jabs in my direction. "You can both be my bestest friends, forever and ever."

With a shake of my head, I laugh and take Skylar's hand, lowering it. "Love you, Sky." I squeeze her hand, then release it. "We should probably switch to something non-alcoholic for a bit."

On a huff, she tips her head back and gives a stiff nod. "Yeah. Probably a good idea.

The bartender stops in front of us, takes our empty glasses, and wipes down the bar. "How's it going, ladies?" Her eyes roam over Skylar, a smirk tipping up one corner of her mouth as she tries and fails to hide her amusement.

"A round of water, please."

The bartender nods, grabs three large glasses, loads them with ice, and fills them with water.

"And one Coke," I add as she sets each water glass on a coaster in front of us.

"You got it." She repeats the process, pressing a different button on the drink gun, filling the glass with Coke. "Anything else?" she asks as she places a new coaster down, then my drink.

I glance at Skylar as she drinks water through way too many cocktail straws and shake my head. "Think we're good for now."

Tapping the bar top, she winks, then wanders down the line to refill beer glasses.

Over the next hour, we sip our drinks and move to a high-top near the dance floor. Several patrons stop by the table and wish Skylar happy birthday, offer to buy her a drink or ask her on a date. The more water she drinks, the more sober she becomes, the more I watch her lean away from the attention. Not all of it. A few guys have managed to weasel their way into sitting with us. They seem nice enough. Then again, my common sense meter switched off a couple hours ago.

"Let's dance," Skylar suggests as she pushes away from the table and stands.

Two of the guys hop off their stools and sandwich Skylar between them. "We'll dance with you, birthday girl."

I wince as I watch them touch her hips and shoulders. *This just got ten times more uncomfortable.*

Oblivious to their intentions, Skylar pushes out her lips and shakes her head. "No, I want to dance with my friends." Skylar twists out of their holds and reaches out a hand for me and Delilah. "Please," she says, dragging out the word like a greedy child.

I love dancing. Love shoving money in the jukebox, choosing enough songs to play for an hour or two, then getting lost in the music. Skylar, on the other hand, isn't keen on dancing. At least not in huge public crowds.

But it's her birthday, and she is still very intoxicated.

Who am I to deny her? Especially on *her* day.

I hop off my stool and take her outstretched hand. Delilah does the same, taking her other hand.

Skylar glances over her shoulder and gives the guys a finger wave. "Thanks for hanging out with us. It was fun." Then she blows them a kiss.

I groan. "Don't goad them any further."

Delilah chuckles. "Makes no difference to me. Their chance remains the same. Nil."

Weaving between the small crowd on the small dance floor, we find a small opening, throw our arms up, and start dancing to the sultry beat of a song I don't know. For a moment, I get lost in the song. Forget about everything else except this night with my two closest friends.

The song transitions to a pop number. We continue to dance, but I shift closer to Delilah. "They may have no chance with you"—I glance back at the table, one of the guys no longer there—"but they don't know that. They don't know you prefer the glove over the bat."

*Thwack.*

"Ow!" I rub my upper arm. "No need to hit."

"Then don't be crude." Delilah imperceptibly shakes her head. "Say I only date women. Call me a lesbian." Her brows tug together. "But don't use baseball equipment euphemisms. Or any other weird alternatives. Just don't."

"Got it." My lips curve into an apologetic smile. "Won't happen again."

"Thank you," she says softly.

When the current song ends, I tap Skylar on the shoulder. She spins around, brows raised in question. I lift my hand and make a tipping motion toward my mouth, then throw a thumb over my shoulder. She nods, then follows me back to the table with Delilah in tow.

The three guys from earlier are nowhere to be seen. Probably found new *prospects* for the evening. Can't say I blame them. I drain the last of my Coke, then switch to water. As Skylar drinks the last of her water, she sways in place.

"Doing okay, birthday girl?" I ask. This is the first time our trio has been publicly intoxicated. The initial excitement is long gone. The thrill of ordering drink after drink and being allowed to do so has faded. At least, tonight it has.

"Think I need to lie down. Or maybe curl into the corner of the couch and watch a documentary."

Delilah and I chuckle. Skylar and her damn documentaries.

Not sure how she stomachs watching those things. Serial killers and creepy as hell people doing fucked up shit to strangers. She watches them as if they soothe her like nature documentaries do most other people. Sometimes I question whether or not I should be concerned. So long as *she* doesn't go psycho on us, it's all good.

I step into her space, toy with her fiery curls, then wrap her in my arms. "Go home. Watch your shows. Drink more water."

When I step out of the embrace, her eyes lazily trail up to mine. A ridge forms between her brows. "Are you staying?"

I glance past Skylar to Delilah, and she mouths, *"I got her. You stay."*

With a subtle nod, I meet Skylar's gaze again. "For a couple more songs. I'll be right behind you."

Delilah opens the rideshare app on her phone and requests a ride. Skylar rises from her stool, her hand quickly gripping the table to steady herself.

"Whoa!" Delilah wraps an arm around Skylar's shoulders. "Easy now." With measured steps, they head toward the door. "The car should be here in a few minutes." Delilah glances over her shoulder, her eyes more sober than I feel. "You good?"

"Yeah." I nod. "Probably leave in twenty."

"See you at home," she says, then disappears in the thickening crowd.

Dalton's is always the place to be in Stone Bay, especially on Friday and Saturday nights. Though it's busy once the sun sets, the real crowd doesn't show until after ten. Between ten and two, Dalton's is packed with townies and tourists alike and definitely hits max capacity.

I down the last of my water and return to the dance floor. Closing my eyes, I move to the music and get lost in the sea of bodies. As the current song fades out and the next starts, I open my eyes and feel momentarily unsteady. Heat blankets me as someone presses against my backside. Sweat slicks my skin and trails down my neck to my cleavage and shirt. My breaths come in short, shaky bursts.

Winding through the crowd, goose bumps erupt on my skin when I hit cooler air. The momentary reprieve alleviates some of the dizziness, but not all. I scan the pub in search of a familiar face, someone I trust. Half the town is here, but no one I know well enough to ask for help.

Slow and steady, I walk to the nearest abandoned table. Dragging out the stool, I slide onto the seat, rest my hands on the cool wood, and take a deep breath. As I pull my phone from my pocket, a man sits on the stool next to me.

"Your friends abandon you already?" His gravelly voice isn't familiar as his words fuse together in an underwater bubble.

My face tightens, my brows and eyes and lips squashing together. "No," I say as I look up at him.

*Why does my head feel so heavy?*

I study his somewhat blurry face. Roam over his messy, dirty blond hair. Stare into his dark eyes for a beat. Squint and search for familiar features to tell me who this man is, but come up empty.

"Who are you?" The question comes out in a garble.

He lays a hand on mine and chuckles. "Just a guy trying to enjoy a night out."

I yank my hand back, but it barely moves. Every muscle in my body slows, grows heavier with each new breath. "What the hell?" I mutter.

"Come on." The man stands and reaches for my elbow. "Let me get you a ride home. Looks like you're done for the night." His voice is softer, gentler, a lullaby to my ears.

Gripping the edge of the table, I slowly rise to my feet. "Okay." I stow my phone in my pocket. "Thank you."

The closer we get to the front door, the heavier my eyes feel, the more the room starts to spin. And when the damp bay air sweeps across my face as we step outside, I close my eyes and inhale deeply. Everything muddles together as I become weightless.

I try, and fail, to open my eyes. My legs dangle in the air, nausea crawling up my throat as we move much quicker. Metal creaks a moment before I'm seated and strapped in. I beg my mouth to open. Implore my voice to form words and ask what is happening.

But I don't get the chance.

The scent of bacon grease and pancakes stirs me from sleep. I roll over and groan as pain radiates from every inch of my body.

"Never again," I croak out, my voice scratchy and almost inaudible.

Cracking one eye open, I squint at the faint rays of sunlight slipping through the blinds. *Ugh, I forgot to close the curtains.* I pat the nightstand in search of my phone, locating it after a moment. Bringing it close to my face, I note it's just after eleven and my phone is minutes from dying.

"What the hell?" I never sleep in this late. Ever. Let alone forget to charge my phone.

Throwing back the covers, I hiss as I sit up. I stare down at my body and narrow my eyes in confusion. Scan the cotton covering almost every inch of my skin. *I don't sleep fully clothed.*

No matter how much I drink, I never go to bed in full pajamas. I only have those for company.

I strip off the pants and gasp when my eyes hit the inside of my thighs.

What. The. Actual. Fuck?

Spreading my legs wider, I wince as pain radiates from my thighs. The source? Massive purple bruises and a plethora of small, surface-level cuts crusted in dry blood.

"Oh my god," I whisper as my vision blurs. I reach out a tentative finger and graze the bruised skin. Inch by slow inch, I trail my finger toward one of the cuts, flinching when I reach the edge.

Grabbing the blanket at the foot of the bed, I wrap it around myself and close my eyes. I think over last night and try to remember how the hell this happened. What *exactly* happened.

Drinks. Lots of drinks. Too many drinks. The guys we brushed off. Dancing. Skylar and Delilah calling it a night. More dancing.

But then things start to get fuzzy.

Images and sounds and people blurring together. And then... nothing. Not until minutes ago, when I woke up in this cloud of confusion.

Was it the alcohol? I may not be a shots kind of girl, but I've been sloshed before last night. I never felt like this the next day. Never forgot hours of time. Never woke up amnesiac and marred. No way all this happened from shots.

Maybe I was drugged. But when? How?

I replay what I remember, then mentally slap myself. "Dumb. Ass."

When we left the table to dance, we abandoned our drinks. And like a total fucking idiot, I picked it up and downed the entire thing minutes later. We may live in a small town, and I may know most of the townies, but it doesn't mean I *know* them.

Pissed at myself, I rise from the bed. I roll my shoulders and move my legs to stretch my limbs. Hesitantly, I reach down and slip my hand between my legs. Gently trace the junction of my thighs for other signs of abuse, and note nothing feels tender or painful or different. Thank God.

Another hiss slips from my lips as I amble toward the attached bathroom. I crank the hot water in the shower and spin around to face the mirror as it heats. Tears sting the backs of my eyes as I drop the blanket and pull off my tank top. As I stare at my reflection. As I take in the bruises on my breasts, thighs, and arms. As I survey the minor cuts. Slowly, I spin to look at my back and cringe. Dark purple colors both cheeks of my butt. Finger marks on my shoulders.

Nausea claws its way up my throat, but I swallow it down and step into the shower. Under the hot spray, I close my eyes and imagine the water washing away the demons I see but don't really know. And when the water runs cold, I shut off the shower. I decide whatever happened ends here and now. Mentally, I bury the hurt and confusion clouding my thoughts.

Drying off in a daze, I slip on a pair of leggings and a long-sleeve hooded shirt. Pull my hair up in a messy top knot and plaster on a smile as I open my bedroom door. Mask the pain as my skin chafes the fabric. Inhale one more deep breath and extinguish any assumptions about what happened last night during my blackout.

*You can't live in a constant state of what-ifs and maybes. Let it go, Kirsten. Move on.*

"There she is," Skylar greets as I emerge from the hallway and into the open living area. "Bacon, eggs, pancakes, and fruit are ready."

I step up to her at the kitchen counter, wrap her in my

arms, bite the inside of my cheek as my body screams, then kiss her hair. "Thanks, birthday girl." Grabbing a plate, I load it up. "You have a good night?"

"Best birthday yet."

My brows twitch for the briefest of seconds before I turn to face her. "Good. Glad it was memorable."

I sure as hell will never forget it.

# ONE

## TRAVIS

*Present*

*I will not stare. I will not stare.*

Lifting a steaming mug of coffee to my lips, I blow on the hot morning elixir before taking a sip. I stare down at the black coffee and force myself to focus on *it* and not *her*. Focus on the important things—like the meeting with my father in a couple hours—and mentally preparing myself for every possible outcome.

What I shouldn't be focused on is the curvy blonde with a green guest check pad in her hand and a spellbinding smile on her perfect, pouty lips. But fuck, I can't seem to look away.

Do I instigate daily flirt sessions with Kirsten? Damn right I do. I live for her bright smile, for the moment she leans in closer. My day would be shit without her.

Occasionally flirting—or all the time, if I'm honest—is one thing, but unabashedly gawking is wholly different.

As gentlemanly as I want to be, it's downright impossible to not ogle Kirsten during my thirty minutes on this stool. Every morning, with my eyes on my coffee, I chant the same line over and over in my head. *I will not stare.* And every morning, without fail, my unfettered gaze locks on her curves.

Hips swaying, Kirsten weaves between chairs before reaching a couple seated at a window table. She sets plates down, reiterating orders as she does, then asks if they need anything else. They politely decline, and she tells them to enjoy their breakfast before spinning on her heel and waltzing back toward the counter.

I drop my gaze back to the mug in my hand before taking another sip. As I go to set the mug on the counter, Kirsten is there with a fresh pot of coffee in her hand.

"Refill?"

My eyes lift to hers, and my pulse stutters. I swallow and tell myself to snap the hell out of it. "Please," I say, pushing the mug closer to her. "Still not awake yet."

Kirsten fills the mug, slides it back in my direction, sets the coffee pot down, then drops her elbows to the counter and leans forward. And it takes every ounce of strength I own to not look down the V of her shirt. Not that it matters, I can still see her cleavage in my periphery.

"Me either, to be honest." That bright smile of hers I live for lights up her face. "With a little more caffeine and Max's superb cooking, you'll be ready for the day in no time."

"Max makes the best breakfast in town. Hands down." I lean forward and inwardly groan when her sweet scent hits my nose. "But you didn't hear that from me," I say, a breath above a whisper. "People may have me arrested for choosing a town favorite."

Her smile tugs impossibly higher as she rolls her eyes. "And who will put you in handcuffs, *Officer* Emerson?" Kirsten reaches across the counter and taps the Stone Bay Police Department patch on the sleeve of my uniform shirt.

Damn, I love when she flirts back. Even if it's just a little, I love the rush in my veins when she teases in return. "In this small town, you never know what the day will bring."

Isn't that the truth. Majority of the time, the department responds to non-emergency calls. Lonely elderly that need human interaction. Someone who burned food on the stove and wants to be sure they won't burn down the house. Lost pets. Parents "teaching" rowdy children lessons.

Every once in a while, we get serious calls. But it's been years since Stone Bay's been on the map for a grievous crime such as murder, arson, trafficking, or kidnapping. Kirsten's friend, Skylar, being held hostage months ago by a small group of embezzlers was the biggest news since my time on the force. But the news never left Stone Bay. And if that's the worst I have to deal with during my service, I consider myself lucky.

Stone Bay isn't a sleepy town. With wealth comes problems. None of us are ignorant of that fact, but we do our damnedest to keep the town as calm and pleasant as possible.

A bell chimes from the counter separating the kitchen from the server alley. Kirsten leans back and stands tall and I immediately miss her proximity. Her scent. Her.

"Looks like yours." She grabs the ticket beneath the plate and stabs it on the check spindle. Swiping up the plate, she spins around and delivers my breakfast. "Egg white omelet with onions, peppers, and steak, no cheese, and a side of fruit." She pops a hip and rests her hand on it. "Anything else?"

I unroll my silverware as my stomach rumbles. "Not at the moment."

"Perfect." She flashes me a smile. "Be back shortly. Need to check on my other tables."

Kirsten wanders off as I dig into my breakfast. The first bite of omelet hits my tongue and I moan. As always, Max has outdone herself. She adds the perfect amount of her unique spice blend to my breakfast every day. Though I tend to eat simple meals, Max's small touches make basic eggs taste magical.

Years ago, before Polk the Yolk was part of my daily routine, I'd gotten the worst upset stomach after dining out. At the time, I thought it was food poisoning. But when it happened again and again, I visited the doctor and learned all about lactose intolerance. The news had been upsetting. No one wants to stop eating cheese or ice cream.

Shortly after the news, I'd stopped in Polk the Yolk for breakfast and asked what did and didn't have milk in it. Sweetheart that she is, Max showed me how to enjoy old favorites in a new way. She whipped me up the best dairy-free scrambled eggs and biscuits with sausage gravy. Since that day, Polk the Yolk has been my primary breakfast source.

The quaint breakfast and brunch restaurant has since made adjustments to the menu, offering a variety of options for dietary restrictions. I like to believe it was done for me, but Max would smack me upside the head if I voiced such an egotistical opinion.

Boisterous laughter fills the air and I glance across the dining room, spotting Kirsten as she nervously smiles at a man in the booth against the far wall. She lifts a hand to the base of her throat and toys with her necklace while the yuppie prick smiles back. Then he leans in closer and says something only for her ears. Her cheeks flush a beautiful shade of pink, her smile falters momentarily, and my stomach twists.

A loud clang draws the attention of everyone as my fork hits my plate. I make no move to apologize as I pick up my coffee and drain the mug.

*She isn't yours, Emerson. Get a fucking grip.*

No matter how much I remind myself of this small fact, it still pisses me off to see someone flirting with her five minutes after she leaned across the counter and flashed me her smile—and cleavage. She does it for better tips, this much I know. Almost everyone in hospitality flirts to some degree. Comes with the territory. Smiley, happy people who seem interested in *you* earns a fatter paycheck. Period.

Most days, I'm willfully blind to her flirting with other patrons. And it isn't odd for me to be so lost in thought or stressed about work that I ignore my surroundings when here.

But seeing her flirt with other men... did I really believe I was so fucking special she only gave *me* her attention?

*Fucking idiot.*

Sour mood firmly in place, I pick up my fork and tap the tines against my mug. Kirsten stops giving Mr. Pretentious her sparkly eyes and glances in my direction. I hold up my mug and purse my lips. Her cheeks flush a darker pink as she nods. Resting a hand on his shoulder, she apologizes, then heads my way.

"Sorry," she says, grabbing the coffee pot and refilling my mug. "The guy would not let me leave."

"From here, it seemed you were into the conversation."

Her brows twitch as she reads my expression. Yep, I am officially the asshole acting possessive over someone I have no right to claim. And by the look on her face, she wants to tell me as much.

*Fucking idiot.*

She turns away, giving me her back as she sets up the coffee maker to brew a new pot. "You want coffee to go today?"

Taking a deep breath, I hold it and count to ten. On the exhale, I relax my shoulders and shove aside my ego. "Kirsten." Her name is soft on my tongue. "I'm sorry."

She shakes her head, her ponytail swishing across the nape of her neck. "Yes or no to the coffee?"

Why do I like her stubbornness? Why does it make me want to push her further?

"If you turn around, I'll answer you."

She huffs, annoyed with my brute behavior. Funny how she is the only person I act this way with—domineering and selfish and comfortable. As the coffee percolates, she spins around and plants her hands on her hips, lips in a flat line and brows raised, waiting.

"I'm sorry," I repeat. "Truly." I drag a hand through my hair and sigh. "I have a meeting with the Chief this morning and it's made me more of an asshole than usual."

"Isn't your dad the Chief?" Her frame relaxes imperceptibly.

I stab an apple chunk and tap it on the plate. "Yeah, but that doesn't mean a thing on the clock. And he's on the clock more often than not."

She drops her hands from her hips and takes a step closer. "Look, I get it. Parents suck sometimes. But don't take it out on other people. No one needs the ripple effect of someone else's negativity. Choose not to let it bother you."

Easier said than done. My father has a way of getting under my skin. He learned it from his father and grandfather, and they learned from the previous generations. All men raised in an era of severe repercussions for not falling in line. Men raised to believe their superiority was more important than expressing love or devotion or kindness to family, friends, or complete strangers. Men raised to be cold and callous to get results.

I don't fault my father for his blunt and sometimes fierce nature. Those harsh qualities aided him in becoming who he is —who I am—today. But I want to break the cycle and be the bigger, better person. Soften myself before I decide one day whether or not to add to the family tree.

"Thank you," I say. "I'll do my best." I smile and lift the fork to my lips, not missing the way her eyes stay fixed on my mouth. *Interesting.* "And I'd love coffee for the road." Popping the apple in my mouth, the corners of my lips curve higher when she doesn't look away.

Then, as if my words took a moment to catch up in her mind, she blinks and lifts her gaze to mine. A fresh layer of heat blooms on her neck and cheeks, and damn, I love her reaction.

"Be right back." She blinks a few times. "Need to get more takeout cups from the back." Then she darts off and disappears through the kitchen doors.

I eat the last of my breakfast with an infectious smile on my face. But it's not until I spot a stack of to-go cups beneath the counter a few seats down that I chuckle under my breath.

The yuppie across the room may have made her blush, but it was me who made her overheat. I call that a win.

Minutes later, I slide a twenty under my mug, rise from my stool at the counter, and head for the door. "Thanks for breakfast, sunshine." The nickname rolls off my tongue as if I've been calling her sunshine for years, and not like I manifested it seconds ago. "See you tomorrow."

She lifts a hand and waves from behind the counter. "Stay safe, *Officer*."

What is it about the way this woman calls me officer that gets me fired up? Hell if I know. But I live for the way she makes my pulse soar. "Always, sunshine."

I step into the cool November air and jog to my department-assigned SUV. Cranking the engine, I sip the large, steaming cup of coffee until the engine warms enough to turn on the heat. My eyes scan the street as residents start their day. Not many commute near Opal and Chalcedony this early unless they're one of the Seven or coming to the restaurant for breakfast.

Across from Poke the Yolk on Chalcedony Way, Tobias Graves pulls into the small lot for the Stone Bay Gazette. I kick on the heat and let the cabin warm as I watch him enter the town newspaper's hub. The Emerson family has a love-hate relationship with the Graves family. Tobias and Phoebe, his youngest daughter, always seem to stick their noses where they don't belong, all in the name of *news*.

Much as I don't want to be another cutthroat Emerson, with the Graves family, there is no alternative. When it comes to Tobias and Phoebe Graves, you have to be assertive.

I set my coffee in the cup holder and buckle my belt before backing out. With a little time to spare, I turn left out of the lot and cruise north on Chalcedony. The woman outside the Savings and Loan waves as I drive past and I return the gesture.

Lampposts still glow in the early morning hour. A touch of frost coats the birch trees and potted plants along the street. Landscape crews move down the sidewalks on either side of the street and clear the fallen foliage from the walkway.

At the corner of Chalcedony and Garnet, I stop and wave to Dr. Belton as she flips the sign on the front door of the veterinarian's office to open. Then, I steer the SUV onto Granite Parkway, the main thoroughfare in Stone Bay. A line of cars wraps around the small bagel shop as residents grab a quick bite before they head to work or school.

Far too soon, I park the SUV in the lot at the police station, fetch my jacket from the passenger seat, and slip it on before exiting the car with my coffee in hand. I tug open the front door, wave to Doug at the front desk, then weave through the small cluster of desks in the bullpen.

Though crime in Stone Bay is low, the police department

never sleeps. Chief Emerson would never allow it. *"If you have nothing to do, why do I need you here?"* he'd propose to anyone slacking on their duties. *"The citizens pay us to keep this town safe. Not to sit on our asses and play Wordle on our phones."* No matter how menial the situation is, if someone in town needs law enforcement assistance, we show up. Always.

I drop my keys and phone on my desk, pull out my chair and sit, then wake up my computer. As I enter my credentials to log in, I hear the telltale squeak of the chief's door open.

"Emerson," he calls out louder than necessary. "Two hours."

I smash the enter key on my keyboard hard, plaster on a smile, and spin around to face my father. "Yes, sir."

He retreats into his office, never giving his back, and closes the door. Story of my life.

# TWO

## KIRSTEN



I snap out of my wandering thoughts, thoughts I should definitely *not* be having at work, and glare at Oliver. His brows lift in challenge, goading me to disagree. Silently begging me to give him the opportunity to say more. To make me confess what had me so distracted that I've been rolling the same set of silverware for the past five minutes.

Not happening. Those naughty daydreams are locked up tight.

"You're one to talk," I throw back at him. "I didn't miss you walking into the counter the other day when Levi walked by." I reenact what I saw, adding a touch of dramatic flair. "But you don't hear me calling you out on the spot." Coming back to my stack of silverware, I start a fresh roll. "Because it's not nice."

"I did not—"

Holding up my hand, I shake my head. "Yes, you did."

He rolls his eyes. "Whatever." Grabbing the bulk salt and pepper containers below the counter, he starts filling the shakers along the diner counter. "Have you done more than flirt with the man? I mean, if there was any chance he was bi, I'd shoot my shot. Gotta love a man in a uniform." A dreamy look takes over Oliver's expression.

Eyes glued to the counter, I don't answer. Instead, I focus on the task at hand. *Napkin, knife, fork, spoon. Roll, roll, roll. Napkin band. Repeat.*

Honestly, I've never been serious with a guy. Not really.

First off, flirting is fun. It's a different brand of energy than those serious relationship moments. Everything is new and alive and edgy. The smoldering eyes, the constant need to lean in closer, the suggestive smiles, the occasional wink, and that addictive pull.

Not a chance in hell I'm the only person addicted to the high those firsts deliver. The swirling nervousness in your chest. The buzz of anticipation on your skin when he sets his hand near yours and almost touches you. Those minute-long seconds when he stares at your lips, then you stare at his, wondering if he'll make the first move and kiss you.

God, I live for the rush of those moments.

And second... what if I'm not ready for more than one night with a random guy? What if I don't want to choose one person to spend the rest of my life with right now? Commitment isn't a guarantee of keeping someone forever. Pledging your heart and claiming someone else's doesn't prevent nightmares from happening. Tragic events painted with lifelong scars.

Life doesn't come with a guide on what to do and when to do it. We make it up as we go and hope for the best. A ring on your finger doesn't equal happiness. Doing what feels right in your heart... that is happiness.

I'm not ready to settle on one person. Not now, but maybe one day. And if that day comes, I'll do my best to welcome it with open arms.

"He does look good in uniform," I finally say. "Though I much prefer the casual police attire over the dress uniform."

Oliver wanders off to collect more salt and pepper shakers from tables. I take the momentary reprieve to lose myself in daydreams again. To imagine what Travis Emerson looks like *without* his uniform on. As heat crawls up my neck and stains my cheeks, Oliver returns with a trayful of shakers.

With a hum, he says, "The man obviously takes care of himself. But distracting me with muscles won't work. Quit evading my question." Oliver uncaps all the salt shakers, then gives a pointed stare. A fixed look that says he is not moving on without an answer.

Inwardly, I groan. *Fine.*

"No, Ollie. I have not done anything other than flirt with Travis." I purse my lips. "Happy?"

He sets down the salt canister, turns to face me, and rests a hand on my shoulder until I stop rolling silverware and look at him. I half expect to see pity when I meet his basil-green eyes. Instead, I see the complete opposite. Tenderness. Empathy. Support.

"Didn't mean to upset you, K." After a quick squeeze, he drops his hand from my shoulder and shrugs. "Just like seeing my friends happy is all."

Silence settles between us as we resume our menial tasks. I clear dishes from tables, offer to pack leftovers, and deliver tabs to patrons.

"Always a good day when I see you," Bill, one of our regulars, says when I collect his payment. "No change, beautiful."

I rest a hand on his arm and, in return, he gifts me his smile. "You're a sweetheart, Bill."

Bill lays a hand over mine, his thumb slowly stroking my skin as he licks his lips. "Only for you."

I swallow and step out of his hold, a halfhearted smile on my face. "Enjoy your day." With a wave, I walk away.

Poke the Yolk slowly clears out, most promising to see us tomorrow. Kenzie, a part-time server, locks the front door and flips the sign from open to closed for the day. Oliver continues to refill condiment jars while I roll silverware and Kenzie wipes down tables. Finished, I gather a stack of paper placemats and lay them on tables, followed by rolled silverware and mugs. Monotonous as the work is, it gives me time to clear my head after a busy shift.

"I'm headed out," Kenzie says. "Unless you need something else."

"All good." I wave her off. "Have fun at school pickup."

Kenzie gives a playful roll of her eyes. "Thanks."

As I place the last setting on the counter against the large street-facing window, an idea strikes. "Ollie?"

His hands still as he looks over his shoulder. "What's up?"

"Got plans tonight?"

"Couple hours of band practice after work. Other than that, nope." Oliver turns back to the coffee maker and wipes the warmer plates. "You have something in mind?"

I enter the server alley, set the excess placemats and silverware in the bins below the counter, then sidle up to Oliver near the coffee maker as he cleans it.

"Movie night?" I suggest. "I'll message Sky and Dee Dee in the group chat, see if they're down." Inching closer, I push out my bottom lip. "I mean, after all your probing"—I cock a brow, pun somewhat intended—"it's the least you can do."

Dropping the cleaning rag, he turns and mirrors my stance, incredulity written all over his face. For a beat, we simply stare at each other, both of us doing our damnedest not to break. In the end, it's me who laughs first. He rolls his eyes, then joins in on my laughter.

"You don't need to guilt trip me, K. Of course, I'll be at movie night. Pizza?"

"Yes, please." I pull my phone from my back pocket and unlock it, tapping the screen until I open our group chat. "Let me confirm with Sky and Dee Dee."

"If I'm buying dinner, I vote no sappy romance movies."

My eyes lift to his, my brows scrunching together. "What the hell kind of bullshit is that?"

"Hey, I'm not the one who tried to guilt trip me." He shrugs. "No romance if you want me to get dinner."

I narrow my eyes. Wait a moment to see if he'll cave under my stern gaze. My phone locks during the staredown and, against every instinct, I give in. "Fine," I huff out. "You win."

Waking my phone up, I type out a text.

> Movie night at Chateau K & Dee Dee? Ollie says he'll feed us pizza.

Oliver digs out his phone and unlocks it. His fingers dance across the screen as he responds to the group. My phone buzzes in my hand and I look down to see what he wrote.

OLLIE

Not like I had much choice 😼 Ms. Blackmail

I stick my tongue out at him as my phone buzzes again.

SKY

Count me in. Law has a late last minute meeting.

Skylar moved out of our house a little over a week ago and moved in with her new beau, Lawrence. We text almost daily, but I miss her face already. I keep that to myself, not wanting to add more to her plate as she adjusts to her new place and living with her boyfriend.

I press down on her message and tap the heart reaction as my phone buzzes with a text from Delilah.

**DEE DEE**

Shift at the bookstore ends at 4. Stopping by Sage Whisperer to see if mom needs help. Then I'll be home.

I tap the heart reaction on Delilah's text too.

Later babes

"Am I also a babe?" Oliver teases.

I playfully slap his arm and laugh. "Shut up." I clamp down on my lips for a beat before adding, "And yes, you are."

We finish the last of our closing duties in relative silence, then say goodbye to Maxine as we exit through the back door. Oliver wanders toward his gray Camry as I head toward Ruby, my red SUV.

"Probably be at the house around six," he says as he opens his car door.

"Six o'clock," I repeat the time and nod. "Later."

Oliver cranks his car to life and drives out of the lot before I buckle my seat belt. Before driving off, I scroll through my playlists and choose one for the drive home.

As music floats through the speakers, I get this strange prickle on the back of my neck. A shiver rolls up my spine, the hairs on my arms standing straight up. I peer up and scan the lot, but see no one.

*Weird.*

I shake off my paranoia, chastise my intuition for being off, smash the door lock button, buckle my seatbelt, and put the car in gear.

As I drive through town, the edgy awareness stirs back to life. An uneasy feeling churns beneath my breastbone. Demands I listen and give it attention. But as I peek left and right, inspect every person on the sidewalk, everything looks… normal.

Shaking my head, I scold my erroneous thoughts and push down harder on the accelerator. I crank the music and let the blaring chords and vibrating beats drown out my thoughts.

*Everything is fine. Your intuition is obviously on the fritz.*

# THREE

## BEN

Railroad lights flash up ahead, the loud *DING, DING, DING* rings around us as the gate arms lower. Aaron slows to a stop and throws the truck in park as the train whistle echoes through the air. Car after car passes on the track as we sit and wait.

"Been to Stone Bay before?" Aaron asks me as he points out the window.

On either side of the road, large gray and white granite blocks frame a wooden sign that reads, "Welcome to Stone Bay, Washington. Established 1908." A smaller sign near the base states, "Founding Families: Barron, Langston, Emerson, West, Graves, Fox, Imala."

Warm air spills from the vents near the floorboard as I stare at the sign, momentarily confused. How odd and pretentious it is to list the founding families on the welcome sign. As if they want everyone who crosses the town border to be aware. As if every person who sets foot in Stone Bay needs to extend some special courtesy to these specific people.

I'd completely understand the founding family names in a guide to the town's history. Showcasing how the families came together and built the town, I easily picture it in a museum. Small placards on town benches and playgrounds, signs in or on historical buildings or specific landmarks—those make perfect sense.

But on the town sign? Seems a bit ostentatious.

"First time," I say, tipping my head left then right, cracking my neck. "Just needed to get out of town and this job came at the perfect time."

He hums, tapping his thumbs on the steering wheel. "Carolyn?"

I wince at the sound of her name. "Yeah."

"Sorry, man." He shifts his gaze to my profile, my eyes still on the town sign. "You ever need to get shit off your chest, I'm here."

"Appreciate it," I say with a nod. Wanting a change of subject, I ask, "What about you? Been to Stone Bay?"

He reaches for his water, uncaps it, and guzzles half the bottle. "Few years back. Woman I was seeing begged me to bring her to the town's Independence Day Festival." Laughter fills the truck cab as he sets his water bottle back in the holder. "Had no clue what I was getting myself into. Thought it'd be hot dogs, burgers, and fireworks." He shakes his head. "Sure, they had those things. But there were also fancy pastries and hand pies, grilled shrimp and lobster, cheese plates with fruit and olives, and more." He runs a hand through his hair. "I'd never seen so many dressy people for an outdoor holiday."

"Hmm. Interesting." Maybe the entire town has overinflated egos. *Wonderful.*

I look in the side mirror and see part of our crew in the box truck behind us. Luke tousles Dylan's hair and she backhands him in the chest. Business as usual. Behind the box truck is a pickup matching ours, *Creekside Construction* hand-painted in green on the driver and passenger doors, our boss behind the wheel.

Several train cars later, the lights stop flashing, the incessant chirp dies, and the gate arms lift. Aaron puts the truck in gear and presses the accelerator, driving us into Stone Bay.

A train station sits off to the left when we cross the tracks. Skyscraper-tall evergreens line the right side of the road and then the left after the train station. Our tires eat up a couple miles before the trees start to thin and glimpses of Stone Bay come into view. My brows lift as my eyes take in the sheer opulence of each building.

From what I gathered before leaving for this job, Stone Bay is roughly the same size as Smoky Creek. Small. Less than five thousand people in both towns. Both towns named after nearby bodies of water.

But that's where the similarities end.

Stone Bay is the definition of "affluent." Smoky Creek... not so much.

We pass the Stone Bay Community Church, a Victorian Gothic cathedral with its gray and black stone walls and elaborate stained-glass windows. I'm nowhere near religious, but as we pass the church, I suddenly feel the need to pray.

The farther into town we drive, the more I feel this is a completely different world than the one I live in. I assumed the town's name came from the stony cliffs surrounding the bay. But with each building and street sign we pass, it appears to get its name from the minerals and gemstones in the area.

And man, do they love to flaunt their wealth.

"Jesus." The word slips from my lips as my eyes widen. "Is the entire town this garish?" I ask as the courthouse and town hall—one massive structure—come into view.

Beside me, Aaron laughs. "Not the entire town." He glances my way, sees my mouth hanging open, and laughs harder as his eyes return to the road. "From what I gather, if the structure belongs to or is run by one of the founding families, or they have a special interest in the business, the building screams wealth."

We stop at a red light and I stare at the two-story, white granite courthouse. The foundation sits higher than the street, a series of steps leading up to the entrance. Both floors are easily fifteen to twenty feet in height. Intricately carved stone pillars draw your attention to the entrance, while arched windows similar to the Gothic church give it life. On a ledge beneath the roof gable are seven men and women carved from stone, all of equal height, sitting tall on thrones with various relics in their hands. Above them on the roof is a nonbinary person in a robe, one arm up and holding scales, the other arm at their side with a sword in their grasp. At the heart of the roof is a clock tower with a belfry and spire, a large golden glass flame on top. The base of the structure is surrounded by granite walkways, ornamentally-shaped bushes, granite statues, a massive fountain, and neatly trimmed evergreens.

"Overwhelmed yet?" Aaron asks as we turn at the light and head north.

"Something like that," I say as I take in more of the town.

The storefronts on this road are less gaudy and closer to what I see every day in Smoky Creek.

Two- and three-story buildings, most butted up to each other, but a sporadic few freestanding. A soft color palette brightens the stone or wood siding, while medium tones accentuate and give the building life. Scalloped awnings extend from each storefront, placards with the store name above them are painted to match the color palette. Vivid flowers bloom in tall pots on either side of store entrances. A-frame chalkboard signs sit on the sidewalk with daily specials or positive quotes listed. Dark gray lampposts line the sidewalk, a potted plant hangs on the store side, and a banner highlighting the town is posted on the street side. Midway between each lamppost are lush evergreens, a bench on one side, and a trash can and recycle bin on the other.

The farther we drive, the more at ease I am.

"This must be the ordinary part of town," I say with a laugh. We pass Sloppy's BBQ, Cheese Us Pizza, then Dalton's Pub and Billiards. "Yep. Definitely more my vibe now."

Aaron laughs as he turns right just before the post office, a stone structure similar in appearance to the courthouse. Then he turns left into the Stone Bay Library parking lot and I gasp at the sheer size of the building.

"Holy shit, man."

Again, Aaron laughs. "Obviously, you didn't look up pictures before taking the job."

Look up pictures? Why the hell would I look up the town library? When John mentioned the job, he said, *"We're adding on to the existing structure. Adding a new wing to the current library."* In my head, I pictured us laying cinderblock and matching the exterior. Creating walls and a stairwell inside. I imagined it was similar to the Smoky Creek library—five thousand square feet of flat walls and thousands of books.

Now, I'm thinking we bit off more than we could chew.

"This looks older than the damn town," I suggest.

Aaron parks the truck in the rear lot, the rest of the crew following suit. "Well, I *did* look up the library online."

I roll my eyes. "You get the gold star," I say, sarcasm thick in my tone.

He rests a hand over his heart and flashes me an artificial smile. "It was one of the first large, non-residential structures built in Stone Bay and wasn't always the library. Originally, it was the hospital. The build took five years, with the doors first opening in 1914."

"Another gold star." I unbuckle my seat belt, open the door, and exit the truck, stretching my limbs.

"Goddamn," Luke says, whistling as he and the others sidle up to me and Aaron. He stares at our job for the next forty-five to sixty days. "Did we land in medieval times or some shit?" He hooks an arm around Dylan's shoulders and hauls her into his side. "Think we'll find some old, kinky torture devices inside?"

Dylan ducks out of his hold and shoves him away. "Stop it already." She lifts a hand, pinching her thumb and forefinger together. "I'm this close to junk punching you."

Luke raises his hands in surrender and takes a step back. "No need for violence, oh spunky one."

"Then quit being an ass."

John joins us, a worn baseball cap on his head and storage clipboard in his hand. "Y'all done goofing off?" He looks pointedly at Luke.

"All good, boss man."

An exasperated huff leaves John's lips before he drops his gaze to the job details on the clipboard. He scans the page a moment before meeting our waiting stares and getting down to business.

"Materials will be delivered tonight. Today, I want everyone to walk the site. Get familiar with the terrain. Review the project one last time." He passes us each a copy of the construction plan. "Go inside the current library and get a feel for the structure. The building is over a hundred years old and a Stone Bay landmark. We were hired to erect walls, build a stairwell, and roof the structure. Make the new wing look like it's been here the entire time."

He tucks the clipboard under his arm and rubs his hands together.

"Expect cold days and dress accordingly. If all goes as

planned, the foundation gets poured tomorrow and the exterior walls should be completed by the end of week three. The roof done by the end of week four. Then we can move inside. It won't have power, but we'll be able to run extension cords or run the generator and plug-in heaters."

John walks toward the sidewalk lining the grass and we follow in his wake. The grass where the addition is being built has already been removed and leveled. String connects a series of stakes and creates a perimeter. Several colored flags are stabbed into the ground to mark utilities, while capped pipes for plumbing shoot up. Borders and welded wire mesh are in place for the concrete pour. John steps over the string and into the construction space, all of us on his heels.

"We may not be building today, but that doesn't mean we aren't working. I want everyone on the same page before we leave today." He removes his hat, scratches his head, then puts it back on. "We'll hit the diner for a late lunch, then head to the inn." Gaze moving from one crew member to the next, he asks, "Questions?"

We remain silent.

"Good. Let's get to work."

From the outside, RJ's Diner and Dive looks similar to every other storefront in Stone Bay. Two stories, large windows, the base color a soft wheat and the trim a bold papaya orange, brightly colored flowers near the door, and a large sign displaying the business name. The only noticeable difference is the lack of a fabric awning. In place of an awning is a pillar-supported metal and wood canopy shading several two-top tables, all of which are taken.

We step inside and I have to blink a few times. Because this is definitely *not* what I expected.

Throughout the dining room, the same wheat color on the exterior coats the top half of the walls, black grouted white subway tiles take up the bottom half, and a six inch plank of stained wood separates the tile and painted wall. Two-top wood tables and chairs line the front windows. One long bench flanks the left and right walls, tables for two or four available with individual chairs opposite the bench. At the heart of the diner is a U-shaped service counter with backless stools, the counter's base tiled with small teal, papaya, and white hexagonal tiles. Between the service counter and tables lining the walls are several two- and four-top tables. At one end of the service counter is a place to order and pick up takeout.

What stands out most… the place is *packed*.

Is this because of early bird specials? Or is RJ's *the* place to eat in Stone Bay?

"This is a diner?" Jake, our newest crew member, asks. "Fanciest diner I've ever seen."

We all nod in silence as we take in the place. It *smells* like a diner—fried potatoes, bacon grease, brewed coffee, chili spices, burgers, and breaded chicken. But that's where the diner vibes end. For me, at least. Everything is so bright and vibrant and chic.

A server pushes two tables together and seats us not far from the window. He hands us menus, relays the specials today, then takes our drink orders.

"I'll be back in a moment."

After perusing the menu and receiving our drinks, we place our orders. While the rest of the crew sparks conversation, I lean back in my chair and watch the people beyond the window.

Bundled in coats, scarves, and gloves, residents stroll the sidewalks without care. In a sharp suit, a woman with a wide smile opens the door to the accountant's office across the street and gestures for an elderly couple to step inside. When the door closes, she hugs them. Next door to the accountant and directly across from the diner, Bean and Leaf has a line out the door. I squint to see people purchasing bulk coffee and tea, as well as fresh-brewed beverages. On the opposite side of the accountant's office is A Touch Crafty. Without further detail, I surmise the store sells all things hobby-related.

Carolyn loved—*loves*—crafts. So many times, I drove over an hour to take her to the craft stores in Olympia. Sometimes to browse. Other times to stockpile her candle and soap making supplies. She could have ordered them online, but I knew how much she loved to see and smell and touch the actual products, especially if they were new.

When we broke up, I gave back all the candles and unused soaps she'd made and gifted me. Felt like the right thing to do. A clean break.

My gaze drifts down the sidewalk, closer to the diner, and I stop breathing. I sit up straighter in my chair, lean closer to the window, and narrow my eyes as my head inches forward.

On the sidewalk across the street, a blonde woman shuffles into line at Bean and Leaf. She lifts her clasped hands to her lips, blows on them, then rubs them together. I catch a brief glimpse of her profile and this odd twist in my gut hits. An old yet familiar ache. As if I *know* her.

I've never been to Stone Bay, but... a memory from long ago smacks me in the chest and steals my breath.

*"Mom says we have to move." She reaches for the small, rose gold crescent moon on her necklace and slides it back and forth on the chain. "I don't want to move," she says, loud enough for her mom to hear.*

*Carrying boxes into the moving trailer, her mom ignores her harsh tone. There's been a lot of harsh words and tears since she found out they were moving.*

*"I don't want you to move either, sparkles. I'll miss you. Who else am I going to beat at UNO?" It's a long-standing joke between us. I said it to make her smile. For a second, it works.*

*"You've never beat me at UNO," she says with absolute surety.*

*And I don't disagree. I can't. Because she is right. I suck at UNO. If "Undefeated Loser" was a title, I'd earn it playing UNO with her.*

*"I know," I say, reaching for her hand and pulling her in for a hug. "And I'll miss losing to you."*

*She constricts me in a breath-stealing embrace. "I won't be mad if you play and lose with someone else." She sniffles in my ear.*

*If only it were that easy. If only I could play cards with someone else and call them my best friend. But I can't. And I won't. It'll never be the same without her.*

*"Maybe," I say, not wanting to upset her further.*

*Loosening her hold on me, she inches back and looks me in the eyes. "Who knows. Maybe if you play with someone new, you'll finally get a Wild card to play," she teases.*

*I think of the Wild card in my back pocket—the one I stole from her UNO deck before she packed it away—and shrug. "If I'm lucky.*

*But I'd rather she stay than ever get a Wild card playing with someone else.*

Luke elbows me in the ribs and snaps me back to the present.

"Ow!" I elbow him back. "What the hell was that for?"

He jerks his chin toward the server, a bowl and plate in his hands. The server repeats the order, looking to verify it's my order.

"Sorry." I rub my side. "Spaced out. Chili and cornbread onion rings are mine."

After he sets the food in front of me, I glance back out the window and scan the sidewalk. The blonde from moments ago is nowhere in sight. And with her disappearance, the twist in my gut vanishes without a trace.

The only thing that doesn't disappear... the tattered Wild card in my wallet.

# FOUR

## KIRSTEN

"Love you, too," I say, blowing a kiss. I dip the brush in the polish and paint the next nail. "When I got home and saw the delivery from Blush Rush, I had to go live and share with everyone." When I finish the nails on my left hand, I hold it up and show my livestream viewers. "Video doesn't do this color justice. And one coat is all you need."

I read comments as they pop up and respond to my followers. In all honesty, I have no idea how I got here—over twenty thousand followers in three years—but am grateful for the online family I've garnered.

Blogging about clothes, beauty products, and the occasional dishware item started with me wanting to show off new purchases and brands I loved. Not once did I imagine it becoming what it is now—free products and paid advertising from my favorite brands. Posting pictures or videos once or twice a day and doing live videos a few times a week while I use the latest product is something I would have done regardless. Getting paid to do it is a bonus.

Halfway through my right hand, I make eye contact with my viewers. "Serious question, everyone. Should I get a pet?" I coat the polish brush and move to the next finger. "I've never really had a pet." Finishing the nail, I read their answers.

*Girl, doooo it! Could so see you with a cute little kitten* 😸

*#catmomforlife*

*Cocker spaniel would fit your style to perfection* 🐾

*I love my little bun-bun* 🐰

*#chinchillalife*

*Living that puppy life* 🐕

Comments roll in too fast to read, but the consensus is a resounding yes. "Loving this feedback! Thanks everyone." I finish the last nail and cap the polish. "My family owns a farm, but it's not quite the same. Cows and chickens never cuddle me on the couch." I chuckle. "But I guess I never really tried."

This garners several laughing emojis.

"Between now and my next live, I'll narrow it down to two possibilities and put up a poll so you can help me decide." I show off the final result of the nail polish. "Head over to Blush Rush's website and use KGIRLK for my exclusive discount."

Lifting the bottle, I display the brand and color one last time, then reiterate why I love the brand and what they will get with each order.

"Thanks for hanging out. Love you all." I blow them a kiss. "Time to prep for movie night." With a parting wave, I end the live feed, save it to my profile, then turn off the ring light beside my vanity.

Sliding my nail dryer closer, I press a couple buttons and

stick my hand under the cover. When the dryer shuts off, I switch hands and repeat. Nails done and dryer back in place, I fetch my phone from the ring light holder, swipe up the bottle of polish, and exit my room.

Before the natural light fades, I take pictures with the polish bottle and the new color on my nails in the living room. I open the photo editing app, apply my usual filter, make a few adjustments so the polish color is a true representation, and save it to the camera roll. I schedule posts for the next week, some with the polish, others with pictures I took over the last few days.

I close the app, stow my phone, and prep for movie night.

With Oliver on pizza duty, Delilah and I have popcorn, drinks, and the movie covered. Skylar may stop at the store for her favorite movie snacks since they no longer take up shelf space in the pantry. We vow to keep movie nights stress-free. Agreeing on a movie is the hardest part of the evening and Oliver added to the challenge tonight.

*No romance.*

Psh. What is wrong with him?

Wandering into the kitchen, I grab sodas and the sparkling flavored water Delilah loves from the pantry and stock the fridge. I fetch the jar of popping corn, the air popper, and the flavor shakers and set them on the kitchen island. Then I shift my focus as I wait for everyone.

While I tidy the house, I mull over the question I asked my followers during the live. *Should I get a pet?* I was serious when I confessed to never having a pet. I've wanted a cat or dog for years, but the timing never worked out. Until now.

Before we moved to Stone Bay, Mom and Dad said they'd consider a pet when I got older and could better care for it.

*"Pets are more than something cute to cuddle. They are family and need lots of care," Dad says, then bops my nose.*

He promised we'd find the perfect addition for our family when the time was right. Unfortunately, he and I never got the opportunity to return to the pet store and make good on his promise.

The summer before fifth grade, Dad passed away while I trembled under my bed with my hand over my mouth and tears rolling down my cheeks.

Wanting to pad the summer vacation fund, Mom had picked up the occasional extra shift at the factory and wasn't home when the thief shattered the glass front door. She wasn't there when Dad dashed into my room and told me to hide, to not come out until he said it was safe. She wasn't there when the gunshots rang throughout the house, followed by a distinguishable *thump* when Dad hit the floor. And she wasn't there when red and white lights lit up my bedroom and police entered our home, asking if anyone else was in the house.

As dawn peaked over the horizon, Mom parked in the driveway and ran to the front door, mascara streaks on her cheeks. She wrapped me in the fiercest hug as I watched sunlight dance on the shattered glass. Her tears wet my hair as I cried in silence, numb.

Not long after Dad passed, we moved to Stone Bay. Neither Mom nor I were able to sleep or feel safe in our own home. So she packed our bags, sold everything with no personal meaning, and drove us to Stone Bay. It wasn't far from Smoky Creek, but far enough for a fresh start.

Mom worked at Northcott Farms while I went to school. When school was out, Mom was with me every minute. Money was tight, but we made it work. We found our way.

A couple years later, Mom sat me down and asked if I would be okay with her spending time with Joseph, the man who ran Northcott Farms. For weeks, we fought. I yelled and asked how she was able to love someone else. Each time, she handled my fits with grace. Told me she would never forget Dad, but that she was also lonely, and Joseph made her smile.

It took a while for me to warm up to Joseph. But after spending time with him and seeing how he looked at my mom, I opened my heart to him too. Gave him the chance to make Mom smile every day. Gave her permission to love someone new without guilt or shame.

In return, I got the best stepdad and stepsister. Was gifted a second family with so much love.

Joseph will never replace Dad. On our first family date, he told me he had no plans to take Dad's place or snub out his memory. All he asked for was a piece of our hearts, and he'd share a piece of his. With time, our families blended together, and Mom and I moved onto the Northcott Farm.

The cows and chickens were a source of company when I needed someone to spill my secrets to, but I never considered them pets. Not like a dog or cat or bunny. Not like the pet I wanted as a young girl.

"What pet would Dad have gotten me?" I mutter as I shift furniture in the living room, making more room to sit on the floor between the couch and table.

I picture me and Dad in the pet store years ago, me swooning over puppies while Dad scratched kittens behind their ears. Dad calm and content while I laughed uncontrollably when I'd all but tipped over as half a dozen puppies begged for my attention.

Flipping to another memory, I recall a different trip to the pet store. Sitting cross-legged on the floor, I held a bunny in my lap, stroking its unbelievably soft fur for almost an hour. God, I'd wanted to leave with that little bundle of fluff, but Dad encouraged me to spend time with another animal. *"How will you know which is your favorite if you don't give all of them a chance?"* And while ferrets were oddly cute, I only played with them a few minutes. Not only were they a little smelly, but they also had more energy than expected.

But what I remember most about every trip… Dad only loved on the cats.

"A cat," I say, without giving it another thought. "Dad would've gotten me a cat, so a cat it is."

"How's life in the new digs?" Oliver asks Skylar before stuffing pizza in his mouth.

"Different, but good." Skylar loses focus a moment, a dreamy look on her face. I love seeing her like this—blissful, at peace, in love.

I envy my friend. How easily she found and fell in love. How being in love lifts her up and makes her smile more. How love doesn't scare her.

*Star Wars: Attack of the Clones* plays on the screen as we devour pizza. Cracked open cans sit on the coffee table, the room lit only by the television and a low-burning fire. All four of us sit cross-legged on a large, soft blanket sprawled across the floor, half paying attention to the movie as we chat.

While scrolling movie options, a grin lit my face when I hit the *Star Wars* films. Technically, it isn't romance. But the budding love in this particular movie is enough to make me, Delilah, and Skylar happy while not listening to Oliver groan.

"Hope Law can make it to the next movie night," Oliver says.

Skylar covers her mouth as she swallows. "Unless another last-minute meeting pops up, he'll be here."

Oliver shifts his attention to me and the corner of his mouth tips up in a sneaky half-smile. "And maybe K will invite Travis. I mean… *Officer Emerson.*" He bats his lashes, then sighs as if swooning.

I throw a pillow at his head and hit my mark. "You're ridiculous."

In a blink, the movie is forgotten, food is pushed away, and three hard stares heat my face.

"Um, what?" Skylar asks.

"It's nothing." I narrow my gaze on Oliver. Tell him with a single look to shut up.

Oliver chooses to ignore my silent demand as he picks a piece of ham off his pizza and pops it in his mouth. "Didn't look like nothing." He chews and swallows, chasing it with a swig of soda. "Yeah, she flirts with all the customers. I do too. Worth the boost in tips." His expression grows a touch serious as he meets my eyes. "But you're different with Travis. You always have been."

I sift through memories of work and the countless times I've talked with Travis. The man is at Poke the Yolk daily, ahead of the breakfast rush. He sits in the same spot at the counter. Orders one of three breakfasts with black coffee. Flashes his dazzling smile and flirts with me without reservation. When I walk off to help another customer, his gaze trails me across the restaurant.

No sense in denying I love his dark-rimmed honey eyes on me. I love that he can't *not* look. As if he fears he'll miss something vital. As if I'll vanish. His eyes on me stirs a buzz beneath my diaphragm and kicks up an endless whirl of nervous energy in my rib cage.

And god… I live for the addictive high it creates.

But none of it means anything.

Flirting with Travis comes naturally. I'm good at it. He's good at it. And we both don't seem to get enough. But it doesn't mean anything. Not really.

Or does it?

*Am I different with him?*

I shake off Oliver's comment. "I am not different with him," I say, not convincing anyone in the room, including myself. Half-eaten slice of pizza in hand, I add, "New subject," then take a huge bite.

Delilah chooses a tamer topic of conversation and talks about the new addition to the library. Construction begins tomorrow and has been the talk of the town among the older generations and investors. The rest of the town is excited for the expansion but not as engrossed with the specifics.

"Paige is confident the bookstore will see a boost in foot traffic, sales, and events," Delilah says, referring to Page by Paige, the only retail bookstore in Stone Bay.

"Less time for reading on the job," Skylar teases.

Delilah waves her off. "Shush you." With a roll of her eyes, she shakes her head. "I'll have plenty of time to read." She sticks out her tongue, then shifts her attention to the movie.

Conversation tapers off as we finish eating pizza and shift to sweets and popcorn. We lay in a haphazard pile on the floor, none of us complaining or uncomfortable.

This is what we do, this is who we are. Friends—a found family—that share the good, bad, and horrid. We joke and tease and call each other out. When life is hard, we lift each other up. When something good happens, we cheer and party. Most importantly, we are there for each other through thick and thin.

I get up and go to the kitchen for more drinks. As I close the fridge, I hear what sounds like light knocking at the front door. Thinking it's Lawrence, I smile for Skylar and pad over to the door. Unbolting the lock, I open the front door and am met with nothing. My brows tug at the middle as I lean out, looking left then right. Nothing.

I shrug, step back, close the door, and lock it. Grabbing the drinks from the kitchen, I return to the living room and plop down between Skylar and Oliver.

"Someone at the door?" Oliver asks.

I shake my head. "Thought I heard something. Was probably the movie echoing in the foyer." But as I stare at the screen and the words leave my lips, a shiver rolls down my spine.

# FIVE

## TRAVIS

I steer my officer-assigned SUV into the lot at Poke the Yolk, a smile on my face when I spot Kirsten through the window. Weaving between tables with loaded plates in either hand, she beams at the older couple as she reaches their table and delivers their breakfast.

For a beat, I remain behind the wheel with the engine running and observe her from a distance. Watch as she smiles and interacts with other townsfolk in my absence. A softness touches the corners of her eyes as she leans in and listens to the older woman. Smile widening, Kirsten rests a hand on the woman's shoulder and says something. Both women smile and an unfamiliar ache blooms in my chest.

On a deep inhale, I cut the engine, unbuckle my seatbelt, and exit the car. My eyes stay trained on her as I approach the entrance and tug on the door. But before I step inside, a diesel engine roars at my back. I glance over my shoulder as two large trucks pull into the lot and park near the back, *Creekside Construction* prominent on each truck.

*Wonderful.* There goes the start of my morning.

Foot in the door, I ignore the boisterous crew outside and head for my spot at the café counter. Before I land in the seat, Kirsten is there, a smile on her face as she flips over my mug and fills it with coffee.

"Morning, officer." Setting the coffee pot on the counter, she rests her hands wide on the counter and leans closer. "Scramble, oatmeal, or omelet?"

Not sure why, but I love that she has this part of my day memorized. That she knows my breakfast routine and the three meals I alternate between. That I can tell her which one I'm in the mood for and she knows everything else I want on my plate.

Those small details are part of the reason I come here every day. Her brilliant smile, flirty nature, and delicious curves are others.

"Scramble," I say as the door opens, cool air sweeping in with the noisy crew. On a groan, I roll my eyes. "Please."

Her soft smile turns playful as she pushes off the counter. "Yes, sir, officer." She enters my order into the system, then grabs a tray, adds six glasses, and fills them with water. "I'll see if we can tame the rowdy bunch in the back."

My hands wrap around the mug and soak up the warmth. "Appreciate it."

She takes the water over to the table and gathers their drink orders, giving them a minute to decide on food. As she moves around the restaurant, I chant the same mantra in my head I do every time I see her. *I will not stare.* And as per usual, I struggle with the follow through.

More early risers arrive, the chatter in the restaurant growing louder by the minute. Kirsten and the other servers pick up speed as they move from table to table. As Kirsten keys in a new order, Oliver taps her chest with a finger, then his own name tag. With a quick *thank you,* she digs in her apron, pulls out her name tag, and pins it to her shirt.

The sweet yet pungent smell of onions wafts from the kitchen passthrough window as the sizzle of food on the grill hits my ears, and my stomach growls. I swallow half my coffee, zeroing in on the mug and tuning out my surroundings. After a beat, my vision blurs. The conversation with my father at the precinct surfaces and I close my eyes.

*"Need you to step up more, Officer Emerson."*

*Whether at work or home, it is a rare occasion if Dad calls me son or by name. If he shows any form of affection.*

*Does Roger Emerson love his children? In his own way, yes. What that way is, I can't be sure.*

*Hands clasped at my waist, I straighten my spine. "Yes, sir. Whatever you need, you can count on me."*

*"Think you have it in you to be a role model? Train rookie officers? Show everyone in this office and town what it means to be an Emerson?"*

*Some days, I love my job. When I slip on my uniform and serve our town, it feeds my soul. Gratitude surfaces as residents and officers look to me when they need assistance. Exhilaration swells in my chest when others regard me as valuable, an asset to the community.*

*I do my damnedest to focus on those days. Let the good outshine the bad.*

*But it isn't always easy. Not when the Chief—your father— knocks you down a peg day after day. Not when he reminds you every chance he gets that the last name on your uniform—a brand carved in your bones you didn't ask for—is "God-worthy" in the town of Stone Bay.*

*I may have been born an Emerson, but all I want is to be myself. Whoever that is and whatever that looks like.*

*"Yes, sir," I state, voice steady and strong. My thoughts drift to*

Pepper and an idea forms. "May be good to add more K-9 officers to the team."

As of now, Pepper is the only K-9 officer in Stone Bay. I adopted her at eight weeks old and trained her for a year before she earned her badge. It isn't often her services are needed, but I maintain her training daily for when the time comes.

Chief Emerson hums, his eyes narrowing imperceptibly. The longer he remains silent, the more I question the idea. But as I hold his stare, the answer hits me in the chest. A truth he won't admit, but I feel it deep in my bones.

He approves of the idea. But he dislikes that the plan didn't come from him.

Though I know he'll take credit.

"Right there." He steps closer and slaps a hand on my shoulder, tightening his grip. "That's what an Emerson looks like. A man with foundational concepts to benefit the town. An innovative man with a good head on his shoulders. A respectable man the town looks to in hard times."

Each of the traits he listed is admirable, virtuous. Most of my life, the man across from me has drilled what it means to be an Emerson into my head. How our family is part of the backbone of Stone Bay. How we have a responsibility to the town and its people. That it is our duty to protect others.

When I was a boy, the Emerson name made me feel invincible. As a man, it robs me of freedom and drowns me in the bay. There is nothing wrong with having pride or strength or courage. But what about adventure and pleasure and love? Aren't they equally important and valuable?

"Thank you, sir. I do my best to deserve the name." Acid claws its way up my throat as the words leave my lips.

"Yes, you do." He shifts around his desk, lowering into the chair —a wordless dismissal. "Have a proposal to me for the K-9 training by the end of the week." Translation: Thursday evening for review on

*Friday morning. "I look forward to reviewing the plan." He lifts the file on his desk and opens the folder, dropping his gaze and skimming the pages—his silent way of saying, "see yourself out and shut the door behind you."*

"Yes, sir."

*Thrilled as I am to take on the task, to finally be seen by my father as worthy, even if only for a moment, unease courses through my veins. And I hate that he harnesses this level of power over me and my future.*

*If I don't get this right, if I fail as an Emerson because of this project, I will never earn the respect I so desperately crave from him.*

Smoky maple wafts in the air as Kirsten sets my breakfast on my placemat, snapping me back to the present.

I blink a few times and lift my gaze to hers, a halfhearted smile on my lips. "Thank you."

She tilts her head to the side as her spellbinding eyes trace over every ridge, curve, and peak of my face. Her inspection heats my blood. Awakens the passion in my veins. Calls to the hidden cravings in my bones. I come alive under her observation.

"Everything okay?" She breaks eye contact, reaches for the coffee pot, and fills my mug.

*Loaded question.*

"Yeah." I shrug. "Work stuff."

With a sympathetic smile on her lips, she nods. "Whatever it is, I'm confident you'll be great." She lays her hand over mine on the counter.

How does she do it? Find the right words in the moment. Touch me in the simplest way and blanket me with ease. Hold me with those magnetic, stormy-blue eyes and make the world disappear.

My thumb brushes over hers and she sucks in a breath. The cacophony around us fades, the room and everyone in it blurring as we lock ourselves in this mini bubble. Her tongue darts out to wet her lips and my eyes zero in on the action, my cock swelling as my mind drifts to all the things I'd love to do to her mouth.

*Ding, ding, ding.*

The bubble pops as Max rings the service window bell. Kirsten blinks as she pulls her hand away. While the heat of her touch fades, the buzz on my skin remains.

"That's me," she whispers, then clears her throat. "Be back in a few."

I unravel my silverware while she loads up two trays with several plates. Oliver sidles up to her and offers to help. As they deliver food, I dig into my own breakfast.

Salty bacon with a hint of maple hits my tongue and I moan. I could make breakfast at home any day, but it would never taste this good. And as much as I love Pepper, she's not the only woman I love seeing in the morning.

As I swallow the bite, I glance over my shoulder at Kirsten. I shove the rest of the bacon strip in my mouth and watch as she smiles at the construction crew, handing them their plates. When she calls out an order, a man with curly black hair and tan skin holds his hand up. She moves around the table and hands him the plate.

His body language shifts as she moves back to the tray, his head tilting to the side as a V forms between his brows.

*Who is this guy? And why the hell is he studying her so fucking hard?*

She hands him a second, smaller plate and he grabs her wrist. I drop my fork and spin on my seat, my feet on the floor, ready to charge if this asshole tries anything.

Her eyes drop to his grip on her wrist, worry etching her expression. She lifts her gaze, opens her mouth to say something, then freezes.

*Does she know him?*

"Sparkles?" His head tilts the other way, a subtle smile lifting the corners of his mouth. "Is that you?"

The buzz I felt moments ago vanishes. In its place... fire and rage and the sudden desire to hit something.

# SIX

## KIRSTEN

"SPARKLES?"

I stare at the man with black curls, turquoise eyes, and a soft smile as he tilts his head. Open my mouth, then clamp it shut, lost for words.

*I know those eyes.*

"Is that you?"

*Sparkles.* More than a decade has passed since I last heard that nickname.

I stutter-step closer and squint, studying the man. Compare him to the lanky boy I knew a lifetime ago. A boy I haven't seen or spoken to in far too long. A friend I lost touch with as Mom and I built a different life in Stone Bay.

Chin-length curls frame his sharp, stubbled jaw. Bold and blue, his mythical eyes hold me captive for a beat. I trace the bridge of his nose with my eyes and pause when I reach soft, kissable lips, licking my own before continuing my inspection. Shirt snug on his broad shoulders, his biceps stretch the cotton and flaunt years of hard work.

Swallowing hard, I blink at the man in disbelief. *Is it really Ben? My Ben?*

"Benji?"

His soft smile widens as he rises from his chair, wraps his arms around me, and lifts me off the floor. "Holy shit," he whispers in my ear. Then, as if he realizes what he has done, he sets me on my feet and takes a step back. "Sorry." He winces. "That was way too forward."

Laughter spills from my lips as I shake my head. "Don't worry about it." I lay a hand on his bicep, my fingers molding around his well-defined muscles. Heat crawls up my chest and neck before spreading to my cheeks, undoubtedly painting my face red. Swallowing, I yank my hand away. "Be right back."

Moving back to the tray, I deliver the remaining plates. Oliver takes the empty tray and tray stand, then waggles his brows. I roll my eyes and playfully slap his arm. As I step toward Ben, a clinking sound rings in the air.

"More coffee would be nice," Travis barks, all eyes shifting in his direction as the restaurant quiets momentarily.

Honey eyes assess me from across the room, a hint of irritation in that gaze as it darts between me and Ben. It isn't *me* he is upset with, but the man who literally swept me off my feet moments ago.

I glance around the table. "Anything else you need?"

"No," they mumble as they eat.

Looking to Ben, I say, "Check on y'all soon."

He gives a subtle nod and unrolls his silverware.

I weave through the tables, smile at customers, and ask if they need anything as I make my way back to the grouch at the counter. Coffee pot in hand, I stand opposite him at the counter and fill his mug. More than half his breakfast remains as he scowls at the plate.

"Something wrong with your food?"

His gaze levels with mine, his honey irises darker and more

intense as he cocks his head. "Friend of yours?" Bitterness laces his voice.

I set the coffee pot on the counter and cross my arms over my chest. "Not that it's your business, but yes. Someone I haven't seen since I was a kid." I purse my lips and throw his attitude back at him. "You have a problem with that, *officer*?"

Picking up his fork, he stabs his food over and over. Bringing it to his lips, he says, "Not at all. Just keeping an eye on all the riffraff in town." Then he shoves the food in his mouth.

*Wow.*

Minutes ago, I had the insatiable urge to kiss him. Now, all I want to do is slap him. Seeing as we are both in our perspective uniforms and I'm on the clock, it's best I stick to verbal hits.

"Jealousy doesn't become you, Travis." I pick up the coffee pot and set it on the warmer. "Think on that before you walk in the door tomorrow." Giving him my back, I grab a cleaning cloth and start wiping down the back counter. "Be back with your to-go coffee in a few." Then I walk away.

I scrub the counter vigorously, taking methodical, deep breaths as I move down the line. On each inhale, I tell myself this is *his* issue, not mine. *I did nothing wrong.* With each exhale, the rage and fire blanketing my skin cools a little more.

*Travis is a townie I flirt with at work. Nothing more. I am not his. He is not mine.*

The last thought sours in my gut. Churning and groaning and complaining. As if my body knows lies from truths better than my mind.

Maybe it does. Maybe I am an ignorant fool. A dull-witted woman with her head in the clouds. A dreamer with her heart on her sleeve in the form of witty words and suggestive body language.

Travis and I may only be friends, but we are equally responsible for this blow up. We may not lay claim to one another, but I don't flirt with anyone the way I do with him. Far as I know, Travis hasn't been in a relationship in years. He is never seen in town with anyone on his arm. Not a single member of the gossip mill brags or complains about the company he keeps.

Maybe wearing his badge is easier when he has no one at home. Or maybe there are more layers to Travis Emerson than I have been led to believe.

What I *do* know is since I shut him out minutes ago, he hasn't taken his eyes off my back. I *feel* the heat of his stare on my skin. *Feel* the weight of his silent plea, begging me to turn around and walk closer to him.

Tossing the cloth in the cleaning solution, I fetch a large to-go cup, fill it with coffee, and top it with a lid. Not quite ready to turn around, I set the coffee maker up to brew two fresh pots. Once I've exhausted every second of free time, I take a deep breath, square my shoulders, and grab the cup.

What I see when I spin to face him throws me off.

The strong, bold, playful Travis that challenges me daily, that makes work more enjoyable, that makes me smile brighter, is nowhere in sight. The man I see now… this is a new side of Travis. Elbows on the counter, he hangs his head in his hands. More than half of his breakfast is untouched. Every other breath, he curls his fingers into his scalp and exhales audibly. Frustration colors his aura a murky red.

A desire to comfort him hits me square in the chest and knocks the air from my lungs.

Then I remember his shitty attitude led us here. If I forgive him so quickly, if I breeze past it as if it were no big deal, it opens the door for him to repeat the behavior.

And I refuse to be spoken to with such disrespect.

I set the cup on the counter in front of his plate. "Want a box for your breakfast?"

Dropping his hands to his lap, he lifts his head but doesn't make eye contact. "Please," he says softly. He reaches for his wallet, takes out a few bills, and sets them under his mug. "Thank you."

I hand him a takeout box and watch as he scrapes the food off his plate into the box. It takes every ounce of my strength to not speak up and offer him some form of solace. Arguing is something I prefer to avoid, but I also won't lie down and take shit from anyone.

Rising from his spot at the counter, he lifts his chin and meets my waiting gaze. Regret swirls in his honey irises as a ridge forms between his brows. He lifts a hand, rubs his collarbone through his shirt, then reaches for the to-go cup.

"I was an asshole." His lips flatten as he nods. "Not sure what came over me." Golden eyes hold my stormy blues. "I'm sorry."

Reaching for his plate, I clean up his dishes to busy my hands. "Thank you, Travis."

He raps two fingers on the counter before picking up his leftover breakfast. "Until next time, sunshine."

All it takes is hearing his nickname for me and I smile. "Later, Officer."

I stand with his plate in my hand and watch him weave through the tables. A gentleman near the door says something to him and he nods with a smile as he pushes the door open and walks to his car. Frozen in place, my eyes track his every move as he sets his cup and food down, as he starts the car, as he buckles his seat belt.

Then his eyes meet mine through the glass and a hint of a smile tugs at the corner of his mouth. I lift a hand and wave. In return, he winks, then backs out and drives off.

"Can you daydream later?" Oliver grumbles under his breath. "Old lady Hensen grabbed my ass as I passed her table." He fills two glasses with orange juice and a mini teapot with hot water. "I can't work in these conditions."

I snort-laugh. "You think she doesn't grab my ass?" My brows shoot up as I give him a pointed stare. "At eighty-six, that woman gives no fucks what she does anymore." Another laugh bursts free. "She probably *wants* to be arrested in the hopes of a pat down."

"Ugh." Oliver shakes head to toe. "I did *not* need that image in my head."

"You're welcome," I tease as I set Travis's dishes in the wash tub. I wipe down the counter, lay a new placemat and roll of silverware in his spot, then place a mug upside down.

I check on the rest of my tables, refilling drinks, clearing dishes, and settling checks. Then I head toward Ben and his construction crew.

"Y'all doing okay?" I survey the table, seeing more empty plates than not.

"I'll take the check, darling," an older gentleman says.

I nod in his direction. "You got it."

As I reach the kiosk to print the check, I glance back at the table. Eyes locked on me, Ben stares without shame. I hold his gaze for a breath, then drop my eyes to the screen.

*"Why do you have to move?"*

*I pluck a piece of grass and tear it into small bits. "Mom says she can't live in the house anymore."*

*He toys with his shoelace, his knee touching mine as we sit in the backyard under a tall evergreen. "There are other houses in Smoky Creek." He rolls the plastic at the end of his lace between his fingers. "You don't have to move away."*

*Angry at the idea of leaving my home, my friends, the only place I've ever known, I grab a fistful of grass and pull hard. "I told her that too." I growl and throw the grass. "She says moving to another town makes it easier to start over." My shoulders sag as I look at my best friend. "I don't want to start over, Benji."*

*Without hesitation, he wraps me in his arms and pins me to his chest. "This sucks."*

*It does suck. But no matter how much I argued with Mom, she wouldn't budge on her decision. Since Dad died, Mom has been sad all the time. She tries to put on a brave face. Forces smiles so people don't see her misery.*

*But I hear her crying in the shower. I hear her sobs as I lay awake in bed and she attempts to sleep on the couch. With Dad gone, she refuses to sleep in the bed they once shared. When she decided we were moving, she sold the bed. She sold almost everything we own. Because too much of it reminded her of Dad and what happened to him, and the fact she wasn't there to try and save him.*

*"Yeah, it does." I lean into my friend and rest my head on his shoulder. "Maybe you can come visit me during school break. Convince your parents to take a beach vacation."*

*He reaches for my braid and toys with the end. "I'll never stop trying."*

*If there is one thing I know about my best friend, it's that he never gives up.*

*I sit up straight, stare into his bright turquoise eyes, and memorize his face. "I know. Me either."*

A little more than thirteen years have passed since I last saw Ben. The boy I once knew is so different from the man across the room—except for his vivid, distinct eyes. This man is unfamiliar, yet a piece of me recognizes him. A part of my soul, buried deep with past memories, knows his soul.

And I don't know what the hell to do with this… this hum inside me as it swims for the surface.

Wandering back to the table, I hand the bill to the gentleman who requested it. As I start to walk off, Ben rises from his seat and steps toward me, shoving his hands in his pockets.

"That guy"—he juts his chin toward the counter—"the cop." He swallows. "Is he your… are you…"

I warm as Ben fumbles over his words, as he figures out how to ask if Travis and I are a couple.

"Is he your boyfriend?" he finally asks.

My lips twitch and I bite the inside of my cheek to fight off my smile. "No. Travis and I aren't together." I wipe my hands on my apron. "He's here every morning. We flirt and give each other a hard time."

His eyes drop to my lips for a fraction of a second before meeting my gaze again. In my periphery, his Adam's apple bobs. "Do you have a boyfriend?"

Well, that escalated faster than expected. "Um, no."

He rocks back on his heels, his gaze caressing the line of my jaw. "We're in town for the library addition." His eyes fall shut for one breath, then meet and hold mine. "Sorry if I sound like a mumbling fool. I'm still a little speechless at seeing you."

I chuckle. "Been a long time, Benji."

His frame relaxes as a soft smile plumps his cheeks. "Too long." He rocks back on his heels again. "I'd love to catch up later." Gaze dropping to the floor, he reaches up and scratches the back of his head. Then he levels me with his gaze, his striking blues locking me in place. His next words come out in a rush. "If you're not busy."

From the corner of my eye, a woman at their table nonchalantly watches our exchange. Her head appears to be down, but her eyes are on us. Being observant is part of my job. I may not be looking at her, but I feel her inquisitive eyes on me.

For all I know, they may be good friends. If she works for the construction company, they spend most of their days together. Like with any job, you tend to form bonds with people you see so often. They're your family and, naturally, you look out for them.

Maybe that's what she is doing. Looking out for Ben.

"No plans tonight, if that's good with you."

His smile widens, an unmistakable glow to his expression. "Work and the four walls of my room at the inn, that's my life for the next couple of months."

"Sounds fun," I say with a hint of sarcasm.

"Loads." He laughs.

"I'd hate to tear you away..." I snicker. "We can grab dinner at Dalton's. A basket of wings or a burger and some drinks. Catch up on life."

Warmth and an energy I haven't felt in years passes to me from him.

*God, how I've missed my friend.*

Ben and I had only ever been friends. When Mom moved us out of Smoky Creek, Ben and I were too young to be anything more—at least from an emotional standpoint. But he'd been my best friend more years than not. Being torn away from him and later losing touch with him was a knife to the heart.

How can I not take his arrival in Stone Bay as a sign? This is a chance to rekindle a long-lost friendship. An opportunity to know the man he has become and share the life I've built here.

"I'll happily abandon my room for dinner with you, sparkles." My old nickname is sandpaper on his tongue.

I swallow and nod. "See you there at six?"

"Six," he confirms, then sighs. "It's really good seeing you."

Inching back, I collect the check and payment for their table. "Yeah." My pulse hammers in my chest. "Good seeing you too."

# SEVEN

## SEEKER

Sitting at the counter facing the street, I stare at her in the window's reflection. Watch as she smiles and flirts and bats her fucking lashes at some other man. A new man. Watch as he gives her lovesick puppy eyes, fumbling over his words like a fucking idiot.

*Loser.*

I tilt my head down and slightly to the side as some kid with dark hair comes over and asks what I want to drink. I order coffee to make him leave.

If she would stop talking to the stuttering moron, she would be the one to bring me my fucking coffee, gifting me with an uninterrupted view of her curves.

I picture her close. So fucking close. Mere inches away.

Closing my eyes, I inhale deeply. Instantly, her sweet scent invades my memory. Takes me back to…

I pinch my eyes tighter. Imagine *I* am the person she flirts with as she toys with her hair. Imagine *I* am the person she pushes her tits higher for as she leans closer.

My dick swells behind my zipper and I groan as I open my eyes. I rub the heel of my palm over my cock.

*Soon.*

The construction crew is out of their chairs and headed for the door. New man has a blinding smile stuck on his face. A smile I want to slap off.

*She* is nowhere to be seen.

Dark-haired kid comes back with the coffee and asks if I am ready to order. I shake my head.

Once I'm alone again, I twist in my seat and scan the restaurant.

"Where the fuck are you?" I mumble to myself.

Minutes pass with no sign of her. My blood boils as I curl my fingers into fists.

I unroll the silverware, the metal clanging as it hits the table. Pulling a pen from my pocket, I flatten out the napkin and uncap my pen. A few scrawled lines later, I fold the napkin, scribble her name on it, toss the napkin next to the full mug of coffee, rise from my chair, and leave the restaurant.

"Fucking bitch."

# EIGHT

## BEN

EXITING THE INN, I SHOVE MY HANDS IN MY COAT POCKETS AND trek the short distance to the pub. The breeze off the bay adds bite to the November chill and I lengthen my stride. Strung lights between lampposts glitter in the darkening sky, lighting the way. Residents pass on the sidewalk more often than cars drive by on the street.

Pausing at the intersection, I stare at the two-story brick building across the street. *Dalton's* on the wooden placard above the awning now glows in burnt orange. Music and the occasional roar of an excited crowd spill onto the street through the open doors.

My fingers curl into loose fists, then relax in my pockets as I take a deep breath. Checking for cars, I cross the street and head for the bar's entrance. Each step forward tugs at the nervous energy swirling beneath my diaphragm. And despite the temperature, perspiration dampens my skin as my heart pounds a vicious rhythm in my chest.

Can't remember the last time I was this nervous.

I reach the open doors, take another deep breath, and step inside.

For a weeknight, the pub is busier than I expected. A bar takes up majority of the right wall, liquor bottles on wooden shelves against the brick, several beer taps at the heart of the bar. Dozens of stools are occupied by patrons catching up, having an after-work drink, or watching one of several sporting events on mounted flat screens. To the far left, brick archways separate pool tables from tables and a dancefloor.

Stepping farther into the pub, I scan the crowd for her. *Kirsten.* The girl I haven't seen or spoken to in far too long. The girl I'd abandoned countless other friends to hang out with at every opportunity before she moved away.

For years, we'd been attached at the hip. Best friends.

She'd been so different from other girls our age. Sure, Kirsten loved to slip on a dress and put ribbons in her hair. But she also loved mud between her toes and swimming in the creek on hot summer days. Kirsten never acted as if she was better than anyone else. Never said a cruel word to make herself feel better. Kirsten was pure sunshine and I gladly orbited her with a smile on my face.

Halfway across the pub, I spot her. At a tall table for two, she scrolls through her phone with one hand and fiddles with the ends of her hair with the other. Patrons cheer around her after a touchdown on the televised game, but she ignores the cacophony.

A few tables away, her posture shifts and she lifts her gaze, searching the pub. Steel-blue eyes meet mine and a riot thrashes in my chest. Heart-pounding seconds pass and I forget how to breathe. Then she smiles and lights up the dimly lit room. My steps falter for a beat as I suck in a sharp breath.

Sliding off her seat as I reach the table, we both lift our arms and step in for a hug. But like the bumbling dope I am, my arms smack hers.

"Sorry," I mutter as I shift my arms and reach for her again.

But she shifts her arms too, and we repeat the same embarrassing process. Heat climbs up my neck and face as I drop my hands to my sides and give up. But Kirsten isn't having it. Still wanting a welcome hug, Kirsten steps forward and wraps me in her arms. Hints of jasmine and notes of peach hit my nose as I lift my arms and hug her back.

In one breath, with one strong embrace, my soul relaxes for the first time in years. With Kirsten in my arms, I finally feel at home again.

All too soon, she releases me and steps back. "Hey," she whispers, her smile softer as she holds my stare.

"Hey." *Say something else, dumbass.* "Have you been waiting long?" *Lame.*

Kirsten takes her seat at the table and shakes her head. "Five minutes, tops." She plucks a small laminated menu from the holder on the table as I sit across from her. "How was day one of the new build?"

"How'd you know it was the first day?" I grab the other laminated menu and scan the food options.

She snickers and I peer across the table. "It's Stone Bay. Gossip is a way of life here. Working in a restaurant, I hear about *everything* in town. Even the things I don't want to know."

At this, I laugh. "Curse of a small town." Smoky Creek isn't a gossip mill, but it doesn't take long before Viola at Thumbprint's Bakery knows your business.

"Too true."

After a momentary scan of the menu, Kirsten flags down a server delivering beers to a nearby table.

A guy around our age sidles up to the table, standing rather close to Kirsten. "Hey, Kirsten." He flashes her a bright smile but pays me no attention. "What can I get you?"

She orders a local brew and barbecue wings. I opt to try

one of the local brews with a burger and onion rings. Promising to return with our beers in a moment, the server winks at her, then walks off.

An awkward silence settles between us as my eyes drift around the bar. Beneath the table, I tap my thigh to the music, needing something to do with my hands. My thoughts spiral like a cyclone as I fumble over what to say. Phony conversation is the last thing I want with Kirsten, but my mind seems to have forgotten how to start genuine dialogue.

"So," she says, breaking the silence.

My gaze snaps back to her. "So," I parrot as our drinks are delivered.

"What have I missed in Smoky Creek?" She lifts the beer to her lips and looks at me over the rim as she tips the glass.

After a few sips of my own beer, I set the glass down and twist it back and forth as I figure out where to begin. More than thirteen years have passed since her mom packed up their car and drove them out of Smoky Creek. So much has changed, yet a lot remains the same.

"The park near the creek got an overhaul a few years ago. New equipment and coverings over the playground."

"No more metal slide?"

I wince at the memory of my butt and thighs burning as I slid down the old slide over and over. At fifteen feet tall, it was the only slide in Smoky Creek for decades. A neighborhood mom bought a hose and left it at the spigot near the slide. In the hotter months, we unraveled the hose, dragged it up the ladder, and cranked the water to cool the metal.

Chuckling, I shake my head. "Nope. Recycled plastic and rubber. The little kids have no idea how lucky they are."

"Indeed." She takes another sip of her beer. "How are your parents?"

A smile tugs at my lips. "Good. Celebrated their twenty-fifth wedding anniversary in September."

"Twenty-fifth?"

I nod.

"Wow. I should send them a card." In a blink, her expression falls. "Or not. They probably don't remember me."

Without thinking, I reach across the table and lay my hand over hers. Warmth radiates from her skin to mine, a hum just beneath the surface. My breath catches in my throat as my eyes shoot to hers. She holds my stare, unblinking, and I know she feels it too. Our connection, but different from how it was years ago.

Against every instinct, I take my hand off hers and cup my beer. "They'd remember you," I croak out, then clear my throat. I draw lines in the condensation on my glass. "How's your mom?"

A gentle smile tugs at one corner of her mouth. "Great. She's a farmer. Remarried about eight years ago."

The server delivers our food and offers to refill our drinks, but we both opt for water. The table falls quiet momentarily as we eat. Returning with water and extra napkins, the server asks if we need anything else. We shake our heads and, after another wink at Kirsten, he walks off.

A few bites into my burger, I ponder over my next question. Consider if I really want to know about her relationship history. Because the moment the question leaves my lips, she will ask for the same in return. And I'm unsure if I want to share that piece of myself yet.

Kirsten and I were always open and honest with each other, even if the truth stung. But that was before life got complicated. Before either of us hit puberty and sex crossed our minds. Before our peers turned petty and our appearance mattered more than kindness. Before she moved away and my once familiar town became a foreign land.

Part of me is glad we missed those messy teenage years together. Lifelong friendships don't always survive high school. Though I would've loved to have seen her change over the years, I might have bombed our friendship by thinking with my hormones instead of my heart.

"Earlier at the restaurant," she starts, and I look up. "You asked if I had a boyfriend."

*Damnit.*

"What about you? Is there a lucky lady in Smoky Creek waiting for you to return home?"

I swallow the bite of onion ring too soon and choke as the breading scratches its way down my throat.

"Oh my god." Wiping her hands with a napkin, she rises from her chair and moves around the table. "Are you okay?"

Holding up a hand, I nod. I smack my chest a few times and dislodge the onion ring. My face flames with embarrassment as I sip my water. Kirsten returns to her seat, her body poised to leap from the chair at any moment. Sweat blankets the back of my neck, forehead, and cheeks as I calm my breathing.

"Touchy subject?"

I blink up at her as she tilts her head and studies me with curious eyes.

*Something like that.* "Not something I'm ready to talk about yet."

Leaning back in her seat, she crosses her arms over her chest. "Are you seeing someone?" She lifts a hand to her necklace—the rose gold chain with a small crescent moon her dad bought for her tenth birthday—and slides the charm back and forth. "Because I don't need some jealous Betty knocking on my door with a knife in her hand."

"Jealous Betty?"

Her shoulders slump as she huffs. "You know what I mean, Benji. Women can be a lot more territorial than men. And significantly crazier when betrayed."

Thank the gods, I've never experienced an insecure lover on a rampage. Though I've heard my share of stories from friends.

"No jealous Bettys, psycho Susans, or deranged Debbies will come knocking." I laugh under my breath and she narrows her eyes. "I promise." I turn somber. "Last woman I was with... we recently decided to go separate ways." *Okay, I guess I am talking about this.* "She wanted things I wasn't ready for."

Emotion swells in my throat as a memory of Carolyn crying surfaces. Regardless of how much it hurts, breaking off our two-year relationship was for the best. The last month of our relationship was agony. I tiptoed around every word, every touch, every kiss, unsure how to act after rejecting the idea of living together. The entire time we were together, I knew Carolyn's heart. Knew what she wanted her future to look like. Hard as I tried, I had difficulty getting on the same page with her.

Carolyn wants a big house bustling with life. A man to sweep her off her feet, kiss her senseless, and eventually put a beautiful ring on her left hand. She wants babies and messes to clean up after. Crayon-doodled family pictures stuck to the fridge with alphabet magnets. Family portraits hung in classy frames on the hallway wall. She wants to grow old with one person and celebrate golden anniversaries with friends and family.

Nice as her dreams are, I don't share them. Not with her, anyway.

I *do* want to grow old with someone, but I don't want to

settle. Much as I cared for Carolyn, our love didn't make my heart beat out of my chest. It didn't rob me of breath. Didn't make me crave more. With Carolyn, I didn't see or feel fireworks.

I want love to wrap me up and swallow me whole. I want fire and passion. A love so powerful, I can't picture life without it. A partner that challenges me in life and lifts me up when I'm down. An indisputable connection no one can break.

Kirsten toys with the balled-up wrapper of her straw. "I get that," she mumbles. "I've never been in a long-term relationship." She scoffs. "Or any kind of relationship beyond one night." Lifting her gaze, she shrugs. "Can't seem to open up that part of myself."

I ignore the mention of one-night stands. "Because of your dad?"

A sad smile curves her lips. "Maybe." She dunks a celery stalk in bleu cheese dressing. "Probably."

"Hey."

I wait for her to look up. Wait for her stormy-blue eyes to lock onto mine. When they do, I see the years of hurt she has kept to herself. Years of thoughts she locked away and cloaked with smiles.

"There's no rule book on how to live your life," I say. "Just because someone declared centuries ago men and women had to get married, have babies, and live a certain way to be happy …" Leaning in, I lay my hand on the table near her. "It doesn't make it true." I swallow and nod imperceptibly. "There is more than one way to live. The only thing that matters is that you're happy." My knee bounces beneath the table. "And your happiness will look different than someone else's. Some people are content with solitude, while others never want to be alone." I sit back in my seat, pulling my hand away. "There's no deadline. No rush. And you're allowed to change your mind at any time."

Warmth blooms in my chest as she smiles at my long-winded answer. I can't help but smile in return.

"When did you become a philosopher, Benjamin Wilks?"

I chuckle. "Sometime between age ten and twenty-three."

She picks up the last wing in her basket and points it in my direction. "I like philosophical Benji." Then she bites the wing and says nothing more.

The rest of dinner passes in comfortable silence and mixed emotions. Every time I glance her way, she drops her gaze and futzes with a celery stalk. This minor glimpse at a bashful Kirsten—an odd trait for the girl I knew—wakes something inside me. A dull hum from years past. A familiar sensation with a new edge.

It's enthralling yet alarming.

When it's time to settle the tab, I snatch the check from the table and pay. We push back from the table and stand, slipping on our coats. As we walk out of Dalton's, Kirsten waves to a few people while I resist the urge to settle my hand on the small of her back.

I walk her to her car, a red SUV with a pink, moon-shaped crystal dangling from the rearview mirror. *So very Kirsten.*

We reach her driver's side door and she spins to face me, her lips rolling between her teeth. She opens her mouth to say something, then snaps it shut. Then without warning, she steps into me and wraps her arms around my middle.

"I've missed you, Benji," she whispers, her breath warm on my ear.

I circle her waist with my arms, close my eyes, and breathe in her sweet floral scent. "Missed you too, sparkles."

She takes a deep breath, drops her arms, and steps back. Reaching into her purse, she pulls out her phone and taps the screen a few times before holding it out. "Will you add your contact info?" She tucks her lips between her teeth. "Only if you want to. I'm at the restaurant most days."

I take her phone and stare down at the blank contact. Smiling, my fingers dance over the screen a moment before I hand it back to her.

Unlocking her car, she tosses her purse inside and cranks the engine. Then she steps out from behind the door and surprises me with another hug. "Night, Benji." Her lips press to my cheek and I stop breathing.

"Night, sparkles," I whisper.

She hops in her car, waves at me through the window, then backs out and drives off.

Hour-long minutes pass before I unstick my feet and walk toward the inn, my cheek on fire and heart rattling my rib cage.

# NINE

## TRAVIS

D ARK CLOUDS LOOM OVER THE BAY AS I CRUISE THROUGH TOWN, the forecasted storm rolling in hours early, a reflection of my dismal mood.

This morning, my plan was to profusely apologize to Kirsten. Again. Beg for her forgiveness. Swear my undying fealty. Do whatever it takes to be in her good graces again. Yesterday, I not only embarrassed her with my barbaric behavior, I embarrassed myself.

And until I redeem myself, I won't be free of this pang in my gut. Until I see the corners of her eyes lift as she gifts me her smile, I won't take a full breath.

I humiliated her in front of dozens of townsfolk. Treated her like a child. Behaved like an asshole. Her mercy is the last thing I deserve, but I pray she grants it nonetheless.

Unfortunately, I missed the chance to get down on my proverbial knees and plead with her today. Because today is her day off, and I have no idea if she returns to work tomorrow. Either way, it serves me right to suffer a little longer.

To add salt to my well-deserved wound, the construction crew was in the restaurant again this morning. A little quieter today, they shoveled down their breakfast like heathens. But I didn't miss one of the guys asking Kirsten's childhood friend how his date went last night. I also didn't miss the way Kirsten's *friend* looked in my direction as he said, *"Perfect."*

*Asshole.*

I head south on Lighthouse Lane, surveying some of the town's rental properties as I pass. As I roll past the last Fox rental, a call comes in on the radio.

"Attention all units, 10-54 called in by hiker. South of Fossil Mountain Highway, west of Granite Parkway, on the eastern ridge of the mountains butting against Barron Cabin number three. Who is responding?"

*A 10-54? Holy shit.*

I peer into the rearview mirror to see Pepper sitting at attention in the back seat. Today, she may actually get to do police work.

Plucking the radio from the dash, I press the button and reply. "Officers Emerson and Pepper, fifteen minutes out and en route." I flip the overhead lights on but leave the siren off.

As I set the radio back in the cradle, another voice echoes through the cab of my cruiser. "Chief Emerson responding. Ten minutes out."

The second my father's voice fades from the speaker, I smash the accelerator to the floor. Naturally, the chief of police should make an appearance at a crime scene. In a small town, it is to be expected. But if I arrive a minute later than the fifteen minutes I promised, the chief will have my head. Knowing my father, he wants me on scene before him.

*"That's what an Emerson looks like. A man with foundational concepts to benefit the town. An innovative man with a good head on his shoulders. A respectable man the town looks to in hard times."*

His small but poignant speech on what it means to be an Emerson—one of the seven Stone Bay "elite" families—replays in my thoughts as I fly past the general store on Fossil Mountain Highway. The words *"innovative"* and *"respectable"* stand out more than the rest.

Bringing Pepper onto the force—the town's first K-9 officer—and offering to train more K-9 teams fulfills the innovative part of the equation. Though the town hasn't had much need for K-9 officers in the past, their extrasensory skills will only enhance the department and aid in closing cases more efficiently.

As far as being respectable, that comes with time and maturity. Respect is earned, not simply handed over because of the badge on my chest or the surname I bear. This much I know. I'll be the first to admit I still have growing up to do. My blowup in the restaurant yesterday knocked my respect status down a few pegs. Integrity? I have that in spades. Keeping promises? I'd have to be on my deathbed or in the ground to not make good on my commitments.

If my father would recognize how much I've accomplished instead of pointing out all the things left unchecked, I wouldn't have this constant need to prove my worth.

I pull onto the south shoulder of the highway, the first to arrive. *Thank fuck.* Hopping out of the cruiser, I shrug on my jacket, then open the back door and let Pepper out.

"Officer Pepper," I say her name sharper—a tone reserved for work—and she stands taller. "We need your expertise today. Ready?"

Pepper lets out a single bark. *Yes.*

"Let's go. Find the hiker. *Such,*" I command in German, telling her to search.

When I decided to train Pepper to be an officer, I learned it was best to teach commands in another language. Online, I read several articles and most had one thing in common. K-9 officer commands are often in German. It avoids confusion if the K-9 hears other command words in English, especially from someone other than their human officer companion.

We trudge through the woods and I let Pepper lead. She doesn't have a specific scent to guide her, but her nose will differentiate humans from the earth much quicker than my own. A little more than a mile from the road, Pepper slows her pace and drops her nose closer to the ground. I remain silent and let her do her job.

At the foot of the mountain, Pepper veers southeast, drops her nose completely to the ground, and picks up speed—a sign we are closing in on the target. My eyes scan the forest as she guides us toward the hiker. Less than a minute later, a flash of fluorescent orange comes into view.

"Stone Bay Police Department!" I holler. "I'm with a K-9 officer. Do not make any sudden movements."

A man in his late forties or early fifties meets my gaze and nods. "I understand."

Pepper barks as we approach the man. I step into Pepper's line of sight and give a nonverbal command to stop but remain vigilant. She stops barking, holds her position, stands tall, and scans the forest.

Pepper was trained to respond to verbal and nonverbal commands. Nonverbal commands are reserved for uncertain situations and I don't want possible suspects aware of what she will do next.

"*Brav*, Officer Pepper," I praise her. Shifting my attention to the man, I introduce myself. "I'm Officer Emerson. The station informed us you discovered a body."

The man nods, his face paling. "Yes." Slowly, he lifts a hand and points behind him. "On the other side of the boulder. A young woman." Sweat beads his brow as he teeters in place. "I'm staying in the Barron three cabin and decided to hike the base of the mountains." He covers his mouth with his hand. "Oh god."

"Sir, you should sit down. Put your head between your knees and take some deep breaths."

He does as I instruct, seconds before Pepper starts barking.

Hand on my sidearm, I scan the forest, not seeing what has Pepper's attention. The radio on my shoulder crackles before the chief's voice echoes through the forest.

"We hear Officer Pepper. We are approaching."

I don't command Pepper to stand down as I respond. "Base of the mountain. One hiker on scene."

Chief Emerson comes into view with my partner, Officer Wooler, and Theo Black, an EMT from the fire department, and I command Pepper to stand down.

Officer Wooler and I cruise town together on the days Pepper is off duty. Unlike me, Starla Wooler prefers reports and desk detail over responding to calls and driving around town. Because of that, we have a symbiotic work relationship. I respond to disgruntled calls and do the face-to-face work, then deliver all the details to her and let her fill out the report. We both sign off on it after I review it and call it a day.

Until today, there hasn't been a case that required additional officers on scene. Not since I've been on the force. Not for more than twenty years, when Dad was a rookie.

"What do we know?" Chief asks as he surveys the hiker.

"Visitor staying at the Barron cabin was out hiking and came across the body. A young woman behind the boulder." I point toward the large chunk of granite. "I have yet to survey the scene."

Chief takes out his phone. "Capture photos before we touch anything. Once we know what we're working with, I'll decide if we need more help." He snaps a few pictures, then looks at Wooler. "Interview the hiker. I want every last detail.

What time it was when he found her. If anything looked, sounded, or smelled out of the ordinary. If he touched the victim or anything in proximity to the victim. How long he's been at the cabin. If he's hiked this same path any other day since his arrival, and when, if yes." He looks at me, then back at Wooler. "No detail is inconsequential."

"Yes, sir, Chief," Wooler states as she pulls out her phone and taps the screen.

"Emerson, Black," Chief says as he heads for the boulder. "Let's go."

"Officer Pepper, *gehen*," I command her to go and she stays in step beside me as we follow Chief and Theo.

Retrieving my phone, I open the camera app and take photos while Chief does the same. Two sets of pictures are better than one. I circle around the opposite side of the boulder from Chief and Theo, getting a different vantage point of the scene.

Pepper becomes agitated the closer we get, whining and squirming, tugging me forward. I flip my camera to video mode and start recording. A simultaneous gasp leaves us all as we round the boulder.

"*Sitz*, Officer Pepper." *Sit.* I point a finger down and Pepper immediately sits. "*Bleib.*" *Stay.* I hold up a hand, my palm facing her, and she sits taller. Proud.

Giving the scene a wide berth, I circle around with my phone held high and record the lay of the land. Chief snaps countless photos, and slowly we move closer to the woman. Theo tugs on a pair of gloves and sets his medic bag down before moving in closer.

Pale lips peek through fallen foliage, along with a hint of dull, blonde hair. Most of her body is covered with leaves and evergreen needles, but enough is exposed to show her lack of clothing and see specific features.

"Get your pictures," Theo states. "I'm calling in for addi-tional help."

Chief nods and we continue capturing the scene. A moment later, I'm handed a pair of gloves. "Continue with the video as we uncover her."

Gently, we clear the foliage from the body. I tunnel my vision and focus on the task, detaching emotionally. Finished, we straighten and take different shots of the scene. Close-ups of her face and body. Theo steps in, scoops his hands under her torso, and lifts her slightly.

"She's been here eight hours, minimum," Theo announces. He jerks his chin toward her backside. "See the purple hue on her skin?"

"Yes," we say simultaneously.

"Lividity," he says with surety as he gently lowers her to the ground. "Happens post mortem. Blood 'sinks' in the body" —he air quotes the word *sinks*—"in the direction of gravity." He lifts her and checks the underside of her limbs. "The purple discoloration happens after about eight hours." He looks over his shoulder at us. "But given the cooler temperature, it could've taken longer."

Ending the video, I stare down at the young woman. She appears to be in her early twenties. Cuts and bruises mar the front of her torso. Blood crusts the hair at her temple, but her face appears otherwise clean. Her body lies perfectly straight, as if she laid down for bed and never woke up.

And when I take a step back and look at the scene as a whole, I stop breathing. At my sides, my hands shake. Nausea rolls in my stomach and I swallow past the fear clawing up my throat. The backs of my eyes sting and I blink several times, fighting the tears that threaten to fall.

I don't personally know this woman; I don't recall ever seeing her in town, but her resemblance to Kirsten is uncanny.

Same build, same facial structure, same color hair. The similarities are eerie.

"Take five," Chief orders, his eyes locked on my face. "We'll be here a bit longer."

Nodding, I step around the boulder and suck in a deep breath.

*It's not her. It's not her. It's not her.*

No matter how many times I chant the words in my head, my mind refuses to stop comparing the lifeless woman to Kirsten. My gut twists, bile climbing up and burning my throat. I curl my fingers into fists and inhale deeply, begging the mental image to disappear.

But I know it won't. Not until I lay eyes on her again. Kirsten may only be a friend—a woman I see thirty minutes a day, five days a week—but my soul begs to differ. Deep in my bones, Kirsten has always felt like more than a friend.

I care about her more than I realized until minutes ago. And the way I left things yesterday, the way I treated her... I *need* to see her. I *need* to apologize. More than anything, I *need* to set things right.

Because if this had been her, I'd never forgive myself.

# TEN

## KIRSTEN

An ominous cloud swept in yesterday, blanketing Stone Bay in fear and curiosity.

Within an hour, news of the dead woman discovered at the south end of town spread from one gossipmonger to the next. Gasps filled the air as the story passed from one resident to another with too much ease. Scrutinous eyes scanned sidewalks and stores and every unfamiliar face.

On a normal day, I ignore the gossip mill. Shove aside the whispered rumors that spread faster than cancer and pollute the town. But this story isn't your average small-town scandal.

A woman is dead. A fact, not a rumor.

And for the first time, I want every single detail. I want to know who we lost in our town. Her name, what she looks like, if she lived in Stone Bay or was passing through. How she died.

If we are safe.

Along with the circulated news, I've learned more than twenty years have passed since the last reported local murder. Delilah was in kindergarten when it happened. Though her parents didn't share the details with her at the time, they talked about the girl for years, divulging more of the story each year.

Several years before Mom and I moved to Stone Bay, the quaint and quiet town brimmed with chaos when a sixteen-year-old girl was found dead on the playground. Her limbs outstretched on the climbing dome, her wrists and ankles tied to the coated metal bars, a switchblade in her chest. Hours before she was found, her parents had reported her missing to the police department.

After weeks of rigorous detective work, the killer was caught. A disgruntled young man passing through town. When asked why he did it, he said he had too much to drink and the girl reminded him of his ex-girlfriend.

Shortly after the case was solved, the town dismantled and removed the climbing dome from the park.

Not that one is better than the other, but the newest murder, from what I've heard, is considerably worse.

I turn off my ring light and tug my phone from the holder. Wanting some positivity in my day, I did a short live online and showed off the leggings, joggers, top, and hoodie from a fitness company. For a moment, reality slipped away and I got lost in the world of social media.

But as soon as I ended the live, all the joy I felt extinguished too.

Staring at the pile of fitness attire, it dawns on me I haven't worked out in weeks. Would be nice to get in a run, but I may have to visit the gym and use the treadmill. Though I love running near the bay or on trails, with a killer on the loose, it's best not to run solo or in secluded areas.

Tugging a hoodie over my head, I free my hair, opting to leave it down today. After one last look in the mirror, I pocket my phone, key fob, and wallet, exit my room, and step out the front door. I jog to my car, hop in, and crank the engine.

My phone connects with the car's Bluetooth, music from my favorite playlist echoing through the cab as I text Skylar.

> On my way

An immediate response vibrates my phone.

SKY

> I'm driving with Do Not Disturb turned on. I'll see your message when I reach my destination.

I smile down at the screen and type out another message.

> Look at you being a good girl 😊 See you soon

Depositing my phone in the cupholder, I buckle my seat belt and back out of the driveway.

As I make the short trek to the deli, a chill rolls down my spine at the eerie stillness of the neighborhood. On any given day, no matter the season, I wave to neighbors out for a walk. I spot people decorating their porch for an upcoming holiday or season. Reminisce as kids play on the lawn. See some form of *life* outside.

Today… nothing. Not a single soul.

Within minutes, I park on the street in front of Rosenberg's Deli. Skylar stands inside next to the door, smiling when she sees me approach.

"Hey, girl," I greet, pulling her in for a hug.

She embraces me with equal strength. "Hey." Then she releases me and takes a step toward the order line. "I'm starving."

We place our orders then find a table. Though we arrived

earlier than the lunch rush, the deli is quiet. Too quiet.

Like every other food establishment in town, some days are busier than others. Select times of the day are busier than others. Rosenberg's always has a line, whether it's for sandwiches, deli meats, premade salads, or heat-and-eat meals. There is always someone roaming the small selection of groceries.

Not today. One other person waits for their lunch, but not at a table.

"Feels like we've entered some parallel universe," I say, peering out the window at the empty sidewalk.

"Right?" Skylar follows my line of sight. "Where is everyone?" She unwraps her straw and takes a sip of her Dr Pepper. "Law is freaked out, too." Light green eyes hold my steely blues. "Made me promise to check in with him anytime I leave or arrive somewhere."

Skylar and Lawrence's relationship is still young, but I've never seen someone as fiercely protective of another person the way Lawrence is with Skylar. He gives her freedom to spread her wings while simultaneously keeping her close.

Our night out at Dalton's six months ago went from a girls' night—with the possibility of hooking up with a guy—to the start of their relationship. I watched him eye-fuck her from the opposite end of the bar as we sipped our drinks. When we hit the dance floor, he rescued her after a wrong move that led to a sprained ankle.

Their relationship turned heads and stirred up gossip, but I loved watching my friend fall hard and fast.

Love may not be something I'm actively seeking, but a part of me wishes I had *my person*. Someone who would drop everything when I texted or called. Someone who wanted every available minute of my time and craved my affection.

But in the same breath, having someone consume such a

large piece of my heart terrifies me to no end.

"We should all check in with each other until this passes over. Especially if we're alone."

Skylar nods as her eyes lose focus.

In record time, our food is delivered to the table. We eat in relative silence as a few other patrons come in for lunch, somber smiles on their faces when they look our way.

Sick of the silence but unsure what to talk about, I speak what's on my mind. What's on everyone's mind. "Why do you think someone killed her?" I keep my voice low.

Skylar dunks her grilled cheese in her soup over and over. "Your guess is as good as mine." She shrugs. "Why does anyone do crazy shit like that?" Bringing the softened sandwich to her lips, she pauses. "'Cause something isn't right with their mind." Then she bites into her sandwich.

I hum. "True."

I guess there is no appropriate explanation as to why people commit heinous acts. But part of me is curious what makes the switch flip in their heads. What moment triggers them to think it is a good idea to hurt or take another life.

"I hate that this happened," she says, setting the spoon in her now empty soup bowl. "I hate that one person has the power to darken countless other lives with their actions."

Her words revive memories from my childhood. Memories that, no matter how many years pass, will always haunt me. Memories of the darkest time in my own life I see clear as day when I close my eyes. And one specific memory I wish would fade away rather than suppress all the good memories before it.

I drop my chin to my chest, close my eyes, and inhale deeply. One breath at a time, I shove the dark memories down, down, down. Force them into an invisible box in my mind labeled *Do not open*. Push past the dark days that followed the worst day of my life. Swallow past the emotion suddenly clogging my throat as I try my damnedest to shake off the past.

"Hey." Fingers squeeze my hand. "You okay?"

*One more deep breath.*

I lick my lips, open my eyes, and lift my gaze to meet hers. Concern tugs her brows in as worried eyes flit between mine.

"Yeah." I flip my hand over and grip hers tightly. "Old memory."

"About your dad?"

Skylar was my first friend in Stone Bay. For years, I didn't share much of myself with anyone in town. But she was patient and kind and always there when I needed a friend. She stuck by my side on the good and bad days, solidifying the foundation of our friendship each time she wrapped me in her arms while I cried. At the time, she had no idea why I cried so much. She didn't ask, which made me love her more. And when I finally felt strong enough to share my story, she held my hand and listened without interruption.

Only a select few in Stone Bay know about my dad and what happened to him. I don't want anyone's pity, and neither does Mom. We choose to celebrate the good times we shared with him.

But every now and then, the darkness slips back in. It doesn't last as long as it once did, but is still a clenched fist around my heart when it does.

I nod, forcing a sad smile. "I wish there was a way to delete that memory." My gaze drifts out the window. "A way to push it to the very end of all my memories of him."

"Me too." She gives my hand one last squeeze, then releases it. "What are you doing after this?"

Skylar and I planned our lunch date days ago. If today were a normal day, we would cross the street after lunch and wander town. Stop in the bookstore and harass Delilah in the romance section. Visit the thrift store in search of new clothes on the racks or curious knickknacks on the shelves.

Instead, Stone Bay is a dismal ghost town without a ray of sunshine.

"Grocery shopping," I say with false enthusiasm.

"Mind if I tag along? There are a few things we need anyway."

"Girl time at the grocery store." I roll my eyes and chuckle. "Why do I suddenly feel twice my age?"

Our laughter fills the air and garners the attention of everyone in Rosenberg's. An older woman narrows her eyes at us while a man closer to our age stares on like we've lost our minds.

And maybe we have.

But if death has taught me anything, it's that you have to live in the present. You have to experience every moment as if it may be your last. Live life to the fullest because you never know what tomorrow will bring.

End each day with a satiated soul, not a hungry heart.

"Come on." I rise from my chair and offer her my elbow. "Let's go tear up the grocery store."

"Wow," we say in unison as we survey the grocery store parking lot.

"Are we getting a snowstorm neither of us heard about?" Skylar asks.

Middle of a weekday and almost nowhere to park at the grocery store. Add that to the list of things you have never seen in Stone Bay.

"Either that or there's one hell of a sale," I muse.

We scurry through the doors and grab carts from the corral. Residents mill about, tossing anything and everything in their baskets as they clear shelves. Skylar and I freeze near the entrance, both of us awestruck.

A woman with a full cart of bagged groceries heads in our direction on swift feet. I hold up my hand as she approaches, hoping she will stop. After a tentative look, she rolls to a stop.

"Excuse me, ma'am," I say. "Why is the store so busy?"

With a tilt of her head, she narrows her eyes and regards me a moment. "You didn't hear?"

*Hear what?*

When I don't answer, she continues. "A young woman was murdered near the Barron property."

Slowly, I nod. "Yes, I heard about that." My face grows tight as I try to figure out what that has to do with the town emptying the grocery store.

Me not connecting the dots must grate her nerves because her expression morphs from one of concern to indignance. "You younger people keep living life as if nothing's going on around you. Someone died." Her stare turns icy as she looks from me to Skylar. "We should all be at home, where it's safe." She shakes her head. "Not out having fun." Shoving her cart between ours, she darts out the door.

"Since when is grocery shopping fun?" I mutter and steer my cart toward the pharmacy. "I need to pick up my prescription."

"Meet me in produce?"

I nod. "Be there in a minute."

Second in line, I tap my fingers on the shopping cart to the overhead music. Before the song ends, I step up to the window.

"Miss Sparks," the pharmacy assistant greets, his tone as indifferent as his expression. "Picking up?"

"Hi, Charles." I smile at the grumpiest employee in the grocery store. "Yes. One script."

He types on the computer in front of him, then spins around to fish through the prescriptions waiting for pickup.

"So crazy to hear about the lady they found in the woods," I say, trying to make conversation with him.

Through the gossip mill, I overheard a diner in the restaurant say Charles's wife recently divorced him, took their child, and left town. He'd been surly before his ex-wife turned his life upside down, but at least he smiled once in a while. Now, I don't think his facial muscles remember *how* to smile.

Doesn't stop me from gifting him one. If mine is the only smile he sees, then at least he's seen one today.

Bag in hand, he turns around and rings up my order, stony expression firmly in place. "Maybe she provoked her attacker."

*I'm sorry. What?*

Dazed, I sign for my prescription and swipe my card on the reader. When he hands it over, I meet his gaze. "No one *asks* to be killed and thrown in the woods."

Blinking a few times, his expression softens. "I didn't mean that." He runs a hand through his shaggy hair. "It's been a long day." He waves a hand toward the store. "Half the town has lost their damn minds. And all I hear about is this woman, whoever she is, and everyone's opinion on what happened."

I drop my prescription in the cart. "Hopefully they'll catch the person soon. Then everything will go back to normal."

He points to my prescription—my birth control—and says, "Be careful." He straightens a display of cold medicine near the register. "There's a killer on the loose."

*What the hell?*

From head to toe, every muscle in my body locks up. My face distorts as my lips purse and my forehead wrinkles. I get it; some people are socially awkward. They mean well but say the strangest things with good intentions. This may be one of those moments, but I have no clue if it is.

Unsure how to respond, I steer the cart away from the pharmacy and start walking. "Have a better day," I throw over my shoulder as I breeze past a display.

Finding Skylar in produce, I opt to not share my weirder-than-normal interaction at the pharmacy. *Maybe I should start ordering my pills through the mail.* Whatever. It's done now.

We move through the aisles, filling our carts with less than everyone else in the store. Because this isn't the apocalypse and more groceries will be delivered.

As we approach the checkout, an uneasy feeling washes over me. I glance over one shoulder and spot a woman in green scrubs. She smiles and I return the gesture. Looking over the other shoulder, I catch a man blatantly staring at my butt. When I tug my hoodie lower, dark eyes lift and meet mine. His tongue darts out and licks his lips. I face forward and shuffle with the line, the knot in my stomach more pronounced.

I close my eyes and take a deep breath. Work to shove down the nausea bubbling beneath my diaphragm. One breath later, scribbled words on a curled napkin flash behind my closed lids.

*Every morning, you flash him your cleavage and tease him with your words. And when he pisses you off, you make plans with other men. You drink and dance and fuck like a whore. One day, you'll be my whore.*

A hand on my arm makes me jump, and I open my eyes. Skylar studies my face, concern etched in her brows as she mouths, "What's wrong?"

I shake my head and move my groceries from the cart to the belt. The cashier rings up my items and I smile as he tries to make polite conversation. As we wheel our carts back to the corral and remove our bags, I peek over my shoulder into the store, my nervous belly churning and twisting.

No one pays us any attention. No one approaches us.

*It's nothing, Kirsten. Just your mind fucking with you.*

We step outside, the cooler air dancing over my exposed skin and soothing my anxiety.

"What happened?"

I glance at Skylar briefly and keep walking, not saying a word.

"Did you have another flashback of your dad?"

No one except Oliver knows about the note from work the other day. And all Oliver knows is someone left one. It was folded in half, with my name written on the outside. Thank goodness he didn't snoop. Had he read it, I'd literally be escorted everywhere.

If I was smart, I'd share the note with Travis. Though I don't think the person who wrote it is the same person who killed the young woman, it's definitely someone who needs help.

When this dies down, when they catch the person responsible for the woman in the woods, I'll share the note with him. The last thing Travis needs is a heavier workload.

"Yeah," I lie far too easily. "Another flashback."

No sense in creating unnecessary concern. No sense in making a big deal out of what could be nothing.

When the time is right, I will tell Travis. Until then, I'll remain vigilant. Text the group chat when I go places on my own. Keep my head high and eyes on my surroundings.

You only get one chance at life. And I refuse to let anyone steal mine.

Head down and hand braced on the tile, I pinch my eyes shut as water pelts my hair, my neck, my back. Silently, I beg for the heat to soothe my tense muscles. To release the ache in my bones. To give me some form of respite.

Two days have passed since the woman was discovered in the woods. And in those two days, I've aged two decades.

At the police academy, they train for countless scenarios. Standard speeding tickets, domestic disturbances, murder, and an endless list of crimes in between. They hand out mock case files and guide you on how to deal with each situation. How to shut off your emotions, focus on finding a resolution, and close the case. We all dealt with a made-up murder case, photos included in the file, and handled it with ease.

But being presented with a case study is wholly different than seeing the victim firsthand. Seeing their lifeless body and knowing you can't save them.

Her irises and pupils were cloudy and vacant, eyes wide in fear and aimed skyward. Lacerations marred her pale and bruised skin as she laid impossibly still on the earth. Deep cuts on her bare breasts and inner thighs. Smaller cuts on her abdomen, hips, and pelvic region. Dried blood—too much damn blood—blanketed most of her skin and hair. Earth caked under her nails.

The woman fought for her life. Clawed and thrashed and watched every second as her killer overpowered her lithe frame. As they stole her life.

And fuck... I can't get the fucking image of her lifeless body out of my head. Every time I close my eyes, her clouded irises stare back. Awake or asleep, those colorless, desolate eyes torment me.

To make matters worse, my mind won't stop comparing the woman's features to Kirsten's. The resemblance between the two women is beyond eerie and unsettling.

Night or day, I'm tortured with an endless loop of nausea-inducing images. One moment, the woman in the woods haunts my dreams. Outstretched arms, a silent scream ripping from her throat, her red-rimmed eyes implore me to bring her killer to justice. A breath later, the woman morphs into Kirsten. Mascara-stained tears on her cheeks, Kirsten calls out to me and begs for my help. Pleads with me to save her.

The nightmares jolt me awake. Body blanketed in sweat, my heart pounds, pounds, pounds in my chest as I try to catch my breath. As I try to wipe the horrid dreams from my mind.

No matter how exhausted I am, no matter how quickly I pass out, I wake up after four or five hours of sleep, run to the bathroom, and drop in front of the toilet. No matter how many times I tell myself the woman in the woods isn't Kirsten, my brain still crosses its wires and replaces the woman with her.

*I just need to see her. Kirsten. I need to know she's safe.*

"Fuck," I mutter as I drag a hand through my soaked hair.

Inhaling deeply, I push off the wall, straighten my spine, and reach for the shampoo. *Lather, rinse, soap up, rinse.* The daily routine passes without an ounce of thought. *At least some things don't require brain power.*

Shutting off the water, I towel off and step out of the shower. Towel slung around my waist, I shave and brush my teeth. Zone out as I swish mouth rinse for minutes instead of seconds.

*Snap out of it, Emerson. You have shit to do.*

Spitting the mouth rinse out, I amble into my bedroom, pull a uniform from the closet, and dress for work.

As I slip my legs into my slacks, I give myself a pep talk. Remind myself of my duty to the community. Remind myself that residents depend on me to keep them safe. When I tug on my shirt, I picture a shield of armor slipping into place. A force meant to guide me in the right direction and give me strength on the difficult days. To keep me human but also teach me how to separate work from emotion.

Mildly better, I head for the kitchen. I feed Pepper breakfast and brew the first of many cups of coffee in my day. Inhale the robust caffeine as it fills the mug and breathe a little easier.

When Pepper finishes, I let her out to roam the backyard and do her business.

I sip my coffee and stare down at the blue file folder on the kitchen island. Two days and the folder is the thickest to grace my desk. Reports and photos and anonymous tips poke out of the crammed folder and threaten to spill out. A copy of the Consent for DNA Testing form at the top of the stack.

Eager as I am to find the person responsible for this woman's death, I don't have the stomach to look at the crime scene and coroner's photos this early in the morning. Hell, I closed the folder less than seven hours ago.

*A couple more hours, then I'll dive back in.*

Pepper rings the bell on the back door, signaling she is ready to come inside. I slide open the door and let her in. Give her some morning cuddles on the couch while I finish my coffee. Scratch behind her ears as the sky morphs from inky to a golden pink.

I rise from the couch, give her one last scratch behind the ears, then wander into the kitchen.

"After breakfast, I'll come pick you up," I tell her as I rinse my mug and set it in the dishwasher.

She gives a low bark, letting me know she understands.

Pocketing my wallet, keys, and phone, I shrug on my jacket and tug a beanie on my head. I fetch the file from the island, then head for the garage. In the car, I check updates on the dash monitor while I wait for the engine to warm up.

On my drive to Poke the Yolk, I scan the streets and side-walks with fresh eyes. Most of the town is still asleep, and I use the momentary peace to survey Stone Bay in a new light.

Since early childhood, Stone Bay has maintained the same elusive vibe. Quiet and small, yet prominent and larger than life. We take care of our own, some more than others. We pride ourselves on the community we built and vow to preserve what the seven founding families created.

Stone Bay was founded on dreams. It is the mission of the seven founding families to keep those dreams alive.

I park near the entrance of the restaurant and exhale days of stress. For the first time in days, a smile tugs at the corners of my mouth. Genuine relief floods my veins.

*Because she's here. Kirsten is safe.*

I cut the engine, unbuckle my seat belt, and exit the vehicle. Gaze locked on her, I refuse to look away as I scan her features. With each passing second, with each sweep of her face, her smile, the warmth in her cheeks, I prove to my irrational mind Kirsten is alive and well and as beautiful as ever.

*Thank fuck.*

With a foot in the door, her stormy blues lock onto my

ambers and my breath catches in my throat. Her eyes dart between mine, neither of us moving as we assess the other. As if we both need the same reassurances.

Heat blooms in my chest as I close the distance between us. The vicious rhythm of my pulse silencing everything in the room as I stand a foot from her. Hands at my sides, my fingers twitch with the need to reach for her. To touch her. To make sure she is real and whole and unscathed.

But I resist the urge. Swallow past the swell building in my throat. Blink back the sting behind my eyes. Gift her a soft smile that says all the things my voice won't say. How sorry I am for the way I behaved when I saw her last. How grateful I am to see her smile and know she is safe and well.

"Hey," she whispers with a shaky breath.

"Hi." I lick my lips. "Good to see you."

She nods, a subtle smile softening her expression. "Same." Tipping her head toward my usual spot at the counter, her eyes brighten a little. "Breakfast?"

My hand brushes hers as I slip past her for the counter, an undeniable buzz simmering under my skin from the contact. I pause and close my eyes momentarily, the whir intensifying when I hear her suck in a sharp breath.

*Damn.*

I will be the first to admit I am not in the right headspace for an intimate relationship. Years later, the bullshit with Gracie still has me fucked up. She did more than break my heart. She shattered my soul. And though her deceptive actions are not my burden to bear, guilt still gnaws at my psyche.

An imbecile would have spotted the signs long before I did. But I'd been blinded by love.

One day, she whispered words of love in my ear. Told me she couldn't imagine life without me by her side. Wrapped me tight in her arms and kissed me as if no one else existed. The next day, she confessed her sins and shredded my heart. Looked at me as if I was some schmuck at a seedy bar and not the man she wanted to share a life with.

After four years together, I'd trusted Gracie explicitly. She'd never given me a reason not to. Then she told me about her trip to Florida with a few of her girlfriends. Months after the spring break getaway, she sat me down and admitted to cheating. Not once, but twice on the same trip. Stone-cold sober, she went back to their rooms and betrayed her commitment to me. All because she wanted to "live a little."

The worst part… not an ounce of remorse filled her chocolate eyes as she tipped my world upside down. If anything, she looked relieved when I screamed at her to get the fuck out.

And since the dreadful end of that relationship, I've been a bachelor. The sporadic hookups satiate my primal nature, but I prefer my own company.

No one can hurt me if no one is in the picture.

But Kirsten… she has me seeing the world with fresh eyes.

Life is less daunting when she holds my gaze. The world is more stable every time she is near. For years, she has been a constant light in my life. Someone I look forward to seeing, to speaking with, to spending time with. And over the past several months, she has awakened something inside me I thought died years ago.

Kirsten may only be a flirty friend, a woman I can't take my eyes off of, but I refuse to deny the part of me she revived. Without effort, Kirsten gives me a reason to smile, to push forward, to *live* again.

She may not be mine, but that doesn't stop me from wanting more, from wanting her.

Flipping over a mug, she fills it with coffee and sets it on my paper placemat. Coffee pot back on the warmer, she glances over my shoulder at the only other person in Poke the Yolk.

"Be right back."

I follow her with my eyes as she sidles up to his table and pulls out her order pad. The older gentleman peers up at her over his reading glasses, ignoring the newspaper in his hands. A gentle smile stretches across his face, deep wrinkles settling around the corners of his mouth and eyes. I fail to hear their exchange, but glimpse the fondness in his expression as she jots down his order.

Small moments such as this are what I love about Stone Bay.

It's obvious he comes in daily and knows the staff. The ease with which they talk is as if they've known each other for years. As if they are family. Wouldn't surprise me if he waited for the door to unlock each morning. Wouldn't surprise me if he sat at the same table every day for hours, sipping coffee and chatting with other townsfolk.

Kirsten leaves his table, taps his order into the kiosk, then comes back to stand across from me.

"You're here early today."

I curl my hands around my mug and bask in the warmth. "Couldn't sleep." Lifting the mug, I sip my coffee and meet her waiting stare.

"Are you... okay?" Her brow furrows, a deep crease settling in the middle.

The impulse to tell her I'm fine rests on the tip of my tongue. The last thing I want to do is upset her and cause unnecessary anxiety. But I bite my tongue and swallow past the need to sugarcoat reality.

With a subtle shake of my head, I admit, "No. Not at all."

She reaches out and wraps her fingers around my wrist. When she tightens her hold, I stop breathing. Her eyes fall shut, a mix of agony and elation etched in her expression. The buzz from earlier feels minuscule compared to the current now dancing beneath my skin, the fire scorching my veins.

*Damn... has anything ever felt this intense, this monumental?*

No. Never.

I release my grip on the mug and slowly twist my wrist, capturing hers in my hand. Gaze locked on her still-closed eyes, my thumb caresses her skin in slow, hypnotic strokes.

*So soft. So fucking perfect.*

Her stormy eyes blink open and meet mine, more blue than gray, as she holds my gaze. She doesn't say a word as her pulse pounds beneath my fingers. Neither do I. And it's our silence that speaks volumes.

*She feels it too.*

With a soft clearing of her throat, the corners of her mouth turn up as she loosens her grip. "You know I'm here if you need anything." Her voice is scratchy yet soft.

Inch by painstaking inch, she withdraws her hand. But as her fingertips dance over mine, she grips them once before disengaging fully. Immediately, I miss her touch. Miss the fire she ignites on my skin, in my veins, in my soul.

As the daze of her touch fades, I become keenly aware of the swell behind my zipper. The deep ache in my groin. From one simple touch, she has my mind, my heart, and my body begging for more.

Clasping my mug, I focus on *her* and not my throbbing cock. I cradle the mug in my palms and nod. "Thank you." My fingers absently trace the cup handle. "The last two days have been... grueling."

Eyes on me, she fiddles with the salt shaker. Perhaps something to distract herself. "I imagine so." A strained smile tugs at her lips as she spins, spins, spins the shaker. "My friend, Skylar, and I got lunch at the deli yesterday"—her hands still

—"and it was so… bizarre to see the town empty." She laughs without humor. "Like everyone is on self-imposed lockdown."

I finish the last dregs of my coffee and sigh. "The quiet streets are good and bad."

"How so?" She reaches behind her, grabs the coffee pot, and refills my mug.

"Thank you." I tip my head toward the mug. "Good because there's less people to watch. And bad for the same reason."

She hums, the soft sound almost indiscernible. Her eyes lose focus as she stares at the counter and gets lost in her thoughts.

Rapt, I allow my own mind to wander. Think of the case in a big picture way rather than in the fine details.

Chief limited the number of officers working on the case, hoping to thwart gossip and minimize hysteria in town. But no one in the department was shocked to learn half the town knew of the woman in the woods within hours of the call. Mighty as they are, the gossip mill spreads the news faster than the flu. And before the sun set on Stone Bay, the sidewalks and businesses were desolate.

"It's early, but do you want something to eat?"

My mind screams *no*, while my body pleads for *something*. Staring at horrific crime scene photos for hours zaps all desire for food. For the last forty-eight hours, I've run on fumes.

"Maybe some oatmeal," I suggest.

She lays her hand on mine again, as if her hand belongs in mine. I blink up at her, silently asking if she feels it too. The swirl of energy around us. The invisible thread pulling us closer, refusing to let go. Her lips part and she draws in a stuttered breath.

"I, uh—"

The door swings open and her gaze shifts to whoever

walked in. A strained smile stretches her lips as she releases her hold on my hand. Glancing over my shoulder, I spot the construction crew working on the library expansion. They file in and head for one of the larger tables. All except one.

*Him.*

*The friend.*

I grind my molars as his eyes flash from mine to hers, a long list of questions written all over his face. *Who is this guy? Are you with him? What are we if he's in the picture?*

Kirsten may not be *mine*, but damn, do I feel the sudden need to claim her.

Gone is the peace I gained less than thirty minutes ago. Gone is the addictive buzz beneath my skin as Kirsten took my hand. Gone is our blissful little bubble.

In its place, an inferno of jealousy flares to life. An incendiary hellstorm ready to ignite.

Reaching across the counter, I trail my fingers over hers and take her hand. Wide, stormy eyes flash to and hold my ambers as she swallows.

"What were you going to say?" I ask, softening my tone.

Her gaze falls to our hands for one, two, three breaths. Then those tempestuous irises latch on to my ambers and hold me captive. Steal my breath and jumpstart my heart. Tongue darting out, she licks her lips, then traps them between her teeth. Seconds feel like minutes as neither of us moves, breathes, speaks.

"I…" Her brows twitch. "I don't remember."

*Because of him?*

I mentally curse him and nod. "Okay."

She steps back and my hold on her falls away. Pointing to the kiosk, she says, "Going to put your order in, deliver Mr. Taylor's food, and get drinks for the other table." Tension radiates off her, and I do my damnedest to remain unfazed.

Kirsten and I may have undeniable chemistry, but we have yet to lay claim. Though we never see each other outside these walls, something more than friendship exists between us. This inexplicable bond, this indisputable *ache*, draws us together. It begs for attention. Pleads to be satiated. Gets on its knees and prays for more than simple touches and breathless minutes.

She may not be mine, but in the deepest corners of my heart, a piece of me wishes she was.

# TWELVE

## BEN

At the head of the table, I ease into the chair between Luke and Dylan, my eyes glued to Kirsten. She taps the counter, says something I can't hear, and steps away from Officer Asshat.

*Is this guy always around?*

*Ignore him. Focus on her.*

Secured in a ponytail, her buttery blonde locks dance over her shoulders as she moves behind the service counter. Dusty rose gloss coats her lips, giving them a poutier look. A hint of eyeliner draws attention to her hypnotic steely-blue eyes, while a dusting of rouge highlights her cheekbones.

*Damn, she shines. Sparkles.*

After more than a decade, my nickname for her still fits. Only now for a new reason.

A smile tugs at the corners of her lips as she grabs a plate from the kitchen window. Looking over her shoulder, she rolls her eyes at *him*. The prick cop. The jerk that barked orders at her the other day, making a scene in a packed restaurant and embarrassing her.

*Asshole.*

Wonder if he knows Kirsten and I had dinner the other night. It may wipe the smile off his smug face.

Luke kicks my shin under the table and I hiss. My eyes flash to his as I jerk my leg away from him.

"What the hell, man?"

Expression deadpan, he shakes his head. "Quit staring like a perv." His gaze shifts to Dylan and softens a beat. Then his eyes are back on me as he shoves a menu in my direction. "It makes us uncomfortable."

I tilt my head and hold his stare. "What are you talking about?" I snatch the menu, but don't look at it. "She's a friend. Someone I haven't seen since I was ten." My eyes drop to the menu, the words blur as his accusation sinks in. "I'm not a pervert," I mumble.

"Sure thing," he says, tone thick with sarcasm. "A friend you went on a date with."

"It's too early for this shit," John mutters from the other side of Luke. "Save the jibes for later." He flips over the mug on his placemat. "When I can't hear them."

Can't fault John for speaking the truth. It is too early for snide comments. But once we step foot on site, Luke will regret poking fun.

"Morning, everyone." Kirsten sidles up to the table, her hip inches from my shoulder. "Coffee?"

"A gallon, please," John says with a laugh before rattling off his breakfast order.

One by one, everyone orders drinks and food. After Kirsten jots down Luke's order, I toss a mocking smile his way as I rise from my chair. His eyes narrow before he shakes his head and mutters, "Perv."

"Morning, sparkles."

I lean in, wrap my arms around her middle, and lift her from the floor. Her arms snake around my neck as soft laughter spills from her lips. I close my eyes for a beat, nuzzle the crook of her neck, and inhale her sweet floral scent. Absorb her warmth and home in on every curve of her body flush with mine.

*Damn, she fits my body perfectly.*

When my eyes open, they land on *him*. Across the restaurant, his fiery gaze holds mine, the muscles in his jaw stiff and unforgiving. Fingers curled into tight fists, his nostrils flare. He doesn't blink as his head cocks to the side.

Against every instinct, against every kindness in my bones, I smirk at him as I secure my hold on her. Eyes locked on his, I nestle the curve of her neck again and press my lips against her soft skin. She shivers in my arms and playfully slaps my back.

"Put me down, Benji."

Setting her on her feet, I keep my hands on her waist. "Not sorry." I give her hips a quick squeeze, release them, and return to my seat. "Happy to see you."

Luke groans. "Will you order something already. Your sappy bullshit is making me nauseous."

I slap him with my menu. "Shut. Up." Turning my attention back to Kirsten, I order coffee, juice, and a breakfast platter.

"Be back with your drinks." Kirsten darts from the table to the service counter.

More people file into the restaurant, light chatter floating in the air as they take their seats. Morning greetings mixed with halfhearted smiles. Whispered words about the recent murder in town.

Tuning out my crew members, I eavesdrop on other conversations. Listen to the townspeople's concerns over a crazed killer in Stone Bay. Note the slight tremble in their voices as they pray for the woman who died. Hear their rising panic as they question if it's safe to leave their homes. Zero in on one voice that says he saw a picture of the young woman.

"The woman," he says quietly, leaning closer to his table-mate and shaking his head. "Was a pretty one." He peeks over his shoulder briefly, then drops his voice further. "Our waitress would easily pass as her sister."

The hairs on the back of my neck stand at attention. *What?*

My eyes drift to Kirsten as she mills about behind the service counter. At the end of the counter, she chats with an elderly man with a bright, toothy smile. She rests a hand on his and he says something that makes her blush. After a quick squeeze of his hand, she moves to the coffee maker.

I study the slight plumpness in her cheeks as she works. The softness of her shoulders and ease of her movements. Relaxed and happy as she fills a carafe with coffee, I doubt she's aware of her resemblance to the victim. She's too care-free, too at ease.

Begrudgingly, my gaze shifts to *him*. Leaning back in my chair, I cross my arms over my chest and watch him watch her. For a moment, I cast aside my feelings and watch them with fresh eyes.

A mug of coffee clasped in his hands, he follows her every move. Makes note of who she speaks with and smiles at as she works. I study the lines of his face as his eyes trail her throughout the restaurant. The faint twitch of his lips when she says or does something he likes. The slight lean of his posture in her direction, no matter where she is in the room. The smile he gifts her every time their eyes meet.

Anyone paying attention would see his attraction for Kirsten.

But the longer I observe, the more I note slight changes in his expression when she isn't looking at him. The minute pinch of his brows and distant look in his eyes. The blanch of his knuckles as he tightens his hold on his mug. The rigid set of his shoulders and stiffness in his posture. The frequent bounce of his leg beneath the counter when her back is to him.

A body language expert, I am not. But from top to toe, this man flaunts his concern, his fear.

And damn, it makes my heartbeat erratic.

The gossip compared Kirsten's features to the victim's. If that holds an ounce of truth, it explains why hotshot cop can't sit still today. And if it's one hundred percent true, does that mean Kirsten is in danger?

My stomach sours as a guy with brown hair delivers our drinks. I read his name tag as he sets a glass of orange juice next to my rolled cutlery.

*Oliver.*

"Thanks," I mutter.

"No problem," he says, voice chipper. "Food should be out soon."

As more tables fill and conversations drown out the low-volume background music, I grow more uncomfortable with the news. My foot taps the floor as I follow Kirsten with my eyes. I tug at the hem of my shirt beneath the table as she smiles and chats and laughs, oblivious to the whispered rumors.

*I can't just sit here. I can't do nothing.*

Shoving away from the table, the chair legs grate the wood floor as I stand. The table falls silent as five sets of eyes swivel in my direction. *Great.*

"What's wrong?" Dylan asks.

Luke grumbles under his breath, "Jesus fucking Christ."

I ignore them both and walk away. Weaving between tables, I head for the one place I don't want to be in this restaurant—the counter. And before I talk myself out of it, I sit in the seat next to him.

"Good—" His greeting cuts short when he sees it's me who sat down. He faces forward with his eyes on the wall while he grinds his molars. "I'm not in the mood, *pal*."

Eyes never leaving his profile, I clasp my hands in front of me on the counter. "Don't care, *prick*." I twist in the seat, my knee knocking his leg. "What I *do* care about is the gossip spreading near my table."

He rolls his eyes but still doesn't grant me his full attention. "Small town." He shrugs. "What do you expect?"

I lean into him and he bristles at my proximity. *Good. You should be uncomfortable.* Lowering my voice, I say, "I live in a small town, *prick*. Gossip doesn't generally faze me." I pause and suck in a breath. "But when *your* town is talking about Kirsten..."

At this, his head whips in my direction. "What did you just say?"

Unaffected by his scrutiny and sharp tone, I sit immobile and glare at him. Purse my lips and bite my tongue as he waits for me to fill in the blanks. And for a moment, I bask in his irritation. But not long enough. Much as I'd love to torment him, much as I'd love to knock the smug prick off his high horse, this isn't about me and him. This is about Kirsten.

"For a minute, can you set aside whatever the hell you feel about me and listen?" I inch closer. "A man at a table near mine said the woman in the woods looks like Kirsten." I lean back, study his shifting expression, and read all the things he *isn't* saying. "Is it true?"

He pales a breath before his eyes fall shut and his face twists in pain and distress. With one indisputable reaction, his nonanswer speaks volumes. Tells me I already know the answer.

Bile burns the back of my throat as my pulse hurtles into fifth gear.

*Damn it.*

"Is she safe?"

Fierce amber eyes all but slap me in the face. His chest heaves as he swivels his chair in my direction. "She. Is. Safe," he grits out between bared teeth. "Nothing will happen to her. Not on my watch."

"How?" I challenge.

A ridge forms between his brows as his eyes narrow to slits. Leaning into me, he opens his mouth to answer, but I cut him off.

"How?" I ask, the word a growl in my throat. "From your desk at the police station? Or maybe behind the wheel of your car as you drive the streets?"

Red crawls up his neck and spreads across his cheeks.

*Good. Get angry.*

"Will you be here when she leaves work? Will you follow her home? Make sure she gets there safely? Check every room of her house before she goes in?" I invade the last of his personal space. "Who will watch her home while she sleeps?"

His lip curls as his nose hits mine. "No one hurts Kirsten. Not. On. My. Watch," he vows, voice low and lethal. "Now back the fuck up, pretty boy." He looks over my shoulder. "Go play with your Legos at the kiddie table."

I open my mouth, a curse on the tip of my tongue, when Kirsten enters my periphery.

"Ben, go back to your table," she says softly. "Please."

"Yeah, *Ben*. Go back to your table," Officer Asshat repeats.

"Travis, stop."

Much as I want to be the bigger man and walk away without another word, I refuse to let this go. I refuse to be silent when she has every right to know—about the woman in the woods and how the town is gossiping about her.

Rising from the seat, I throw a sneer his way. Then I soften my expression and turn my gaze to her. "Don't worry, sparkles." I wink. "One of us will keep you safe." I level him with a hard stare. "And it won't be *him*."

And as I step away from the counter, she hisses at him. "What the hell is he talking about, Travis?"

# THIRTEEN

## KIRSTEN

Travis's confession from two days ago resurfaces as the restaurant empties.

*"Somehow, a townie saw a picture of the woman in the woods."* His chin trembles slightly, a light sheen of sweat coats his forehead. *"And they're telling others how much she looks like you."*

The admission stole the air from my lungs. Had me running for the restroom, cracking my knees on the tile, and hurling into the toilet. Made me question every person in the restaurant, on the street, in our town.

*She looks like you.*

Paranoia has me scrutinizing everyone within eyeshot. Analyzing every verbal exchange for hidden meaning. Dissecting every expression, every shift in body language, as I scribble down orders or walk from point A to point B.

Nerves shot, my mind refuses to focus on anything other than his revelation. And every time I close my eyes, all I see is the terror in his honey irises.

*She looks like you.*

Exhausted beyond measure, sleep evades me the moment my head hits the pillow. My thoughts refuse to stop, my brain refuses to shut down and unwind. And when my body finally crashes, the little sleep I do get is restless. Horrid dreams of some faceless person dragging me into the woods and doing heinous things as I scream for help that never comes.

Worst of all, old, overcome habits have emerged in response to my anxiety.

For years after my father passed away, I felt like I had no say in my life. No control over what happened next. I lived in a swirl of fear and anger every day. Though the person responsible for Dad's death was no longer a threat, panic and rage existed in my marrow. Guilt gnawed at my soul. Life spun in dizzying circles.

*I hid while my dad died. I hid and did nothing to help save his life.*

Dad's ashes sat in a box on Mom's nightstand, a constant reminder of what was missing in our lives. A constant reminder of what was stolen from me in seconds. A constant reminder that you don't always have a say in what happens to you.

The lack of power lit a fire in my soul. Had me thirsty to take my life back, even if only my adolescence. Had my young mind pondering things no preteen or teenager should consider.

In an effort to assert control, I hurt myself. For years, only I knew of my unhealthy habit. Only I had a say. And I fed off that power while my body withered to skin and bones.

Mom joked about me becoming Stone Bay's running legend. My sneakers ate up miles daily while I starved my body of nutrition. Mom had no idea what laid beneath the baggy graphic tees and tightly tied drawstring shorts I wore at the dining table. She had no idea I ate measly portions of breakfast and dinner, only to throw them up minutes later.

I was emaciated by the time she put the pieces together. Become a living, breathing skeleton.

Naturally, she blamed herself. So preoccupied with the loss of her husband—her best friend—she turned a blind eye to the world around her. I tried to take the blame, tried to remove the burden from her shoulders, but she wouldn't allow it. She cried until her eyes turned red and puffy. Held me in her arms until our limbs went numb. Promised me she'd be a better parent. Vowed to be more present and help me heal. In return, I pledged to help her heal too.

Months of therapy later, I learned new ways to harness power over my life. Healthier habits and coping mechanisms.

But since Travis's confession two days ago, since I ran to the bathroom and heaved over the bowl, my rationality is gone. Once again, it feels as if my power has been stolen.

*She looks like you.*

Silverware clangs on the floor as I jump back, withdrawing from an unexpected hand on my shoulder. Stomach in my throat, my heart bangs against my rib cage.

"Sorry, sorry, sorry."

One breath at a time, my vision clears, and an apologetic Oliver comes into view. The concern in his eyes does nothing to soothe my building anxiety.

I press the heel of my hand to my breastbone, close my eyes, and count to ten. On a steady exhale, I open my eyes, skim my hand up, and finger the small crescent moon resting at the hollow of my throat. Clutch it between my fingers and slide it back and forth on the chain as I compose myself further.

"K, I'm so sorry. I didn't mean to..." Hands hovering over my arms, his basil-green eyes dart between my alarmed steely blues. "Can I?"

Before I register what is happening, his arms wrap around

my shoulders. He hugs me to his chest and forces the air from my lungs. And as much as I want to loosen his hold on me, I snake my arms around his waist and hug him back. I rest my forehead on his shoulder and close my eyes. Breathe steadily in his embrace, knowing I am safe.

"Thank you," I mumble, fisting his shirt once before releasing him. I step back and attempt to smile. "I needed that."

"You're welcome." He squats, picks up the silverware, and tosses it in the dirty bin. "Sorry I startled you in the first place."

An unwelcome twinge stirs to life beneath my diaphragm, a fresh wave of paranoia hitting me hard in the chest. My eyes sweep the restaurant and find it empty. Not a soul in sight, only evidence that they were here not long ago. A half-glass of water and dirty plate on one table, balled-up napkins on plates, and coffee-stained mugs on another.

*How long did I zone out?*

Tentatively, Oliver reaches for my arm. With a gentle squeeze, the corner of his mouth tips up in a half-smile. "I'll get the tables if you finish roll-ups."

I nod and we get to work.

Oliver switches the background music from café acoustic to alternative rock and cranks the volume. Silently, I thank my friend for knowing exactly what I need right now. Distractions. Something else to focus on other than my endless, unsettling thoughts.

*She looks like you.*

Shaking out my hands, I take a deep breath. "Worrying won't help," I chastise myself. "So stop it."

Head down, I focus on my task. *Knife, fork, spoon. Roll, roll, roll. Secure, next.* I repeat each step in my head. Give myself a focal point. A way to limit the intrusive words from days ago.

I wrap the last roll-up minutes before Oliver finishes the tables. Emptying the pockets of my apron, I tug the strings apart, pull it off, and toss it in the dirty hamper near the office in the back. Oliver steps through the swinging kitchen doors, apron balled up in his hands as he shoots it toward the basket like a basketball. It flies past me with a whoosh and lands on top of mine.

"Five points," he declares.

I clap and make a muffled hissing noise, mimicking a cheering crowd. "And that's the game, folks."

As we do one last sweep of the restaurant, Oliver pipes up. "So…" He falls silent as he double-checks the lock on the front door.

When he doesn't continue, I parrot, "So…"

"What did I walk in on the other morning?"

A fool, I am not. Oliver is talking about the shitshow starring Travis and Ben.

After their pissing match and Travis's confession, I shut down. Went into protection mode as I processed his admission. The irrational part of my mind commanded I keep his truth locked up tight. The stone-cold truth is something I want contained.

Yes, the gossip mill whispers this fact more than anything else related to the woman in the woods, but I won't validate it. Won't flinch under their longer inspections. Won't add fuel to their chatter fire. Best to save any breakdowns for home, when I am alone.

Thank goodness, not everyone in Stone Bay believes the town gossipmongers.

Which is why I play stupid as I answer Oliver. "The other morning?"

Sidling up to me, he rolls his eyes and knocks my shoulder with his. "I know you know what I'm talking about. The testosterone fest between our favorite Stone Bay policeman and a certain out-of-town construction worker."

Indecision rests heavily on my shoulders as I ponder whether or not to share the news. Without a doubt, Oliver has heard the townies mumbled words about the woman in the woods. You'd have to be a hermit to be oblivious.

While some of the chatter is low-key and tight-knit, the rest is forthright and loud. Too many people in Stone Bay wear their blabber badges with pride. The second something out of the ordinary happens, the scandalmongers are on the prowl for more details, ready to tell anyone who will listen.

The whispers remind me of the game "Telephone." A group of people sit in the same room. The first person passes on a word or phrase to the next. This continues until you reach the last person. Then, everyone hears what the last person heard to see if it's different from the original word or phrase.

Spoiler alert… it's never the same.

Knowing this, I do my best to ignore what people say as I wind my way through the dining room each day. I tune out everything except what I need to hear for my job.

But how much has Oliver paid attention to? Has he heard *it* too?

*She looks like you.*

My need for control says to bottle up the information. The less who know, the better.

But my rational side says to speak up and tell my friends. Be vulnerable and shed some of the anguish the news caused. Share my thoughts after speaking with Travis and the possible emergence of old habits.

I need to tell someone. More than anything, I need the support of my friends.

Swallowing down the ball of nervous energy in my throat, I lock eyes with Oliver and sigh. "Ben overheard someone talking about the woman in the woods." I reach for the charm on my necklace, sliding it back and forth on the chain. "Ben and Travis were arguing over my safety."

Wrinkles mar his brow as he stares at me, confused. "Your safety?"

I release my necklace and nod as my eyes lose focus. "Yep." Closing my eyes, I tip my head back and take a deep breath before leveling my gaze with his. "Because I look like the woman in the woods."

His eyes widen in shock as his jaw drops.

*So… this is new information to Oliver. Great.*

"What the hell, K?" His fingers fist his hair as he inhales steadying breaths. Hands falling to his sides, he shakes his head. "Why didn't you say something sooner? God… you must be freaking out." He steps away and paces the back room.

Rooted in place, my eyes follow him. I give him time to process the revelation. Hell, I haven't truly processed the depth of it.

Does our similar appearance mean anything? Or is it coincidence? Not as if me and the woman are the only two people with our features. We are two of millions on the planet. And until she was discovered in the woods, no one in town said they'd seen my long-lost twin moments earlier.

Oliver stops pacing and reaches for my shoulders. Holding me at arm's length, he locks me in place with worried eyes. "Tell me you're safe."

Am I safe?

Travis says not to worry. That he will keep me safe. The conviction in his tone… I trust he believes as much.

*But am I safe?*

"Travis says I am." I shrug. "Don't have much else to go off of." I wiggle out of his hold, my fingers tapping at my sides. "Can we talk about something else, please?"

He doesn't want to drop the subject. I see as much in the narrowing of his eyes, clench of his jaw, and rigidity of his posture. The news hit him minutes ago and has his emotions in hyperdrive. I get it.

But I don't want this to be the center of every conversation. I don't want to be the friend or woman people look at and think, *"How's she doing? Is she scared? How can I help?"* I am not some pity project that needs tending to. Good friend, upstanding citizen, and flirty woman at the restaurant are who I am.

The last thing I need or want are more sympathetic smiles. I got more than a lifetime's worth after Dad passed.

Sending Oliver one last pleading look, his shoulders fall. I sigh and send a silent *thank you* to the universe.

"Fine," he huffs out. Then the corner of his mouth tips up in a wicked smirk. "Friendsgiving is days away."

When he doesn't say anything further, I grow suspicious. "It is," I say, and leave it at that.

Stepping back, he crosses his arms over his chest and cocks his head. "Travis and Ben invited?"

"Sweet fucking hell," I mutter and shake my head. "No."

"Oh, come on. Invite them. It'll be *fun*." He waggles his brows. "I'd pay good money to see that measuring contest."

"Yeah, you'll be the first in line with the measuring tape." I chuckle. "You're ridiculous."

"Don't be a spoilsport. Invite them. When was the last time two men fawned over you? Plus, your construction buddy is probably missing Thanksgiving with his family."

I don't remember much about Ben's parents except that they were kind, gentle people. The type of parents every child wishes for. Parents that love you unconditionally and without reservation.

An ache stirs in my chest at the idea of Ben being alone on a family holiday, especially after his recent breakup. Does he have plans for the holiday? Will he drive back to Smoky Creek to spend the day with family? Or is he staying in Stone Bay alone?

"You're considering it, aren't you?" Oliver nudges my arm with his.

I tilt my head and give him my best mean mug. "Have I told you recently how annoying you are?"

He sticks out his tongue. "You love me."

"Sometimes," I tease.

Without warning, he plants a sloppy, wet kiss on my cheek. "Always."

I shove him away. "Ew. Gross." I playfully slap his arm and laugh at his antics. "Come on, let's go."

"Say yes." Oliver fetches his hoodie and tugs it over his head.

I slip on my jacket and shoulder my purse. "You're not giving this up, are you?"

"Nope." He turns the handle on the back door and steps out. "Not until you say yes."

The door slams and locks behind me as I cross my arms over my chest and shiver. Oliver bounces from foot to foot but doesn't take a step toward our cars.

*Such a pain in the ass sometimes.* But it's one of the reasons we all love him.

The likelihood of Ben saying yes is much higher than Travis. Cops don't get holidays off. The town and its residents still need protection. My guess is Travis will either be patrolling town, sitting at his desk trying to find the killer, or at the Emerson estate with his family. Ben will either drive back to Smoky Creek for the day or be alone in his room at the inn.

With a smile plastered on my face, I say, "Fine, I'll ask them tomorrow when they come in."

Oliver goes wide-eyed. He opens his mouth to respond, but I hold up a hand.

"But only if you ask Levi to Friendsgiving."

His expression falls. How Oliver feels about Levi is no secret to me, Skylar, or Delilah. He hasn't come out and confessed he is in love with Levi, but we aren't oblivious to the way he looks at Levi when his attention is elsewhere.

Oliver shoves his hands in his hoodie pocket. "Yeah, sure." He nods. "He is my friend, after all." We amble toward our cars in silence. His eyes lose focus as he stares at his car door, lost in thought.

Since high school, Oliver has been in love with Levi. Anyone with a heart can see the way he pines over him. The subtle glances that last a little longer. His constant desire to hang out with him. The blinding, endless smile on his face when Levi comes to his shows. And the way he keeps Levi to himself, not sharing much of what happens between them or bringing him to gatherings often.

If only Oliver's love was reciprocated. If only it was more than friendship. One day, my friend will find love and happiness—with or without Levi.

We hug and say goodbye at his driver's side door. Then he's in his car, a solemn expression on his face as he cranks the engine to life. As I open my car door, he drives off.

And that's when I see it.

# FOURTEEN

## SEEKER

Her golden hair glitters in the sunlight as I stare at her from down the street. The shimmer gives her an ethereal look. Angelic. Divine.

But looks are deceiving.

She left the restaurant with the dark-haired kid, a smile plumping her cheeks. Did that little fucker give her my note? Her carefree expression says no, while her eyes, scanning every inch of the street, scream yes.

The past two days, she hasn't walked to her car alone. No matter the time, she exits the door with someone at her side. After surveilling her for months, I imprinted her work routine in my memory. And the change in her usual habits pisses me off. Her time outside of work is less scheduled and harder to track, but I keep an eye on her when time allows. But if people continue to steal *my* time, I may need to step up my game.

Did my note on the napkin scare her?

Skin pale and clammy, limbs trembling under my scrutiny, voice and breath shaky with fear…

Fuck, it makes me hard.

They stood outside talking until his face soured. Then he all but ran from her. Gave her a halfhearted hug and shut himself in his car.

What did she say to piss him off? Would it please me or piss me off too? Would I want to punish her?

My dick twitches in my pants at the idea of bruising her creamy skin.

Hidden behind a pickup truck, I gawk at her as she stands motionless, watching him speed off.

"Any second now," I mutter, then suck my teeth.

Car door open, she tosses her purse inside. As she bends to slip behind the wheel, she pauses.

Thrill shoots through my veins as my heart thunders in my chest. I don't dare look away as her eyes roam the parking lot, the sidewalk, the street.

The fact she doesn't see me but *knows* I'm close… My eyes roll back as I palm my cock.

Eyes on her, I rub the length of my dick through my pants as she plucks the folded paper tucked beneath her windshield wiper. I cup my balls as she unfolds the note and reads my message.

As she reads, I mentally recite.

*I dream of your curves. Of my hands on your skin, my fingers bruising your tits and ass and cunt. I dream of my cock in your mouth, down your throat, choking you until your lips turn a pretty blue. In this dream, you beg for air, for help, for freedom. In this dream, I laugh and tell you I am your freedom, your salvation. And in this dream, you come to realize you are MY whore. You will always be MY whore. Only mine.*

A green pallor blankets her face as a hand covers her mouth. The hand holding the note shakes uncontrollably.

My steel-hard cock begs for relief as fear consumes her. Precum leaks from my tip and dampens my jeans. I squeeze the tip of my cock and hiss as the denim chafes the skin.

She hops in her car, slams the door, and taps the steering wheel as she waits for the engine to warm up. A moment later, she eases out of the parking spot and drives toward the street. Stopping, she looks both ways, and I swear she spots me hidden behind the truck.

But her eyes shift too soon. If she'd seen me, we would have had a staredown for far longer.

Instead of turning left out of the lot, today she turns right. Fuck, I love when she keeps me on my toes.

"Time for a new game," I mutter as she turns onto Opal Trail. "Can't wait until we really play."

# FIFTEEN

## KIRSTEN

I all but scream at the steering wheel as I stare at the entrance to the police station.

"Just stop already."

I stare down at my hands in my lap and mentally will the tremors to cease. Implore my body to calm, if only for a moment, so I won't appear the distressed damsel when I enter the police station. Curl my fingers into tight fists, close my eyes, and beg for more strength than I feel.

Funny thing about fear… no matter how strong you are, fear is always one step ahead. Regardless of what you have overcome, fear learns how to use that triumph against you.

Despite my resilience, despite my pleas, despite every ounce of willpower I summon, my hands continue to shake.

"Please," I plead, the five-letter word almost inaudible. "Please."

Lifting clenched fists to my chest, I tuck my chin and repeat the word again and again as I rock in a gentle rhythm. After several deep breaths, I lift my chin, lower my hands, and open my eyes. Numbness blankets me as I stare at the granite and brick structure, *Stone Bay Police* in neat, metal letters above a large window.

*Go inside. Give Travis the note. Drive home.*

*Then, you can lose your shit.*

Cutting the engine, I inhale one last deep breath, tug on the door handle, and exit the car. I shoulder my purse and clutch the strap with both hands. Appearing more confident than I feel, I stride up the sidewalk, one foot in front of the other. I focus on my destination and disregard my surroundings as I open the front door.

A blast of warm air hits me as I pass the threshold. Behind the reception desk, an older man with dark hair and kind eyes meets my gaze, a bright smile on his lips. Out of courtesy, I return the sentiment, though it feels forced and disingenuous.

"Good day," he greets, straightening his spine. "How may I help you?"

Inching closer to the counter, I scan the desks behind him in search of Travis. A fresh dose of panic hits when I don't find him. My rib cage feels too small, too tight in my chest, as my breaths come in short, labored bursts.

*Maybe he's in the back.*

"Ma'am?"

My eyes snap back to the man at reception as he rises to his feet. His brows tug inward as he scrutinizes every line and twitch of my expression.

"Ma'am, are you alright?"

Undeterred by the panic coursing through my veins, I nod. "Yes," I choke out, then clear my throat. "Yes," I repeat with more confidence. "Is Officer Emerson available?" My hands wring the strap of my purse, the words on the note inside heavier than anything I've ever lifted.

"Officer Emerson is unavailable at this time." He peers

over his shoulder and surveys the active bullpen before returning his attention to me. "What is this regarding? I may be of assistance."

Head shaking, I hug my purse closer to my chest. "No. I need to speak with Travis."

His stare burns as concern gathers at the corners of his eyes. With slow, calculated steps, he walks around the desk, opens a door off to the side, and stands within arm's reach. He regards me as an injured animal. Maybe I am.

Raising his hands slowly, he inches closer. "Ma'am, Officer Emerson is off duty. Whatever you need to speak with him about, any of us can help with." His eyes shift toward the entrance for a split second and scan the lot. Before my next breath, sober brown eyes meet my stormy blues. "I'll ask again. Are you alright?" The question a gentle staccato.

All this man wants to do is help. At the very least, he wants to figure out why I am ready to crawl out of my skin. Why I look pale as a ghost. Why I refuse to speak with anyone other than Travis.

My eyes drift to the badge on the left breast of his starched uniform shirt and lose focus. I wish I trusted him. I wish I had the courage to share what I discovered on my windshield less than an hour ago. To hand over the second note since the woman in the woods was unearthed. To explain my worst fear —that I will be next.

But this man is as nameless and foreign to me as the person who left the note on my car. He may have worked hard for his badge, he may have earned it with flying colors, but that still doesn't change facts. I don't know him. And right now, that means I can't trust him.

Pinning my purse under my arm, I pluck a business card from the holder on the desk. Flipping it over, I grab a pen from the nearby cup and scribble my name and phone number on the back. I glance down at his name tag as I hand him the card.

"I appreciate your offer to help, Officer Fritz."

He takes the card and reads what I wrote.

"If you'd please reach out to Officer Emerson and ask him to call Kirsten from Poke the Yolk." I tug my jacket tighter, cross my arms over my chest, and step back. "I'm more comfortable speaking with him."

Officer Fritz regards me, then looks back down at the card. Then does it again. After a beat of silence, he tucks the card in his palm and gives a subtle nod.

"I'll let him know you stopped by."

A faint dose of relief replaces some of the panic. "Thank you."

I pivot, step toward the door, and inhale deeply. One foot in front of the other, I tell myself everything will be okay. I repeat the words until it's all I hear in my head.

In no time, Travis will reach out. When I share the news of the notes, I expect nothing less than his anger and frustration. With some sicko on the loose, he will give me a hard time. Ask why I didn't mention the first note sooner. Dole out his concerns for my safety. Preach how he can't protect me if he doesn't have all the details.

After he gets everything off his chest, that's when the mood will shift. When realization will hit.

*Someone is watching me.*

The unrelenting knot in my gut tightens. It twists and turns and constricts. Robs me of breath and forces bile up my throat.

As I slip into the driver's seat and start the car, I gasp for air. The tremor from earlier returns, stretching, expanding, crawling its way along my limbs as a chill rolls up my spine. Perspiration dampens my skin as my heart bangs, bangs, bangs in the confines of my rib cage. I pinch my eyes shut and pray for this to end. Pray for enough solace to make it home safely.

I peel off my jacket, crank the air conditioning as high as it will go, and take slow sips of cool air. Hour-long minutes pass before my pulse eases to a reasonable rhythm. Inhaling deeply, I count to ten and try to gain some form of composure.

Hands less shaky, I buckle my seat belt, back out of the parking space, and exit the lot. The drive home is brief, but the entire ride is a blur of empty streets and silent sidewalks. Not a soul meanders through town. Front yards are void of children and laughter and fall fun.

Since the woman in the woods, Stone Bay is a ghost of its former self. Eerie and cold and desolate.

The pang in my gut eases a fraction as I park in the drive-way. I bolt from the car to the front door, scurry inside, and twist the deadbolt immediately. Then I take my first true breath since leaving work.

*I'm home. I'm safe.*

My fingertips are prunes by the time I step out of the shower. While the hot water soothed the ache in my muscles, it did nothing to alleviate the chill in my bones.

I towel off as I amble into my bedroom. Fishing my softest sweatpants and baggiest shirt from the dresser and closet, I dress in a daze. I toss the towel in the direction of the laundry basket, crawl onto the bed, and burrow under the covers. My body shakes from head to toe as I curl into a ball and close my eyes. An image of the note flashes behind my lids and my stomach flips.

Eyes wide open, I reach for my phone on the nightstand and check for missed texts or calls.

Nothing.

"Please call," I beg, my voice hoarse.

I unlock my phone, check my message and call history as if I disbelieve the lack of notifications, then whine when I get the same results. Nothing.

*It's Travis. He will call.*

Needing a distraction, I open social media and scroll, scroll, scroll through one of my happy places. Bright, cheery pictures and videos of my favorite influencers with new products flood the screen. Makeup tutorials, workout attire, lotions, handbags —the list goes on and on. I read the captions or react to the posts as per usual. Contemplate posting something in my stories to keep my page active but decide not to. Instead, I scroll to divert my attention.

Time passes as I get lost in the secondary world that brings me joy. The more I scroll, the more I slow down. The more time that passes, the more captions I read. I lose sight of why I opened the app in the first place. For the briefest of moments, I feel light and carefree.

Until a notification appears at the top of the screen. A text message from an unknown number. With one notification, a knife pierces my chest. I gasp and grip the phone tighter, pain shooting up my arm as I tap on the notification.

UNKNOWN

This is Travis

My thumbs hover over the keyboard, unsure what to say first. The phone vibrates in my hand as another message appears.

UNKNOWN

I'm calling

I type out *okay* and go to press send, but don't get the chance. *Unknown caller* fills the screen as my phone vibrates over and over in my hand. Thumb over the accept button, I close my eyes, press down, and bring the phone to my ear.

"Hey."

# SIXTEEN

## TRAVIS

After three painfully long rings, her voice fills the line. "Hey." The three-letter word is scratchy and frail as it hits my ear. A muffled message of panic disguised as a simple greeting. But her *hey* is far from simple.

I grind my molars, more pissed at myself.

With no new information and several hours of staring at the same pages and photos, the file spread out on my desk morphed into a kaleidoscope of more unanswered questions. Desperate for undiscovered evidence, I'd searched nearby towns for similar cases but came up short. Unexplained deaths weren't always common in small towns. Most were hiking accidents. Some ruled as natural causes after a thorough autopsy.

Exasperated but unwilling to give up, I expanded my search to include the state. Scoured the internet for anything remotely close to our case. Went cross-eyed as I inspected articles and horrific images. Got a fresh reality check on how off-kilter the world is outside the town's borders.

The end result of my day-long search? Nada. My feet

hadn't left square one, but my head was drowning in sights I wish I could unsee.

Frustrated with the lack of progress, I grabbed my coat and left for the day. Drove home with the intent of vegging on the couch and watching hours of mindless television.

When I walked through the front door, Pepper was on my heels. Her excitement to see me alleviated some of my disappointment. Seeing her shifted my evening plans. I wanted to devote my attention to her. Spend time with her without distractions. Focus my energy elsewhere and clear my head.

Thoughtlessly, I abandoned my phone. With all the shit going on, I should have known better.

One selfish decision was made. All I wanted was a break. An hour. A thirty-minute run through the Emerson property. A small reprieve while I trained with Pepper in the backyard and unwound from the day. A moment to breathe and reset.

When I swiped my phone up from the table, guilt slapped me in the face. Because ignoring my phone for less than an hour today turned out to be the worst decision.

Bypassing her greeting, I dive in head first. "What's wrong?"

Rustling echoes through the line. "I… erm…"

Kirsten is one of the most exuberant people in my world. Her smile has the ability to blind you. Her laughter embeds itself in your bones. But it's *her* that brands your soul.

And the woman on the other end of this call, she isn't *my* Kirsten.

"A million horrible scenarios are running through my head, sunshine. I need you to tell me what's going on."

More rustling as her breathing grows more labored.

And damn, her silence sets me on edge. Has me bounding up the stairs and down the hall, yanking clothes from my dresser, and swapping my joggers and SBPD shirt for street clothes with the phone pinned between my ear and shoulder.

"Please talk to me," I beg as I strip my shirt off and tug another over my head. Her hesitation to speak up is a hot knife slowly sinking into my soul.

"A note was on my car," she confesses in a whisper.

*A note?*

Instinct coils my gut. "What kind of note?" I grab my boots from the closet and head for the living room. Dropping on the couch, I slip my feet in and lace them up.

"Travis…" My name is shaky on her tongue and it sours my stomach.

"Can I come over? Please?"

I can't fucking do this over the phone. Listen to her shaky voice and not be able to comfort her. Our relationship may be platonic, but she *sought* me out at the station. We may only be friends, but she *needs* me right now.

And I refuse to sit idle when I have the chance to do more. When I can be there for her.

"Yes." Voice timid, she rattles off her address.

"Be there in ten," I promise. "I'll text, then knock."

The call disconnects and I shove my phone in my pocket. In a rush, I feed Pepper, then tug on my SBPD hoodie. Pocketing my wallet and swiping up my keys, I flick on the porch and foyer lights.

Out the door, I lock up, bolt to my SUV, and kick up gravel as I whip out of the driveway. Gear in drive, I smash the accelerator too hard the entire trip to her house. But it's not until I read the house number on her mailbox, until I see her car parked in the driveway that I take my first real breath since reading Doug's message.

Parking my SUV behind hers, I cut the engine and send a text to let her know I'm here. Soon as I hit send, I exit the car and head for the front door. As I raise my hand to knock, the door swings open just wide enough for her to fill the space. Wrapped in a blanket, she meets my gaze with a blank expression.

I should feel relief at the sight of her. Knowing she is home and safe should be a comfort.

But the dread darkening her eyes and obvious tremor in her limbs robs me of all solace. Seeing her like this—void of her natural charm, absent of her sunny disposition—rips a hole in my chest.

Shoving my emotions down, I soften my voice. "Can I?" I gesture past her, silently asking permission to come inside.

Brows bent in confusion, she blinks a few times, then shakes her head. For a moment, it's as if she doesn't remember why I am here. In a blink, the bewilderment vanishes. "Yes. Sorry." She steps aside and allows me room to pass.

First thing I take note of is how dark the house is inside. No lamps or overhead lights turned on. All the curtains drawn, staving off the last of the daylight from entering the house. No roaring fire in the fireplace to ward off the chill in the air and light the main part of the house in a soft orange glow.

The house is dark and cold and eerily quiet. The complete opposite of the woman at my side.

She slams and locks the door, then ambles past me without a word. I follow in her wake, unsure what to say or do as my eyes adjust to the darkness. After a few turns, we step into a dimly lit bedroom. She climbs on the bed near the foot, crawls toward the headboard, and curls in on herself.

I wilt at the sight.

Unlacing my boots, I toe them off and pad toward the bed. I ease down on the mattress and inch closer to her. My hand twitches at my side, but I resist the urge to reach out and touch her. Now isn't the time. Not when she is vulnerable and scared and not herself.

"Can I turn on a light?"

Her ragged breaths mingle with the loud whoosh of my pulse in my ears, filling the silence. Frozen beside her, I wait for a response. Breath by breath, time stretches longer and longer. And for a beat, I take advantage of the moment, make use of the darkness.

My eyes dance over her face. Trail the angle of her jaw down to the curve of her chin. Drift up and over her plump lips to dip in her cupid's bow. Sweep up the slope of her nose to the arch of her brow.

This woman… damn, she is a punch to the gut. A hit I will gladly take again and again.

The mattress dips and I suck in a sharp breath as she inches closer, hints of peach and jasmine invading the air. I bask in her scent, her nearness, her warmth. Let it consume me for this small blip in time.

In a literal blink, the moment ends. Light filters through the room and I squint at the sudden brightness.

"Sorry." She inches away and resumes her spot on the bed.

Easing my eyes open, I truly take in the sight of her. Curled in on herself, she stares at the bedding tugged close to her chest. She fists the blanket tighter and tighter with each breath. And when my gaze dips to meet hers, when I *see* the alarm in her dilated pupils, a snake slithers around my heart and constricts the pained organ.

The need to comfort her, to hold her, to protect her surges in my veins. And before I second-guess my instincts, I move across the bed and wrap her in my arms. She stiffens at the contact, but doesn't pull away. Heart pounding against my rib cage, I hold her steady. Minute-long seconds of silence pass before I sense her shift on the bed. Her frame relaxes in my arms as her body melts into my chest.

My eyes fall shut as my arms band tighter around her. Lost in the moment, I breathe her in. Absorb her weight as she gives me more of her. Let my mind wander for the briefest of seconds as she shares a piece of herself with me she never has—her vulnerable side.

Holding her as if she is mine is surreal. Buried in the crook of my shoulder, her warm breath on my neck... god, I've fantasized about holding her in my arms. Molding my body to hers. Kissing her hair, her forehead, the tip of her nose, her lips.

For months, my daydreams of her have been the best distraction—from work and responsibilities. Our early morning flirt sessions always stoke the fire I feel near her. Every smile, every laugh, every look in my direction fuels my need for her. As for my nightdreams... explicit doesn't begin to cover them.

Her arms circle my waist as her fingers fist my hoodie. She breathes slower as the tremor in her limbs dissolves. As if I've done it countless times, I press my lips to her hair. Kiss her crown in an effort to lull her worry and alleviate my own. To my surprise, she inches closer. Holds me tighter. Nestles deeper into the curve of my neck.

Living in this moment for hours and days and weeks would be sublime. A literal dream brought to reality.

But she came to me for a reason. She needs help, protection, someone to keep her safe. Much as I want to exist in this bubble with her, ignoring the reason I am here in the first place is irresponsible and selfish.

Loosening my hold on her, I inch back and cup her cheek, my thumb brushing her soft skin. A finger drifts down the line of her jaw, my eyes following the action as I lift her chin. I bring my gaze to hers, a storm brewing in her steely-blue irises.

Fuck, I want to kiss her.

*Not now.*

Mentally shaking off my desire, I swallow and find my voice. "Talk to me, sunshine."

"I found—" A loud grumble fills the room and cuts her off.

My thumb caresses her chin. "When's the last time you ate?"

Her eyes drift to the side, lost in thought a moment before she shrugs.

"Let's order food. Then you can tell me about this note."

Takeout boxes and soup containers cover the coffee table in Kirsten's living room. Hints of basil and mint and fish sauce mingle with pine and smoke. Warmth fills the expansive living room as a fire roars feet from where we sit on the floor.

From the corner of my eye, I peek over at her, mesmerized as she melts into the couch behind us. I pretend not to notice as she gravitates closer. As her arm brushes mine. As she subconsciously seeks my touch.

I love the idea of her wanting me close. Too much.

*Not now,* I chastise myself.

Kirsten shoves shrimp after shrimp in her mouth, followed by a meatball. She slurps a heap of rice noodles between her chopsticks before gulping the warm phở broth. A moan rumbles in her throat a beat before a sigh leaves her lips, as if the soup is a balm for her soul.

But with one simple act, an odd spark of jealousy flares in my chest, and I mentally growl at myself.

*It's a bowl of soup, dumbass. Get your shit together.*

This woman turns me into a horny, bumbling fool. When it comes to Kirsten, all my rationality goes out the window. Shamelessly, I'm addicted to her flirtatious demeanor, sunny smile, and kind heart. But oh, how I wish I was the bearer of her solace. The one to make her moan.

I dip my egg roll in the tangy, sweet sauce and bring it to my lips. "So, about that note." I shove half the roll in my mouth and arch a brow when she twists to meet my stare.

"I..." She clamps her lips between her teeth and turns, giving me her profile. "I, uh..." She sets her soup on the table, crosses her arms over her chest, and fidgets.

Much as I want to drop the subject, much as I want to wrap her in my arms and tell her not to worry, I bite my tongue and remain rooted in place. I refuse to interrupt her thoughts or downplay her concern. If something made Kirsten a shell of herself, I want every damn detail.

Shortly after the woman in the woods was discovered, Kirsten learned of her resemblance to the victim. Days later, she stumbles into the police station, pale and panic-stricken, asking to speak with me and refusing any other help. Fritz said she looked on the cusp of fainting.

Damn, I still hear the shakiness in her voice from the call— a potent cocktail of distress and alarm.

*"A note was on my car."*

One bite after another, I keep my mouth shut. Keep my thoughts to myself. Grant her time to find the right words and the strength to tell me about the note. Give her breathing room while staying close, my silent way of saying I am here.

Were it some cutesy note from a regular diner, she would smile and brush it off. Maybe tease them the next time they stop in for a hot meal. And I'd be none the wiser. There would be no need to share a harmless note of adoration.

The fact that she went to the station and sought me out says the note is far from friendly.

Minutes pass without a word. I study the silhouette of her profile against the fire. Once, twice, three times, her lips part to speak, but she snaps them shut. Pain twists her expression, and I fight every instinct to drag her into my lap, band my arms around her middle, and never let go.

I reach for her, ready to say *Fuck it*. But as I do, her voice breaks the silence.

"After work, I found a note on my car." Her fingers curl into tight fists as she nibbles on her bottom lip and turns to face me. She closes her eyes, inhales deeply, then knocks the air from my lungs when her stormy blues meet my ambers. "It wasn't the first note."

It takes a beat for her confession to register. For the words to really sink in. When they do, I drop my takeout box on the table.

"What?" The single word comes out harsher than intended.

Kirsten winces and I immediately hate myself.

"Sorry." I count to five in my head and force myself to calm down. She needs cool and collected, not senseless and hysterical. "Sorry," I repeat. "Do you have the notes?"

With a nod, she rises and shuffles toward her bedroom. She reemerges with her purse and drops back to the spot next to me. After a little digging, she hands over a crumpled napkin and a tattered piece of paper. Unraveling the napkin, my molars gnash together as I read the sloppy scrawl.

What the *actual* fuck?

Whoever this is, they obviously visit the restaurant while *I* am there. Some sick pervert watching us interact. A psycho deviant with nothing better to do than trail innocent women.

I read the note again. And again. My gut churning more

with each pass. Leveling Kirsten with a softened gaze, I ask, "Have you gone out with someone recently?"

Pink stains her cheeks. "Wasn't a date." She shakes her head, grabs the blanket from the floor, and covers herself. As if the blanket will shield her and make this creep disappear. "I met Ben at Dalton's to catch up. We talked over dinner." She shrugs. "It was casual. Two friends who haven't seen each other in years. Nothing happened other than an innocent hug and peck on the cheek." The words rush out of her. "He walked back to the inn and I drove home."

Jealous as I am that *he* got time with Kirsten away from the restaurant, I can't be angry. They were grade school friends that went in different directions. Them reconnecting and sharing a meal after more than a decade apart is normal. Still, an envious flame burns green in my chest.

"Okay," I say, much calmer than I feel.

I unfold the second note and read, my eyes scanning the lines over and over. My fingers curl into fists and crush the paper. The chill in my bones a juxtaposition to the magma-hot rage in my veins.

*Sadistic motherfucker.*

One breath after another, I work to settle my boiling fury. Last thing I need to do is exacerbate the situation with undiluted anger aimed at the wrong person.

Kirsten needs someone to trust. Someone to protect her and assure her everything will work out. Someone to be her strength while we hunt this lowlife down. And I'll be damned if that person is anyone other than me.

I hold up the tattered paper. "This the one from today?"

She nods.

"Have you seen anyone new, other than the construction crew, in the restaurant?"

"Not really." She tugs the blanket higher. "Most of the tourists are gone."

"No other notes before the napkin?"

She shakes her head.

"And no sense of someone watching you before that?"

Again, she shakes her head. Her arm snakes out from under the blanket and she grabs a spring roll. After drenching it in sauce, she shoves half the roll in her mouth.

*Stress eating.*

I've seen it countless times, but in less traumatic situations. After a test while waiting for results. At a sporting event when your team is down and the adrenaline is high. During a tense day at work when you're under the boss's thumb for a project.

But this is different. Kirsten isn't eating to fill time or pacify her nerves. No, she is shoveling food in her mouth like a starved, desperate woman. It feels wrong in more ways than one.

"Hey." I wait for her to put the food down and look in my direction. Minute-long seconds pass without any acknowledgment from her. I set the notes down and scoot in her direction. Lifting a hand, I trace the length of her arm through the blanket. "Hey," I repeat, a touch softer.

Red, glassy eyes meet mine and I swallow past the emotion in my throat.

Taking the food from her hand, I set it on the table. Then, I erase every bit of space between us and wrap her up in my arms. Like before, she stiffens at my initial contact. But a breath passes and she melts into my embrace.

I hold her tighter, press my nose to her hair and inhale, close my eyes, and get drunk off her warmth, her curves, the intimacy.

"Promise I'll keep you safe, sunshine. Always." I kiss her hair.

At this, she shifts and crawls into my lap. She straddles me, hooks her legs around my waist and arms around my neck, and hugs me with unimaginable strength.

"Thank you."

One arm around her middle, I trail soothing lines up and down her spine with the other. Time slips away as I get lost in the feel of her in my arms. As my body sings at holding her like this. As if she is mine.

Her hold loosens and she inches back. My eyes fall to her lips and I fight the urge to lean in and kiss her.

As if she hears my thoughts, Kirsten puts more space between us. Goose bumps blanket my skin in the absence of her warmth. Still needing some form of contact, I reach up and twirl her wavy blonde strands between my fingers.

I *feel* her watch me as I study my fingers in her hair.

"Travis." My name on her tongue is soft, sweet, a prayer.

My eyes meet hers. "Hmm?"

She licks her lips and inhales a stuttering breath. "Do you have plans this weekend?"

Is she… asking me on a date?

"No." I wince at the higher pitch of my voice.

The corners of her mouth tip up slightly. "Want to come to Friendsgiving?"

# SEVENTEEN

## KIRSTEN


interest.

Eyes on my flour-coated hands, I knead bread dough with more gusto, needing an outlet for my elevated anxiety. "Mm-hmm."

Hours after I asked Travis to Friendsgiving, I pulled Ben aside in the restaurant and asked if he'd like to join us for the day. His instant smile was a burst of warmth and light, and something I'd missed for far too long. That gentle, boyish smile slowly stitched together the hole in my chest he'd semi-filled before I left Smoky Creek. And for a beat, that smile made me forget all the craziness in my life.

Wrapped in soft blankets next to the fire on a snowy day, unabashed laughter and endless smiles, a beacon of light and love and hope—this is Ben.

Those earlier years we shared, Ben was always by my side. He was as glued to me as I was to him. Every ounce of free time was spent together. Our parents joked about us getting married one day. We played along and had a fake wedding in the field near our houses.

In a box of photos in my closet, I still have the picture Mom took of us that day. Me in a white sundress with yellow flowers stitched in the fabric and Ben in jeans and a white polo. Our feet were bare and our smiles stretched ear to ear.

When Mom drove us out of Smoky Creek, I cried for weeks. Not only had I lost my dad, but I'd also been torn away from the one person I wanted most. The person who soothed the pain. My best friend. Ben.

Him showing up in Stone Bay is kismet. A second chance at a long-lost friendship.

"Please tell me I'm sitting across from the action," Oliver teases. "I need a front-row seat to the brawl."

I pinch off a piece of dough and hurl it at his head. It hits him right between the eyes. "Don't be an ass."

Delilah shakes her head as she stirs cheese shreds into her homemade macaroni and cheese.

Skylar flings a green bean in his direction. "Seriously, Ollie?" She rolls her eyes. "Could you be more immature?"

Oliver ambles to the sink and starts to wash his hands. A second later, water sprays across the room. Maniacal laughter bounces off the walls as Oliver drenches me and Skylar. "To answer your question…"

Skylar charges Oliver, irritation in her eyes but a smile on her lips. "You little shit!" She steals the spray nozzle from his hand and turns it on him. "You'll pay for that." Her laughter mixes with his as they wage war in the kitchen.

Delilah adjusts the dial for the stove burner, puts a lid on her macaroni and cheese, and backs out of the kitchen. "Let me know when it's safe to return." She plops down on the couch, swipes her book from the coffee table, and flips it open to the bookmarked page.

By the time the sprayer is back in its rightful place, the floor is as equally drenched as Oliver and Skylar. We drop dish towels on the floor and shimmy our way across the tile as we soak up the water. Delilah puts her book down, disappears down the hall, and returns to the kitchen with bath towels.

Delilah and I dry the floor while Oliver and Skylar go change clothes. Thankfully, they had the foresight to bring a backup outfit. This isn't our first Friendsgiving or our first messy gathering.

Skylar and Oliver return to the kitchen with bright smiles, playfully shoving each other. I cut the dough into smaller pieces and roll them into balls as they resume their tasks. Delilah samples her macaroni and cheese, then adds a splash of liquid smoke before cutting off the burner.

Out of nowhere, warmth and love and gratitude hit me square in the chest. The backs of my eyes sting as emotion swells in my throat. I tuck my chin to my chest and blink away the impending tears.

Having these incredible people in my circle is the most amazing gift. One I will never take for granted. For days, my life has been *off*. But these people, my closest friends, make every step forward worth it. They make each moment, big or small, count.

A ding fills the air and Skylar picks her phone up from the counter. Her cheeks flush as she reads the message. "Law's on his way with the turkey." She locks her phone, sets it on the counter, and finishes snapping the green beans, her cheeks still pink.

"Since when does turkey make you blush?" I place the last dough ball on the pan and drape them with a towel.

She tosses the last green bean in the colander, then gives me her best evil glare. "Everything Law cooks makes me blush."

"He's good in the kitchen?" Oliver cuts the final potato and throws it in the large stock pot.

Skylar licks her lips and ducks her chin. "You could say that."

Silence fills the room as we all stare at our friend, her cheeks closer to red than pink now.

"Good for you," Delilah says.

Oliver takes the pot of potatoes to the sink and adds water. "He looks like the kinky type."

I pluck a green bean from the colander and throw it at Oliver. "What does that even mean, Ollie?"

He cuts off the water, carries the pot to the stove, and cranks the burner to high. After adding a fistful of salt, he spins around and leans back on the counter. "Older man, sharp suits, thick build..." He shrugs as if it's self-explanatory. "Men like Law love control. In every aspect of their life. It's easy to assume they're kinky in the bedroom." Oliver pins Skylar with his stare. "Or the kitchen. Am I wrong?"

Cheeks still flush, Skylar stands a little taller. "Not wrong at all."

Oliver winks. "That's what I thought?" He grabs the sponge and starts cleaning his work area. "Just like I know the difference between our favorite officer and your long-lost construction beau."

I stick my fingers in my ears and hum loudly like a child. "Don't want your opinion, Ollie."

Seconds pass and he holds up his hands in defeat. I unplug my ears and start cutting carrots while Skylar adds the green beans to a sauté pan with butter and lemon. Delilah dumps her macaroni and cheese in a casserole dish and tops it with bread crumbs before putting it in the oven. Then she gets to work on the cranberry relish.

We move in sync with one another, stepping out of the way when necessary or silently offering help.

But that silence is broken when Oliver sidles up to me with

a shit-eating grin on his face. "You may not want my opinion now, K." His smile stretches wider when there is a knock at the door. "But I'll validate it soon enough."

I playfully shove him. "You're ridiculous." I shake my head. "Go let Law in. We need his maturity to balance you out."

What the hell was I thinking?

Obviously, my brain was out of service when I decided it was a good idea to invite Travis *and* Ben. In what world did I see today going smoothly?

Oliver, on the other hand, hasn't stopped smiling since either of them arrived. *Little shit.*

"So, Ben," Oliver says as he plucks a small piece of turkey from the platter. "You have someone special back home?"

"Ollie," I chastise. Turning to Ben, I roll my eyes. "Please ignore Oliver. He's a pot stirrer."

Ben chuckles, lifting his beer to his lips and taking a sip. "You remind me of my buddy, Luke. Always asking the uncomfortable questions." He sets his beer down and shakes his head. "And to answer your question, no. I don't have anyone back home."

"Ah." Oliver reaches for another piece of turkey and I slap his hand. "Hey." He gives me his best pout.

"Take the turkey to the table."

He arches a brow.

"Please," I add. "Then let everyone know we're ready."

Shortly after Law arrived, Skylar dragged him to the back-yard and had him light a fire in the pit. Delilah followed them when her baked macaroni and cheese came out of the oven. Oliver opted to stick around for Travis and Ben's arrival.

I wish he would have gone outside. Troublemaker.

Oliver walks off and I breathe a little easier. Until reality sets in.

A weighted blanket of claustrophobia swallows me as I stand in the kitchen with only Travis and Ben. With the faintest shifts in their posture, each shuffles closer to my side, sandwiching me between them. Though I refuse to look and confirm what I *feel*, since stepping foot in the same room, neither has stopped sizing the other up.

Travis arrived first with a bottle of wine and a warm embrace. He held me longer than a friend would, his thumb stroking my spine once, twice, three times before he kissed my hair and stepped back. The absence of his warmth made me desperate to reach for him, to wrap him in my arms once more.

Somehow, I resisted the urge.

Minutes later, Ben knocked at the door. Beaming smile in place, I opened the door and greeted my friend. A second after he saw Travis over my shoulder, Ben swept me up in his arms, lifting me off the ground. His soap and leather scent invaded my nose and muddled my thoughts.

Until Travis literally growled.

A slight twist of my head, my eyes flicker to Travis. Just as quickly, I shift my gaze to Ben. Two sets of addictive eyes fixed on my profile. Two different fires blazing and swirling beneath my breasts, between my thighs.

Acoustic music plays softly in the background as a thick bubble shrinks the room. Perspiration that has nothing to do with the fire in the living room dampens my skin. A pleasant shiver rolls up my spine as I look from Travis to Ben again and again. Hunger pulses in my veins, building, expanding, converging at the junction of my thighs. I clench my legs; my breaths come in shallow sips.

Closing my eyes, I think about anything other than the two men at my side. Think of anything other than how it feels to be in either of their arms.

As my arousal tapers off, something else swarms in and replaces it. An unnameable throb in my rib cage. A slow-building ache in my soul. A different type of need. An incomparable desire. Swelling. Begging. An irrefutable longing for something I've never truly had.

Vulnerable, another sensation wiggles its way to the surface. One that refuses to be denied. More than anything, I hate it. Like a viral infection, the sharp pang expands in my chest. Growing. Festering. Stealing my happiness. Robbing me of light and love and pleasure.

Much as I hate that damn sting, much as I wish I was strong enough to quash it, that painful reminder has guarded and protected my heart for years.

There is a reason I don't get emotionally involved. There is a reason I flirt and hook up and don't do repeats.

If I never fall in love, I have no one to lose. And if I have no one to lose, I will never know hurt. Not like before.

# EIGHTEEN

## BEN

Awkward as this is, there is nowhere else I'd rather be.

Doing my best to ignore the prick on the opposite side of her, I focus on the conversations floating around the table. Glimpse the people Kirsten is closest to now. Get an intimate look at this piece of her life.

Oliver talks about his band, Hailey's Fire, and their first official performance schedule. For a local band, they have several dates on the books—a few between now and New Year's, then a regular schedule starting in late January. Though they've played small venues in the past—including a bar and grill in Lake Lavender—this is the first time they'll have a confirmed schedule for months.

Loaded fork pointed in my direction, he mentions the tavern in Smoky Creek. A tavern I visit once or twice a week to catch up with friends over a beer.

"Have you seen us play?"

I cover my mouth and shake my head. "Not yet. Let me know next time you're in town. I'll invite my buddies."

"Will do." He shoves the excessive bite into his mouth.

The conversation quiets for a beat as we savor the meal and enjoy the company.

When was the last time I did this? Sat down with friends, talked over a mountain of great food, and simply existed in the moment?

On occasion, I meet with the crew after work for drinks and a bite as we bullshit for an hour. Not only is it a great way to wind down from an intense day, it also brings us closer as a crew.

Once a week, I join Mom and Dad for dinner at their place as we catch up on life. Without fail, Mom asks about my love life and Carolyn. Before last month, she would ask when we were taking the next step. Now, all she wants to know is why we broke it off. I spelled it out for her the first time. Since then, I simply change the subject and ask about her and Dad.

But those regular nights at the bar or dinner with my folks feel routine. When was the last time my friends and I did something like this? Gathered with individually made dishes and shared meaningful conversations. Connected on a deeper level, then razzed each other about nonsense. Friendsgiving.

Never.

Now that I've gotten a taste, I want more days like this. Significant moments with people I hold close. Smiles and laughter and elbows to the ribs. Asking to pass the potatoes or rolls. Letting go of everything outside this room as we strengthen our bonds.

"How's the library expansion coming along?"

I shift my gaze to the raven-haired woman across the table. Delilah, Kirsten's roommate, appears to be the quietest of the group. Though reticent, she speaks up when she has something notable to say or needs to put someone in their place. Most times I glance her way, she is simply observing the room.

"Good. Faster than anticipated." I spear a few green beans

and swipe them through mashed potatoes. "We wanted to have the walls and roof intact before December. We're a couple days ahead of schedule."

"Dee Dee is an avid reader," Kirsten says. "The day she says she's not reading anything is the day we should all be concerned."

Delilah shrugs. "Books are good for your brain and your soul. In some cases, your heart too."

"I like that." I wash down my bite of food with a sip of beer.

When was the last time I had a lazy day with a book? Too long ago to recall.

"Could probably use more brain food," Travis mutters under his breath.

*Prick.*

Kirsten elbows him. "Knock it off."

He grunts and rubs the spot where her elbow made contact.

Internally, I snicker. *Keep it up and you'll push her away.* The thought makes me smile. Gives me a boost of confidence. Adds a hint of fuel to the fire.

Before I lose the nerve, I lay my hand over hers on the table. Trail my thumb over her soft skin. Close my eyes for one breath as a low hum courses through my veins from my fingers to the center of my chest.

*Damn.*

She is the first breath after an endless free dive. The whirlwind of a summer storm you didn't see coming. The jolt your heart needs to keep beating.

I lick my lips, swallow, and lean into her side. "Thanks, sparkles." My breath warm on her skin makes her shiver. And fuck, I love that shiver. "You don't need to defend me, though."

Quiet blankets the room as I inch back into my seat. And I *feel* more than see everyone's eyes aimed my way.

On the other side of Kirsten, his fingers curl into a fist on the table. A growl filters through the silence. His ragged breaths are loud enough for everyone to hear.

And I bask in his jealousy.

Chatter erupts around the table as I remove my hand from hers and pick up my fork. I scoop up mashed potatoes and spear a piece of turkey, slathering the bite in gravy. As I bring the forkful to my mouth, I can't fight the widespread smile on my lips.

"What's Smoky Creek like?" Skylar asks as she hands Lawrence a glass of wine. She sits on the floor between his legs and leans into him. Molds herself to him as he toys with her fiery curls from his seat on the couch.

Though there is a noticeable difference in their ages, it isn't off-putting. They just *fit* together.

I lift my beer to my lips and take a sip. "Small like Stone Bay, but not as flashy."

Bellies full and clothes a bit tighter, we cleared the table and stowed leftovers after dinner. Needing a reprieve before dessert, we gathered in the living room with drinks. Lawrence, Oliver, and Delilah took over the couch. That left Skylar, Officer Prick, Kirsten, and me on the floor.

Naturally, he and I are on either side of her. Again.

Skylar sips her wine. "Stone Bay is flashy."

I chuckle. "Compared to Smoky Creek, definitely." I set my hand on the carpet, leaning back and a touch closer to Kirsten. "Smoky Creek has more neutral tones. Earthy. Shaker shingles and cottage-style homes." I pick at the label on my beer bottle. "A more laid back vibe. Less pretentious." Holding up a hand, I wince. "No offense."

"None taken."

With a shrug, I add, "Life is simple in Smoky Creek. You have what you need." My eyes meet hers. "And that's what matters."

Skylar raises her glass. "To what matters."

Everyone but Travis lifts their drink. "To what matters," they announce.

As attention shifts away from me, side conversations spark to life. Delilah slides off the couch and chats with Skylar about her newest read at the bookstore. Oliver asks Lawrence about work and if things have returned to normal. Lawrence pinches the bridge of his nose, then nods, relief evident as his shoulders relax.

I nudge Kirsten's arm with my elbow as I lean into her. "You have great friends, sparkles."

Bright smile on her pouty lips, her stormy eyes meet my blues. "Thanks. Like it or not, they're stuck with me."

"Who wouldn't want to be stuck with you?"

She lifts a hand to her throat and pinches the moon charm between her fingers. "I, uh…"

I set down my beer and bring my hand to hers. Brush her fingers a moment before tracing the rose gold chain around her neck. Her hand falls away as she inhales a shuddering breath. Then that shiver from earlier makes another appearance. And damn, it lights a fire in my chest.

"I remember when your dad gave this to you." My eyes drop to the small crescent moon as I trace the edges of it with my finger. "God, you wouldn't shut up about how pretty it was." I chuckle, and she joins in. Then a beat of silence passes before I lift my gaze to hers. "All I remember thinking was how I wanted to get you a gift you loved as much as this necklace."

"Benji…" Her nickname for me is soft on her lips. A litany as tears rim her eyes.

"You were my favorite person." I swallow past the lump building in my throat as I release the necklace. "I wanted to be yours too."

"You were mine too," she confesses in a whisper.

The room around us disappears as gravity draws us closer together. She licks her lips and my gaze drops to follow the action. Inch by painstaking inch, an invisible chord pulls me toward her. Into her orbit. My breath comes in short bursts as my pulse soars. Our lips so close I all but *feel* them pressed to mine. And as I make the final move, as I close that final breath of space between us, reality pops our fantasy bubble.

"Anything new since I was here the other night?" Officer Asshat asks.

Kirsten sits straighter, her brows bending as his words sink in. She clenches her teeth, the muscles in her jaw tightening.

"Not now," she mutters.

"Yes, now." His eyes bore her profile. "Obviously, you haven't shared with the group."

She turns away from me to face him and I curl my fingers into a tight fist.

Why the hell is he here? What does she see in him? The pompous prick is an ass more often than not.

But what if she brings out his softer side? Hard as it is to believe, maybe his ego only makes an appearance when someone else threatens what he wants. Challenges him. If that is the case, why aren't they together? Not that I want them together. But I'd be a fool to miss the chemistry between them.

Kirsten doesn't have a boyfriend. Is there a reason why? If

this asshole flirts with her daily and she welcomes his playful advances, why are they only friends?

"Travis," she begs under her breath. "Please, don't."

He lifts a hand to her face and caresses her cheek with his knuckles. "They need to know, sunshine."

Rage boils beneath the surface of my skin as he touches her with ease. As if they are lovers.

I fight the urge to yank her from his touch. My teeth grind to the cusp of cracking as I open my mouth. "What's he talking about, sparkles?"

"It's nothing," she says, pulling out of his hold and scooting farther away from us both.

He shakes his head. "It's definitely something, and everyone should be aware."

"Should be aware of what?" Skylar asks.

Kirsten winces, then glares at Travis. "I hate you," she mutters.

The corner of his mouth tips up in a cocky half-smile. "No, you don't, sunshine." He reaches out, pinches her chin, and traces the pad of his thumb across her bottom lip. "You hate what's happening. You hate that I want to protect you." He closes the distance between them, his lips a breath from hers. "But you could never hate me."

She sucks in a sharp breath and swallows.

And for hour-long seconds, he captures all of her attention. It's in those seconds I see exactly what I am up against. A man who wants her as desperately as I do. A man who hasn't found the courage to take the next step with her. But a man who won't let anyone take what he wants.

They may share an undeniable connection, but there is no mistaking the bond between us either.

Will I fight for her? Without a doubt, yes.

Will I come out unscathed? That remains to be seen.

He releases her chin and sits straighter, turning to face the group. "Kirsten has an admirer," Travis says, his expression as sober as his voice. "And not the good kind."

My eyes dart to her profile as she pales. One breath after another, her frame wilts.

"An admirer?" Lawrence sets down his wine and rests his elbows on his knees as his forearms cage Skylar in place. "You mean a stalker?"

Travis nods. "Yes. A stalker."

"When did this happen?" Oliver butts in, his attention shifting from Travis to Kirsten. "Does this have to do with the napkin note?"

All eyes shoot to Oliver.

"You know about the napkin?" Travis's growl vibrates through the room. "Why didn't *you* say anything?"

Oliver holds up both hands in surrender. "One—I had no idea it was some psycho shit. The guy left it under his mug and it was addressed to K. I didn't read it. I don't invade people's privacy." He pauses, takes a deep breath, then continues on the exhale. "Two—don't bark at me. I'm on your side. So chill the fuck out."

For someone who comes off as passive, Oliver gets fired up when provoked.

"Do you remember what the guy looks like?" Travis goes into investigator mode.

Oliver tips his head back and closes his eyes as he pinches the bridge of his nose. Still as stone, our eyes fixed on him, we wait for his response. Wait for the slightest clue. He levels his gaze with Travis and shakes his head. "Dark hair." He shrugs. "Older than me, but maybe younger than Law."

Silence falls over the room as we all process his vague description.

"That's it?" Travis's nostrils flare.

But Oliver doesn't bend to his wrath. "Yeah. That's it." He swipes his beer off the table and downs the last of it. "It was weeks ago. He kept his head down. Seemed pissed. Didn't drink any of his coffee or order food."

He rises from the couch and trudges toward the kitchen. A clang echoes in the air as he tosses his bottle in the recycle bin. From the kitchen side of the island, he slaps his hands on the counter and faces us.

"One second, he was there. The next, he was gone."

Grabbing a knife off the counter, he cuts one of the pies with too much aggression. Then he goes to the fridge for the whipped cream. He adds a slice of apple pie to a plate and smothers it with the dairy confection.

Not another word is said about the note as everyone ambles toward the kitchen for dessert. I pull up the rear of the line behind Kirsten. I tug the end of her hair as we wait to pile our plates high. When she peeks over her shoulder, I give her a sad smile.

"You okay?"

She half-shrugs. "I guess." Her lips roll between her teeth. "Kind of."

Wanting to lighten the mood, if only a little, I tease, "You know, I considered moving here." I faux-wince. "But y'all have psychos in the woods, so..."

She snorts and rolls her eyes.

I lean into her, my front inches from her back. My breath dances across the skin of her neck. "Psychos aside, I'd love to be closer to you again."

She shivers and I smile.

"Let me be closer, sparkles." I ghost my knuckles along her spine. "Give me a chance."

When I peer up and see half the room staring at us, I put a little distance between us. Travis peeks over his shoulder to see what everyone else is looking at. His growl of irritation is unmistakable.

But it's Kirsten who verbally knocks me on my ass. "Let's talk about this later," she mutters. "In private."

Her rejection is a dull knife to my fragile heart, but I nod like my heart didn't crack a little. "Yeah. Sure."

# NINETEEN

## KIRSTEN

Crossing my arms over my chest, I tip my head back and stare as snow flurries trickle through the tree canopy. Flurries land on my bare shoulders and I shiver, rubbing my hands up and down my forearms.

Where is my jacket?

Leaves crunch beneath my feet; evergreen needles jab between my toes as I wander through the woods. Daylight fades with each step forward. Or is it backward?

I stop, spin in a slow circle, and try to get my bearings. I've hiked several trails in and around Stone Bay, but I've not seen a familiar marker for hours as the trail vanishes in the trees.

Lips numbing, my teeth chatter as a tremor ripples through my body.

So. Damn. Cold.

A twig snaps nearby and I turn to locate the source. In no time, the day has quickly transitioned to night and I can't see more than a few feet away.

I open my mouth to ask who is there, but nothing comes out. Hand at my throat, I clutch my neck and try to speak again. But my attempt at saying hello is met with a scratchy, faint whisper.

*Another twig snaps, followed by the rustling of leaves. Whatever —whoever—it is, they're closer now.*

*I shuffle forward, the earth squishing between my toes as I try to escape. Extending my arms in front of me, I feel for trees or boulders. Somewhere to hide.*

*My hands land on a thick tree trunk. Fingers sweeping over the bark, I discover a dip in the trunk. A hollow cave within the tree.*

*Squatting down, I crawl into the small alcove, sit down, and draw my knees to my chest. Lips pressed to my legs, I count until my breathing calms, listening to the sounds outside the tree.*

*Owls hoot in the distance. Snow hits the forest floor faster, harder. Cicadas chirp from every direction, closer, louder. The one noise I listen for, the one sound I try desperately to focus on, I no longer hear.*

*I close my eyes and curl into a tighter ball. My body shakes uncontrollably; my toes and fingers numb, lifeless. I rub my hands up and down my shins, begging for warmth from the friction. Up and down. Up and down. As I try to stave off the cold, it dawns on me what I am wearing. A summer sundress, most of my body exposed to the elements.*

Why am I wearing this dress in the winter?

*Before I get the chance to backtrack my steps, a hand is in my hair, fingers in a tight fist. Yanked out of my refuge, the hidden figure drags me across the forest floor by my hair. I slap at their hand, opening my mouth to scream. Again, nothing comes out. No voice to cry for help. No hope of begging for my life.*

*Then they let go. Drop me on the ground.*

*My head hits a nearby rock and I dizzy. But my muddled brain clears when something icy grazes my bare skin.*

*"Help," I force from my throat, but it is less than a whisper.*

*In the next breath, my skin is on fire. Raging, blazing, a brand sears my skin and slashes my soul.*

*The sound of fabric tearing bounces off the trees as my dress is ripped away. Fire scorches my skin again and again, on my thighs, my belly, my breasts. Slashes filled with hatred and disgust and anger.*

*Snow pummels my face, blinding me, drowning me, but I don't attempt to brush it off. I can't. My arms refuse to move, to act, to fight.*

*Warmth caresses my cheek, one puff followed by another. Knuckles stroke the line of my jaw, stopping when they reach my chin. Grip firm and punishing, they tip my head back, their lips dancing over mine.*

*"My whore."*

I shoot up in bed and slap a hand to my chest. Lungs burning, I gasp for oxygen. Sweat slicks my skin, my body shakes from head to toe. "Just a dream," I mutter as I fist the comforter. "Only a dream."

My eyes scan the room with desperation. I search for an anchor. One tangible thing to link me to reality. A touchstone to ground me when my mind wanders down uncertain paths.

Scooting off the bed, I pad across the room to my dresser. Pat the surface in the dark. Watch—*no*. Candle—*no*. Picture frame with a photo of four-year-old me on Dad's shoulders at the beach—a vacation I don't remember, but my favorite picture of us—*no*.

Tears well my eyes as I pause my scavenger hunt. God, I wish Dad was here. Alive. Whole. By my side. Able to wrap me in his arms and make the world disappear.

More than thirteen years have passed, yet I miss him as if it were yesterday.

Dad was everything good in life. He had this uncanny ability to turn bad days into the best days. A sliver of good was all he needed to make life better. With his brilliant smile and vibrant aura, he won the hearts of everyone in his orbit.

Regardless, there were only two he pursued constantly—Mom's heart and mine.

Matthew Sparks was too generous, too loving, too magnificent for this world. And taken far too soon from this life.

I reach for the small rose gold chain around my neck. Trace a finger along the metal until I meet the small crescent moon at the hollow of my throat. Close my eyes and send a silent prayer to him.

*Love you, Daddy.*

And when I open my eyes, they land on a small paper bag on my dresser. The day before Thanksgiving, Travis brought it into the restaurant. *"It's not much, but it may help you feel safer."* I'd stowed it next to my purse and had forgotten about it until it was time to leave for the day. As I exited Poke the Yolk, I carried it alongside my purse and didn't give it much thought.

Five days have passed since I set the bag on my dresser. Distracted by the holiday and uptick in restaurant business, I forgot about the pity present. Then this nagging twinge would flare in my gut, my intuition instantly on high alert. In the moment, it was an instant reminder to open the damn bag. Still, I never did.

Maybe the real reason I've ignored the bag is because I don't want to *need* to feel safer.

More than anything, I just want life to return to normal.

Fingers curled around the handles, I carry the bag back to my bed and sit cross-legged under the comforter. I flip on the salt lamp next to my bed, peel apart the flaps, and reach inside. One piece at a time, I remove the contents and lay them on the comforter.

All in red, the first few pieces make me smile. A poofy pom pom on a keyring. A lip balm holder with red and pink kissy lips printed on it. A glittery red sanitizer holder.

"And *how* will these keep me safe, officer?"

Reaching into the bag again, the next item I remove is shiny, red, and cylindrical. I roll it over in my hand and see a cutout. *A whistle.* The next piece resembles a car fob. On the back, it reads *40-minute continuous 140db personal alarm with an 85 lumen LED light.* Gingerly, I lay it on the bed, then reach into the bag again. My fingers curl around the ridged tube and, without seeing it, I already know what it is. *Pepper spray.* With equal ease, I set it next to the alarm.

"Really know how to charm a lady, don't you, Travis?"

With a roll of my eyes, I check the bag for any additional items for my new self-defense kit. My fingers brush a small cloth pouch, the final item, and remove it. I loosen the cinched fabric and turn the pouch upside down over my open palm. A small, solid item hits my palm but is quickly covered by a folded slip of paper.

Tossing the pouch aside, I pick up the paper, unfold it, and smile at the simple note in Travis's messy scrawl.

*My sunshine.*

*xo*

*Travis*

I never expected a growly man like Travis to have a soft heart. His hard exterior is up for the world to see, but a lucky few see the real him. The man behind the mask. Someone who gives his all to protect those he cares about.

Lifting my hand higher, I stare down at the golden charm in my palm. A sun. *My sunshine.*

Similar in size to the moon on my necklace, the sun's rays swirl out from the heart of the charm. In the center, several diamond chips make the sun sparkle in the light. And like the moon at the hollow of my throat, the sun charm is simple but says more than words.

I caress the small token of his affection with the pad of my thumb and smile. Unlatching my necklace, I slide the sun on then fasten the clasp. I brush the two charms and take a deep breath.

Without effort, Travis gifts me rare comfort. A dose of peace. An invisible hug from a distance. A silent promise, in the shape of a sun, that says he will always be with me.

"Such a softy." I chuckle.

Swiping my phone from the nightstand, I unlock it and click on the messaging app. But before I get a chance to type out a teasing text to Travis, my phone buzzes with several notifications. Over and over, notifications from several social media apps pop up on the screen.

I open the first app, an alert over the notification icon indicates several new followers, likes, and comments. My eyes dart across the screen, reading some of the comments, and I gasp at the unexpected crudeness and vitriol.

*rouge_rebel* someone paid you for this content?! Ew. Pass.

*bb.06* them red lips around my c*ck tho

*frankengrind* stfuattdlagg

*bb.03* MY whore

Pulse whooshing in my ears, I close the app and open another to see much of the same.

*hey.itssophie* minutes of my life I'll never get back

*bb.01* red is for pretty little whores

*vanhoe* *don't quit your day job*

*makupbycali* *@vanhoe right?! *unfollow**

*bb.04* *check your DMs*

*bb.09* *check your DMs*

*bb.02* *check your DMs*

*bb.08* *CHECK YOUR FUCKING DMS*

Hands shaking, I swipe out of the app. Ignoring the other notifications, I return to the messaging app and open my chat history with Travis. My thumbs hover over the screen as I urge my trembling limbs to stop. One letter at a time, I type out a message and hit send.

> Probably just trolls, but I got several unsavory comments on SM

I glance at the time stamp above the message. *Today 4:34 AM*

Cursing under my breath, I pray I didn't wake him. Though he comes in for breakfast around six every morning, that doesn't mean he is an early riser. He may be the type that gets ready in ten minutes and is out the door shortly after he rolls out of bed.

Dots dance in a bubble on the screen, and I reach for the sun and moon at the base of my throat.

> TRAVIS
>
> Be there in 15

My thumbs fly over the screen.

You don't have to come over

His response is instant.

TRAVIS

Yeah, I do

I stare down at the screen until his words blur and the screen dims. When my phone locks, reality hits.

Bolting out of bed, I toss the self-defense kit items back in the paper bag and return it to the dresser. Digging through the drawers, I grab pajamas and slip them on. I dart from one side of the room to the other, tidying up my space.

I swipe the bra I wore yesterday off the bed footboard, followed by the shirt and jeans on the floor beneath it, and toss them in the laundry basket. Move to one side of the bed and straighten the bedding, then do the same on the other side. Open the nightstand drawer, grab the pump bottle of natural air freshener, and spritz the room.

Scanning the room for missed undergarments, my eyes land on the attached bathroom door. I pad across the room, flip the bathroom light on, and wince. Once my eyes adjust, I survey the vanity. "Too much to fuss over."

As I reach for the light switch, my eyes land on my toothbrush. I cup a hand over my nose and mouth, huff out a breath, then inhale. It isn't bad, but no one likes morning breath funk. With a hefty squirt of toothpaste, I quickly brush my teeth.

Lights flash through the blinds as I exit the bathroom. Not wanting to wake Delilah, I rush to the front door on bare feet. I unlatch the metal security guard, flip the deadbolt, and swing the door open.

Travis steps onto the porch, his golden eyes scanning the length of my body as if searching for wounds. Then, his honey irises turn fiery as they trail ever so slowly up, up, up. He licks his lips before biting the bottom one. And when his eyes finally meet mine, the heat of him sears my flesh.

I swallow and his gaze drops. The corner of his mouth twitches as he lifts a hand to my neck. With the softest caress, he brushes his knuckles down the column of my throat. Goose bumps dot my skin as he traces my necklace with a single finger, stopping when he reaches the sun charm.

"You put it on," he whispers.

Rolling my lips between my teeth, I nod.

"Going to let me in, sunshine?"

A bumbling fool, I nod again.

Shuffling to the side, I let him in, close the door and lock the dead bolt. His warmth and presence devour the foyer as I face him. An everlasting buzz dances over my skin as I step past him and walk toward my bedroom. Quiet on his feet, Travis follows without a word. With a soft click, I close my bedroom door and lean against the wood. Inhaling deeply, I get hit with the full force of Travis's addictive scent—fresh cotton, a hint of spice, and something distinctly him.

For a moment, I forget why he is here. Forget my world is off its axis. Forget about everything except him. Until he breaks the silence.

"Define unsavory?"

Padding across the room, I pick up my phone and unlock it. Open the first app, tap on the notification icon, and hand him my phone.

Telling him what I consider offensive is pointless. What bothers me may not disturb someone else, and vice versa. With thousands of followers online and a customer-facing job, I've developed thick skin over the years. Brushing off the occasional snide remark is as easy as taking out the trash.

But previous comments never felt this personal. And they didn't come in a massive wave.

The muscles in Travis's jaw tic as he scrolls and reads each one. He hands back my phone. "Can you screenshot the comments and send them to me?"

"Yeah. Sure."

His phone dings with the messages, and he pulls it from his back pocket. "Thanks."

I close the app, then open the next, and hand him my phone again. "There's more."

A low growl echoes in the air. "More?"

I nod.

He takes my phone, his knuckles blanching as he grips it tighter. Closing his eyes, he thrusts the phone in my direction. "Send them to me too." Head tipping back, he takes a fortifying breath. Then another. Dropping his chin, he rolls his neck, opens his eyes, and moves past me to sit on the edge of the bed. "*Fuck.*" Elbows on his knees, he drops his head and runs his hands through his hair. "*Fuck, fuck, fuck.*"

I text him screenshots of the comments and lock my phone. Hesitant, I shuffle across the room, each measured step stitching the fissure between us back together. Within arm's reach, I toss my phone on the bed and wait for him to look up. Wait for those amber eyes to lock me in place.

One breath. Then another.

Watery eyes lift to mine and, in one step, I erase every inch between us. Hands outstretched, he spreads his legs and hauls me to him. I crash against his chest as his arms band around my middle and constrict. As if we've done it countless times, I snake my arms around his neck and comb my fingers through his thick, dark hair.

Heat radiates off him and soothes the ache in my bones. I close my eyes, press my cheek to his crown, and let the world disappear. All too soon, Travis pops my bliss bubble.

"No one will hurt you, sunshine. I swear it." He buries his nose in my neck and inhales. "Morning, noon, and night, I'll keep an eye out. On your house. The restaurant. *You.*"

I relax my hold on him and try to step back. But he pins me in place, unwilling to unravel his arms from my waist. With a huff, I deflate and sag against him. For a beat, he breathes me in. Then, after a quick squeeze, his hands fall to the bed.

"Travis," I warn, taking a step back and putting distance between us. "No." I shake my head, my hand reaching for my necklace. "No," I repeat.

His brows scrunch together before he drags a hand through his hair. "No?" He pushes off the bed and paces to the other side of the room. Back and forth. Back and forth. "No?" he parrots, disbelieving. Turning on his heel, he cocks his head. "What do you mean, no?"

"Travis, I—"

"He will *not* touch you." He growls, storming across the room to stand a breath away. "*No one* will touch you." The muscle in his jaw tics. "No one," he affirms.

Breath caught in my throat, I stare into his molten amber eyes. Read the emotion etched in his unforgiving gaze. Decipher all the things left unsaid, all the things he hasn't given a voice.

A palpable, red, pulsing cloud, his anger steals the air in the room. Sends my heart into overdrive. Has my fingers twitching at my sides.

On a deep, cleansing inhale, I remind myself his rage isn't directed *at* me. No, it is aimed at those treating me with cruelty. It's aimed at the person leaving me indecent notes. The person threatening my livelihood.

Exhaling, my eyes roam the arch of his brows and slope of his nose, his thicker-than-usual stubble and angle of his jaw. For a moment, I look past his anger. Look beyond the surface. Look for something deeper. Something to take hold of and strengthen. Something to assuage the panic drowning him.

On instinct, I inch closer to him. Invade his personal space. My breasts pressed against his chest, his breaths come faster. I lift a hand to his cheek and cup his jaw, my thumb stroking his stubble.

Eyes falling shut, he leans into my touch. Shivers under my caress. Swallowing, he turns and kisses the heart of my palm. Then he meets my gaze with unyielding determination. "No one," he repeats, the words a whisper on his tongue.

"I love that you want me safe." I rest my forehead on his. "But you can't be with me all hours of the day."

"Says who?"

I close my eyes, take a steadying breath, then hold his stare. "Your job. Your dad."

"Fuck my job." A hand clutches my hip and draws me impossibly closer. "Fuck it all." His other hand skims up the opposite hip, then dances along the hem of my tank top, his fingertips caressing my skin.

I open my mouth, ready to counter him. But before I get a word out, his mouth crashes down on mine. Dumbstruck, I freeze.

Warm lips brush mine as his arms circle my waist and pin me to him. His tongue darts out, licks the seam of my lips, and rouses me from my stupor.

After one erratic beat of my heart, I kiss him back. Meet his fervor with my own hunger. Lick and taste and devour him as I claw at his shirt. Nip at his bottom lip. Fist the cotton of his tee and crush the length of my body to his.

He licks my top lip before he breaks the kiss long enough

to tug his shirt over his head and toss it on the floor. Then his lips are back on mine, my face framed by his hands. A moan spills from his mouth into mine as he steps back, taking me with him. We jolt as his legs hit the bed, his brutal kiss softening.

Needing to touch more of him, my knuckles graze the light dusting of hair on his abdomen, just above the waistband of his jeans, and he hisses. That single break in his control sparks a fire in my chest. Gifts me a power over him no one else wields.

But I don't want to overpower Travis. When it comes to this, us—whatever we are—I want an equal. Someone willing to go toe to toe with me in life and love and all things in between. I want hunger and passion and desperation. But not at the expense of losing who he is at his core.

With all his faults, Travis Emerson is a good man, and I want him as he is.

I rest my forehead on his and dip my fingers beneath the elastic of his briefs, relishing the way his entire body shudders under my touch. Eyes rolling closed, he audibly swallows. Our ragged breaths mingle as I memorize the lines of his body. The dips and curves and ridges of lean, hard muscle. The twitch of his abdomen each time my fingers dance over his happy trail, then dip lower.

"Fuck, sunshine." His shaky breath coats my lips as his fingers in my hair curl tighter, his thumbs stroking my cheeks. "I'm dying."

"Take off my shirt, Travis," I whisper, bolder than I feel.

Amber eyes clash with my stormy irises. "You're sure?"

My fingers trail up his midline and he shivers, his jaw going slack. I nod. "Yes." I lean in and lick his lips. "Need to feel you." My fingers drift down, down, down and pop the button on his jeans. "All of you."

My words are a switch in his brain flipping on.

Before my next breath, my tank top is ripped from my body and flying across the room. Then his mouth is on mine again, bruising my lips with gloriously punishing kisses. The fire in my chest moments ago burns hotter, builds, expands. Wildfire licks my skin, singes my veins, scorches my bones, forever brands my soul.

And goddamn, I want more. *Need* more.

Of his fevered skin pressed to mine.

Of his frenzied kisses stealing my breaths.

Of his brutal fingers kneading my waist, my hips, my ass.

Of him.

Just him.

Fingers in the elastic of his briefs, I shove them down with his jeans. He kicks them away as he kisses and nips a trail along my jaw to my ear and slowly, ever so slowly, down the column of my neck. I tip my head back and gasp at the delicious buzz his lips and teeth and tongue leave in their wake.

Calloused fingers knead their way up, up, up until he palms my breasts. One unrestrained kiss after another, he drifts down my body. Tastes my skin. Licks a path to my nipple, circles the tight peak with the tip of his tongue, then devours it with unrivaled hunger.

"Travis…" Breathy, I invoke him like a god.

A yelp rings through the air as teeth pierce my nipple. I feel more than see the corners of his mouth curve up. My grip on his hips tightens, my nails digging into his flesh. On a hiss, he releases my nipple.

"Fuck, sunshine."

Before a witty comeback leaves my lips, his mouth clamps down on my other nipple. Sucking and ravishing and bruising. Arching my back, I give him more. Silently beg him to punish my body with his.

A muted pop echoes through the room a beat before a thud. Dropping my chin, I gape at the sight of him on his knees. Wild eyes hold mine as his hands skim up my thighs, over the curve of my hips, and stop at the waistband of my pajama pants.

A silent request for permission lingers in the air as his honey-eyed stare holds me captive.

And I love how he wants my reassurance one last time.

Bottom lip between my teeth, I give a subtle nod.

Goose bumps dance over my skin as the last of my clothes hit the floor. But they don't last.

Jaw slack, I comb my fingers through his hair and fist the thick strands. Inch by painfully slow inch, he leans in and presses his lips to my hip bone. Hands palming and massaging my ass, he kisses and licks and nips his way to my other hip.

And then he kisses a path along the hinge of my hip, drifting down, down, down to the junction of my thighs.

My knuckles scream as I grip his hair harder, my nails digging into my palm. The welcome sting mingles with the vicious beat of my heart. Air rushes in and out of my lungs as he dips lower, his hands thrusting me into him.

On unsteady legs, I suck in a sharp breath as his tongue darts out and tastes me for the first time. Melting into the feel of him, a moan vibrates my chest, the back of my throat, and spills from my lips and mixes with his.

He hikes my leg over his shoulder, hauls me closer, tilts my hips, and feasts on my flesh, my body, me.

Closing my eyes, I tip my chin to the ceiling and get lost in the pulse-pounding dizziness.

"Eyes on me, sunshine," he growls against my center.

Blinking open, I level him with my gaze and swallow at the fire in his.

One of his hands drifts down the curve of my ass to trail

through my drenched pussy. He groans again, louder this time. Finger teasing my soaked center, he sucks my clit harder. I mewl without shame as I stare down at him and he sinks a finger into my core.

Our brazen moans bounce off the walls.

And then my hips thrust in time with the pump of his finger. His teeth nip my clit, his tongue flicking it once, twice before he sucks it between his lips. I pin him between the mattress and my body and grind my sensitive flesh over his deliciously scratchy stubble.

He doesn't fight for air. If anything, he smothers himself more by crushing me to him.

Heat expands low in my belly. Thrill buzzes through every nerve ending in my body before rushing, swirling, swelling between my thighs.

"That's it, baby," he cajoles. "Come on my tongue."

Eyes on his, breaths coming out in short, throaty bursts, my vision blurs at the sensation overload. I cry out as my body detonates, my walls constricting around his finger.

"Such a good girl," he praises a second before my back lands on something soft. His mouth is on mine, the salty tang of my orgasm on his tongue as it tangles with mine. "So fucking perfect."

Crinkling hits my ears and my vision clears as I look up at him, watching as he tears open a foil package, then rolls a condom down his length.

Tongue darting out, I lick my lips, already hungry for him again.

"Keep looking at me like that and we'll break the bed, sunshine."

I arch a brow, goading him.

The corner of his mouth kicks up in a smirk as he shakes his head. He lowers himself, bracketing me with his forearms like parentheses. His hips rest in the cradle of mine. Neither of us moves as the seriousness of the moment settles between us. A finger caresses my temple and twirls a lock of my hair, his addictive ambers never leaving my stormy blues.

He drops his lips to hover over mine, rocks his hips forward, and fills me fully. Our unified gasp floats in the air as we pause and relish the overwhelming sensation of our connection.

Breath hot on my lips, he shakes his head. "So damn tight."

I lift off the bed and crush my lips to his. Fingers thread through my hair and guide me back to the bed. He kisses in time with the rock of his hips, slowly at first before growing desperate. Hiking my leg up and over his shoulder, he drives harder, deeper, grinding against my clit. Needy fingers caress the skin of my neck a beat before wrapping around my throat and pinning me in place. Thrust for thrust, loud slaps mix with moans and grunts and the thump, thump, thump of the bedframe hitting the wall.

I clutch the globes of his ass and meet each of his thrusts with equal fervor. Fire spirals low in my belly and he reaches between us, stroking my clit with his thumb. I open my mouth to tell him not to stop, but don't get the chance.

My eyes roll back as my orgasm hits, this one harder than the previous.

"Goddamn," he rasps out a beat before rolling us over. "Ride me, sunshine."

I groan as my body wilts, and he laughs.

He grips my hips with strong hands and rocks me up and down his length. Sitting up, he kisses me with such tenderness. "Watch."

He jerks his chin to where we're joined and I drop my gaze. Grip firm, he rocks our bodies in time. His growl vibrates through me as I stare open-mouthed at his cock disappearing inside me. It's one of the most erotic things I have ever witnessed.

"Was fucking made for you."

Arms draped over his shoulders, I rock my hips harder, reenergized by the sight of us coming together.

"That's it, baby." He palms my ass, spreads my cheeks, and impales me on him. "Fuck. Me."

I ride his body hard, his thrusts meeting mine with equal intensity. When he tries to assume control by guiding my hips, I shove him into the mattress and pin his hands above his head. Bounce up and down his cock like it's my new favorite toy. Ride him harder and faster than any fucking cowgirl ever could.

Releasing his hands, I palm my breasts and pinch my nipples in time with my rocking hips.

"Fuck, I'm not going to last." His fingers paint rough lines up my belly. Then he sits back up. Grips my hips and slams me down on him painfully. "One more, sunshine."

*Slap. Slap. Slap.*

Our bodies crash together over and over and over. Heat crawls across my skin and resonates deep in my bones.

"That's it, baby," he croons. "So fucking beautiful." His fingertips dance over the fire on my skin.

My body detonates without warning. Frantic and forceful, it steals the oxygen from my lungs.

Lips at my ear, he growls and holds me down on him. "Holy fucking hell." His hips jerk, his cock twitching inside me as his orgasm consumes him.

My eyes fall shut as I nuzzle the crook of his neck, our fevered breaths the only sound in the room. One of his arms bands around my waist, his other hand trailing up the length of my spine to clutch the back of my neck. For endless minutes, we sit like this. Unmoving. Silent. Reveling in the moment.

*I had sex with Travis Emerson. The best damn sex of my life.*

Now what?

His hold on me tightens, as if he hears my thoughts. Turning toward me, he kisses my cheek. "We'll figure it out, sunshine." Another kiss. "Promise."

A simple vow, yes. And somehow, I trust Travis. With my body, my heart, and my safety.

# TWENTY

## TRAVIS

Gravel crunches beneath my tires as I pull onto the shoulder. Pepper sits taller in the backseat, eyes scanning the forest, guard up as she waits to be let out. Silence greets us when I cut the engine. An eerie chill slithers its way around my bones that has nothing to do with the early December temperature.

I grab my police-issued jacket from the passenger seat and slip it on, followed by a pair of leather gloves. Police vest secured around her torso, Pepper paces back and forth on the bench seat. Her soft whimper bounces around the SUV's cabin. Her eagerness to get to work evident in her body language.

Tugging on a beanie, I exit and round the car. Once Pepper is leashed, she hops down and sits at my side while I double-check my gear. The second she hears the locks beep, she stands and inches toward the woods.

"Let's see if we missed anything, Officer Pepper. *Such*," I command in German. Lengthening the leash, I give Pepper a wide berth to sniff and search as we enter the forest.

After almost a month of sifting through evidence, we are no closer to catching the killer than we were the day the woman in the woods was discovered. Or, as Chief announced to a crowded bullpen yesterday, *I haven't made any progress with the case.* Never mind the fact that my partner, Wooler, and other officers with less urgent grunt work have been tasked with helping.

The way Chief sees it… if an Emerson is on the case, an Emerson is held accountable. Period.

Roadblock or not, I need this case solved. I need this sick fuck off the street and behind bars. Yesterday. Not only to appease my father and get him off my back, but also for Kirsten.

I have zero proof the man behind the letters is the same person responsible for the death of our victim. Not an ounce of DNA or a single fingerprint to search for a match. No note was left with the body, so there's no cross-referencing the handwriting.

But from the moment Kirsten told me about the notes, a sixth sense prickled in my gut. With each passing day, that inclination grows stronger. Twists low in my belly. Exists just out of reach in my mental periphery.

The murder followed by the sinister notes may be a complete coincidence. But what if they aren't? What if this is how it starts? What if this lunatic gets his jollies out of scaring victims before committing the ultimate crime?

My instincts have never steered me down the wrong path in the past. I refuse to believe they will now.

Nose inches above the ground, Pepper sniffs the air and earth for scents she has been trained to identify. As a dual-purpose K-9 officer, Pepper hunts for several scents. Select drugs commonly found in the area, humans—living or deceased—accelerants, and miscellaneous crime scene evidence.

Right now, I will take the smallest piece of evidence.

Anything. Even if it's only a minor step forward, some momentum is better than nothing.

While Pepper guides us through the woods, my thoughts drift to Kirsten. To the shift in our relationship.

It's been a week since I read her text and manically drove to her house at four thirty in the morning. I defied the speed limit and blew every stop sign and red light to get to her. And I'd do it again.

Which worries me.

Kirsten and I have known each other for years. We have smiled and flirted and talked shit over breakfast at the restaurant almost every day. On countless occasions, she has lifted my mood. Added a dose of sunshine to my cloudy life. Given me a reason to smile.

The last thing I want is to be deprived of her solace or affection, and that terrifies me more than the fugitive I'm hunting.

The skin near my left collarbone burns as memories of the past flicker through my mind. Pain flares in my jaw and temples as I grit my teeth. "Don't want to think of *her*," I mutter.

Regardless, an image of Gracie pops into my head. Her frigid brown eyes cutting me in half. Her acrid admission flaying me wide open. A glimpse of her wicked sneer before she straightened her spine and walked out of my life.

Heat claws up my neck to my cheeks. I ball my fingers into tight fists as I will every memory of her away.

"Was all a lie," I say through gritted teeth.

Gracie didn't just gut me, she stole my ability to fully trust. She embedded the tiniest speck of doubt in my bones. Made it difficult to confide in someone completely or believe every word out of their mouth.

Hate may be a strong word, but I fucking hate her. For

what she did and that she still harbors an inkling of control over me and my life.

Nearly a year post-breakup, I reached the acceptance stage. Visited the tattoo shop and had a reminder permanently etched into my skin. *Survive the storm.* Determined to never be in this position again, I promised myself I'd never fall in love so carelessly in the future. That I'd go slow and get to know someone before handing them my heart.

A week ago, Kirsten traced the tip of her finger over the swirly font of the tattoo while we lay in her bed. I'd held my breath and waited for her to ask the meaning behind the ink. But she never did.

To say I was grateful is an understatement.

With that single action—her not prying for details I'm uncertain I am ready to disclose yet—the hum she elicits morphed into this persistent, delightful effervescence. A collection of tiny, fizzy bubbles in my chest.

That mini-explosion... I love it with as much force as I despise it. It makes me want something I once thought I had. It makes me want Kirsten more. Makes me want her heart.

Above all, it opens doors to vulnerability. Places I locked up tight. Emotions I shoved in the dark recesses of my mind, determined to never let them see the light of day again.

I want more for my life—love, rapture, to wake up every morning and wrap my arms around my favorite person, a future full of smiles and laughter and growing old together. All it would take is letting go—of the past, of what *she* did, of the reality that none of it was *my* fault, of this incessant bruise on my heart that whispers never to trust the organ again.

Am I ready to release the ghosts of my past and vanquish them for good?

Am I ready to take back the power I so easily handed over in my broken state?

Am I ready to move forward and admit not everyone hurts others with a malicious grin on their face?

Damn, I wish I had definitive answers.

Pepper drops her nose to the ground as she picks up the pace and homes in on whatever new scent has her attention. I snap out of my thoughts and focus on her every move and reaction.

Through the trees, roughly ten yards away, is the boulder where the woman was discovered by the hiker. Last time we approached the crime scene, it was from the north. This time around, I chose to proceed from the east.

In the initial moments, crime scenes are processed with hyperfocus. Our mind rapid-fires to collect as many details as possible before the location gets disrupted. But with that tunnel-vision focus, we sometimes miss minor pieces of the mystery puzzle.

Without that extra boost of adrenaline or a million *what-the-hell* thoughts clouding my head, I survey the area with fresh eyes and an open mind. Pepper tugs me left, away from the path toward the boulder and into more forestry. With my eyes on her, I keep my mouth shut and let her work.

Sun filters through the tree canopy, but does nothing to stave off the December chill in the air. Labored breaths come out in small white clouds as Pepper picks up speed. She zigzags in short bursts for one, two, three strides before her direction has a focal point.

And then she stops, sniffs the ground, lifts her head an inch from the earth, and barks at her discovery.

"*Brav*, Officer Pepper." I step to her side. "*Sitz. Bleib.*" I aim a finger at the ground, then show her my palm, directing her to sit and stay.

I squat down and study the foliage blanketing the terrain,

visually sifting through each leaf, twig, and needle. But I have yet to find what grabs Pepper's attention.

With careful, deliberate movements, I brush aside leaves and needles. Gingerly shift sticks and small branches out of the way. Stone Bay has yet to see its first snowfall of the season, and I am grateful for one less obstruction.

Beneath a needled bundle of Ponderosa pine cones, a faded piece of paper snags my attention.

Digging in my coat pocket, I pull out an evidence bag and open it. I pick up what looks to be the corner of washed-out yellow cardstock, a hint of something darker near the tear. Dropping it in the bag, I flip it around to look at the other side. More bleached than the other side of the card, I see faint lines of two or three letters.

Again and again, I study one side then the other.

"Argh!" I bellow out, my frustration echoing through the trees. "This cannot be a coincidence. It has to be a clue." I turn the bag over in my hand once more. "But what? *What is this?*"

I seal the bag, fill out the identifying information on the front, then stow it in my pocket. Rising to my full height, I hook Pepper's leash on my arm and say, "*Such,*" telling her to search once more.

The sun shifts overhead as we trudge through the forest. We pass the location where the victim lay, nothing. We walk along the base of the mountains, nothing. We take a more southern path back to the car, nothing.

But we aren't leaving empty-handed.

I only hope forensics is able to figure out what this paper is or where it came from. And if we are damn lucky, maybe it will have a hint of DNA in its fibers.

"What am I looking at, Emerson?" Chief asks, his tone severe as he stares at the scrap of paper in the evidence bag.

I swallow down the expansive ball of anxiety in my throat, square my shoulders, and hold my father's gaze. "Officer Pepper and I returned to the crime scene and did another sweep of the area. This was thirty feet east of the boulder under some brush."

An exasperated huff leaves his lips as he tosses the bag on his desk. "This *evidence* could be one of a thousand things." The word "evidence" is laced with disbelief and ridicule. As if there is no fathomable way *I* would ever find something on my own. "A piece of a hiking map. Litter from the highway. The corner of a takeout box."

Pain erupts in my palms as I curl my fingers into tight fists, my blunt nails biting my flesh.

"Why is it so hard to believe?" The question comes out harsher than intended. But I don't apologize. Nor do I stand down. "Why don't you have faith in a damn thing I do?"

Dark eyes pin me in place, but I don't waver. I glare at him with evenly matched frigidity.

For once, would it kill him to say, *"Great job, Travis."*? Would it be so difficult to give me a pat on the back and praise me for my discovery or effort?

Hell, with a rookie badge pinned to his shirt, Jacob is the opposite of serious. When an opening presents itself, Jacob is the first to make a joke—clean or far from appropriate for work. Yet our father manages to reward his shitty work and behavior with smiles and positive recognition in front of the department. He lifts him up while he buries me deep.

And I am so fucking tired of people making me feel less than to serve themselves.

"Watch your tongue, Emerson," he warns.

I take a step in his direction. "Show some respect, and

maybe I will, *Emerson*." With a shake of my head, I add, "Time to redefine your double standards. If you're going to treat me like trash for busting my ass, I better see the same with every other person in this building. If not, prepare to be more furious with your most disliked child."

The muscles in his jaw flex as he picks up the evidence bag from his desk and thrusts it my way. "Log this in the system, then have it analyzed. Report back to me with the findings."

And just like that, we are back to business as usual.

I snatch the bag from his hand, spin on my heel, and move toward the door with thunder in my step. "Fine."

Ignoring everyone I pass in the bullpen, I sit at my desk and log the evidence in the system. With my eyes on the computer screen, I feel Wooler's questioning stare on my profile. But I refuse to acknowledge her. It will only lead to questions I am too fired up to answer.

Once the evidence is with forensics, I fetch Pepper and walk out the front door. No *goodbye* or *see you tomorrow*. I leave without a word.

The drive from the station to home is a blur. After stripping off my uniform and slipping into comfortable clothes, I spend time outside with Pepper, praise her for her work today, then reward her with treats.

And once my blood pressure stabilizes after the conversation with Dad, I pull my phone out, open my chat history with Kirsten, and type out a message.

How's little Trixie today?

Friday evening, Kirsten coerced me to visit the town pet store with her to ogle kittens and bunnies. My first inclination was to say no. Pepper is the only pet I've owned, and she is more of a working dog than a pet. But Kirsten was persistent, batting her lashes and pushing out her perfect, pouty lips, and I caved.

For hours, we sat cross-legged on the floor, surrounded by furry babies. To say I was uncomfortable for the first few minutes would be an understatement. I was in the eye of a furr-icane, unsure how to proceed safely.

But when this tiny ball of gray fluff crawled into my lap, pawed at my chest, and showed me the sweetest face before mewling, my heart melted on the spot. While others vied for both my and Kirsten's attention, the little gray one curled up in my lap and purred the entire time.

When the shop owner told us the store was closing in thirty minutes, I did not anticipate what would happen next.

*"I'd like to adopt this cutie,"* Kirsten proclaimed as she pointed to the gray kitten in my lap.

On the way back to her house, kitten in a carrier on her lap and my backseat loaded with everything a kitten may possibly need, Kirsten rattled off a long list of names, waiting for some sort of reaction. It wasn't until we were in her room, the kitten sniffing every inch of the space, that Kirsten said, *"Hey, Trix-ie?"* and the kitten gave a scratchy meow in response.

My phone vibrates with Kirsten's reply.

> **SUNSHINE**
>
> When she's not kicking litter out of the box, she's great 😺

My body shakes with laughter as I type.

> Maybe she needs one of those covered boxes after all

Kirsten argued it was silly to get a covered litter box for a kitten. *"It's a baby. How much of a mess can she make?"*

Question answered.

SUNSHINE
Yeah, yeah 😊

Dinner?

Entering my bedroom, I fetch boots and a hoodie and slip them on.

SUNSHINE
Burgers?

Jogging down the stairs, eyes on the screen as I type out a response, I head for the mudroom, grab my jacket from the hook, and wiggle it on over my hoodie.

Send me your order. I'll call it in.

She texts an order that could possibly feed two people, and I chuckle. Indecision is a bitch, but leftovers are delicious.

Got it. See you soon.

After I let Pepper out one last time, I pocket my wallet, phone, and keys and walk out the door.

It's not until I call the restaurant to order that reality smacks me in the face.

I *am* in a relationship with Kirsten. We may not have defined *us*, but there is definitely an *us*. And with this realization, I lose my appetite.

# TWENTY-ONE

## BEN

Wind howls outside, a shiver curling up my spine, shaking me from boot to beanie. Arms crossed over my chest, I tuck my fists under my arms and inch closer to the heat lamp. The glowing orange bulb wards off the initial bite but doesn't warm me fully.

At least the space has windows now. Last week, a commissioned antique window specialist delivered massive windows to match those in the current library. With their team, our crew, and the help of a crane, the windows were placed. The next morning, the heat from the lamps stayed longer, which made working in the winter a little easier.

Eyes cast across the room, I stare at the bare bones of what will become a grand fireplace. At ten feet wide and eight feet tall, it is the largest fireplace I have laid eyes on. Reminiscent of the days when central heating was a fool's dream. Though the fireplace won't be the only source of heat for the library's new addition, I picture it becoming a coveted spot to sit and read or hang out with friends.

After the holidays, an artist from Colorado will join the build. Flying more than a thousand miles, he will spend weeks bringing the fireplace to life and matching the medieval stone details on the windows' exterior. John took no offense when the town committee shared the news. The artist works with various types of stone, carving intricate details for hours and days and weeks until a new masterpiece takes shape. Considering the town wanted the library to maintain its medieval Gothic vibe, this artist was more appropriate for the job than anyone on our crew.

"You pussing out on me, Wilks?" Luke feigns a punch to my arm as he huddles next to the heat lamp, rubbing his hands together.

With a gentle shake of my head, I roll my eyes. "If by 'pussing out' you mean not letting my fingers go numb so *I* can do my job, then yeah."

His hands still, his entire frame stiff and unyielding as he sears my profile with his stare. "Calling me a slacker?" His voice toneless, I study the tense line of his lips. Look for hidden meaning in his question.

*Is he mad? Or is this just him giving me shit like always?*

"I, uh..."

This is what we do; pretend to be irritated by the other. But truth be told, everyone on this crew is family. The amount of time we spend together, the level of trust our job requires as we put ourselves in risky situations, how can we not be close? Though some of us have stronger bonds, it's impossible to picture my life without anyone in this room.

*Whack.*

Luke slaps my bicep and laughs. "Just giving you shit. Everyone knows I work ten times harder than you." He says that last part loud enough for the crew to hear over the music echoing off the walls. "And my lines are cleaner."

I slap him back. Every muscle in his face scrunches to the

middle as he lifts his arm and pretends to be hurt. All I want to do is laugh—at him, with him—so I do.

"Are you laughing at me?" he asks in mock offense.

This makes me laugh harder, louder, until my abdomen aches.

"I may have chiseled muscles, a sharp jawline, and a panty-ripping smile"—he pauses, clamping down on his lips briefly before continuing—"but I am a delicate flower, Wilks."

At this, every sense of rationality I have lets go. An embarrassing snort-laugh rips from my nose and mouth as I clutch my stomach.

"What're you two blathering about?" John sips water from a jug, his eyes darting between us.

I reel in my laughter long enough to say, "Luke is… a delicate flower."

A classic holiday song ends and a modern rendition plays next. The heat lamp cycles off for one, two, three breaths before kicking back on. Aaron, Jake, and Dylan join our muted conversation, their eyes darting from one person to the next in question.

"Did I hear Fitzpatrick call himself a delicate flower?" Dylan arches a brow, then levels Luke with her formidable gaze. A single snort bounces off the bare walls. "Delicate my ass." Fingers inches from his nose, she flicks the air. "If you're a flower, you're definitely a pansy."

At this, everyone clutches their stomachs as booming laughter crowds the room, Luke included.

"Alright, children," John chimes in when our merriment fizzles out. "Let's call it a day." Weathered eyes survey the room for a beat. "Our time in Stone Bay is almost up. If we push hard, we should be on our way home early next week." A bulky, long arm spans my shoulders and grazes Luke's farthest shoulder, John's other arm drapes across Dylan, Jake, and barely touches Aaron. "Proud of you all and the hard work you've put in the past five weeks."

Bright smiles light the room as we huddle closer to John.

Of all the people I have worked for and with, John and this crew are unparalleled in skill, motivation, and compassion. We are a true team. What impacts one of us influences all of us. We handle ups and downs as if they're our own, cheering on good days and lending a shoulder or an ear on bad days.

"Aw," Luke coos, sarcastic as ever. "You're such a softy, boss. Like a mega teddy bear."

John slaps Luke's back, loud enough to hear but not hard enough to hurt.

But Luke being Luke, he plays into it. "Ow, John. That hurts my feelings."

We break apart and clean up for the day.

"Oh, I'll hurt your feelings, you grouser."

Once the worksite is tidy, we shrug on our coats and head for the parking lot. Midway to the truck, Aaron asks if I want to join everyone for dinner at the barbecue joint in town. I nip the corner of my bottom lip as I mull over the idea. Much as I'd love to share laughs, good food, and a couple of beers with the crew, my mouth refuses to open. My tongue refuses to shape the words *I'd love to.*

And I know exactly why.

*Kirsten.*

The occasional breakfast at Poke the Yolk aside, I haven't spent time with her in weeks—since Friendsgiving and the awkward encounter with Officer Asshat. Though we text daily, it isn't the same. I soak up every one of those little bubbles of conversation, those small glimpses into her life, but they are no longer enough. I need time with her. I need her voice and words and laughter. Her smile, her warmth.

Filling each other in on the past thirteen years feels akin to coming home. Sharing pieces of my life and little things she has missed in Smoky Creek warms my chest while simultaneously stitching the Kirsten-shaped void in my heart back together. Memories I've taken for granted have been given new life as I share them with her.

"I may have plans," I mumble as he cranks the truck's engine.

Taking out my phone, I unlock it and type a message to Kirsten.

> Would like to see you. Dinner?

Clicking the seat belt in place, I stare down at the screen, praying she will say yes.

"That your girl?" Hands in front of the vents, Aaron nods toward my phone.

Thrill courses through my bloodstream at his question. Is it wrong to go along with it? Allow him to think Kirsten is mine?

Unsure if he means romantic or platonic, I simply say, "Yeah."

A buzz followed by a little gray bubble is an instant shot of adrenaline to my bloodstream.

**SPARKLES**

> I could eat. Where? When?

Knowing the crew is headed to the barbecue place, I steer clear of the intersection. Last thing I need is Luke being an ass in front of Kirsten. The man has no filter unless absolutely necessary.

> Bay Chowder House, 6?

Aaron pulls out of the lot and drives toward the inn,

thumbs tapping on the steering wheel to the beat of the Christmas tune on the radio. The library is a mile from the inn, and it'll take no time to park beneath the snow-dusted evergreens.

"Grabbing a bite with Kirsten," I say, wanting to let him know before we're out of the truck and Luke is in earshot.

"Sounds good, man. Glad you two reconnected."

Me too.

SPARKLES

Perfect. Need a ride?

With the swift drop in temperature and snow flurries this week, walking that far without decent layers isn't the best idea. Nor do I want to risk Luke spotting me on the street and razzing me for the next year.

A ride would be great.

Quirky sea-themed tchotchkes blend with weathered boat parts and pieces on blue walls inside Bay Chowder House. Nets and rope hang from the ceiling with no set rhyme or reason. Classic rock plays loud enough to hear but quiet enough not to steal conversation. Smokiness and herbs and the salty bay water scent the air.

A young man seats us at a table for two near the back, hands us menus, and rattles off the daily special before walking away.

At the heart of the wood plank table sits a votive candle in a glass holder. Beside it, small-stemmed blue flowers fill a slender glass vase. Netting rests beneath both, while dried coral, starfish, and sand dollars have been artfully placed around them.

At first glance, Bay Chowder House is a unique mix of rustic seafood restaurant charm and borderline fine dining. As if the owner couldn't decide which they wanted and came up with a new concept to make themselves happy.

I shrug off my coat and drape it over the back of my chair, then offer to help Kirsten with hers. Cheeks pink from the winter chill, she gifts me her smile and nods. Stepping behind her, I hold the lapels of her coat as she pulls her arms free. Innocent as the act is—taking off her coat—I startle when my fingers brush hers.

A burst of warmth steals the last of the cold from my skin. Arms frozen on either side of her, my fingers twitch with the need to touch her again. Spasm with the urge to drop her coat and wrap her in my arms.

Until she peeks over her shoulder and meets my gaze, her brows bent in confusion.

Heat crawls up my neck to my cheeks. I shake off my daydream and hang her jacket on her chair. "Sorry."

Soft laughter hits my ears as I return to my seat. Eyes on the menu, she says, "No need to apologize. Just glad there's nothing wrong." Her eyes lift and meet mine across the table. "Thought maybe I had something in my hair. Since adopting Trixie, I've been gifted many undesirable things."

"Trixie?"

Dropping her menu, she winces. "Obviously, I've lost my wits too." With a roll of her eyes, she shakes her head. "I adopted a kitten. Swear I told you."

"With a name like Trixie, she's bound to be a handful," I tease.

"Shush you."

The server sidles up to the table, deposits a glass of water at each of our place settings, and greets Kirsten by name after welcoming me in. After minor deliberation, we order drinks and dinner.

Silence forms a tense bubble around our table as Kirsten traces the condensation drops on her water glass. In the time I've known Kirsten, she has never been so reticent. The last time she was this reserved—that I recall—was when her dad was killed. The happy-go-lucky girl I'd known most of my formative years retreated into herself. Smiles she once gifted so easily—gone. Laughter and teasing I heard more often than not—absent. The goofball I wanted to spend every minute with—nowhere to be found.

The woman across the table has a hint of that dark cloud hovering over her now.

Arm extended, I lay a hand on the table as I glimpse her features.

Shoulders caved, she slouches in her seat as she draws patterns in the condensation on her glass. Chin slightly tucked, she rolls her lips back and forth, occasionally biting one corner, then the other. But it's the constant scrunching then smoothing of her brows that throws me the most.

Is she nervous? Has something else happened? Have the gossipmongers made her more uncomfortable? Is she safe?

Not that I trust him, but that prick of a cop said he'd keep her safe. I may not be a violent person, but knocking the smirk off his face would bring me extreme pleasure.

"Everything okay?" I sip my water, then return it to the table. "You seem down."

Stormy irises meet my gaze, more gray than blue today— like her mood. The corners of her mouth tip up in a strained smile as she sits a fraction taller. Her fingers fall away from her glass. "I'm good." The words hold no conviction.

I narrow my eyes at her.

"Really, everything is fine."

Still, I'm not convinced. So I try another tactic. "They apprehended the killer?"

Her momentary wince is all the answer I need.

"Let's talk about something else," she suggests. "How's the library coming along?"

For now, I humor her and go with the change of subject. But the topic is far from dropped.

I update her on the project and that we hope to wrap up next week. I don't mention wanting to stay in town longer to spend time with her. Something tells me that will only spark another redirection of our conversation. Smile wide on my lips, I share more about my work crew and what has changed in Smoky Creek since she left. The more I share, the brighter her smile becomes.

And damn, I want to see that smile every day.

Steamy bowls of chowder are deposited on the table—hers with shrimp and lobster, mine with shrimp, clams, and bacon —followed by a loaded basket of crusty garlic and herb bread.

Eager for the first bite, I scoop a little of everything onto my spoon and bring it to my lips. But just as I open my mouth to taste it, a moan floats across the table and cuts me off. Beneath the table, my dick twitches against my zipper and I mentally tell it to stand down. Spoon an inch from my mouth, I stare at her closed eyes. Two breaths pass before our gazes lock and she swallows.

In the middle of a bustling restaurant, we are statues—still and silent and unsure of what to do next.

Kirsten chuckles, breaking the silence. Lifting a napkin to her lips, she wipes her mouth, her cheeks a little flush with embarrassment. My eyes refuse to look anywhere but at her.

"Been a while since I've had their chowder. Sorry."

"All good." My affirmation comes out throaty.

Swallowing past the sudden dry patch, I bring the spoon to my mouth and take the first bite. An explosion of flavor hits my tongue—tangy and salty, buttery and creamy, smoky with a hint of sweetness—and I moan loud enough to garner attention from other patrons.

"Damn, that is good."

Kirsten laughs as my cheeks heat. Then my laughter blends with hers, and it is the lightest I have felt in a long time.

This invisible structure forms around us—weightless and carefree—for the rest of dinner. The sullen woman who greeted me at the start of the evening is nowhere to be seen. Boisterous and flirty Kirsten is back in full force. *My* Kirsten.

After I settle the bill and we don our coats, she leads me out a side door and on to an enclosed wood deck. We climb a flight of stairs, her hair whipping as we reach the top. Guiding me toward the rail, she leans against it and sighs.

"I love this part of the restaurant," she whispers into the wind. "In the summer, they throw parties up here. Good food, great people, and the best view."

While she stares at the bay, I memorize her profile in the fading light. How the shadows dance over the arch of her brow, the slope and flare of her nose, the perfect pout of her lips. My eyes roam over the dusting of freckles on the bridge of her nose and beneath her eyes, less noticeable than they once were. And the stars… they twinkle behind her but are no match to her beauty.

The glow of the lighthouse bulb flashes over her face and she twists in my direction, blinking a few times.

With one look, she locks me in place. The salty air hums between us, growing thick and warm and potent. On instinct, I inch closer to her. Breathe faster and harder when the hum expands, morphs, becomes more intense, palpable.

I lift a hand to her cheek, trailing the back of my finger

down the line of her jaw, my eyes following the action. Her lips part as she inhales a shaky breath, her body trembling beneath my touch. Unhurried, I trace the column of her throat, pausing just before the hollow. And before I overthink my next move, I lean in and press my lips to hers.

Soft and warm and sweet, her lips quiver beneath mine. I lick her bottom lip and she gasps, her breasts pressing my chest, her body melting against mine. Barely a beat passes before I dip my tongue inside and taste her. Salty and sweet and something distinctly Kirsten. Her tongue sweeps over mine and heat explodes beneath my sternum.

I moan into the kiss a second before I'm shoved away. The wind is a slap to the face, but not as hard and painful as the icy glare from Kirsten. The hum from moments ago is long gone. Now, the space between us is loaded with shame and regret and embarrassment.

"Did I do something wrong?"

"Yes." Her brows furrow. "No." She stares up at the stars, swallows, and shakes her head. "Yes."

Taking a step toward her, I chuckle. "Gonna need you to be a little clearer, sparkles." Another step. "Yes or—"

"I'm with Travis," she blurts out, cutting me off.

Her confession is a ruthless punch to the gut, robbing me of breath and sense and hope. I repeat the words over and over in my head, swearing I misheard her. Because Kirsten with Travis is a reality I can't seem to grasp.

"What do you mean you're with *him*?" My fingers ball into fists at my sides. "Since when?"

Crossing her arms over her chest, she hugs herself tightly. "We haven't labeled our relationship." The muscles in her jaw flex as she gives me her profile. "But we're more than friends." She swallows, then meets my gaze. "For a couple weeks."

I lay my forearms on the rail, take a deep breath, then

another, as I stare at the now inky sky. Closing my eyes, I focus on my surroundings. The salty, cool air on my skin. The waft of spices from the kitchen below. The cheers and chatter from patrons at the restaurant's bar watching sports games over a beer. The sturdy rail beneath my arms.

Determination floods my veins as I open my eyes. I refuse to lie down and give up.

"Are you sure?" I ask a breath above a whisper.

She grips the rail but keeps a foot of space between us. Heat blankets me as I eye that gap in my periphery. "What?"

Figuring I have nothing to lose, I turn to face her and shift closer. "Are you really with him?" *Closer.* "What kind of man makes a woman *think* they're more but gives no clear indication?"

"Ben, don't." She takes a step back.

*Uncomfortable topic? Good.*

I shuffle forward. "Why? Because it makes you question if you *are* in a relationship with him?" I reach out and capture her hair between my fingers, staring at the buttery locks. Swallowing, I inch closer. Meet her stormy gaze with nothing but deep affection. "You would never have to question how I feel for you." I release her hair and trail my fingers down her jacket-clad arm. "You would never have to question whether or not I am yours. Whether I belong to you and you to me."

Her eyes fall shut as she trembles beneath my touch. "Ben, I'm begging you." Shaking her head, she opens her eyes. "Please. Don't do this."

"Where is he, Kirsten?" Voice soft, I invade every ounce of her personal space. "You're here with me, not him."

"He knows where I am," she responds without hesitation. "He knows who I'm with." Her eyes flick to mine with new resolve. "And he knows where I'm going when I leave." She licks her lips and inhales deeply. "Home. Alone."

"You don't have to go home alone."

She shuffles back, her head shaking as she growls, and heads for the stairs. "Yes, I do. And if you want a ride back to the inn, I suggest you knock this shit off and follow me to the car." Foot on the first step, she stops, grips the rail tightly, and stares down the stairwell. "I was happy to have you back, Ben." She inhales a shaky breath. "But if you can't respect my wishes, if you aren't capable of being my friend…" Glassy eyes meet mine and knock the air from my lungs. "Then maybe all we'll ever be is strangers."

# TWENTY-TWO

## KIRSTEN

*Argh!*

Never in my life have I wanted to punch someone. Truly beat the crap out of them. Throw strike after strike at them until common sense kicks in. Get in their face and scream. Ask why.

*Why, why, why?*

Leave it to Benjamin Chace Wilks, my childhood friend next door, to bring that urge to the surface. For years, he was my best friend, my person, one of the few people I thought I could trust with my heart, my secrets, my everything. Seeing him after so many years apart is like coming home. Rekindling our friendship and having the chance to know him again has been the best gift.

In one swift move, he ruined it.

I hate this itchiness beneath my skin. I hate that I now have this bitter guilt pulsing in my veins. Guilt and shame for something *he* did, something he pushed me to do.

Although it was merely seconds, I kissed him back. I softened in his embrace. I gave into the feel of his lips and mouth and tongue on mine. So warm and inviting. So exhilarating and impeccable. For a blip in time, kissing Ben felt right. Sublime. Unparalleled.

Then his moan ripped through the air and brought me back to reality.

Travis and I may not have defined our relationship with words like boyfriend and girlfriend, but we are definitely more than a one-night stand. Though neither of us is eager to announce or flaunt whatever our relationship is to anyone else, we stepped out of the friend zone and into something more.

And until we sort out our relationship, until we decide what our future looks like, other people are off limits. Regardless of how I feel about them.

Turning into the lot for the inn, I drive up to the loading zone by the doors and throw the car in park. Eyes forward, I drop my hands to my lap and let my eyes lose focus.

"Please don't be mad, sparkles." Soft and stilted, his plea fills the cab. "I, I..."

I wait for him to finish his thought. To explain further. To give me *some* form of understanding.

An idiot, I am not. Friends don't kiss other friends the way Ben kissed me without wanting a relationship beyond friendship. But I admit it was foolish of me to not see what was right in front of my face. The smiles he gives me and no one else. The way he challenges Travis at every turn. Texts and calls I assumed were two friends catching up and making up for lost time. The dinners he most likely saw as a date that I regarded as two friends hanging out.

*Idiot, idiot, idiot.*

Inhaling deeply, I count to three and compose myself. "You what?" I twist in my seat and take in his pained expression.

His gaze drifts and loses focus out the window. In the faint light from the inn, I study his expression, the lines of his profile, *him*.

Ben is more than a beautiful man. He is more than defined muscles and arm candy. More than surface-level appeal. If you're lucky enough to know him, really know him, he'll unveil his soul. The gentle, reserved, sweet, and irresistible side of him. Traits I glimpsed in our formative years but didn't have the faculty to grasp yet. Traits that have matured well with him over the years.

Is it selfish of me to want this side of him? The piece he should only gift to someone willing to give just as much, if not more, in return.

Yes. It's thoughtless and indulgent and unfair.

A ridge forms between his brows a beat before his gaze returns to mine. Adam's apple bobbing, his audible swallow echoes in my ears. "I misread the moment," he confesses, voice thick and raspy. He gives a subtle shake of his head, then laughs without humor. "Seems to be a talent of mine."

Reaching across the console, I take his hand. Probably an unwise move on my part, but I need his attention on me and not elsewhere. He drops his chin and looks at our joined hands. His face twists in pain.

"Ben…"

I squeeze his hand and his eyes close. With that simple action, I know no matter what I say, a fissure will always exist between us. Only time can stitch it back together. Even then, we will never be whole. Not in the way he wants. Not in the way either of us wishes.

Licking my lips, I ignore the pang in my belly. "There will always be a part of me that loves you, Ben."

Veiny, turquoise eyes flit up and pin me in place. I love and hate the hope I see in them.

"But I'm not the same little girl anymore."

Calloused fingers slowly stroke my fingers, my palm, my wrist. "I know."

"What happened to my father"—the backs of my eyes sting as my chin trembles—"it changed me."

He lifts his free hand and cups my cheek. Brushes his thumb over the apple of my cheek with such tenderness. "How could it not?"

I close my eyes and let my mind drift momentarily. Give him my weight and sigh. Relish the feel of his rough fingers on my soft skin. Bask in his warmth, his affection. Let it flow through me and give me strength.

With Ben, life could be so simple and perfect. Uncomplicated. Lazy weekends reading books or exploring forests or mountains. Breakfasts and dinners across from each other as we talk about our day. Summers spent splashing each other in the creek or bay. Endless laughter and smiles and joy.

But love... the love I have to offer seems inadequate or unbalanced when compared to what Ben has to give. I love him, but not the way he believes he loves me. Letting him think otherwise makes me a horrible person. Giving him a false sense of hope is wrong, a setup for failure.

My eyes open and meet his patient gaze. "Ben, when I told you weeks ago I'd never been in a relationship, I wasn't kidding." My truth barely audible as it leaves my lips.

He subtly shakes his head. "Still blows my mind." His thumb brushes my cheek with lazy strokes. "How has someone as beautiful and incredible as you never been in a relationship?"

Unable to fight it, I lean more into his touch. Bask in the warmth and comfort only Ben delivers. "No *romantic* relationships." My brows scrunch together. "I've been with people." I drop my gaze to our joined hands. "But I don't make a habit of hooking up with a person more than once." Gnarly energy swirls in my belly and I take a deep breath. "Things with Travis..."

His hand in mine locks, his body going rigid. "Things with Travis, what?" A growl highlights his words.

God, why is this so fucking hard? Why does this hurt so damn much? Each piece of truth is a jagged blade being slowly pushed into my heart.

I lift my gaze and search the depths of his for a hint of understanding. "It's different with him."

His head jerks back as if I slapped him. "What does that even mean?"

Fire sparks beneath my skin as my heart bangs, bangs, bangs against my rib cage. Irritation crackles in the air and I grind my molars. I release his hand and move out of his reach. "In our own way, we're both messed up." I shrug.

"Unbelievable," he mutters.

"What?"

He laughs without humor, faces forward, and reaches for the door handle. "So because I don't have some fucked-up past, I'm not worthy." He shakes his head, then slaps me with the iciest glare. "But hey, at least I'll have more baggage for the next person."

Ben yanks on the handle, exits the car, and slams the door hard enough to rattle the window. My heart splinters, a shiver rolling up my spine that has nothing to do with the December temperature, as he storms to the entrance and disappears inside.

*It is the right thing to do. It will never work with Ben.*

Regardless of how many times I repeat the words, the spasm in my chest doesn't let up. Regardless of how much I try to convince myself this is for the best, the knife in my chest only goes deeper.

*What have I done?*

My phone buzzes a second after the message flips from delivered to read. Travis's name flashes on the screen, and I picture him pacing the room, frantic.

In the history of conversations, no great ones began with *We need to talk.*

I tap accept and bring the phone to my ear. "Hey."

"What's wrong? Did he do something?" I all but hear his teeth crack through the phone.

A sigh leaves my lips. "Travis, I don't want to talk about this over the phone."

An engine roars to life on the other end. "Headed over now."

"See you—" The call disconnects. "Soon..."

I kick off my shoes and strip out my clothes. Pulling on something more comfortable, I barely have the long-sleeve, oversized sweater over my head when I hear Travis's truck outside. I tug up my pajama pants and amble toward the front door.

Before he knocks, I open the door and step out of the way. He breezes past me and storms inside. I close the door, lock it, and head back toward my bedroom. Travis is on my heels but doesn't utter a word.

As soon as the door clicks shut, his hands frame my face. Then his lips are on mine, hungry and desperate and claiming. He brands me with his kiss as he shoves me against the door.

Quickly as he pounced, he rips his mouth from mine and steps back. Drops his hands and pins me to the door with feral eyes. "What happened?" The question more a growly demand than a basic request for information.

Pushing off the door, I take his hand and cross the room to the bed. I sit on the edge and hug my legs to my chest. Travis opts to stand, his fingers tapping his thighs.

And then I relay my dinner with Ben. I share every detail—the meal, our conversations, going out on the deck, the kiss, the conversations following the kiss. The only time I pause is when his fingers curl into fists or his face flames with anger.

Honesty is important to me and Travis, even when it hurts. Ripping off the bandage and getting hit with it all at once is better than drip-feeding details over time and appearing deceptive.

"Motherfucker." *Thump, thump, thump.* His boots pound the floor as he paces the length of the room.

"He misread the situation, Travis." I drop my feet to the floor and stand. "Believe me, he's upset and embarrassed."

Travis whirls around and jabs a finger in my direction. "He should be."

I take a step toward him, then another. Reach out and wrap my fingers around his wrist. Shuffle closer to him. Lift a hand and cup his cheek. Stroke the scruff of his beard with my thumb.

The fury in his eyes morphs into something else. Softer. Deeper. He sucks in a sharp breath, his amber eyes darker as they dart between mine. Searching. Probing.

He drops his forehead to mine, skates the tip of his nose along the length of mine, then lowers his mouth to mine and kisses me with unparalleled tenderness. No two kisses with Travis are the same. This kiss… is the softest yet.

And all too soon, he breaks the kiss.

He takes one step back, then another, and another. Hand on the door handle, he meets my puzzled expression with a subtle smile. "Just need some air, sunshine." He takes a deep breath. "Call me in the morning?"

Nausea churns beneath my diaphragm. "Are you mad at me?"

"No, baby." He shakes his head. "Just need to work out my feelings." Lips trapped between his teeth, his jaw rocks back and forth a moment. "Old wounds messing with my head. Nothing a run with Pepper won't solve."

"'Kay." I let his words sink in and assuage the queasiness. "I'll walk you out."

Steps from the front door, it swings open and Delilah walks through. An awkward exchange of hellos and goodbyes happen, then she ambles into the kitchen.

Travis frames my face with his hands and brushes my lips with his. I melt into the kiss, into his touch, into him. Forehead pressed to mine, he whispers, "In the morning."

"In the morning," I repeat.

Then he is out the door and headed for his truck. I stand on the threshold, watching as he walks away.

*He's not mad at you. It's not you.*

I close and lock the door, then make my way to the kitchen. Delilah is at the island, eating leftover Vietnamese from the box. Going to the fridge, I grab a Coke and pop the top.

"Everything okay with you and Travis?"

Delilah may not know a lot about Travis personally, but she knows quite a bit about his family.

Like Travis's family—Emerson—Delilah's family—Fox—is one of the Stone Bay founding families. The Stone Bay Seven. And with each of those seven families comes some level of secrecy. The contributions of each family when the town was founded are public record. Such information is accessible at the town hall and the town history museum.

But much has changed since the town charter was created.

The seven families that came together in 1908 and the beliefs they shared in that period are not the same as today. Greed and jealousy and power change people—some for the better, others for the worse.

Delilah's grandparents changed for the better. And every day I have her in my life, I am grateful for her family and the courageous strides they have made.

"Yeah." I lean a hip on the counter and take a long pull of my Coke. "He's irritated with Ben."

She finishes chewing a bite of rice noodles and tofu. "What happened with Ben?"

I huff out a breath, my shoulders slumping forward.

"That good, huh?" She chuckles.

With a roll of my eyes, I suggest, "Maybe we should sit down." Then I laugh. "I need ice cream for this."

Swiping up her leftovers, she exits the kitchen and heads for the hall. "Gonna change really quick. Your room or mine?"

"Mine," I shout as she disappears from sight.

I rummage through the freezer, grab the peanut butter chocolate fudge ice cream, then fetch my ice cream pint koozie from the drawer. Spoon in hand, I flip off the kitchen light and head for my room.

Two bites into the pint, Delilah walks in and plops down next to me on the bed. Cozy in her fuzzy pajama pants and matching shirt, she slurps her noodles and waits for me to start. After one more bite, I stab the spoon into the ice cream and begin.

For hour-long minutes, I spill every detail about me, Travis, and Ben. By my side, she listens to every word, only asking questions when I pause. When I reach the end, she sets her takeout box aside and sits up straighter, turning to face me head-on.

"You care for them both?"

I nod. "I do."

"But you only want friendship with Ben?"

I wince. "Yes." My face twists tighter. "No." My head tips back and I close my eyes. "Yes." An audible exhale leaves my lips. "Gah! I hate this."

Delilah chuckles. "Want to know what I th—"

*Snap. Whack.*

Both our heads whip toward the window. Breath trapped in my lungs, my heart thumps viciously in my chest. Neither of us moves. Slowly, Delilah peeks over her shoulder at me and mouths, *"What was that?"*

Eyes wide and bouncing between Delilah and the window, I shrug and shake my head.

I put the lid on the ice cream and set it on the nightstand. Dropping my feet to the floor, I rise from the bed and tiptoe toward the window. I drift to the side of the window as I get closer.

A brutal thrum, my pulse is white noise in my ears. I suck in a deep breath and hold it. My limbs shake as I inch closer to the curtain. One step, then another. Sweat slicks my brow as I reach for the heavy material and pinch it between my fingers. Ever so slowly, I peel the curtain back and peer through the gap and out the window. All I see is blackness.

Lightning flashes, thunder claps shortly after. I jump out of my skin with a shriek, letting go of the curtain and slapping a hand to my chest. "Holy shit!"

Then we both laugh, loud and hard, until our stomachs cramp.

No one is outside. It's only a storm rolling in.

# TWENTY-THREE

## SEEKER

A SLUSHY LAYER OF SNOW BLANKETS MY HAIR, MELTING AND dripping down my neck one flake at a time, soaking my collar. The booming storm from hours ago is long gone, frigid temperatures and a thin coat of ice and snow left in its wake.

I don't mind the cold. Never have.

And right now, the sight of her keeps me warm. Heats my skin and engorges my cock.

For the first time in weeks, her cop hook up isn't here—outside in his car or in her bed.

*Whore.*

No, she managed to piss off both her boy toys in the same night. All but kicked one in the nuts after he kissed her. Let the other drive away, dazed and confused.

*Whore.*

Parking up the street after she dropped dipshit number one at the inn, I walked around the block and approached her house from the opposite direction. I was two houses away when dipshit number two hopped in his truck and drove off.

At least I don't have to look at his pretty boy mug tonight.

At least I don't have to watch him fuck her tonight. Don't have to listen to her moans while she begs him for more.

*Whore.*

I peek through the small crack in the curtains. A crack I swear she leaves open for me. Only me. Until my first note, she rarely had that crack between the curtains. Or left the small lamp on while sleeping.

*For me. She does this for me.*

I trail my eyes over her body as she sleeps. Each night, before she drifts off, the covers are yanked high. Pulled to her chin, blanketing her bare flesh. She may own pajamas, but she never sleeps in them. And as the night progresses, as she dreams and rolls and shifts, the covers slide off her body. Move to the opposite side of the bed or down toward the footboard.

Unless that fucking pig is in her bed.

*Whore.*

Unbuttoning my jeans, I jerk down the zipper, shove the denim down a few inches, and pull out my cock. Hard and thick and needy, I wrap my fist around my dick and yank. I stare at her perfect little tits and stroke myself. Lick my lips and imagine I'm licking those rosy, pert nipples.

Drifting down her body, I memorize her dips and curves. When I reach the small tuft of hair on her cunt, I jerk my dick harder, faster, greedier.

She shifts in the bed, her legs spreading a few inches wider. Even in sleep, she wants to give herself to me. She wants me to have what is mine.

*My whore.*

I stare at her pink cunt and hiss as I tug my cock forcefully. Precum spills out and slicks the head. I spit in the direction of my cock and lube myself, imagining it's her pussy soaking my dick.

Lightning bolts through me, drawing my balls up. My

breath comes in ragged bursts as sweat soaks the back of my neck. And just before I come, I release my cock, reach for my balls, and yank down.

I want to come—on her face, on her breasts, down her throat, in her cunt. But I won't waste my cum on the side of her house. I won't waste it on the snow blanketing the ground or the shrub near her window.

No, I will wait. A little longer, I will wait.

Stuffing my cock back in my pants, I zip and button up. Take one last look and step back from her window.

One step, then another, I move to the front porch. Remove the slender box tucked in my coat and lay it on the welcome mat. I pivot with a smile on my face and head for the sidewalk.

In the cover of night, I return to my car and drive away.

*My whore.*

# TWENTY-FOUR

## TRAVIS

Ripping the blanket off my body, I throw my legs over the side of the bed and sit up. I drop my head in my hands and press the heels of my palms into my eyes until the pain becomes unbearable.

"*Fuck…*"

I need sleep. Uninterrupted, dreamless sleep for half a day. Maybe more.

But that isn't happening today. Hopefully tonight.

First, I have to clear the air with Kirsten. Apologize for my reaction. What happened with Ben isn't on her. Kirsten wants to rekindle a lost friendship and he misread their time together as something more. Or he took advantage of the situation.

For his sake, it better not be the latter.

Pepper perks up from her bed near mine and I extend a hand in invitation. She does her morning stretch routine, then crosses the space and nudges my hand with her head.

"How's my girl this morning?"

With both hands, I scratch behind her ears, along the back of her neck, and under her collar. Giving me her weight, she presses the top of her head into my thigh. Her way of showing affection.

I drop a kiss on the top of her head and push up from the bed. "Let's go outside, then get you breakfast, pretty girl." When we're home and not in our gear, our relationship is like most other human-canine relationships. The only difference with me and Pepper is there are no unwarranted treats or playful behavior that may confuse her later when we are working.

Pepper trots out of the room while I tug on sweatpants and a hoodie. I pad across the house and meet her at the sliding doors, opening one and letting her out into the yard. She bolts out into the darkness and disappears from view in seconds. With the light dusting of snow on the ground, she will likely be outside longer than usual. Pepper loves snow, no matter how little or much falls.

A shiver rolls through my limbs as I close the door and head for the kitchen.

"Coffee," I mutter.

Far back as I recall, I've been an early riser. Probably instilled from Dad and him waking at four in the morning my entire childhood. Most days, I get up around five. Gives me time to wake up slowly, tend to Pepper, get ready for work, and make it to the restaurant a little after six.

I flip the hood light over the stove on and squint until my eyes adjust. Considering I barely slept last night and it's now —I look at the clock on the range and mentally curse—three fifty-two, I need a triple dose of caffeine if I'm to make it through the day.

Hitting brew on the coffee maker, I head for my bedroom and swipe my phone from the charger. I sift through emails, deleting most as I fill my mug. As the first sip of coffee hits my tongue, Pepper rings the bell by the door. I set my phone down, shuffle across the room, and let her in.

As I flip the lock on the door, my phone buzzes on the counter.

Most likely another email to delete. Probably a sale on those damn bamboo underwear I love. Not that I need a new pack, but I'd buy one.

But it's not an email notification I see when I pick up my phone. It's a new text alert.

SUNSHINE

Found a box on my porch

I read the message three times before my brain catches up. Before it dawns on me that the box was probably unexpected.

Tapping her contact picture, I hit call and bring the phone to my ear. The two rings last too long.

"Hey." Her voice has that early morning rasp I love.

"Hey, sunshine." I sip my coffee, then set the mug down. "You found a box?" My brow tightens. "Why were you outside? It's barely four."

Something rustles on the other end. I close my eyes and picture her in bed, covers drawn to her chin, hand tucked under her cheek on the pillow.

"Didn't sleep well." Her confession is a whisper, and it lingers a moment before she continues. "For whatever reason, I remembered I didn't check the mail yesterday. So I went out for the mail."

I trace the handle of the coffee mug with my finger and try to sound more composed than I feel when I speak. "And you found a box on the porch?"

"Yeah. Like a small shirt box." Her shuddering exhale ripples through the line. "With my name on it."

If this is the same person that left her the notes, they're stepping up their game. Escalation. Not a good sign. At all.

"Did you touch it?"

"No."

The distinct sound of purring reverberates through the phone, followed by a scratchy sound and a muffled, *"Love you too, Trixie."*

Cats were never pets I looked at with fondness. But knowing Kirsten has that little ball of gray fluff loving on her makes my chest constrict.

"Are you working this morning?" I lift the mug to my lips and chug the rest of the coffee.

"Start at six. Might get there earlier."

I set the mug in the sink and head for the bedroom. "Try to get the box in a bag without touching it and bring it with you." I enter the bathroom attached to my bedroom, flip on the light, and move toward the shower. "I'll head there once I'm ready."

"Okay." Her voice cracks on the second syllable and I hate how feeble it makes her sound. A word I would never associate with Kirsten.

"Try not to think about it. Get ready like you always do. Love on Trixie for a bit. And I'll see you soon."

"Soon," she parrots. "Thanks, Travis."

"Always, sunshine."

I park next to her SUV in the restaurant lot, cut the engine, and hop out. Lights inside Poke the Yolk flip on one by one as I approach the front door and knock. The restaurant doesn't open for another twenty minutes, but she will let me in.

With a soft click, the lock disengages and she opens the

door. I shuffle past her and stomp my boots on the mat. Shrug off my jacket and head for my usual spot at the counter. Hang my jacket on the back of the chair, but don't take a seat.

Music mixes with the occasional clang and chop, chop, chop in the kitchen. No doubt Maxine is cutting produce, baking quiche, and mixing batter to get a jump on the morning crowd before the doors unlock. Instinct has me wanting to wave and greet her. But I ignore the inclination and focus on why I'm here early.

I bite the inside of my cheek and swallow down the command on my tongue. Were this anyone else, I'd cut to the chase and demand to see the box. But this is Kirsten, and she will hand it over without a word.

Just out of reach, she meets my gaze. "Coffee?" Dark crescents blotted with makeup shadow her eyes.

Guilt gnaws at my soul for leaving her house last night. For walking away to cool off and making a bad night worse.

I should have stayed, at least outside, to watch the house. I should have walked the block a few times to clear my head, apologized for my frustrations, kissed her good night, and stayed.

But like a self-absorbed ass, I did none of the above.

So of course, the person behind the notes makes an appearance. *Fucking great.*

I nod. "Please."

Kirsten moves behind the counter and loads the coffee maker. Within seconds, the rich, nutty scent wafts across the counter as a steady stream of coffee drips in the pot. Part of me relaxes at the familiarity of being here with her in our daily routine.

Until she spins around, reaches under the counter, and fishes out a canvas tote.

*The box.*

As she sets it on the counter, I dig in my jacket pocket and take a pair of gloves out. Slipping them on, I remove the box from the bag and inspect the exterior. Nothing notable stands out. The box is lightweight, white, and something you'd get in a package of clothing boxes in the gift wrap aisle.

"You got it in the bag without touching it?" I ask for confirmation.

She nods, grabs my mug, and moves to the coffee maker.

"I'll have it dusted for prints at the station."

"Okay." She places my full mug on the counter, eyes glued to the box.

I finger the edge of the box top then pause, look up, and wait for her to meet my gaze. Three pulse-pounding seconds pass before our eyes connect.

"You don't have to watch."

Not sure I want her to see what's inside. The contents may be strange, but innocent. Most admirers gift things they think the devotee would like. Or it may be the complete opposite. Something perverse or disturbing.

Based on the notes, my gut says it is far from innocent.

Staring down at the box, she nods. "I want to know what it is."

I nod. "Okay."

My fingers move back to the base of the lid and slip under the lip. Gingerly, I lift the top and purposely tip it at more of an angle to block the initial reveal from Kirsten. At first glance, the contents appear innocent. Tissue paper and another note. I set the lid aside and pick up the note.

*So many nights, when the blanket slips from your naked body, I trace your alabaster skin with my eyes.*

*Jack my cock as I stare at your cunt. Lick my lips when you spread your legs while you dream.*

*Soon, I won't do any from a distance. Soon, I'll feel every inch of your skin with my bare hands. Soon, I'll hover above you, pound your sweet cunt with my cock, and fill you with my cum.*

*When that day comes, when we finally get to play, I want you to wear this. My pretty little whore. I'll bruise you and break you until the day you say you're mine. Until you beg for more. Until all you see, all you want, all you crave is me.*

Fingers curled around the note, my eyes fall shut as I fight the urge to vomit. One breath after another, the bile settles in my gut. The twisting knife, however, continues to spin and dig deeper.

"What does it say?"

The shaky desperation in her words has me opening my eyes.

"Nothing good, sunshine." I give her a halfhearted smile and take my seat at the counter.

She worries her bottom lip between her teeth. "As bad as the last one?"

*Worse.*

This fucker just admitted to peeping through her damn windows. To jacking off while she sleeps in the privacy of her own home. And if I show her the note, if I relay what it says, she won't sleep at all.

I nod, flip the note upside down, and set it on the counter between me and the box. "Yeah."

Wanting to get this stashed away before the doors unlock, I peel back the tissue paper, take a deep breath, and mentally prepare for what lies underneath.

Pink fabric brightens the ominous box as I release the tissue paper. At first glance, it appears to be a satin tank top. Maybe a dress. But as I shift it in the box, realization hits me like a brick wall.

*Lingerie.*

"Is that..." Kirsten's voice trails off as she leans closer and inspects the negligee. "Oh, god." Skin paling, she steps back and covers her mouth. "Oh, god," she repeats, almost inaudible.

The door between the kitchen and dining area swings open and Oliver comes into view. "Morn—" His eyes dart between me and Kirsten, then drop to the counter. "Everything alright?"

I toss the tissue paper back in place, deposit the note on top, replace the lid, and stow it in the bag. With a shake of my head, I peel off the gloves and say, "Not really."

Oliver shifts his gaze to Kirsten a beat before he dashes to her side and wraps an arm around her shoulders. "Want to cut out? I'll cover for you."

She leans into his side and grips his waist. Takes comfort from one of her closest friends. Were it any man other than Oliver, I'd be around the counter, ripping him off her. But Oliver has no romantic interest in Kirsten, and he never will. From what Kirsten told me, Oliver's had a crush on his best friend, Levi, for years.

"No," she whispers. "But I need to sit for a few."

Oliver drops his arm from her shoulders, steps back, and nudges his head toward the kitchen. "Go in the back so no one bothers you." His gaze meets mine. "Sit with her?"

As if he has to ask, but I nod anyway. "Yeah, man."

Oliver gives Kirsten's arm a quick squeeze, then he walks toward the front door to unlock it.

I pick up the bag, toss my jacket over an arm, and down the last of my coffee. As I round the corner of the counter, I pause in front of Kirsten.

"What?" Her eyes dart between mine as she rubs the sun and moon charms on her necklace.

"Maybe we should get out of here for a few days. Shake things up." I shrug. "Maybe it'll draw whoever this is out."

Wide, stormy eyes hold my stare. "I can't just leave, Travis." She waves a hand toward the dining area. "What about work? My bills won't be magically paid without money."

"We'll figure out your bills."

"What about Trixie?" Her chin wobbles as she blinks a few times. "I just adopted her." Tears rim her eyes. "I can't leave her."

I step into her and bend my knees so we're eye-to-eye. "Trixie comes with us. Pepper too."

"What if they don't like each other?"

"They will," I promise her, though I have no idea if it's true.

Silence blankets us while I wait for her to agree. I won't force her to do anything. Strongly suggest? Absolutely.

Until this nutcase is apprehended, I don't want Kirsten out of my sight. Come what may at the station and with my father, I will protect her. This very well may be the same person that killed the woman in the woods. With his level of obsession, it is difficult to believe otherwise.

And I'll be damned if I let this motherfucker get Kirsten too. Not a fucking chance.

"I'll text Skylar and see if CKI is cool with last-minute time off."

*Oh, thank fuck.*

If either Calhoun or Kemp gives Kirsten any shit, I'll storm into their office and swiftly change their minds. One of the only perks of being a founding family member... people do almost anything you want.

"They will be." I press my lips to her forehead. "I'll sort out where to stay. We should leave tonight."

Kirsten opens her mouth to respond, then jerks back, eyes wide. A flash of red catches in my periphery and I spin around, drop my jacket and the bag and shift to block Kirsten. I reach for my sidearm just as I register Ben's face.

He throws his hands up and shuffles back. "Whoa, whoa, whoa." He takes another step back. "Didn't mean to startle you, man. Sorry."

I drop my hand. "Stupid fucking move, *man.*"

His eyes shift to Kirsten. "Came over to apologize again." Then he shifts his attention back to me. "You're taking her somewhere?" He narrows his gaze. "Why?"

Widening my eyes, I grit out, "Not here."

The muscles in his jaw flex. "Fine. Whatever." He peeks over my shoulder, softens his gaze for a beat, then levels me with an icy glare. "But wherever she goes, I go."

*For fuck's sake.*

Ben wants to tag along? Fine by me. But by the end of the trip, he'll likely regret the decision.

"Then pack your bags."

# TWENTY-FIVE

## KIRSTEN

This is a bad idea. A *really* bad idea.

I don't like the idea of running away. What will it accomplish? Travis seems to think it may draw out my admirer. That in my absence, they will slip up and reveal themselves.

All I foresee is pissing them off and making it worse.

The cherry on this whacked out sundae... Ben insists on joining the escape party.

After the kiss disaster last night, Ben tagging along is nowhere near a good idea. Yet, a piece of me wants him there too.

Years ago, I loved Ben. He was my other half. The brother I never had but couldn't imagine my life without. We spent as much time together as our parents allowed. He picked me wildflowers every spring and tied them with twine or ribbon. He taught me to climb trees in the woods behind my house and his. Told the corniest jokes that were impossible not to laugh at.

A lifetime has passed since Ben was my person. And as much as I loved him then, we are no longer those sweet, innocent versions of Ben and Kirsten.

Losing my dad impacted several facets of my life. For years, anger and depression were my closest friends. I love Mom, but I'd loved Dad more. Not seeing him every morning, not sharing updates with him over dinner, not wrapping my arms around his neck for the best hugs... it'd been brutal. Missing him shredded my heart. Selling our home in Smoky Creek—though I understood why—and moving to Stone Bay felt like betrayal.

Skylar eased some of the hurt. Delilah too. They held my hand or hugged me breathless when I needed it most. So many days, they sat with me while I cried or screamed or ransacked my bedroom.

But they also spoke up when my body withered away. Not once did they criticize me for my choices. Control was something I'd lost when Dad died. Though I'd found a way to be in control again, it wasn't healthy. With tears in their eyes, they expressed their fears. How distraught they'd be if my bingeing and purging stole me from them. Tears staining our cheeks, their confession hit me hard. The heartache I felt more often than not over the loss of my dad, Skylar and Delilah would live with that level of pain if I kept hurting myself. And I wanted no one to feel that kind of pain.

Though the past is incomparable to the present, it's unwise of me to ignore this pang beneath my breastbone. The heavy and slow-expanding ache as I walk the narrowing path to heartbreak. As I tiptoe the tightrope with arms widespread and hope in my eyes.

Hurting either of these men will scar my heart. But in the end, devastation is inevitable.

I want Travis and Ben in my life, but can't picture either of them clearly. For weeks, Travis has been front of mind, invading every moment with his flirty smile or calloused hands or lips on my skin. But after one heady kiss, Ben is front and center with Travis in my thoughts, battling for my affection.

Warm arms wrap around my waist and steal my attention. I blink a few times, then scan the dining room. From one table to the next, several sets of eyes home in on my face. Study the worry lines on my forehead and clamped lips between my teeth. Expressions blank, they simply stare.

And I hate my first thought: *which of them is my admirer?*

"Let's go sit," Travis whispers in my ear. He steers me toward the kitchen door and I go without hesitation.

"Text me with details," Ben says as his fingers circle my arm.

Beneath the sleeve of my shirt, my skin tingles from his touch. Brows tight, my gaze darts to his. A mix of blue and green and deep affection stare back with unflinching resolve. The pad of his thumb strokes up and down, up and down, adding a subtle spark to the tingle.

A tornado of confusion swirls in me and upends every ounce of certainty.

The touch of a friend shouldn't make your body buzz. Shouldn't light small fires beneath your skin. Shouldn't make you gasp or lean in. Their touch shouldn't make your pulse soar.

Yet, my traitorous body doesn't care I friend-zoned Ben.

With a forced smile, I nod. "I will."

Soon as the words leave my lips, Travis whisks me into the back and sits me at a small table we use for breaks. Maxine stops chopping fruit and eyes us a moment.

"Not feeling well?"

Travis sets his jacket and the bag down. "A little woozy." He flashes me a soft smile, then looks at Maxine. "Nothing some food and a break won't fix."

Maxine nods. "I'll whip up something quick." Eyes on

Travis, she points to the walk-in fridge with the knife in her hand. "Grab her some juice."

Travis enters the walk-in and comes out with a jug of orange juice. He finds a glass, fills it to the top, and sets it in front of me before filling another glass for himself.

Within minutes, Maxine sets two loaded plates on the table and returns to her spot between the range and prep station. I inhale deeply, my shoulders sagging as smokiness fills my nose.

Fetching clean forks near the dishwasher, Travis and I dig into fresh fruit, dairy-free scrambled eggs, home fries, and bacon. I moan as the first bite hits my tongue, and Travis freezes with his fork halfway to his lips. He cocks a brow, and I roll my eyes, a small smile tugging at the corners of my mouth.

When our plates empty, I take them to the dirty tub for washing. We thank Maxine and she waves us off, but not before making me promise to come back and sit if I feel light-headed. Travis shrugs on his jacket, grabs the bag, and hooks an arm around my waist as we head back toward the dining room.

On shaky legs, I pass the threshold and pause as the cacophony of the early morning crowd hits me all at once. Crowds never bothered me in the past. But with everything that has come to light, the last place I want to be is in the middle of a packed room with all eyes aimed my way.

Breath warm on my ear, Travis whispers, "Want me to stay longer?"

The twist in my belly screams *yes,* while my somewhat rational brain calmly says *no.*

"I'll be fine." I repeat the words in my head and will them into existence. "Ollie's here. Max is five seconds away. Deidra should be here soon, and Trudie in a few hours."

Travis drops his arm from my waist and lifts a hand to cup

my cheek. "Call me if something happens. I need to do some work at the station and talk to my dad, then I'll be back."

He presses his lips to my forehead, then tips my head back and drops a kiss on my lips. Fire roars in my veins when my tongue strokes his. The noisy conversations and curious stares fade into the background. Every thread of worry fizzles out.

Far too soon, Travis breaks the kiss and rests his forehead on mine. "Text you soon." With one last chaste kiss, he releases his hold on me and heads for the door. Eyes glued to his back, I wilt when he steps out the door and disappears from view.

"That was hot as fuck."

I startle, then turn and smack Oliver in the chest. "Don't sneak up on me."

"Sorry." He rubs a hand up and down my back. "But in my defense, I whistled seconds before."

"You did?"

He nods.

"Oh." I scan the tables—not missing Ben's scowl as he and his crew rise to leave—and change the subject. "Who needs what?"

Oliver rattles off what tables need attention and we get to work. Deidra arrives just before seven, says her morning hellos, then goes into the office for fifteen minutes as per usual. Tossing on an apron, she alternates between the kitchen and dining room to lighten the load.

When the first rush tapers off, I ask to speak with her. She directs me to the office and I relay the CliffsNotes version of what's happening. I rarely ask for extra time off and feel guilty the second I voice the request. But Deidra assuages my concern with an unexpected hug.

"Take the week, honey." She releases me and inches back, holding me at arm's length. "We'll manage here. Kenzie may gripe when I ask, but she'll thank you for the tips later."

"Are you sure? I don't want to put anyone out."

"Although it's not, think of it as a vacation." She gives my arms a squeeze, then lets go. Opening the office door, she gestures for me to exit then follows in my wake. "We all need extra time away." We wander through the kitchen, enter the dining room, then pause behind the service counter. "Work has its upside, but so does time for yourself. Taking care of yourself is more important than taking orders and serving breakfast."

"But—"

"But nothing." She digs the pad of paper and pen out of her apron. "We aren't robots, honey. We aren't meant to work every minute of every hour of every day. That we think otherwise is unfortunate."

Before I argue further, she dashes off and sidles up to a table. With her best smile in place, she scribbles their order on the pad and winks before walking off.

Pulling my phone from my back pocket, I open the group chat with Skylar, Delilah, and Oliver. My fingers fly over the keys, filling them in on the latest news.

> Admirer left a gift and note on the porch. Travis said the note's worse than the others. Gift was lingerie 😬 Travis suggested we get out of town. Don't have details yet, but Ben wants to tag along.

I pocket my phone and distract myself by wiping down tables and refilling coffee mugs. A few of the regulars stop me as I pass and update me on their own lives. It irks me to fake interest, but I simply can't focus enough to care right now.

Tossing the cleaning rag in the bleach water, I move to the empty end of the counter and take out my phone.

OLLIE

Yeah, I bet Ben wants to come 😏

SKY

How very 13 of you Ollie 😌

SKY

Keep us posted. Sorry you're dealing with this
bullshit. Love you!!!!!

DEE DEE

Really, Ollie? FFS

DEE DEE

Need me to watch Trixie?

I react to Oliver with a thumbs down, then type a response.

Any other time, I'd laugh Ollie. Travis said to
bring Trixie. I'll let you know if that changes.

Love you 😊

*Buzz, buzz, buzz.*

SKY

Love you more xo

DEE DEE

Love you too

OLLIE

Yeah, yeah. Love you most!

# TWENTY-SIX

## BEN

"Wʜᴀᴛ ᴛʜᴇ ʜᴇʟʟ ᴡᴀs I ᴛʜɪɴᴋɪɴɢ?"

In what universe is joining Kirsten and Travis in the middle of nowhere a good idea? Easy answer… I have no fucking clue. But it's too late to turn back now.

After a few hours on site at the library, my phone dinged with a text from Kirsten.



A second text came through with the address of where we're headed. Still in Stone Bay, but outside the main part of town. The map showed it on the outskirts, in the southern mountains.

After breakfast, I pulled John aside and explained the situation. At first, he was confused as to why I was involved with the matter. Once I shared who Kirsten was to me, it took a little less convincing. With our part of the project nearing the end, he gave me the go-ahead to leave with the promise to update him.

An hour before the rest of the crew called it a day, I went back to the inn, packed my duffel, and headed to Kirsten's house. Hyper-focused as we loaded the vehicles, I didn't allow myself to think about what would happen when we arrived at our destination.

But now… the farther we drive, the more I question my decision. And my sanity.

Travis throws on his blinker, so I do the same in Kirsten's car behind them. We turn off the main highway and onto a two-lane road with tall evergreens lining either side. Our tires eat up several miles before we turn again. Slowing our speed, we drive deeper into the forest. The broad canopy of thick evergreens shadows the road, the fading sunlight barely lighting the way. Snow-capped mountains peek through the trees moments before a brown sign labeled *Bay Cliff Mountain Range* appears on the side of the road.

When Travis flips his blinker on this time, we turn onto a gravel drive. He slows to a crawl and stops beside a post with a keypad. Punching in a code, he waits a few seconds, then hits the gas. I follow him through a large gate that closes after I pass.

Thick forestry lines the gravel drive as we trudge forward. After almost a quarter mile, the trees thin and Travis slows down. A large A-frame cabin comes into view as Travis steers right and parks his truck under a wide carport off to the side. Parking next to him, I cut the engine, hop out, and take a better look.

Not bad. Maybe two or three bedrooms.

*I can do this.*

Moving to the back of the SUV, I open the hatch and reach for my duffel bag. Kirsten climbs out of the pickup with a blanket fashioned into a baby sling on her chest. Twigs and pine needles crunch beneath her feet as she closes the distance between us.

"Hey," she mumbles, a perfunctory smile in place.

My gaze drops to the sleeping kitten in the blanket nuzzled to her chest. The smallest yet longest blip of time passes as my vision blurs and fantasies of the future flash in my mind.

A two-story bungalow with clapboard and shaker siding stained a rich brown. Large windows on the east and west sides of the house, so we never miss a sunrise or sunset. A large porch that extends out to a vast yard with a tree house and playset. The bubbling creek mingled with young, sweet giggles and pleas to be pushed on the swings.

Then the daydream bends and shifts, an invisible thread slowly wrapping itself around my heart and cinching.

Lazy days beneath fluffy blankets, our limbs tangled for hours. Skin on skin, fingers gentle and leisure one minute, then bruising and greedy the next. Desperate kisses and unbridled moans as hips rock and fists tug hair. Whispered confessions of *I need you* and *I crave you* and *I love you*.

And it is the last thought that snaps me out of my heart-pounding daydream.

After an audible swallow, I choke out, "Hey," and haul the duffel over my shoulder. Shifting my attention from Kirsten to the cabin, I blow out a low whistle. "If this is what he calls a cabin, the ones I've stayed in must be outhouses."

Kirsten inches closer, her arm grazing mine as we study the A-frame that appears to be more windows and roof than wood frame. It takes everything in me to keep my eyes on the cabin, to not snake my arm around her waist and tuck her into my side.

If I have even the slightest chance of winning Kirsten's heart, I need to be mindful of every step forward. I may want to dive headfirst into uncharted waters without a life preserver, but that doesn't mean she feels the same. Our years of childhood friendship are unparalleled to her years of flirting and familiarity with Travis. Both hold significance, but one has been more front of mind in the present.

Inserting myself into her life, rekindling the bond we shared for so many years, letting her know I will be there for her through thick and thin... this is how I win her heart.

Like a good friend, I squash my emotions and focus on something else. The cabin.

Black stains the wood framing the windows, the front deck, and the plank stairs leading to the front door. Several weeks' worth of firewood is stacked beneath the deck, while two black basket chairs and a tree stump table sit on the right side of the deck. Snow dusts the black metal roof and blankets the forest floor between the cabin and a stone fire pit.

This place would be a great escape any time of the year. If only we were here for pleasure and not to hide.

A large German Shepherd rounds the tailgate of Travis's truck, a black vest wrapped around its torso. Dark eyes size me up as a black nose sniffs the air.

"*Rechts*," Travis orders, voice thick with authority. The dog sidles up to Travis but doesn't take its eyes off me. "*Sitz.*" Without hesitation, the dog sits tall. Travis levels me with his gaze. "This is my dog, Pepper. She's also a K-9 officer." He drops the tailgate of his truck. "Don't take this personally, but please don't feed or pet or tend to her unless asked."

I nod in agreement. "Got it."

Travis may not be my favorite person, but I respect his and Pepper's roles and bond. Last thing I need is an open wound in the middle of nowhere.

He hefts bags over his shoulder and starts for the cabin. "*Komm.*"

Pepper rises off her haunches and follows Travis immediately.

Kirsten and I trail behind, taking in the scenery and our temporary home for the next several days. I gesture toward the stairs and let her lead the way to the front door. After a quick stomp of our boots on the door mat, we enter the spacious cabin. Travis drops the bags just inside the door and jogs back outside.

Bright and open and airy. My eyes scan every surface. The spacious living room with a wood stove fireplace. The quaint kitchen with a slender breakfast bar and two stools. A short hall with what I assume to be a bathroom on one side and storage on the other. My eyes drift up, following a spiral metal staircase that leads to a loft. With only one bed.

Worst of all, it's completely exposed to the living area below.

*"Fuck..."*

# TWENTY-SEVEN

## KIRSTEN

Beautiful as this cabin is, being secluded here with Travis and Ben is a recipe for disaster.

During the drive, Travis said we were headed to one of the rental cabins his family owns. With the holidays fast approaching, many of the rentals in town are unoccupied. Seeing as I have no desire to rent a place in the town I live in, the only rentals I've seen are those owned by Delilah's family. She visits one in particular solely because it's her favorite spot to disconnect from the world.

The Emerson cabin looks nothing like the Fox rental, which has more of a beachy, cottagecore vibe. Both grab your attention and speak to how different the founding families are in Stone Bay. Both make you never want to leave.

I follow Ben's line of sight, take in the loft, and understand why he muttered a curse seconds ago.

One bed. No door or wall to close it off from the rest of the cabin. Zero privacy.

*Great.*

My stomach cramps as I survey the rest of the cabin. The only other place to sleep is a couch in the main room, which is aesthetically pleasing but small with stiff cushions, and the hardwood floor.

From the outside, the cabin appears much bigger. The vast windows and colossal roof give the illusion of a grander space. For one or two people, the cabin is perfect and intimate. For the three of us…

Stepping farther into the room, I inspect the kitchen. Butcher block sits on pewter base cabinets with more space than expected in such a small room. Live edge wood creates a partition between the living and kitchen rooms and is a perfect spot to sit and eat. Near the corner is a single-basin sink and dish rack tucked in the recess. To the right is the narrowest gas oven range I've ever seen and a fridge big enough to hold basic necessities.

Back in the living room, I glance up the stairwell at the only bed. Though it may have been a challenge, the loft could have been made into a full second floor with additional sleeping space. Yes, it would have darkened the space a little. Nothing strategically placed lights and softer paint couldn't fix.

All I'm certain of is if the guys refuse to get along, I will be the only one in the loft. Well, me and Trixie.

Unraveling the blanket from my chest, I set it and Trixie on the couch. "Check out our little cabin in the woods, Trixie girl." I pet her soft fur and she mewls.

Pepper's eyes dart to the blanket, but she stays in her spot on the area rug a foot away, tail wagging with what I hope is excitement.

Travis walks back in with a cooler and grocery totes, eyes Pepper on the rug staring at Trixie, and passes her for the kitchen, setting everything down. Then he's at Pepper's side, squatting down beside her. "*Vorsicht.*" Travis pets Trixie with slow, soft strokes. "We have to be gentle with little Trixie, Pepper."

Pepper whines and scoots closer to Trixie, leaning in to sniff her. Trixie jerks back, studies Pepper for a moment, then pads across the blanket and meows. After a few more whiffs, Trixie jumps off the couch and weaves between Pepper's legs, purring.

"Fast friends," Travis says, the smile in his voice matching the one on his face. "Let's unpack."

I unload the cooler and totes, leaving the guys to figure out who gets what drawer in the dresser next to the stairwell. Shouldn't cause too much drama, right?

While I figure out what to make for dinner, Travis starts a fire in the wood stove in the living room, then goes upstairs. Ben scans the built-in shelves on the wall opposite the couch, perusing the decent library of books and board games. I have yet to see a television, but there is a Bluetooth radio and land-line phone on one of the shelves.

I cook the most basic of meals—lightly seasoned chicken breasts, brown rice, and broccoli—but both guys smile when I set their plates on the bar... on the same side. Not that I am *forcing* them to get along, but they need to find middle ground. So while we eat, I stand with no one at my side.

Since it's still somewhat early when we finish dinner, Ben suggests we play a game. He grabs UNO off the shelf and a wave of nostalgia hits.

As kids, Ben and I played UNO so much the cards had curled and peeled and torn. Every time he won, I huffed and tossed my cards. He would laugh far too long at my tantrum, shuffle the cards, then ask to play again. Mad as I was, I always said yes, swearing I'd beat him. Because more often than not, I won.

Sitting on the floor next to the coffee table, Ben takes the cards from the box and shuffles them. "Ready to get your ass handed to you, sparkles?"

Eyes narrowed, I purse my lips and stomp across the room, lowering to the floor to sit at the table. "In your dreams, Benji."

Lips pursed and eyes slightly narrowed, Travis joins us at the table. He doesn't say a word as Ben deals the cards. Doesn't look at either of us as the muscles in his jaw flex. Envy pulses off him in red, insecure waves. My fingers twitch, eager to reach under the table and touch him. Gift him a small token of reassurance, silently convey there is no need for jealousy.

But I keep my hands to myself.

Everyone has a past. Ben was part of mine for several years. Circumstances ripped us apart and we lost touch over the years. But this version of Ben, though much of him is the same, a lot of him is different. This Ben is new to me too.

One round after another, we relax and lower our walls. Grow more comfortable around each other. We tease and laugh and cheer like lunatics when we win. A few games in, the guys make a pact to beat me, regardless which of them it is. I smile at their camaraderie but pout that they are ganging up against me. At one point, when we all have too many cards in our hands, I whip out the big guns. Slap action card after action card on the table. Watch the guys wince while I belly laugh.

When I lay my last card on the stack, a Wild card, Ben shakes his head and laughs.

"Always the Wild card, sparkles."

Although he means the game card, a tightness forms beneath my diaphragm. An eerie silence settles in the room and no one moves. Thick, palpable tension bounces between us as I lick my dry lips.

I jolt with a squeal when a hand rests on my thigh under the table. My eyes shoot to Travis and he mouths, "Sorry." With a stroke of his thumb, he scoots back, rises to his full height, and extends his hand my way. "It's late. We should get some sleep."

If the air was thick seconds ago, it's downright insufferable now.

Not sure why, but this feels like a test—of my will, of my allegiance, of my sanity. Travis and I may not have explicitly defined our relationship, but we *are* in a relationship. To make anyone believe otherwise would not only hurt Travis, it would be a lie.

I take his hand and let him pull me up. "Where is the extra bedding?"

He presses his lips to my forehead and steals my breath. "Be right back." He wanders to the back of the cabin, into the alcove behind the kitchen.

I scoop up Trixie, rub behind her ears, then kiss the top of her head as I cuddle her to my chest.

With sheets and a blanket in one hand and a pillow in the other, Travis returns and places them at the end of the couch. "There's more if you need 'em, man."

*Yeah, this is awkward as hell.*

Ben rubs the back of his neck and nods. "Thanks." His eyes shift to mine for three wild heartbeats. "Sweet dreams, sparkles."

I roll my lips between my teeth. "You too. Night, Benji."

And as Travis and I climb the stairs toward the bed, Ben's unrelenting stare heats every inch of my skin.

# TWENTY-EIGHT

## TRAVIS

Did I intentionally pull out the nice guy card minutes ago? Yes. Yes, I did. Did I do it to throw Ben off his game? Damn right, I did. I'd be a fool not to.

Ben is a great guy. Down to earth, kind, endearing. The type of guy you want to introduce to your family. The guy that buys flowers just because and showers you with affection and tenderness without an agenda. Ben is that wholesome guy next door women would be honored to have by their side.

With one smile from Ben at any given time, Kirsten visibly softens. Not because she is in love with him. Not because she wants to be more than friends with Ben.

Quite the opposite, actually.

Those doses of tenderheartedness come from a place of deep affection. Unfortunately for Ben, those drip-fed bits will never be anything stronger. In her own way, Kirsten loves Ben. But she isn't *in love* with Ben.

And as I ascend the stairs to the loft behind Kirsten, I school my expression and peer down at him in the living room. Say more with a single glance than any string of words.

*Kirsten is mine.*

Ben inches forward, his eyes shifting from mine to Kirsten's profile. With each step up she takes, his shoulders cave more inward. When she reaches the landing and doesn't acknowledge his eyes on her, he deflates completely.

Could I toss a victorious smile in his face? Absolutely.

Will I be that asshole right now? No, I won't.

Is every molecule in my body thrumming with triumph? Hell yes.

Turning my attention back to Kirsten, I take a wiggly Trixie from her. "I'll hold this little lady while you change." I press my lips to Kirsten's temple, then step back and hold Trixie high. "You gonna steal my snuggle spotlight tonight, little Trixie?"

Her dark eyes close as her sweet purr vibrates my hands.

In a graphic tee that hits the tops of her thighs, Kirsten pulls back the covers and slips between the sheets, shivering. "Shit, it's cold."

I set Trixie on the bed and she trots up to the pillows. After a few gentle nudges of Kirsten's head, Trixie crawls onto Kirsten's pillow and curls up by her fanned out hair.

Stripping down to my underwear, I duck under the covers and hiss as the frigid sheets swathe my skin. Darkness blankets us as the light on the first floor shuts off. I roll onto my side, band an arm around Kirsten's middle, and drag her across the bed until no space exists between us.

Chin tucked in the crook of her neck, I inhale her sweet floral scent. Skim the tip of my nose up the column of her throat. Kiss the soft spot below her ear and smile when her pulse soars beneath my lips. Tighten my arm around her and hum as every inch of her molds itself to me.

"Mm. Night, sunshine." I press a kiss to the angle of her jaw.

Laying her arm over mine, she sighs. "Night, Trav."

Skin hot and damp, I groan and shove the blanket down my body. Goose bumps flare to life as the chilly air hits my bare chest. After several steady breaths, my body temperature starts to regulate. I reach for the sheet at my hip but pause when Kirsten rolls her hips slightly.

Breath caught in my throat, my eyes blink open. Unflinching, unspeaking, I wait to see if my semiconscious mind plays another trick or if Kirsten rolls her hips again. A slow-burning fire expands in my lungs as I lay motionless, my solid frame pressed firmly against her supple curves. Beside me, her muted inhales and exhales give nothing away. Her back to my front, her steady heartbeat declares I must have been dreaming.

Exhaling, I grip the sheet. And just as quickly, I pause again. Because this time, when Kirsten rubs herself over my length, there is no denying it is intentional.

I drop the sheet, grip her hip, and rock my hips into her. Her raspy hum of appreciation echoes in the confines of the steepled loft, spurring me further.

I trail kisses along the length of her shoulder, the curve of her neck, and up to the spot beneath her ear that makes her back arch. Breath hot on her ear, I grind my hardening cock between her cheeks. "Something you want, baby?"

"Mm-hmm." Her hips gyrate in slow, measured circles as she reaches back and clutches my thigh.

Fingers bruising her hip, I nip her ear with my teeth. My hand drifts over the curves of her body, tugging her shirt up, up, up. On the next breath, she sits up, rips it over her head, and tosses it aside.

And then she twists, shoves me flat on my back, and straddles my hips. Palms on my chest, blonde waves curtaining her face, she grinds over my length. I latch on to her hips, curl my fingers into the thin band of elastic, and drag down in silent request.

Forearms framing my face, essentially on all fours, she sways forward and gives me room to slide her panties down while simultaneously smothering me with her breasts. I moan into her cleavage and she giggles. And after some momentary finagling, she hovers bare and radiant and horny as fuck above me.

With a lick of my lips, I stare up at this goddess, *my* goddess. *Mine.* "So fucking perfect."

Eyes on mine, she teases the head of my cock through my underwear. "Need you," she confesses in a whisper.

My fingers dance over the flare of her hips, over the base of her rib cage, over the swell of her breasts. I sit up, roll one perfectly pink nipple between my thumb and finger while my lips wrap around the other. Slick with arousal, she rubs her center over my length again and again, grinding and seeking and desperate.

Once I've paid equal attention to her breasts, she shoves me down on the mattress. I open my mouth to protest but stop when her fingers dip beneath the waistband of my briefs. With a swift shuffle down my thighs, she rips my briefs off and throws them behind her.

And then her warm tongue is on my cock, licking a torturous trail from root to crown.

A throaty moan spills from my lips as I fist her hair. "Goddamn, baby," I hiss as she swirls her tongue around my crown once, twice, then swallows my length.

I feel her smile a second before she takes me deeper, her throat spasming as I hit the back.

"Such a good fucking girl," I praise, rocking my hips in

time with her. Fire licks my veins and swirls low in my balls. I open my mouth to tell her to stop if she doesn't want me to come down her throat.

But before I get the chance, she releases me with a pop, kisses her way up my abs, and settles her hips over mine. And it is in this exact moment, I mentally berate myself.

"Condoms are in my bag," I whisper. "Downstairs."

She rolls her hips, coating the length of my cock with her arousal. "I'm on the pill."

I palm her breasts and roll her nipples between my fingers. "Only if you're sure, baby."

Her hands cover mine, her fingers encouraging me to pinch harder, to tug her nipples. An unrestrained moan fills the cabin as I tweak her nipples with a little nail.

"God, yes."

Up and down, she strokes the underside of my cock with her pussy. With a slap of her palms to my pecs, she digs her nails into my chest and sheaths me fully with her heat.

"*Fuck...*" I hiss as she takes me bare. Dropping my hands to her hips, I bruise her flesh with my grip. "Fuck me like you're mine, baby."

After a few rhythmic rocks of her hips, she sits taller, cups her breasts and twists her nipples, then bounces hard and fast and mercilessly up and down my cock. My eyes roll back as I meet her thrust for thrust.

Moans and skin slapping skin pulsate off every surface of the cabin. Sweat dampens her skin and shimmers in the faint moonlight peeking through the window at the head of the bed. I trail a thumb to her clit, circling that bundle of nerves, loving the flush that paints her skin in response.

Her hands drop to my rib cage as she shifts her hips and takes me at a different angle. Deeper.

I sit up, band one arm around her waist while the other pins her to my chest. "Come on my cock like a good girl."

On a guttural moan, she tips her head back and exposes her throat. I lift my hips as she slams down again and again, until her body starts to tighten.

"That's it, baby. Let go."

With those words, her pussy constricts my cock and refuses to let go, triggering my own release. And fuck, it is the most glorious sensation—coming inside her. Not a chance in hell I will have her any other way but bare again.

Her mouth crashes down on mine as we twitch with the last of our orgasms. Hands roam and caress and speak a language all their own. Her fingers drift up my neck and into my hair.

As we come down from our sex-induced high, as our breathing finds its normal rhythm, the kiss slows into something softer, more tender. Something I have always wanted. Something that terrifies me to no end. *More.*

But as much as I crave more with her, I refuse to acknowledge the hum in my veins. Refuse to own the buzz beneath my breastbone. Refuse to recognize the fire in my marrow. More than anything, I refuse to admit she has branded my soul.

Not now. Not yet.

Because the last time I handed over my heart fully, it was pulverized with a wicked smile.

# TWENTY-NINE

## KIRSTEN

Cocooned in a flannel blanket, I scoop Trixie up from the bed and swathe her to my chest. Little paws knead my shirt as she purrs loud enough for the guys to hear downstairs. After a scratch behind her ears, I kiss the top of her head.

"How about some breakfast, pretty girl?" Her motorboat of a purr intensifies. "Smells like Daddy is making sausage."

I wind my way down the spiral stairs, the living room empty below. At the base of the stairs, a shirtless Travis comes into view. Barefoot in gray sweatpants, he stands at the stove, turning sausage in a frying pan. A box of pancake mix and carton of eggs sit next to an empty bowl and a stack of plates on the counter.

Watching Travis cook has been one of the highlights of this unplanned non-vacation. A chef, he is not. But everything he cooks would get five stars on Yelp from me, simply because he cooks shirtless.

Setting Trixie down, I step up to Travis, press my front to his back, slip an arm around his middle, and kiss his shoulder. "Starving," I mumble against his skin.

The corner of his mouth kicks up in a cheeky smile as he

looks over his shoulder and kisses my forehead. "Late-night rendezvous will do that."

Leaning back, I peer around the cabin in search of Ben. Beyond the front wall of windows, I spot him near the fire pit. Beanie on his head and heavy coat warming his torso, he sits inches from a roaring fire, snapping twigs and tossing them into the flames.

Since yesterday morning, Ben refuses to meet my gaze.

At first, I assumed he was trying to put distance between us with Travis here. When he volunteered to come along, he undoubtedly pictured our time in this cabin with one idea front and center. That it would bring us closer. And it has, just not in the way he anticipated.

But as the three of us hiked to a nearby lake yesterday, reality slapped me hard and fast.

Halfway through our trek, Travis laced my fingers with his. As I tightened my hold on him, Ben sighed. Had I asked him if he was okay, he would have waved his audible unhappiness off as heavy breathing. So I kept my mouth shut and put one foot in front of the other.

When we reached the lake, Travis had taken me by surprise, hoisted me up off the ground, and swung me in circles. Laughter echoed across the water as he dug into my ribs. I begged him to stop, to put me down and knock it off. I shrieked, my stomach cramping as his relentless fingers kept at it.

Over his shoulder, several feet back, Ben dropped his chin to his chest. Brow creased, lips twisted in pain, hands shoved deep in his pockets, his knee bounced over and over.

Seeing him so withdrawn sobered me in the moment. I pressed my hands to Travis's chest and pushed back as my laughter died. He apologized with a boyish grin on his handsome face, set me on my feet, then dropped his lips to mine in a chaste kiss.

I tried to smile when Travis inched back and leveled me with a heated stare. I tried to not feel self-conscious. But it was impossible. Because it wasn't me holding hands with Travis that made Ben look away. Nor was it the way Travis and I coexisted with such ease that made Ben uncomfortable.

*Ben had heard us. Last night in the loft, when Travis and I had sex, Ben heard us.*

Though it'd been the middle of the night and I tried like hell to be quiet, we either woke him up or he'd never gone to sleep. It was the only valid explanation.

And now, Ben's discomfort is probably closer to mortification.

Around three in the morning, I woke Travis with slow, gentle strokes of his cock. After a vivid dream of the night before, I stared at his sleeping face for several minutes and tried to fall back asleep. My body wasn't having it. Cock thick against my belly, he'd rolled me onto my back, pinned my hands above my head, and worshipped my body for hours.

Days ago, when Ben kissed me, I told him Travis and I were together. Maybe he thought by tagging along, my mind would change. By spending time with him, maybe Ben thought I'd choose him.

Is it wrong that part of me *wants* him too? That I want to keep both Travis and Ben? No, it's not wrong. But it isn't who I am.

As I stare at Ben, alone by the fire, surrounded by a heavy blanket of snow, my heart wrings beneath my breastbone. It begs me to keep Ben close but also let him go.

I brought this hurt on. Letting him come to the middle of nowhere with me and Travis, what had I been thinking? When he inserted himself into the situation, I should have pushed back. I should have let him down gently. Should have done anything other than let him tag along. Instead, the selfish piece of my heart gave in.

It is my careless indecision, my inability to let him go, that will ultimately drive us apart.

I press a kiss to Travis's shoulder and hum. "How much longer?"

Setting down the spatula, he spins and bands his arms around my waist. "Help me with the pancakes?" He kisses the tip of my nose. "It'll cut the time in half."

My fingers toy with the elastic of his sweatpants. "How?" I chuckle. "There's barely enough space for you at the stove."

Warm fingers trail up my spine, my back arching and breasts firm against his chest. "If you mix…" Hand at the back of my neck, he dips me back and drops his lips to my skin, peppering kisses up the column of my throat. Breath hot on my ear, he continues. "I won't stop…" He nips the sensitive skin over my turbulent pulse. "Cooking."

Cool air hits my fevered skin as Travis straightens to his full height and pulls me upright. Molten ambers lock onto my stormy blues for one, two, three breathless beats before he winks and turns back to the stove. I narrow my eyes on his profile and he snickers.

"You're trouble, Travis Emerson."

He points the spatula at his chest. "Me?"

I nod, lean in, and kiss his cheek. "But I like your brand of trouble."

Trixie weaves between my legs, crying for her own breakfast. Tossing the blanket on the breakfast bar, I scoop Trixie up, hug her to my chest like a football, fetch her bowl, and head for the laundry room behind the kitchen. "Has Pepper eaten?"

"Yeah, she's good."

One scoop of kibble in her bowl and Trixie wriggles to get

down. I set her on the floor and carry her food out to the living room. Bolting in front of me, her string of meows is one unending cry. Setting her food down, I scratch behind her ears as she devours the small bits.

"Save some for later, silly girl."

In the kitchen, I snag the pancake mix and bowl and get to work on the batter. Travis cracks eggs in another bowl and scrambles them. We move in tandem, as if we've been cooking together for years instead of days. And as he finishes cooking the last of the pancakes, I slip on boots, swipe up the blanket, bundle myself in it, and head outside to get Ben.

Hair whips across my face as I step past the eaves of the cabin. Tugging the blanket higher and tighter, I take the stairs one at a time. Snow crunches under my boots, the occasional flake landing on my face or the blanket as I cross the lawn to the still-roaring fire. My heart bangs faster, harder in the confines of my rib cage as I eliminate the distance between me and a broody Ben.

His fingers stop fumbling with the stick in his hands when I sidle up to him. He doesn't look up. Doesn't gift me his soft smile. Doesn't acknowledge my presence in any customary way. He simply stares at the fire, jaw tight and posture rigid.

Rather than spark a one-sided conversation, I tip one of the other chairs sideways and shake off the snow. Then I drag it closer to his chair until the arms touch. Dropping into the seat, I draw my knees to my chest, drape the blanket around them, and rest my chin on my knees.

Silence stretches the seconds to feel like hours as neither of us speaks. Ben goes back to breaking apart sticks while I zone out watching the flames dance.

Peeking at Ben in my periphery, I fight the urge to apologize. Unsure what it is he's upset about, I don't want to apologize for the wrong thing. Maybe he didn't hear me and Travis the past two nights. Maybe he just feels out of place in this messed-up situation.

Without a doubt, Ben wants more than friendship with me. Seeing me share simple intimacy with Travis—holding hands, playful shoves, kisses to my cheek and temple and forehead—after his confession has to be salt rubbed in his splintering heart.

I don't want to hurt Ben. But I don't want to lie to him either.

Travis and I still have yet to define our relationship with titles or proclamations, and maybe that is because we both have pasts to unravel. Wounds that are still fresh mentally. Invisible scars that need extra care. Our hurt may not be the same, but we understand and respect each other nonetheless.

Which is why this is so difficult.

In my own way, I love Travis. And I love Ben.

But could I ever be *in love* with either of them? I want to say yes. I want to believe, after all these years, it is possible to dismantle the brick wall I built around my heart. I want to believe it is possible to fall in love and not worry about losing that person.

Bicep pressing against his, I lean into him. Rest my head on his shoulder and close my eyes. Breathe in his leather and soap scent. Curve my lips up into an almost imperceptible smile as his rigid frame softens, as he gives me his weight in return.

"You know I love you, Benji," I whisper as I open my eyes, the words floating away in a white puff.

The stick in his hand drops to his lap, then falls to the ground. A shudder ripples from his chest, his frame visibly shaking as the small wave of aftershocks passes through the length of his limbs and absorbs into mine.

He rests his cheek on my crown and sighs. "Yeah, sparkles,

I know." On a ragged inhale, he lays his hand next to mine, his little finger lightly stroking mine. "Love you too."

We sit like this—motionless, mute, lost in thought—for hour-long minutes, our cloudy breaths mingling.

In another life, one where my dad didn't die and I stayed in Smoky Creek, Ben and I would be more than this. More than two best friends reconnecting after years apart. More than two people with an unclear future. In that other life, I have no doubt Ben and I would have dated. He would have been my first kiss, my first romantic love, my first everything. And I would have been his. We may have had arguments and heartbreak, but we would have mended those wounds.

If that other life existed, Ben would be the one pulling me into his arms and pressing me to his chest. Ben would kiss me breathless, and I'd kiss him with equal fervor. If that other life existed, I would tell Ben I love him in a way that says *I am in love with you.*

My eyes fall shut as a shiver rolls up my spine.

*In another life…*

I brush the side of his finger with mine. "Hungry?"

With a turn of his head, he presses his lips to my hair, holding them there. "Mmm."

Inching back, I lift my head and meet his gaze. The vivid turquoise of his irises invades my vision, the heat of his breath hits my lips in soft, short puffs. I swallow at his proximity, my heart rattling my rib cage with desperate fists. I lick my lips, then tuck them between my teeth. Such a simple move, but not one that will keep me from making a move. It certainly won't quash the desire simmering beneath the surface. The urge, the impulse, the *need* clawing up my neck and heating my cheeks. The compulsion screaming at the top of its lungs to lean back into Ben, to get sucked back into his gravity once more. To exist in his orbit and cave to this attraction between us. To kiss him again and surrender to this muddled mess in my head and heart.

Closer.

One centimeter.

Then another.

Desire pools low in my belly—building, expanding, searing.

Statue of a perfect gentleman, Ben doesn't move. But I feel him everywhere. Stuttered breaths on my lips. The undeniable buzz on my skin from the smallest contact. The blissful hum in my bloodstream that grows louder the closer I get.

I tilt my head and inch forward, my lips barely caressing his. A loud *pop* comes from the fire and I jerk my head back. Reality backhands me as my eyes meet Ben's hopeful stare.

Heart punching my chest, I scramble out of the chair and tug the blanket tighter around my body. Eyes on the stick Ben dropped, I mutter, "Breakfast is ready." I nod as if needing to remind myself. "We should go in."

Pivoting on my heel, I step toward the cabin. Ben stops me, his fingers clutching at the blanket.

"Kirsten, wait."

"Ben, I..." Unsure what to say, I shake my head.

Heat blankets my back and I close my eyes, basking in his proximity, his energy, the way he makes me feel alive. He releases the blanket, his hand drifting lower to rest on my hip. Curling. Kneading. Holding me to him.

*Th-thump, th-thump, th-thump.*

My heart hammers in my chest. My breath caught in my throat. I will my muscles to move, will my body to step out of his hold, will my mind to make a damn decision and stick with it.

But with each ragged inhale, I sink farther into quicksand.

I can't love them both. I'm not built for it. In the end, loving both of them will break us all. But how do I choose?

Lips on my hair and grazing my ear, he whispers, *"Let me love you."*

God, how I want to let him. If only it were that easy.

"We should go in," I choke out.

With one last knead of my hip, he releases his hold on me, and I deflate faster than a freed, untied balloon. Until he moves to my side and hooks an arm around my shoulders, fingers toying with my hair.

"Suddenly"—he angles closer, pressing his lips to my temple—"I'm famished."

"All has been quiet here, sir." Travis paces the length of the bookshelf, ear pressed to the landline receiver, shoulders back, and spine straight. Attention sharp, but gaze unfocused as he listens to his father update him on town news.

Since the almost-kiss with Ben this morning, all three of us have been on edge. The tension thicker than the chimney smoke.

Travis hasn't mentioned seeing me come within a breath of kissing Ben. Nor has he been his usual grouchy or grabby self, demanding my attention. But I know he saw us. With a wall of windows facing the lawn, how did he not?

From the moment Ben and I walked in, Ben's arm still around my shoulders, Travis has had this vacant expression. Even now—as I sit on the floor with Ben behind me, playing with my hair—not an ounce of emotion mars his features or distorts his frame.

For hours, I have waited for anger to flare and fists to fly.

And for hours, I have been in this bizarre parallel universe. One where the guys don't exchange insults or go toe-to-toe to claim my heart. Instead, Travis tucked my hair behind my ear and pressed a chaste kiss to my lips moments before Ben finger-combed my hair, then clumsily braided the thick strands.

Don't get me wrong, I love the attention and easy affection. But it feels… *wrong*. Ambiguous. Shameful.

They both want me, my heart. With whispered words, subtle and not-so-subtle touches, and inescapable, soul-penetrating stares, they have both expressed their adoration.

But after seeing me outside with Ben, is Travis giving up?

Sharp, unrelenting pain swells near my breastbone. I gasp, pressing the heel of my hand between my breasts. Ben crowds me from behind, his voice distant and wobbly, and white noise in my ears. I can't breathe, can't speak, can't think clearly. My somewhat tranquil life morphs into a discombobulated haze of pandemonium.

Travis stops pacing, his feet aimed in my direction. I lift my chin, my blurry gaze latching onto his anguished stare. Time warps and slows as we take each other in. In his amber eyes, I read all the thoughts he's kept to himself over the last several hours.

Irritation not only with the Ben situation, but also with my stalker still on the loose. Uncertainty with where we stand after I almost initiated a kiss with someone other than him. Jealousy over sharing me, even if only in friendship, with someone else.

Something else lingers in his molten honey eyes. Something he is nowhere near ready to admit or give a voice, but shows me nonetheless. Something that scares the hell out of him.

Love.

I blink back the tears brimming my eyes and search the depths of his. The cabin blurs into a swirl of browns and creams and black. Travis's lips move, but I don't hear a word he says to his father. Pulse thrumming in my ears, I swallow as the rhythm of my heart changes. As my heartbeat learns a new pattern. A tempo I memorized as we drifted off to sleep, my head on his chest and ear above his heart.

Without a single word spoken, without a single confession vibrating the air, I know with absolute certainty that Travis Emerson is in love with me. I see his truth in his soul-deep stare.

And it is with this realization that the room comes back into focus.

Ben shakes my shoulders from behind. "Are you okay?" Concern edges his words as they hit my ears.

On a harsh swallow, I nod. "Uh." The sound scrapes my throat and I clear it. "Yeah." I pat his hand on my shoulder. "I'm fine."

He presses his lips to my crown, breathes me in, kisses my head, then mumbles against my hair. "Scared the shit out of me." He gives both shoulders a quick squeeze, then straightens in his seat.

"Sorry," I mutter.

"If it's still quiet by the weekend, we'll head back," Travis says, and everything in the room sharpens. His father's booming voice echoes across the room a moment before Travis rolls his eyes. "The gun safe is secure, and I've taken... measures for intruders."

*Gun safe? Measures?*

Where the hell is there a gun safe?

As if I asked aloud, Travis holds up a finger. "Call you tomorrow, sir." Then he hangs up the phone. No *I love you,*

*Dad.* No *good night* or *thank you.* Nothing warm or affectionate or familial.

Travis sets the phone back on the bookshelf, crosses the room, and squats in front of me. Eyes locked on mine, he cups my cheek, the softest smile tipping up the corners of his mouth. Pulse throbbing beneath his ear, he nods imperceptibly, a silent confirmation of my assumption a moment ago.

*Travis Emerson is in love with me.*

Swallowing, I lean into his touch and close my eyes, giving a small nod in return. Warm, soft lips meet my forehead and I melt under his touch. But it doesn't last long. With a blink, I meet Travis's solemn expression.

"In the laundry room, the wall butting the kitchen pops open."

My brows crumple inward. "Pops open?"

Travis looks up at Ben for a beat before meeting my eyes again. "Not as seamless as it looks." A brief smile finds his face. "Between the washer and the wall, there is a small button that blends in with the molding."

He pushes up on his feet, stands, and offers me his hand. Leading us to the small room, he swings me in front of him, takes my hand, and guides it to a small notch in the wall. His hand on mine, we press the button and a click echoes in the room. To our left, about three feet down, the wall sticks out a couple inches. Stepping back, he waits until I move around him before he opens the hidden door.

My jaw hits the floor. Between the kitchen and laundry is a small room. Travis tugs a chain just inside the room, illuminating the space. Hesitantly, I take a step forward, then another, and another, until I'm inside. To the left is a tall gun safe with a digital keypad. Straight ahead, a collapsed cot, bucket, non-perishables, and a few gallons of water.

"Below you," Travis says, and I spin to face him. "Under the rug is an escape hatch."

"Jesus," Ben mutters. "Get locked in your panic room much?"

The muscles in Travis's jaw tic a beat before he smirks at Ben. "No, *Benji*. It's called being smart." Travis faces him fully. "If someone pins this door shut"—he waves a hand to the wall—"the person inside needs another way out." He cocks his head. "Sounds intelligent in my mind."

"Whatever," Ben mumbles.

Travis steps in next to me and spends the next several minutes detailing everything about the room—the safe combo, where the escape hatch leads, what supplies and how much are in the room. When the room should be used. With each new thing, I grow more overwhelmed.

The door closes with a soft click once we step out. Though the room is built for safety, something about being in there, seeing the prison-like confines, sends a chill up my spine.

Palm rubbing up and down my back, Travis leans into my side as we enter the main part of the cabin. "We shouldn't need to use it, but knowing about the room is smart. Better to err on the side of caution."

"Is that how we're brushing all this off now?" Ben pipes up.

"Ben..." I say, exasperated.

"What?" Ben holds my gaze a beat before aiming it at Travis. "It isn't *normal* to have panic rooms and emergency exits in the floor."

Stepping in front of Travis, I shield him from Ben's wrath. "True." I pin my fists on my hips. "It also isn't *normal* to have some nutjob leave disturbing notes or gifts at your work or private property." Fire licks my veins and I advance toward him. "It isn't *normal* for some sick fuck to stand outside your bedroom window, peep through the crack in your curtains, and jerk off as he watches you sleep." Fingers curled so tight my knuckles burn, I grind my molars. "Nothing about any of this is *normal*, Ben. But here the fuck we are." I wave my arms around the cabin, take a deep breath, then meet his pained expression with my furious one. "Right now, can we cast aside the bullshit and try to be as *normal* as possible. Please?" The last word comes out in a whispered plea.

Ben steps closer, lifting his hands as if to embrace me. But then his arms drop to his sides. "Shit, sparkles." He lifts a hand and rubs the back of his neck, squeezing the muscles. "I'm sorry."

I fight the urge to tell him it is okay, because going off the rails is never okay. Yes, this situation is outrageous. But it is happening to me. He doesn't get to smother the real problem with his jealousy. Not with this.

"It's early, but let's just make dinner and play some music or something. I can't deal with this right now."

Before either of them says a word, I storm to the fridge and dig through the contents, ignoring their hard stares on my back.

Most of dinner passes in sweet, blissful silence.

I sit on the short side of the breakfast bar, forcing them next to each other once again. Beneath the table, neither attempts to touch my thigh or brush my foot with theirs. Above the table, neither attempts to soothe my blowup with phony or sympathetic smiles.

It's equal parts relaxing and stifling.

When I eat the last bite on my plate, I push back on the

stool, amble over to the sink, and deposit my dish in the basin. Without looking at either of them, I walk by, grab my shoes and coat, and slip both on.

"I need air."

And before either of them opens their mouths to argue, I yank open the door and step out into the night.

I shiver the moment the door closes behind me, my jacket and gloves no match for the frigid mid-December temperature. Regardless, I trek forward, down the stairs, and stop near the bottom, plopping down.

Snow floats down leisurely from the inky night sky, slowly adding to the already thick blanket on the forest floor. By morning, this place will be a magical winter wonderland.

Closing my eyes, I inhale the crisp air laced with pine. Absorb the quiet, the peace, the calm. Let it settle my anger and ease my frustrations. Then I remind myself we won't be here much longer. That this madness will all be over soon.

A click echoes through the trees and my spine straightens.

I twist on the step, thinking it's one of the guys coming out to check on me already. But when I open my mouth to assure whomever I am fine, my brows tug together. The stairs and porch are both empty, the soft glow of the cabin's lights fading into the night.

"Probably a deer," I mutter, turning back to face the lawn.

The distinct sound of feet crunching snow hits my ears. As I twist left to scan the forest, another *crunch* hits my ears. I spin to the right as I shove up from my seat, ready to run up the stairs.

But before my foot lands on the next step, pain ricochets through my skull. A loud hiss rings in my ears. The world tilts left and then right, and I throw my arms out to balance myself.

*Crunch.*

*Thwack.*

Sharp. Fire. Infinite.

Cold burns my cheek. The light of the cabin dims.

Rocks. Branches. Dirt in my mouth. Something pulls at my hair.

The light disappears.

*Thwack.*

Tree.

Then nothing.

# THIRTY

## BEN

"Maybe she doesn't know what she wants, asshole," I bark out, pointing behind me to the front door. "*She* almost kissed *me* this morning." Glare burning a hole in the back of his head, I grip the edge of the breakfast bar.

It isn't in my nature to get so worked up, so heated over anything or anyone. But Kirsten isn't just anyone. And the fact that she was a second away from sealing my lips with hers hours ago says she has yet to decide. If there is the slightest chance she wants to be with me, shouldn't I wait and see?

Smirk firmly in place, Travis keeps his attention on the sudsy plate in his hand. As if he is privy to information I have yet to learn. As if my admission about the almost kiss is pointless.

He just keeps washing dishes, and it pisses me off.

"Anything to say?"

At this, he peeks over his shoulder, his smirk transforming into a beaming smile. Stomach churning, my dinner threatens a reappearance.

"Nah, man." He cocks a brow. "I'm confident of where I stand with her, whether she wanted to kiss you or not."

"Cocky much?"

Throaty laughter fills the cabin as he tips his head back. Rinsing the pot in his hands, he sets it in the rack. Faucet off, he dries his hands and saunters to the opposite side of the bar. He tosses the towel down, flattens his palms on the tabletop, and leans forward.

"One of my best qualities." He shrugs, then looks over my shoulder, his stare lingering a moment before meeting mine again. "Kirsten seems to be a fan."

Such a fucking prick. What the hell does she see in him?

"So you're cool with her wanting me too?" Arms folded across my chest, I purse my lips and raise my brows.

With a shake of his head, he covers his mouth with a loose fist and chuckles.

My fingers ball into tight fists beneath my elbows as I fight every impulse to lean over the bar and punch the condescending smirk off his pretty boy face.

"Listen," he starts, straightening his spine and propping his hands on his hips. "I get that you and Kirsten have years of history. But you were friends. Childhood friends." A sympathetic wince stretches his lips. "Seeing you again is bound to stir up old feelings and prompt several what-if questions." One shoulder lifts in a subtle half-shrug. "But it's comparable to finding a toy you had as a child, one you loved deeply, then cried over when you lost it. For a little while, you keep the rediscovered toy close. Reminisce over all the good times you had with it. Wonder what your life would've been like had you not misplaced it."

White-hot anger pulses through my veins. I open my mouth to tell him I'm not some damn toy. But he holds up a hand and carries on with his stupid toy metaphorical story.

"As the days pass, you stare at that toy with less excitement. It's a great memory, but you've spent more years without it than you did with it. Not to mention, you aren't the same person anymore. You've grown, been hardened by the world, learned to live without childish things." The corner of his mouth tips up a beat before he continues. "You've also fallen in love with new toys."

He pauses to let those last words sink in deeper. To take root and unsettle me. *Asshole.*

"Soon, the nostalgia wears off and you put the childhood toy away. You move forward with your adult life with the toy of your youth as a happy memory." He swipes the towel off the counter and folds it. "The end."

"One." I hold up a finger. "Comparing people to toys is asinine." A second finger pops up. "Two. If she's in love with you, she wouldn't be thinking of kissing me."

He scoffs. "Obviously you've never been in love."

"What's that supposed to mean?"

Tossing the towel near the sink, he shoves his hands in his pockets. "Love is scary as fuck. Giving your heart to someone else…" He visibly shudders. "Every second of every day, I've fought what I feel for her. Since you arrived, I've fought harder. Fought the current pulling me closer to her." On an audible inhale, he closes his eyes. Seconds pass before he exhales and levels me with a fiery gaze. "But I'm done fighting."

His shoulders relax, the lines of his face smooth out.

"You can be madly in love with someone and still find other people attractive. You can want to live the rest of your life with one person and still fantasize about what it'd be like to kiss or touch or fuck someone else." His finger brushes the underside of his nose, a mocking smile on his lips. "We're animals, Ben. It's human nature." He shrugs at the simple yet complex explanation. "As long as you don't step outside of the parameters of your relationship, you've done nothing wrong."

"Thinking about someone else in a non-platonic way when you're in a relationship is cheating."

"I beg to differ."

Alright, you arrogant bastard. Let's put your theory to the test.

"So, if I walk outside to check on Kirsten and one thing leads to another and she kisses me, you won't be pissed?"

"At her? Not at all. At you? One hundred percent."

I roll my eyes in disbelief.

He points to my chest. "Old toy, remember?"

I dust off my shoulder. "More beloved than old."

"Perhaps, but here's where our trains of thought differ." He steps up to the bar and rests his forearms on the counter. "Her thoughts are all over the place, this much I know. Although it bothered me days ago, I've given her the space and time to sift through those thoughts. To decide what it is *she* wants. And now she's made her decision," he says the last part with overt confidence. "She may not have *said* she's in love with me, but she is. Her temporary paralysis when I was on the phone earlier, it was written all over her face. With your hands in her hair, she looked *at me* and silently said she was in love *with me*." He rubs the scruff along his jaw. "And I told her as much in return. Because yeah, I am in love with her." His expression softens. "Have been for years. Just didn't realize it until recently."

Annoyed by his admission, I imagine slapping the gooey, lovesick look off his face. Imagine the thrill in my veins at seeing my red handprint on his cheek. The satisfaction is temporary.

Solemnity takes over his expression as he holds my gaze. "If you kissed her and she kissed you back, I wouldn't be angry with her. She needs to know she's made the right choice. I can't fault her for that. Not in this scenario." He inhales a deep, steadying breath. "I would, however, be livid with you. If she made the move, it'd upset me, but after we talked about it, I'd be fine. Like I said, she's trying to sort out her feelings. And I'm right here." He points to the ground. "She isn't doing this behind my back."

He pauses and shakes his head.

"But if you made the move, inserting yourself in the middle of *our* relationship for selfish reasons, it makes you the asshole. It makes *you* the guy who just won't see what's right in front of him. It makes *you* the selfish prick. It makes *you* the bad guy." He straightens to his full height and purses his lips. "And after this fiasco ends, she may never want to speak to you again. You willing to risk it?"

*Motherfucker.*

Why are his words sinking in and making sense? Why is this prick right? And why the hell does he look so smug?

"Whatever." I back up from the bar, turn on my heel, and head for the door. "Going to check on her."

Running water hits my ears as I tug on my coat and boots. I take one deep breath, then another, in an attempt to clear my head before seeing Kirsten. Last thing she needs is my frustration.

A gust of wind howls and slaps my cheek as I step out onto the empty porch. Zipping up my coat, I shove my hands in my pockets and head for the top of the stairs. Snow crunches beneath my boots and I make a mental note to shovel a path from the door to the steps later.

The farther down the steps I go, the more I lose the light from inside the cabin.

"Weather's getting bad, sparkles. Should probably come in."

No response. Just another howl of wind.

I jog down the snow-covered stairs that are nearly a ramp

now. "Kirsten?" I call out louder this time. "Where are you?"

When I hit the bottom, I pull out my phone, hit the flashlight button, and shine the light on the lawn and surrounding trees. All I see is snow. Way more snow than earlier.

Pulse whooshing in my ears, I scan the forest and cup the side of my mouth. "Kirsten!" I shout, her name echoing through the trees and disappearing. "*Fuck.*"

I bolt up the stairs and through the front door, winded. Travis takes one look at me and stiffens.

"What's wrong?"

"Can't find her."

"What do you—" He sprints across the room, rips the landline off the shelf, and dials out. His knee bounces as he waits for the call to connect. "Dani, it's Travis. I need backup." He pauses while Dani speaks on the other end. He rattles off the address to the cabin, along with the gate code. "Single, white female. Early twenties. Blonde hair, gray-blue eyes. Approximately five ten in height, slender build."

Numbness consumes me as he describes her attire, as the reality of the situation sinks in.

Kirsten didn't go strolling off into the night through an unfamiliar forest with a snowstorm rolling in. Someone *took* her. The person stalking her in town followed us out here and *took her*.

Is she hurt? Scared?

*Alive?*

I shake the dark thought from my head. "Can't go there," I mutter.

Travis hangs up the phone and dashes to the shoe rack next to the door. "Officer Pepper," he commands, and she rises from her spot near the wood stove. "*Rechts.*"

She sidles up to him, on alert. Travis picks up a red, puffy dog windbreaker beside the shoe rack and wraps it around her middle. Along the spine, near the neck, is a small device. Once the jacket is in place, Travis flips a switch on the device, and a green light blinks. Taking out his phone, he taps the screen a few times.

"App connects me to the camera." He points to the device. "It also tracks, in case we lose sight of her." Rising, he grabs his jacket and slips it on as he moves across the room. Beside the communal dresser, he fetches a backpack and hoists it over his shoulders. "One sec." He jogs into the laundry room, returning quickly with a large LED flashlight and his sidearm.

As he passes the chair near the wood stove, he yanks Kirsten's cream sweater off the back. In two strides, he stands between me and Pepper. He holds out the sweater, inches from her nose. "Pepper, *such*. Track Kirsten."

And then we are out the door. Running down the stairs until we reach the bottom. Pepper whimpers softly, then trots across the lawn toward the treeline.

In less than a minute, we lose sight of the cabin. Snow and sticks and rocks crunch beneath our boots. Every fifteen to twenty feet, Pepper lets out another soft whine.

I swallow down the urge to puke the farther into the woods we search. Resist asking what those small whimpers mean as the flashlight shines on the jagged, rocky mountain wall. Fight the voices in my head that echo the Stone Bay townsfolk... *"The woman... was a pretty one. Our waitress would easily pass as her sister."*

Bile climbs up my throat and I slap a hand over my mouth.

*It's not her. Kirsten is okay. She's alive. We'll find her in time.*

I repeat the words over and over, but they won't stick. And as Pepper slows her pace, head held higher, nose sniffing in every direction, dread sinks in.

We are losing the trail.

We are losing her.

# THIRTY-ONE
## SEEKER



She has been on my radar for too damn long. Months before that cunt of a wife left me high and dry, stealing our kid and leaving town. The ink on the divorce decree and child custody papers was still fucking wet when she drove south and as far from me and Stone Bay as possible.

*Whore.*

Is it Kirsten's fault her flirty nature reminds me of that bitch? No.

Do I give a fuck? Also, no.

For days, I've patiently waited. After following her and her precious boy toys out here, I parked near another cabin, not far from the highway, then scoured this property for shelter closer to their cabin. A cave or alcove. Somewhere to make shelter and bide my time.

And that's when I stumbled across the rickety shack in the forest. Dilapidated boards for walls and a mix of boards and branches and foliage for a roof, it looked ready to collapse any moment.

When I stepped inside, I discovered the true prize.

After some looking around, I left the property and did some shopping. With a few tweaks, the space was ready. For *my whore*. For me to take what's mine.

From the door, I trace the curves of her face with my eyes. Lick my lips as my eyes coast over hers. Stiffen in my pants as I glimpse the dried trails of blood on her cheek, near her eye, down her forehead.

Frenetic energy buzzes in my veins. Wakes up every molecule in my body. Gives me a new sense of purpose. New motivation to push forward. To fulfill the sick and twisted fantasies in my head.

*My whore.*

I glance down at the box near her feet—a small slip of paper taped to the top—as a devious smile slowly curves up the corners of my mouth.

"Hide and seek time, little whore."

And before she wakes, I reach for one of two knobs high on the wall outside the room and twist left until it stops. The room goes pitch black and my dick strains against my pants.

Backing out of the room, the door closes with a heavy *thump*. Gripping the steel wheel, I crank until metal squeals against metal as several gears turn and drive the steel bolts into the solid metal frame.

I palm my dick through my pants, tip my head back, and sigh.

"Finally, you're mine."

# THIRTY-TWO

## KIRSTEN

The dank scent of mildew lingers in the air and I wrinkle my nose. But the scrunching of my nose and curling of my lips are immediately cut short by the lancing pain behind my eyes.

On a groan, I drag an arm up and press the heel of my hand to my temple, then to the throbbing spot on the back of my head. Damp syrup coats my hair, some of the strands sticking to the stiff, scratchy ground beneath my back. I lift my hand and peel my eyes open to see the tacky liquid on my hand, but come up empty.

Darkness infiltrates every molecule of air, stealing my sight. I bring my hand closer to my face and slowly narrow my eyes. Search the darkness for a discernible hint of skin.

Nothing.

"Hello?" The two syllables scrape my throat and echo in my ears. Pushing up into a seated position, I clutch my throat and massage either side. I swallow past the dryness and try again. "Hello?" My voice bounces around in the darkness, mocking me as no one answers.

Drawing up my knees, I dig my heels and palms into the ground and push to stand. Legs still bent, I sway and dizzy as

I straighten them. I reach out, hoping to clutch something, anything, to keep me upright and steady. But my hands don't make purchase and I stumble back, one step after another, before my tailbone smacks the ground.

I drop my hands to the ground and push up to alleviate the radiating pain, but get distracted by the fibers between my fingers. Resting on my hip, I focus on the material. Run my fingers through it, curling and plucking the small pieces.

*Is this* carpet? *Am I in someone's house?*

"Hello?" I try again, louder this time. "Is anyone here?" I shift until I'm on all fours, then slowly try to stand again. "I have injuries and need help."

More stable than moments ago, I straighten my spine, stretch out my arms, and inch forward in the dark. Left then right, left then right. On my next step, dim light glows around me, illuminating the room. I squint, then close my eyes, as the pain in my head pulsates.

Inhaling deeply, I open my eyes and let my senses adjust. Little by little, the space comes into view.

Matted, dingy shag carpet under my feet. A wood-frame couch and chair with a vintage farmhouse and watermill pattern on large, lumpy cushions; a spindle-legged wood coffee table centered a foot away with a dusty bowl of artificial fruit and stack of children's books at the heart.

To my left, the carpet ends where orange and yellow linoleum begins. Grimy yellow base cabinets butt against two walls. Pots sit on an electric coil cooktop, kitchen utensils dangling from a rack inches from a tile backsplash similar to the linoleum floor. Two wall-mounted ovens to the left of the stove. On the other countertop, a sink basin, wood wine rack, and yellow-glass cabinet take up most of the space.

Above the sink, a set of windows with wood bars and orange half-curtains garners my attention. I bolt across the room, dizzying as I do, and tug at the knobby wood bars. But my effort is pointless when they don't budge an inch. When my eyes drift up to the uncovered glass, unease creeps through my veins. Behind the glass is a fading image of the forest and mountains.

"What the hell is this place?" I question under my breath.

Spinning around, I take in the rest of the room. In the center of the severely outdated kitchen is a rich brown dining table with enough space for six but only two chairs. Draped over the width of the table, a red-stitched yellow runner serves as a tablecloth, with two place settings, one on either side. Bowls and platters sit on the ends of the table; more fake food on display. Above the table, a chandelier with fake candles as bulbs.

I move across the room, slower this time, and wander through the *house* in search of a way out. There has to be a door or an escapable window somewhere. Behind the kitchen is a pantry, row after row of shelves loaded with shelf-stable food. A utility sink at the end of the room with a washboard in the basin.

My stomach sours and I back out of the room.

On faster feet, I pass a floor-to-ceiling bookshelf loaded with books and games, go to the opposite end of the space, down the short hall past the living area. Two doorless thresholds exist in the hall—one leads to a bathroom, while the other opens up to a bedroom. Blanketed in the same pattern as the couch, the wooden four-post bed swallows up most of the room. The rest of the room is crowded by the lengthy six-drawer dresser, a cabinet beside the drawers, and a wood-framed mirror with shelves on the ends on top.

Dashing back to the living room, I search for a phone and come up empty.

"Hello?" I call out, on the cusp of yelling.

The lights in the space brighten, the soft glow more yellow than white.

"This isn't funny," I add, more leveled.

As if to mock me, the lights glow brighter. Hotter. Blinding.

Sweat slicks my skin, my heart bangs in the confines of my rib cage as I cover my eyes. Several pulse-pounding seconds pass before the air cools. I peek through cracked fingers to find the lights have softened.

When I lower my hands, my eyes catch on a box on the floor, a slip of paper taped to the lid. Dread slithers through my veins as I step closer to the *gift*. Bending, I pick up the illusive package, tear off the note, unfold it, and read.

*Put this on and I'll let you out, my pretty little whore.*

Bile climbs up my throat as alarm mixes with anger.

Who *is* this person? Why are they doing this to me? What the hell did I ever do to them?

Nails bite my palms as I curl my fingers into tight fists. "Mommy and Daddy not love you enough?" I bite out and gnash my teeth together.

I tear open the box, rip away the tissue paper, and yank out the silky material inside. Similar to the nightie in the other gift box, the lingerie is pale pink. Unlike the other piece, this negligee is much more revealing. More sheer and lacy and provocative.

Holding up the offensive garment, I shout, "I'm not putting this on, pervert."

Bright light fills the room and I hiss as I drop the box and lingerie to cover my eyes. This time, the heat and lights stay cranked up longer, as if proving a point. Minutes tick by, my skin heating up like I've been sunbathing for hours. The wound on the back of my skull throbs. The stabbing behind my eyes grows more intense. I can't think, can't process, can't see. My breaths come in short sips as I crumple to the floor. My muscles contract, shriveling against my frame. A dull ache settles in my bones.

On a strained inhale, I hold up my hand. "Fine. I'll do it."

The lights glow hotter, brighter.

I curl my fingers into the rug, muster every ounce of strength, and shout, "I'll put it on. Just turn off the lights."

Just as the last word leaves my lips, the room turns pitch black and the air cools.

With the shield of darkness, I peel off my clothes with shaky hands. Leaving my bra and panties on, I pull the repulsive lingerie over my head and tug it over as much skin as possible.

A creak followed by a deep thud echoes throughout the room. A sliver of light shines less than ten feet away. *Behind the bookcase.*

I straighten to my full height and tiptoe toward my only shred of hope. Time to get the hell out of here.

# THIRTY-THREE

## TRAVIS

Pepper has walked in circles for nearly an hour. As if she smells hints of Kirsten's scent but can't pinpoint where it originates from. The more aimless her search is, the more my gut twists with unease.

Hours have passed since Kirsten stepped outside the cabin for fresh air. It's been hours since Ben and I bickered over Kirsten while some sick motherfucker abducted her and disappeared into the woods.

Did he nab her the second she left my line of sight? Or did she sit at the bottom of the steps, where Pepper picked up her scent, for several minutes?

Is she hurt? Scared?

Nausea rolls in my belly and bubbles up my throat.

Is she *alive*?

I inhale a shaky breath and shove away the last thought. Instead, I focus on what I know. I focus on the facts.

The notes and the gifts... this person is obsessed with Kirsten.

In most stalker cases, the victim is kept alive for nefarious reasons. The perpetrator gets some sick sense of pleasure seeing the victim distraught or frightened. Gets their jollies by watching the target squirm under their scrutiny or touch. In most cases, the stalker wants to live out some perverse fantasy more than harm the victim. By the time they capture their victim, they've lived so long in their delusion, they don't know reality from fantasy.

More than anything, it's the instability of this person that bothers me most. Because if this person killed the woman in the woods, we are on borrowed time.

Aside from their looks, what did the woman in the woods and Kirsten have in common?

Recently, we identified the woman in the woods. Spoke with her family and learned she'd moved to Stone Bay six months ago to start over. After years of substance abuse, she broke up with her boyfriend—who was also her dealer—and left everything behind. She'd told her sister she didn't want to spend the rest of her life high or drunk and oblivious to the world.

She'd been in Stone Bay four months before she went missing. At first, her sister thought she'd gone back to her old life. A week later, the news of the woman in the woods spread like wildfire in town. With a hectic schedule, the news hadn't reached her right away. Once it did, we were able to finally name the woman in the woods. Julia Quinn.

Still, other than their uncanny resemblance, there were no other common factors between Julia and Kirsten. Different job types, different family dynamics, different lifestyles. Their dissimilarities are what kill me more than anything. Because finding that missing link is key to solving this case, to putting this sick fuck behind bars.

In the hands of their stalker, especially those with control and anger issues, abductees have a small window to get out alive. If we don't get to Kirsten in time, she may be the next woman in the woods.

A hand hits my arm and I blink out of my mental spiral to look at Ben. Sad smile on his lips, he zips his jacket higher. "We'll find her," he states with zero confidence.

I stop and look up into the inky tree canopy. Pepper trots to my side and nudges my thigh, her form of consolation while we search. Dropping my chin to my chest, I scratch behind her ears. Then I level Ben with my gaze and voice my fears.

"But will we find her in time?"

Snow hits the forest floor with more frequency, wiping away any possibility of a trail. Scent trails still linger in the snowfall but fade with each new layer of flakes. Pepper won't give up until I call her off the search. And with the heavy snow and lack of light fighting against us, we are likely to freeze or starve before picking up Kirsten's scent again.

Hands shoved deep in his pockets and jaw set, Ben invades my personal space. "Don't say shit like that." He huffs, a thick cloud floating between us. "Don't fuck up our chances with a defeatist attitude." A step closer and we stand inches apart. "We will find her," he proclaims. "Or I will without you."

I nod and nod and nod, absorbing his confidence. "We'll find her. She'll be okay."

"Damn right. Now let's go."

With a boost of conviction, I command Pepper to inhale Kirsten's scent again and search for her. Pepper buries her nose in the sweater, inhales a few times, barks, and guides us deeper into the woods. Snow crunches beneath our boots as Pepper weaves us between the trees. While she leads, I let my mind drift.

Countless times, I have been in these woods. When I was a kid, before Dad turned the additional Emerson properties into rentals like the other Seven did, we came out here and camped two or three times a year. He and Mom brought us out here to get away from the gossip and internet. They wanted their children to not be sucked into digital misconceptions of the world.

We spent days hiking in these woods. Dad taught us how to navigate our way with a compass, marking our way, and by the stars at night, in case we got lost. Mom shocked us with her fire starting skills and ability to trap wildlife for food. My mom wasn't unskilled in the kitchen, but I'd only ever seen her expertise in action when someone wanted to buy or sell property.

But those mini-vacations in the woods were years ago. Though not much has changed in the Bay Cliff Mountain range, my sense of direction out here isn't what it once was. Distinct, curvy tree limbs and rotting trunks and moss-coated fallen trees I imprinted in my memory bear no resemblance to the snow-covered forest around us. The constellations I learned to navigate with are hidden behind clouds.

Every tool I have in my arsenal... useless. Close to a decade of not wandering these woods for hours and days on end has me aimless.

*But I won't give up, dammit. I can't.*

Pepper picks up the pace, her nose lowering an inch or two. A good sign.

"What is—" Ben's stride stutters, then resumes its normal pace.

I glance at his profile to see his eyes narrowed and head forward, trying to make something out. Immediately, I follow his line of sight. My eyes widen as I lengthen my strides.

Maybe a hundred yards away, soft light filters through the trees. I aim the flashlight at the ground and mimic Ben's reaction. The light isn't much—a camping lamp, perhaps. It wouldn't be odd for people to jump the property fence and camp on private land for free.

But this doesn't feel like some drifter. This doesn't feel like some adventurous cheapskate taking advantage of expansive, private property. Not in this weather.

Ben sidles up to me as we rush forward. Eager as I am to reach the source, to find my girl, we need to be smart. I call Pepper to my side and stop my trek toward what I pray is Kirsten.

"This needs to be flawless. If she's there"—I point at the light—"we can't fuck this up. One wrong move could mean life or death."

He nods. "I agree." With a slight bounce of his feet, he rubs his hands together, a wound-up ball of energy. "Tell me what to do."

# THIRTY-FOUR

## KIRSTEN

Tugging on the heavy, metal door-slash-bookcase, I peek through the wider crack and search for any sign of movement. Goose bumps dance over my skin, a shiver rolling up my spine as frigid darkness meets my probing gaze. Hand on the wall, I exit the creepy, 60s-style house and tiptoe through the blackness.

My nose wrinkles after a few steps, an unavoidable blend of mildew and death in the air. Icy metal beneath my fingers and feet raises my tightly wound anxiety up a notch. I draw in a lungful of air and hold it, shuffling my feet faster while my hands explore the wall.

Loud crackling echoes in the space and I freeze. My eyes dart through the darkness, looking for something, anything. I flatten myself against the wall in an effort to make myself invisible. My lungs burn, begging for fresh air. Slowly, silently, I exhale the breath I'd been holding. Then, I breathe tiny, quiet sips of air.

The crackle grows louder, louder, louder. But it is no match against the deafening whoosh of my pulse in my ears.

"There she is." A rough, cloaked voice breaks through the

crackle, through my erratic pulse, and comes at me from every direction. "My pretty little whore."

Oh god.

*Oh. My. Fucking. God.*

Instinctually, I knew whoever had been following me for months brought me to this place. Waking up cold and hurt in a prison disguised as an outdated home raised a thousand red flags. But hearing his garbled voice, hearing him call me a whore, *his whore*… it's one merciless punch after another to the solar plexus. A reality I chose to ignore but knew, deep down, existed.

*I need to get out of here. Now.*

Fingers clawing the wall, I shuffle and search for an exit. Something other than the door to the prison. The crackle simmers in the background, like the faint sound of bacon cooking in a hot skillet a room away. I squeeze my eyes closed and keep moving forward, one step at a time.

*I will get out of here.*

"I'll fuck you better than him, whore."

The backs of my eyes sting. My breathing turns jagged.

"I'll fuck you until you can't walk. Until your cunt and mouth and pretty little ass only know my cock."

I hit a corner and turn onto a different wall. Unlike the other room, this one seems empty. Just metal walls and a metal floor and nothing else.

"I'll fuck you until you beg for nothing and no one but me."

My palm brushes over something sharp, warm liquid coating my skin as I hiss.

"I'll take care of you."

Faint light illuminates the space enough to see inches in front of my face. I lift my hand to see a river of red spilling from my palm. Clutching my hand to my chest, I shuffle forward.

I hit another corner and turn, not a window or door in sight. With each step forward, with each breath I take, the seriousness of my situation becomes more real, clearer, hopeless. The door to the room I woke in comes into view and I wilt. Sliding down the wall, I hug my knees to my chest and drop my forehead to my knees.

With every last bit of strength I possess, I resist the urge to cry. I refuse to let this sicko best me.

Crackling rips through the air a beat before his voice. "Ready for some real fun, my pretty little whore?"

I shove back into the wall and push to stand.

"Time to play hide and seek," he says, voice deep and harsh. "You hide." Manic laughter bounces off the metal walls. "Because I can't wait to seek." The last word comes out as a hiss.

I move toward the door to the fake house, slipping between the crack seconds before metal slams against metal and everything goes black.

# THIRTY-FIVE

## SEEKER

SLIPPING THROUGH THE DOOR, SHE DISAPPEARS FROM VIEW.

But she won't for long.

On bare feet, I bolt for the door separating us. I slink inside and shut the door as my eyes survey the bunker. In seconds, I spot her, one hand on the wall while the other stretches out in front of her.

Just before I announced game time, I shut off the lights in the bunker. With no windows or doors to the outside world—not that that matters in the middle of the night—the soft incandescent bulbs are the only source of illumination. And without even a hint of light, she is sightless. Lost. Afraid.

But I see her plain as day.

Through the green glow of night vision goggles, I follow her every move. Watch her panic rise as she tries to escape and hide. With the rapid rise and fall of her chest, my dick swells, grows harder in my pants.

She moves to the far corner of the living room and squats, tucking her knees to her chest and making herself small. And for a moment, I simply gawk at her. Rub my throbbing dick through my pants. Inhale her sweet scent as it drifts through the room.

With quiet, slow steps, I diminish the distance between us, reach out, and caress the strands of her hair. Then I jerk back as she jolts from the touch. Eyes wide, she scrambles onto all fours and crawls across the room, moving to the opposite side of the couch.

I grant her a moment. Allow her to think she outsmarted me. Let her think I won't find her again.

As her breathing calms, I inch closer. As her frame relaxes, I suck in a deep breath, bend at the waist, then slowly exhale near her cheek. She tips on her side, scrambling to get her legs under her, to get her feet flat on the ground to stand.

Unable to help myself, I laugh, loud and foul and monstrous.

"Help!" she shrieks, the plea bouncing off the steel walls and going nowhere. Just like her.

Hands out in front of her, she rushes from the living room toward the kitchen. She slams into the counter, knocking a pot off the stove before smacking the dangling utensils.

"Run, run, as fast as you can," I singsong in a deep, sinister voice. "I'll catch you, I'm the seeker man."

"Help!" she screams louder as she turns the corner.

I count to twenty. Let her believe she outsmarted me again. Then follow in her wake on quiet feet. In seconds, I find her again, curled up in the corner of the pantry. Trapped.

Reaching for her, I tug at the strap of the negligee. She slams her shoulders into the wall, swatting her hands in the air. I go for the other strap, yanking it hard enough to tear the fabric. She kicks her leg out and hits my shin.

"Fucking bitch," I yell as she shimmies past me on all fours. "For that, I'll freshen your scars."

But she doesn't get far.

Because I am done. I've had my fun.

Now it's time to make her pay.

I lunge forward and clutch her hips. A deafening scream rips from her lungs as I haul her to my chest, her legs kicking the air.

"Shut the fuck up!" I bark in her ear as I exit the pantry and head for the bedroom. "Time to show me how good a whore you really are. And this time, I'll make the cuts deeper. I'll make them last."

# THIRTY-SIX

## TRAVIS

As we approach the shack, the faint light goes out.

"Shit," I mutter under my breath.

"What?" Ben whispers, fearful.

I pull out my phone to see a new message from Dad.

The closer we'd gotten to the light source, the more confused I'd been. The Emerson family owned this property, and others, for generations. My siblings and I had trekked almost every inch of terrain within its borders with our parents and grandparents.

And not once had I set eyes on this structure.

Weathered by years of summer sun and harsh winters, the ramshackle hut looked as if it'd crumble any minute.

*How have we never seen this?*

"Not a good sign." I jut my chin toward the shack. "Either he saw us or…"

I read Dad's message.

CHIEF

On our way. Wait for backup.

"Or what?"

I peer up from the screen and meet Ben's wide eyes. I don't want to lie to him, but more than that, I don't want to give a voice to what else I think it means.

*This sick fuck is about to make his move.*

I type a response to Dad and share my location.

> Can't wait. Situation escalated. Look for hut at my location.

I shove my phone in my pocket, shift my attention to Ben, and school my features. Personal as this is, I need to switch into officer mode and think strategically. Dissociate from the situation and focus on my training.

Detached expression locked in place, I admit, "Or shit just got real and we need to hurry."

Ben's face twitches and twists, then smooths out. I let him process while I map out our next steps.

Squatting down beside Pepper, I speak to her in hushed tones. Praise her for leading us to the shack. Tell her the perpetrator is in the building and I need her help. Command her to stay at my side until instructed otherwise.

"Help!"

I bolt upright, every muscle in my body taut. My heart clutches my rib cage with frantic fists and rattles my insides.

Ben whips around and locks on to the shack. "You hear that?"

Cocking my head, my brows pinch together as I nod. "Yeah." I step closer to the structure. "But it sounded muffled. Distant."

"What does that mean?"

My brain filters through one scenario after another. Countless settings and events taught to us in the police academy. The only thing that stands out…

*Never accept a crime scene to be only what you see with your eyes. Like everything in life, crime scenes are multifaceted. Multisensory. Approach a crime scene with this mindset... it is more than what your eyes tell you it is.*

If this shack is smaller than my bedroom, why did her scream sound farther away? Why did it sound smothered? If the perp gagged Kirsten, we wouldn't be able to make out her cry as easily. Her words would be unintelligible garble.

*Think, think, think.*

And then a memory hits hard. Between freshman and sophomore year of high school, I'd gone to the kitchen to grab snacks and drinks for me and Jacob. He stayed in the basement, battling zombies and trying to beat my high score. Just before I left the kitchen, he yelled for me to grab the red licorice. I'd barely heard him, his voice muted by the house level.

*She's underground.*

I face Ben, my shoulders stiff and muscles tight. "It means there is more to this dilapidated shack than meets the eye." Swallowing, I force out the next words. "It means she is underground."

"What the—"

"Ben, we don't have time to get emotional. We need to get in there. Now."

Ben tips his head back, inhales deeply, then levels his gaze and nods. "Tell me what to do."

An on-the-fly plan spills from my lips. "We'll circle the shack first, make sure there are no other surprises waiting in the wings. Once we have, we will enter quickly and quietly. Pepper will wait up here as we descend, in case the perp attempts escape."

"Seems straightforward," Ben says.

"True, but be prepared for anything. People like this aren't rational. They do crazy shit when provoked."

"Got it."

We circle the rundown hut and find nothing out of the ordinary. When we meet at the door, I give Pepper her commands. Her spine straightens and she huffs a low affirmation bark.

I retrieve my sidearm, and then we creep through the door. Enter the ramshackle cabin with the flashlight set to low. Inspect every crack and crevice and corner of the small space.

To the left is a rusty cot with a yellow and brown stained mattress. To the right, a covered five-gallon bucket and laptop on a splintered makeshift table; no chair. But directly across the room from the door, that is what holds my attention.

Paint peeling off the inside, a metal hatch door stands open on the floor. A yellow triangle with a black exclamation point in the middle warns to watch your head and back.

Not a basement. *A motherfucking bunker*. And by the looks of it, this damn bunker has been here a long fucking time.

My gaze shoots to Ben and I press a finger to my lips, indicating to be quiet. He nods. Leaning into him, I whisper, "I'll go down first." I hand him the flashlight. "You hold on to this." I pause and count to three. "Be prepared for anything."

"Help!" Kirsten's voice rips through the night, laden with panic.

"Now," I whisper-shout. "Let's go."

Pepper sits between the door and hatch as we descend into the unknown. One rung at a time, I go down the steel ladder. Thirteen rungs later, I hit the ground, stepping aside for Ben. Seconds later, he is at my side, shining the light around the room until he lands on a door.

Glock raised and aimed at the door, I advance with long, fluid strides. At the door, I listen for nearby movement. Uncertain of what lies on the other side, I slowly push the door open.

Inch through the opening and leave enough room for Ben to enter but for us to remain flush against the door.

Both inside, Ben does a slow scan of the space with the flashlight. My eyes bulge at the view. Ben leans into my side and whispers, "This is some fucking doomsday shit."

My thoughts exactly.

A stifled cry echoes through the room and both our heads swing right. I turn my aim in that direction and move. Light directed on the floor, Ben remains on my heels. We approach a short hall and her cries grow louder, more frantic.

Pausing, I peer over my shoulder, point to the room, the flashlight, then up as I signal us to walk into the room. An hour-long second passes before Ben nods. Attention back on the doorway, I take aim and proceed. As I pass the threshold, Ben cranks the flashlight to the brightest setting.

Shirtless and hovering inches above Kirsten, a scrawny man with dark, unkempt hair turns his head in our direction. Night vision goggles strapped to his head, his neck twitches as he regards us. Hunting knife in his fist, a sinister smile curves up the corners of his mouth as he presses the blade to her skin, drops his hips in the cradle of hers, and grinds himself against Kirsten.

Pulse deafening in my ears, my vision turns red.

I line the sick fuck up in my sight, inhale a deep breath, and squeeze the trigger on the exhale.

# THIRTY-SEVEN

## KIRSTEN

Pop, pop.

A violent scream rips from my lungs a beat before liquid heat coats my chest, the bed, my back. Weight suffocates me as my stalker collapses. My eyes drift shut as I try and fail to take a deep breath. Limbs tingling, panic swirls in my chest as I fight to move and make no progress. Whiskey and sweat invade my nose as I struggle to escape.

Lungs on fire, I open my eyes and will my arms and legs to move. Demand my body get out from under this demented madman. To escape his nauseating scent and skin on mine.

Light flickers and flashes as I fight against his weight. And then Travis enters my line of sight.

He shoves the man off me and I gasp, filling my lungs with stale, cool air. His hands hover over my face. I sit up and drop my gaze to my torso, taking in the red-soaked nightie. Frenetic energy swirls in my belly, beneath my breastbone as I pat the material.

"Not your blood, baby," Travis whispers. "It's over now. I've got you."

My gaze shoots up, eyes darting between his as my chin

wobbles. I open my mouth to ask if it is really over, but can't find my voice.

Travis looks over his shoulder. I follow his line of sight and land on a pale Ben just inside the room.

"Find her clothes, please?"

Ben looks from the man on the bed to me to Travis, then nods.

When it's just me and Travis, he frames my face with his hands, waits for me to meet his gaze, and softens his expression once I do. "Let's get you out of this." He tugs at the still-intact strap.

"O-okay," I choke out.

Travis drags the material up and off my body, careful not to let the bloody fabric touch me anywhere else. I cross my arms over my chest, an endless shiver racking my body that has nothing to do with the temperature. Travis shrugs off his jacket and drapes it over my shoulders just as Ben returns with my clothes.

"I'll just be…" I glance across the room as Ben thumbs over his shoulder and out of the room.

Rising from the edge of the bed, Travis holds out his hands and helps me up. I hand him back his jacket, then look down my body. Blood stains my bra, my abdomen, most of my panties. The backs of my eyes sting as I curl my fingers so tight my knuckles burn.

"Hey." Travis bends his knees and meets my gaze. He cups my cheek, his thumb caressing the plump skin beneath my eye. "Let me see if the water works. We can wipe this off. Okay?"

I nod and nod and nod as tremors shoot through me, head to toe.

Travis jogs out of the room and I shuffle as far from the bed as possible. Turning away from the lunatic on the bed, I reach back and unclasp my bra. Let it fall to the floor and take a deep breath. Travis returns as I shove my underwear down my legs and kick them away.

Ever so slowly, he lowers his lips to my shoulder and presses a soft kiss on my skin. I tremble under his touch for one, two, three heartbeats before tears spill down my cheeks and the dam lets loose. Travis wraps an arm around my shoulders and holds me up as I fall apart.

"I'm here." He kisses my temple. "I've got you now, baby."

For endless minutes, we stay like this. I sob while he holds me in his arms and whispers reassurances.

The moment is cut short when Pepper's bark rings through the air. A booming, cautious announcement to whoever approaches.

Travis kisses my temple, then steps back and hands me a damp washcloth. "Clean up and dress. That's probably my dad with reinforcements." He moves toward the door, his eyes never leaving mine. "Be right back. It's only me, Ben, Pepper, and whoever just arrived. You're safe now."

My brow tightens as I swallow then nod.

Travis exits the room just as his name is shouted in the distance.

I scrub as much of the blood off my skin as possible before slipping my clothes back on. Grabbing the flashlight from the dresser, I bolt out of the room and search for my shoes. Ben stands in the middle of the living room. I spot my shoes near the couch and tug them on quickly.

"This place is creepy as fuck," he whispers.

I open my mouth to say it's the place where nightmares are made, but don't get a word out. The overhead lights flip on a second before stomps echo through the antiquated bunker. I squint and shield my eyes as several people enter the space, Chief Emerson at the forefront.

Travis steps around him and points toward the bedroom. "Perp's back there." He crosses the room to me and offers his hand. I take it and rise from the couch. "I'm taking Kirsten back to the cabin. Meet us there when you're done."

"Officer Emerson," Chief barks out. "She should stay until we question her."

Travis turns an icy glare on his father. "Anything you need to ask can be done at the cabin." The muscles in his jaw flex. "All due respect, she needs out of here." He laces his fingers with mine and starts for the door. "You know where to find us."

Wrapped in three blankets, tremors shake me to the bone as I sit next to the wood stove on the floor. Trixie nestles in my lap, her sweet purr soothing as I stroke her fur. Pepper lies beside me, head on my thigh, as she surveys the room.

On the couch, Ben sits on the edge of the cushions, his right knee bouncing without restraint. Up and down, over and over. I blink and let my gaze drift up. Arms tightly folded over his chest, Ben's fingers wring the cotton of his shirt. On a hard swallow, tension lines his jaw a beat before his expression twists in frustration or concern.

Chief Emerson walked through the cabin's front door minutes ago. And since then, he and Travis have been bickering in muted tones near the laundry room.

Rather than lean in and eavesdrop, I center my attention on everything else. The crackle of the fire. Trixie's happy purrs. Pepper's refusal to give an inch of space. Ben's fidgety frame. The soft but constant patter of snow on the roof of the cabin.

But all those distractions fade to the background as Chief Emerson and Travis wander back into the room.

Chief Emerson pauses near the breakfast bar. My eyes lock on his, familiar yet foreign golden honey eyes stare back. Soft crow's feet accent the corners. His skin paler and spotted with age. Where Travis has sharp lines and noticeable scruff on his square jaw, his father has softer, clean-shaven edges.

Is this what Travis will look like in twenty years? Prominent genetics that smooth with time.

"Ms. Sparks—"

Travis elbows his father as he mumbles, "Kirsten."

Lips in a flat line, Chief takes a deep breath and starts over on the exhale. "Kirsten, I need to ask some questions. I understand this is a difficult time, but it's best not to wait. The more time that passes, the more specific details may fade."

Dropping my gaze to Trixie, I lightly scratch her cheek. She leans into the touch, purring louder. When I meet his stare again, nervous energy swirls beneath my diaphragm. "He's... dead?" My brows cinch together. "The man in the bunker, he's dead?"

Travis on his heels, Chief eats up the space between us before squatting down a foot from where I sit on the floor.

"Yes, Kirsten. The man is dead." He reaches out and pats my knee before rising back to his full height. Off to the side, he sits in a guest chair, rubs his palms down his thighs, and pauses a beat before meeting my eyes. "Is the name Charles Yatz familiar?"

My eyes lose focus as I search my mind for the name. I repeat countless conversations I've had with patrons at the restaurant. Play back the nights I went out with friends, trying to recall the men that introduced themselves in the hopes of scoring a night of fun.

I close my eyes and clench them until they sting, until white flashes behind my lids.

*Think, think, think. Charles Yatz. Charles Yatz. Charles…*

Holy. Fucking. Shit.

A hand flies to my mouth as the backs of my eyes sting for a new reason. In a flash, Travis is in front of me, hands on my cheeks, thumbs stroking my skin as he soothes my sudden realization.

"You're okay, sunshine." His lips press mine with a chaste kiss. "You're safe."

Leaning into his touch, I give a subtle nod. Travis wipes tears from my cheeks, kisses my forehead, then inches back.

I twist to look at Chief. "Not sure of his last name, but the only Charles I know is at the pharmacy in the market." Confusion is a fiery tornado in my chest as I recall every interaction I had with Charles. His grumpy nature and strange commentary. Most days, he'd been cordial, with generic greetings and obligatory conversation. But our most recent interaction was… bizarre. "Last time I picked up my prescription," I start, flashing back to early November, "he said the most uncomfortable thing." I meet Chief's unyielding gaze and swallow. "It was right around when the woman in the woods was discovered and people were clearing shelves in the market."

Travis rests his hand near my knee, his thumb drawing lazy circles. "Whenever you're ready."

I drop my chin to my chest, blink back tears of disappointment. Disappointment with myself for not putting this together sooner. For not seeing the signs right in front of me. For not saying something to someone, anyone.

Though I only stopped at the pharmacy every three months for my prescription, I saw Charles more often. It wasn't odd for him to eat at the restaurant once or twice a week this past year. Majority of the town pulled up a chair at Poke the Yolk and chitchatted with the staff. I didn't always wait on him, but waved in the hopes of cheering him up.

Obviously, he took my smiles and gestures and politeness as something else.

"Looking back, I still see the judgment on his face as he handed over my birth control." Lava flows through my veins as the memory hits. "He made this snappy comment. Something about being more careful who I take home with a killer on the loose." With a shake of my head, I laugh without humor. "It pissed me off, but I ignored it. Smiled and told him to have a better day. Passed it off as a man still mad at his ex-wife for leaving with their child."

God, I am a fucking idiot.

"Kirsten." I meet Chief's eyes. "This is not on you. He was a sick man that needed help." He takes out his phone, taps the screen a few times, then types a lengthy note. When he finishes, he rises from the chair. "We'll search for the ex-wife and reach out." With one long stride, he rests a hand on my shoulder. "But this is over now."

I nod, then narrow my eyes before meeting his. "What about the bunker?"

Chief winces, steps toward the door, and shrugs on his coat. "Unfortunately, that one is on me."

Travis straightens to his full height and looks at his dad. "What? How?"

Slipping on leather gloves, he zips up his coat. "The bunker has been there since the 1950s." He tugs a beanie on his head. "Your great-grandfather had it installed. Life was pretty rocky at the time and he wanted a safe place for the family in case things hit the fan."

"So Big Papa G put a bomb shelter in the middle of the woods?"

The corner of Chief's mouth curves up as a memory hits

him. "When I was a boy, paranoia was Papa G's middle name." His lips shift to a softer smile. "But he grew up in a different time. And before he went off to war, he wanted to know his family would be safe."

Travis cocks his head as his brows knit together. "But why the middle of nowhere?"

"It wasn't in the middle of nowhere. A wood cabin sat about ten yards from the hatch until the late eighties. Built at the turn of the century, it slowly fell apart with no one maintaining it. Papa G, Dad, and I spent weeks tearing it down. Dad reminisced about playing in the shelter for years as a boy. Mom had redecorated it in the seventies, wanting to modernize it in case we ever used it." He shoves his hands in his pockets and shakes his head. "Of the cabin, we took what wouldn't break down in the forest to the dump but left the rest to decompose." He sucks in a sharp breath. "And some of those pieces formed the shack over the hatch. Had I taken the time to routinely check the properties, maybe I'd have found it ages ago. It's probably been some vagrant's home for years."

Vexation etches lines in the expressions of both Emerson men. Both berating themselves mentally for not doing more. Without a doubt, Chief is angry he and his family didn't drive off with all the pieces of the old cabin. Had they, the shack would never have existed. And Travis is undoubtedly upset he didn't know about the shack or bunker. Had he hiked the woods more recently, he would have stumbled across it and saved all this from happening.

But neither is to blame.

The future is a kaleidoscope of unpredictable uncertainty. No one foresees a person building a shack in the woods above an abandoned bomb shelter. No one predicts an unstable individual will use the space to torture and kill women.

Hell, I missed the signs right in front of my face. After his unsavory commentary at the pharmacy, why hadn't I mentioned it to anyone? Why hadn't I been more uncomfortable seeing Charles in the restaurant afterward? Not a single red flag waved in my head. Not a single alarm went off in warning. Nothing made me connect him to the unwelcome, disturbing notes or gift. My sympathy for Charles's situation obviously overshadowed my common sense and intuition.

If the Emerson men want to blame themselves, fine. Nothing I say or do will change their minds. But if they take an ounce of responsibility on their shoulders, how can I not do the same?

Eyes unfocused on the floorboards, my fingers stroking Trixie's soft fur, the door creaks as Chief and Travis exit the cabin. Their conversation is dull in my ears, but I don't miss Chief's words, "I'm proud of you, Travis. But next time, please wait for backup."

Brown leather boots invade my line of sight, denim-clad legs bending as Ben squats inches from where I sit. He lays a hand on my knee and squeezes. "It's over now, sparkles."

I study the stitching on his flannel. Home in on the tightly woven lines of black and green and blue until my eyes rove over ivory buttons. One button, then another, until my tired, stormy irises land on serene turquoise ones.

With a heavy sigh, I relax for the first time in weeks, months. "I'm ready to go home."

# THIRTY-EIGHT

## BEN

Exhausted is an understatement as daybreak filters through the trees and shines down on the foot of white powder blanketing Stone Bay.

As we pack our bags and put the cabin to rights, the Chief and his team leave the property with a zipped-up body bag. As we load everything into the vehicles, beeping and crunching echo through the trees.

Travis sets the cooler in the back of his truck. "Snowplow." He shrugs a bag off his shoulder and stows it in the bed. "Dad called it in, mainly to get past the gate."

Engines warmed and the last of our belongings in the cars, we drive off the property and toward the heart of Stone Bay. The entire drive, my fingers itch to call Kirsten. To tell her and Travis to meet me at the inn. To grab my duffel from the back, stumble to my room at the inn, fall face first on the bed, and sleep for two solid days. And then check out and drive back to Smoky Creek. Alone.

But I don't call her. I don't give voice to my thoughts.

A glutton for punishment, I park in her driveway. Help unload his truck and her SUV. Amble into the living room and collapse on the couch. Peek at the other end of the couch, frown, then shift my gaze anywhere but at Kirsten as she snuggles into Travis's neck.

Every rational thought in my head screams for me to get up and leave. To give Kirsten one last hug, one last kiss on the forehead. To tell her I'll always love her, even if she doesn't feel the same. To text Aaron for a ride, grab my bag, and walk out the door.

But fuck, my heart begs for one last shot. Pleads with me to try one more time. Implores me to put it all on the line and bare my soul.

Words on the tip of my tongue, a kaleidoscope of butterflies flapping in my chest, I open my mouth to tell Kirsten how much I love her. How I always will, and that she is who I want.

But the words never leave my lips.

Travis buries his face in the crook of her neck, crushes her to his chest, and says, "I love you so fucking much, sunshine." A stuttering breath leaves him a beat before his body shakes and sobs fill the air. "Was so fucking scared."

Fingers in his hair, she curls into his quaking frame. "Love you too, Trav." Muffled sniffles fill the air, her voice chafed and garbled with emotion. "Never been more scared in my life."

The words on my tongue evaporate and I straighten in my seat. And then I'm rising from the couch. Kirsten inches back and heats my profile with her stare. Studies what I'm sure is a pained expression on my face.

Before she says anything, I speak up. "Gonna head out. I'm beat."

She sits up straighter but doesn't leave Travis's lap. "Stay. Sleep in Skylar's old room. Dee Dee won't mind." Wiping a hand under her eyes, she sniffles. "Please, Benji."

A Kirsten-shaped fissure forms beneath my sternum and splits me in two at the sound of my childhood nickname. But I shove down my pain and bury it deep. Don't let her see an ounce of the agony gnawing at my soul.

I fetch my boots in the foyer and slip them on. As I tie the laces, a war wages inside me—my heart says there is still hope while my head yells to bolt now. God, how I want to cave to her pleas. How I want to read more into her words and believe she will run into my arms and never let go.

Minutes pass as I fumble with the simple task. As I fight the urge to take her up on the offer.

Then a moment of clarity strikes.

In her own way, Kirsten loves me. It'd be foolish to ignore such a thing. But her love for me will never be the love I want or deserve from her.

I want endless devotion and adoration. Bubbly laughter from mini versions of me and my future wife. I want adventure and surprise and passion. To hold her hand in mine as we watch our children grow, as our hair grays and skin weathers. To be the person she can't live without, the one she chooses above all others.

Walking away from Kirsten is hard enough. Last thing I need to do is make it worse—for me more than her.

It's time to rip off the bandage. Time to let go of the notion Kirsten and I will ever be more than friends.

Kirsten made her choice. And he isn't me.

Now, I need to move on.

Head high, shoulders back, heart broken, I cross the room to her and Travis. Hinging at the hips, I press my lips to her crown, close my eyes, and inhale one last pull of her sweet fragrance. "Love you, sparkles." I school my features and straighten my spine. "But it's time for me to go," I mutter.

Kirsten scrambles in Travis's lap and he groans. "Ben, no. Stay."

Reluctantly, I step back and shake my head. "Glad you're safe." I glance past her to Travis. "Take care of her, man."

Without a word, he dips his chin. A fool, he is not. Travis knows exactly what I am doing. Knows I am being the bigger person and walking away. Because if I don't, this back and forth will never end. Kirsten's heart is too damn big to let go.

Kirsten bolts off the couch and steps into my space. Tears rim her eyes as she holds my weary gaze. "Benji, no…"

Saliva pools in my mouth as emotion clogs my throat. The backs of my eyes burn, but I refuse to let a single tear fall. I lift a hand to her face and brush my knuckles down her jaw. "It's okay, sparkles." Swallowing, I nod. "No matter what, you'll always be my friend."

"Best friend," she chokes out.

"Best friend," I repeat, tilting her chin up. Then I lean in and press a chaste kiss to her soft lips. "I love you, Kirsten." I drop my hand and step back. "But it's time for me to go home."

And before she says another word, I pivot on my heel, rush to the foyer, scoop up my bag, and walk out the door.

# THIRTY-NINE

## KIRSTEN

One day. Just one.

One day of normalcy. One day without a text or phone call asking if I am okay, if I slept peacefully. A single day without half the town showing up at my front door with a casserole dish or sympathetic smile or random bouquet of flowers or confections.

Just one damn day without people hovering as if I'll break. One day that I don't feel people staring at me as I add groceries to my cart. One day without the whispers and gossip and the occasional *She's lucky to be alive.*

All I want is one day.

To wake up beside Travis and start the day with mind blowing sex and an equally hot shower. To dress in a slightly revealing V-neck and worn denim before adding a light layer of makeup to my face. To hop online and do a live with my followers. To walk into work, tie on my apron, greet everyone who enters with a warm smile, and receive one in return. To hear the Stone Bay gossipmongers talk about something else, anything else.

"One," I whisper as I stare at my reflection in the bathroom mirror.

But that one day isn't today. Unfortunately.

I spit toothpaste into the sink, stow the toothbrush, and rinse my mouth as Travis secures a towel around his waist. He steps up behind me, fists my hips through the terry cloth hugging my torso, and drops his lips to my bare shoulder. Eyes closed, I tip my head back and give him more access.

Arms band around my middle as he peppers kisses up the length of my neck. He pauses beneath my ear, sucks my pulse point, and growls as I rub myself over his length.

"Much as I want to bend you over this counter and fuck you into next week"—he bites his way down to the curve of my shoulder—"the doorbell will ring any minute."

"Ugh!" Fingernails bite my palms as fists form at my sides. Lifting my head, I meet Travis's ambers in the mirror. "Would everyone hate me if I texted and said leave me alone?"

Travis takes my hands in his, relaxing my fingers as he places another kiss on my shoulder. The corner of his mouth crooks up in a panty-melting half smile. "No one will hate you, sunshine." *Kiss.* "But it won't stop them." *Kiss.* "And if not today, it'll be tomorrow and every day that follows for weeks."

I close my eyes, shake like a petulant child not getting what they want, and groan louder than necessary. "Fine," I bite out. "But if anyone treats me like I'm some breakable object, I'm kicking them out."

Chuckling, Travis holds his hands up in surrender. "Your call, sunshine." Then he invades my space again. Fists my hips with strong hands. Brings his lips to my ear and nips the lobe. "But what if I want to break you."

A shameless moan slips from my lips as my eyes roll back. I reach up and release the tucked end of my towel. Tempt him one more time. Bare myself to him as I bite my bottom lip.

Skin hot and pink from the shower, I trail my hands up my body. Over the curves of my hips and dip of my waist. Pert rosy nipples reflect in the mirror and beg for his mouth, his tongue, his teeth. His eyes fixed on my fingers, I cup my breasts and squeeze once before pinching both nipples between my fingers. His hands on my hips grip harder, firmer as I tug my nipples. A brusque moan rumbles in his chest, sending a delicious shiver through my body.

His eyes fall shut as the muscles of his jaw tighten. Rising and falling, faster and faster, his chest crushes my towel pinned between us. His fingers bruise my hips and hold me in place, his erection thickening between my ass cheeks.

Then his grip on my hips loosens. The muscles of his jaw relax. His breathing settles into its normal rhythm.

*He's fighting it.* And fuck, it's sexy as hell.

But when molten ambers possess my stormy blues in the mirror, I *see* his will caving. And before my next breath, he steps back and both our towels hit the floor.

Hand between my shoulder blades, he forces me down until my cheek smacks the mirror. A finger swipes the length of my slick pussy and I moan.

"Does that turn you on, baby?" He lines the tip of his cock with my entrance, slicking the head with my arousal. "The thought of me breaking you?"

I moan. "Yes."

He hinges at the hips and brings his lips to my ears. "Don't have time for that now." His tongue darts out and licks the shell of my ear. "Hours and days and weeks." His tip dips inside me. "I will fuck you until your legs are numb. Until my cum permanently stains your thighs. Until you beg me to stop."

I push my hips back on another moan. "I never want you to stop."

Rising to his full height, one hand takes my hip in a bruising hold while the other trails up my spine, slips around my neck, and clutches my throat. "Good girl," he praises. "Now, brace yourself. This'll be quick."

Travis slams forward and fills me fully. Our moans vibrate the room for a beat before he inches back out and crashes into me again. Seated fully, he tightens his hold on my throat and lifts me off the mirror.

"Look how fucking perfect you are." He bites my shoulder. "Watch as I take what's mine."

And then he pistons his hips, pounding into me over and over, hard and fast and greedy. Skin slaps skin as our grunts and moans and cries fill the air. His hand on my hip drifts between my thighs, his expert fingers circling my clit with precision. Again and again, he hits that spot deep inside me as he fucks me raw.

Fire sparks low in my belly and crawls up my chest, my neck, my cheeks, painting my skin red.

"That's it, baby. Give it to me."

I reach up and pinch my nipples. Twist and tug and tweak them painfully. Whimper as my orgasm builds and builds.

The doorbell rings.

"Time's up, baby." Travis slows his hips.

I level my stare with his in the mirror. "Don't you dare fucking stop."

He chuckles with a shake of his head a beat before all amusement vanishes from his expression. "Might want to hold on to something."

And then he takes both of my hips in his hands and pummels me over and over. I grip the edge of the counter and faucet as he hammers me with his cock. Sweat slicks our skin as high-pitched moans mix with raspy grunts.

"I'll get it," Delilah calls from outside the room, followed by a laugh.

Travis reaches between my thighs, circles my clit once, twice, three times before I detonate. White spots fill my vision as an inferno blazes beneath my skin. My heart bangs, bangs, bangs beneath my breast bone. The hiss of white noise clogs my ears.

As my vision clears, a throaty growl echoes in the room. In the mirror, I revel in Travis's reflection. Jaw slack and eyes on me, lust drunk, his brows pinch together. His hips jerk, his fingers curling and nails biting my skin. And then he buries himself to the hilt as he spills inside me.

Voices seep through the walls as we slowly pull apart. The evidence of our hot, spur-of-the-moment quickie paints my thighs.

Travis kisses my shoulder and mumbles against my skin. "Trouble maker." He grabs a washcloth, runs it under warm water, then cleans between my thighs. "But I like your brand of trouble."

More food, more noise, more people. Today will not be my one day of normalcy. But at least everyone is here for a reason other than my abduction a week ago.

"Merry Christmas Eve Eve," Skylar singsongs as I open the front door. She scurries inside, shrugs off her coat, and wraps me in a fierce hug. "We brought wine and appetizers." She inches back and peers over her shoulder at Lawrence. "Someone distracted me while making them, though." Her eyes narrow on him in mock annoyance before smoothing out to meet my amused expression. "So there's no guarantee on what they look like."

I snort, lifting a hand to my mouth to hide my smile. "Now I can't wait to see what they look like."

Closing the door, Skylar and Lawrence toe off their shoes and follow me to the kitchen. Delilah glances up from her spot at the stove, cinnamon and clove permeating the air as she stirs her spiced apples, a moment before Skylar tackles her with a hug.

Lawrence sidles up to me and sets a tote on the counter. "She may have had some wine while assembling the appetizers," he whispers so only I hear.

A breath of laughter leaves my lips. "I'll take carefree, super-happy Skylar any day of the week."

And the fact she is relaxed enough to not worry over my well-being.

Cheery holiday music plays loud enough to hear but not drown out conversation. Warmth blankets the house from food cooking in the kitchen and a fire crackling in the living room. Herbs and garlic and the sweet scent of spiced apples infiltrate the air. Packages wrapped in silver and blue, red and green, and black and gold lay beneath a brightly lit evergreen on the far wall of the living room.

For the first time in months, a sense of calm washes over me and soothes my soul.

I pluck a grape and square of cheese from one of the appetizer platters and pop them in my mouth. Leaning against the counter near Delilah, my stomach grumbles as I stare down at the apples.

"How was winter solstice?"

She turns off the burner and moves the pot to a trivet to cool. "Great. Peaceful." A smile lights her face. "June made a killer persimmon and pomegranate salad."

"Ooh, nice."

"And Jet invited Shanti," she says with raised brows.

"Still hasn't asked her out, I assume."

Fetching fresh mint from the fridge, she rinses the sprigs, pats them dry, then plucks the leaves from the stems. "Nope. My dear, sweet brother refuses to admit he's in love with his best friend."

Eyes on Travis in the living room with his parents, I take one of the stems and tear off the leaves. "When the time is right, everything will fall into place." I blink and refocus on my task. "Speaking of timing…" I roll my lips between my teeth and bite back my smile. "Bump into Phoebe anymore?"

Before we left for the cabin weeks ago, Delilah told me she literally collided with Phoebe in the library. They rounded the corner of a tall shelf at the same time, neither of them paying attention. Of course, Phoebe snapped and told Delilah to watch where she was going. As if she wasn't equally at fault.

Later that day, Delilah stopped by the Gazette and asked for Phoebe. Her big heart urged her to apologize again. But she didn't get the chance. The woman at reception said Phoebe was unavailable.

Delilah's cheeks flush as she gathers the mint stems and chucks them in the compost bin. "Uh, no." Fetching a small bowl from the cabinet, she scoops the mint leaves up and dumps them in the bowl. "For whatever reason, she avoids me at all costs."

"Her loss," I say, hooking an arm around her shoulders.

"Thanks, K."

Minutes after the buzzer on the stove goes off, plates are loaded up with a little of everything. One by one, we gather around the table and fill our bellies with too much food.

Linda—Travis's mom—asks my mom what she loves about Stone Bay and if she misses Smoky Creek after years away. I don't miss the hint of sadness that shadows Mom's face for a moment before she shares her love for both towns.

Oliver tries his hand at being a smart ass, asking about Ben in a suggestive way. But I spin the conversation immediately and ask why he didn't bring Levi today. That shut him up real fast. We don't make a point to razz Oliver about Levi, but Skylar, Delilah, and I all know he's in love with his best friend. Has been for years. He just hasn't found a way to say or act on how he feels.

Dinner goes by without a single mention of my abduction. Thank goodness.

A week ago, as the sky pinked and the sun peeked over the mountains, Charles Yatz was delivered to Stone Bay Memorial and wheeled into the morgue, a bullet lodged in his heart, a second in his lung. Though we will never know for certain, it is assumed Charles is responsible for the woman in the woods. With all the sadistic things Charles did to me—in the bunker and leading up to my abduction—it's difficult to believe otherwise. His indirect admission about scarring my body years ago and wanting to do it again…

A shiver rolls up my spine.

I have never wished ill will on someone, but Charles Yatz's death brings me peace. Cold as it sounds, the world is a better place without him walking the earth.

"So…" Mom bumps my arm with her elbow. I blink away my wayward thoughts. "Things seem pretty serious between you and Travis."

My cheeks heat as I stab the last potato on my plate and shrug. "Maybe."

A soft smile curves the corners of her mouth. "The way he looks at you…"

I finish chewing my bite, swallow, and widen my eyes at her. "What?"

"Your father would approve."

Warmth blooms in my chest as tears sting the backs of my eyes. Beneath the table, Travis rests his hand on my thigh. I peek at him out of the corner of my eye, but his gaze is elsewhere as he carries on a conversation. Either he was eavesdropping on my conversation with Mom or he simply knew I needed his touch in the moment.

Inhaling deeply, I blink away the tears and nod. "Yeah, he would," I agree.

Our plates empty and we clear the table. Delilah sets up dessert on the kitchen island and we load smaller plates with chocolate cake, spiced apples, whipped coconut cream, and fresh fruit sprinkled with mint. Over the last course, we talk about holidays and gifts and gratitude for time together.

Small gifts between friends get exchanged. Oliver's gift to everyone is a band tee for Hailey's Fire. Delilah hands out gift certificates to Page by Paige. Lawrence tells Skylar her gift isn't appropriate for company and we all laugh. But Skylar and Lawrence give CKI gift certificates good at any of their restaurants. Oliver and I share an unamused look, then laugh. The parents tell us we will get gifts in a couple days at their house.

And then Travis hands me a small box. Small enough to be a ring box.

*No. He wouldn't do that already. Would he?*

All eyes on me, I slowly peel away the paper and take off the lid. My body wilts—in disappointment and relief—when I don't see a jewelry box inside. With nimble fingers, I unfold the tissue paper and stop breathing.

Not jewelry. But equally significant.

"You're killing us, K," Oliver whines from his spot next to the tree.

I roll my eyes at him. "Shush, you." Then I shift my gaze to Travis. "Really?"

Hand on my thigh, he strokes my denim-clad leg with his thumb. "Only if you want to."

My eyes drift back to the key with the question *move in?* etched on the bow, a buzz swirling beneath my diaphragm.

Are we ready for this? To move in together?

Yes, I have known Travis for years. Our chemistry has been fire as far back as I remember. But everything is still new with us. Relationships have never been my strong suit. And his last relationship was when?

Moving in together feels like going from zero to a hundred in a blink.

And I don't know if I am ready for the next step.

# FORTY

## TRAVIS



"Can you give us a moment?" I say to the room, not taking my eyes off Kirsten.

Oliver groans as he sidles up to Lawrence. "I'm always the last to know," he mutters.

Mom rests her hand on my shoulder, bends, and kisses my temple without a word. Seconds later, Dad gives my shoulder a squeeze, then pats it once before he follows Mom out of the room.

Since Kirsten's abduction, Dad has bombarded me less with what it means to be an Emerson in Stone Bay. Something about that night changed him. Hell, that night changed us all. But maybe it was the close call of another victim on his watch that gave him perspective. Maybe it was the fact his eldest son was in the scariest situation this town has seen in decades. Or maybe he got a true glimpse of how precious and short our time truly is on earth.

Whatever the reason, it is nice to see this softer, more affectionate side of him. To know he's proud of me as a man and a protector.

Once the room clears and no one stands within earshot, I

bring a hand to Kirsten's chin and lift her gaze to mine. Tears rim her stormy irises as her bottom lip starts to quiver. With a slow shake of my head, I brush the pad of my thumb over that plump lip.

"Please don't cry, sunshine." I lean in and press my lips to her forehead. "I didn't mean to upset you." Inching back, I cup her cheeks in my palms. Stroke her soft skin with my calloused thumbs. "If you're not ready or if this isn't something you want, tell me. I won't be mad." Dropping my forehead to hers, I hold her stare. "It just feels right… taking the next step with you," I confess on a whisper.

Her brow furrows as her eyes dart between mine. "What if I mess this up?"

"Moving?" Incredulity laces the single-word question.

With a roll of her eyes, she huffs. "No, smart ass." On an audible swallow, she trails her fingers up my forearms and curls them around my wrists. "Us. Our relationship." Her eyes fall shut as her breathing picks up. "I've never done this. Committed to someone."

"Hey," I whisper, my lips a breath from hers. "Look at me, please." Thumbs stroking her cheeks, I give her a moment. Let her do this at her pace. And when her red, veiny eyes meet mine, tears sting the backs of my own. "I love you, Kirsten. Confessing that truth…" I inhale a shaky breath. "It terrifies me."

"I love you, too." Tears roll down her cheeks in parallel lines and I wipe them away. "And I want to say yes, but…"

Silent, I wait for her to say more, to finish her thought. But nothing comes.

"But what, baby?"

"What if I l-lose you?" she chokes out the words as more tears spill down her cheeks.

I swipe at the tears, then kiss the wet stains on her cheeks. "Not a chance in hell, sunshine."

Kirsten inches back and looks over my shoulder. Curiosity eats at me, but I don't turn to see who has her attention. I simply watch her as she stares on and gets lost in thought. I tuck loose strands behind her ear. Trail a finger down her jaw, following the action with my eyes. Study the edges of her soft, plump lips and lick my own. Sweep my way slowly up the bridge of her nose, over the faint patch of freckles, until my eyes meet hers.

"When Mom started spending more time with Joseph," she pauses and takes a steadying breath, "I was so angry." She worries her lips between her teeth. "I thought, how can she disrespect my dad like that? How can she show interest in someone else?"

Something about her confession tells me to remain tight-lipped and give her this opportunity. A chance to release a weight she has carried far too long. To let go of the guilt or shame shadowing her soul.

"It took years for me to accept Joseph and his daughter, Lola. And then one day, Mom had this undeniable glow about her." Glassy-eyed, Kirsten clamps her lips between her teeth and sniffles. "Was the same she had with Dad." A soft smile tugs at the corners of her mouth. "She'd found happiness again. Love."

I cradle Kirsten's hands in mine, my thumbs brushing her knuckles. "That's a good thing. Right?"

Kirsten nods. "It is." She sniffles. "But I wonder if she would've moved on as easily if she'd been home that night, too. If she'd been in the house and heard the gunshot as she hid from the intruder. If she'd had to wait until the coast was clear, only to find my dad in a pool of his own blood."

Emotion swells in my throat as I give her hands a gentle

squeeze. "Had she been home, I'm sure things would've been a lot different."

"I want to wipe that memory away, Trav. I want to move forward." Her chin wobbles as she holds my stare. "I want to believe nothing like this will happen to me again."

God, how I want to grant this wish for her. To tell her what happened when she was a little girl was a fluke. A wrong place, wrong time type of situation. Tell her that her stalker was a sick man who needed help. That his actions are not a reflection of her.

But I can't say such things. I can't promise her an unforeseen future. And I definitely can't say something that would tarnish her dad's memory and what happened to him and her.

I drop a kiss to her tear-stained lips. "Tomorrow isn't promised, sunshine. I wish it was." I reach up and toy with the ends of her hair. "All we can do is live in the now. Live and laugh and love. Keep the memory of others alive as we move forward."

She drags a finger under her nose and sniffles with a nod.

"It's unfortunate I'll never meet your dad. But I bet he'd want you to *live*. Experience all life has to offer and never miss a moment."

"He would," she rasps.

I bring a hand to her chin and lift until her eyes lock with mine. "This is not me trying to persuade you into saying yes." I pause for a beat and she nods. "When you're ready, I want this step with you." My knuckles caress her cheek. "More than anything, I need *you*. Whether in the same space or not."

Warm, salty lips crash down on mine. Dainty fingers trail slowly up my chest, snaking around my neck and up into my hair. A soft sigh spills from her lips and I swallow every drop as my arms band around her middle. Somehow, the kiss doesn't escalate into *not safe for friends and family* territory. And when I hug her closer to my frame, she breaks the kiss.

"Yes," she whispers.

My brows pinch together. "Yes?"

Fingers in my hair, stormy eyes latch on to my ambers, she nods subtly. "Yes, Travis. I'd love to move in with you."

"About fucking time. Ugh!" Oliver groans from the other room.

"Thanks for the privacy, Ollie," Kirsten shouts. "I'll remember that next time Levi comes in for breakfast."

"Got nothing to hide," he says, strolling into the room with everyone in his wake.

"You sure about that?" Delilah pipes up, then shifts her gaze from Oliver to Kirsten and then Skylar. "You forget how long we've known you."

Oliver narrows his gaze, his head tipping slightly to the side. "Right back at ya, Fox."

Much as I love this town, there are too many damn secrets. But as I glance around the room, as family and friends congratulate us on taking the next step in our relationship, there is nowhere else I want to live. No one else I want by my side as we navigate what happens next.

"Love you, sunshine."

The corner of her mouth kicks up in a half-smile that warms my chest. "Love you too, *Officer*."

# EPILOGUE

## KIRSTEN

*Mid-January—Three Weeks Later*

Whispers float from one townie to another as Stone Bay recuperates from the horrors Charles Yatz brought down on our community. But I'll take those whispers over him breathing air any day of the week.

Cold, I know. But it doesn't make it any less true.

Because now that he is gone, I stroll the sidewalks without fear. I live life without looking over my shoulder.

Warm arms circle my waist as I swallow the coffee dregs in my mug. "Have I mentioned how much I love you in my space?"

Three days after Travis asked me to move in with him, the day after Christmas, the whiny persistence began. If I didn't love him, I would have slapped duct tape over his mouth. I swear, every ten minutes he asked when I'd start packing. And after hours of him driving me up the wall, I said, *"As soon as you get me boxes."*

Within the hour, the bed of his truck was loaded with flat

boxes, packing tape, newspaper, and markers. And he'd enlisted help.

It'd been hard not to laugh.

Thirty-six hours later, every possession I owned was in Travis's house.

Travis's house—*our* house—is a breathtaking work of art on the Emerson estate. A three minute trek on a bumpy gravel drive off a road named for their family: Emerson Avenue.

When we approached the architectural masterpiece on moving day, my jaw hit the steering wheel. Stone and wood and steel with more windows than I'd ever seen on a home. Three stories of sharp angles and space for four or more adults to live comfortably. Tall evergreens bordered and shaded either side of the driveway and boardwalk from the drive to the front door. As for the rest of the house, it was exposed to the sky.

The property—like the other founders' lands—is enormous. Acres upon acres of trees with three homes in its borders. At the heart of the Emerson estate is the main house, a massive structure with seven bedrooms occupied by the eldest Emersons—Gaylord and Doreen Emerson, Travis's paternal great grandparents, and Howard and Angela Emerson, Travis's paternal grandparents. On a separate offshoot of Emerson Avenue is a gravel drive to Roger and Linda's house, a blend of the main house's size and the sharp angles of our house.

Travis's younger brother, Jacob, lives with their parents, while his younger sister, Presley, attends the nursing program at Walla Walla University. I have yet to meet Presley, but Jacob doesn't appear to have a serious bone in his body. As a rookie at the Stone Bay police department, his dad isn't keen on his clownish behavior or lackluster job at the station. But so long as he doesn't pull some prank on me, I'll take his mediocre jokes and goofy faces any day of the week.

"You may have said it once or twice," I tease, peeking over my shoulder. "Have I mentioned how much I love being in your space?"

"Hmm… maybe," he says, voice laced with artificial uncertainty as he fights a smile.

"Well"—I give him a quick kiss—"I do."

"Good." He steps back, smacks my ass, then grabs our empty mugs from the counter and takes them to the sink. "Ready to go, sunshine?"

"Whenever you are."

Travis lets Pepper out to do her business, then we head for the garage. Once the engine is warm, we drive off the property and into town. My eyes lose focus out the passenger window as I stare at the trees and buildings.

Over the last two weeks, Travis, Roger, and Howard have spent several hours at the cabin property. The first few days, Travis kept to himself that the Emerson men were ripping down the shack in the woods and burning every scrap of wood. But when I asked about his long days, he winced as the confession spilled from his lips.

Once the furniture and food and luxuries had been removed from the bunker—all donated to charity outside Stone Bay—Travis said the bunker would be sealed shut. It shocked him when I asked to watch.

But I needed the closure.

The relief I felt as the welding torch was lit, when the flame hit the gap of the bunker hatch… every ounce of suppressed weight lifted off my shoulders in that moment. Tears spilled down my cheeks and I didn't fight them. I welcomed them. And as they hit the forest floor, I pictured them taking every ounce of past pain and suffering.

Sealing that bunker was the catharsis I needed to move forward. To live a normal, happy life.

To open my heart fully and love without hesitation or worry.

Past the inn, on the opposite side of the road, we park at RJ's Diner. Snow dusting the sidewalk, we stomp our shoes before entering the modern dive restaurant.

Two four-tops shoved together, our friends talk animatedly as they wait for us. When I scan their faces, a string tugs at my heart when I land on Levi. More the type to game in the dark or sift through crazy shit on the web, Levi doesn't gather with us often. But when he does, Oliver smiles until it hurts.

I slide into the booth next to Delilah, bump her arm with mine, and lean in close. "He brought Levi?" I whisper.

With a subtle nod and small twist, she mutters, "Total surprise."

Just as the words leave her lips, Oliver leans over the table and narrows his eyes on us. "What was that, ladies?"

My eyes dart from Oliver to Levi, then back to Oliver. Lips pursed, I cock my head and hold his stare for three, two, one. "Sure you want it repeated, Ollie?"

He doesn't blink, doesn't breathe, doesn't move an inch as realization sets in. Then he simply shakes his head and sits back in his seat on the other side of Delilah. "Nah, I'm good."

I chuckle and turn my attention across the table. After greetings are exchanged, our favorite server, Sandi, sidles up to the table and we order a mountain of Ray Jr.'s mouthwatering dishes and warm drinks to stave off the winter chill.

Creamy chicken and herb dumpling chowder for yours truly. The Pit Master burger—thank goodness Oliver and Levi decide to share—is topped with cheese, BBQ sauce, crispy bacon, baked beans, and cornbread-battered onion rings. Lawrence orders chili cheese fries with extra cheese and onions, while Skylar gets biscuits with sausage gravy and home fries—because bless places that serve breakfast all day.

Vegan honey butter chick'n biscuit sandwich for Delilah. Though she isn't vegan, she only consumes dairy and eggs from animals. And when Sandi reaches Travis, he orders the healthiest thing on the menu—smoked salmon with brown rice and steamed broccoli.

Sandi walks off with our orders scribbled on a pad of paper, and conversations swirl back to life.

Delilah mentions working more with her family at Sage Whisperer, the metaphysical shop in town. When I ask if she needs more money since I moved out, she assures me she doesn't need the extra income. Like Travis, Delilah's family is one of the Stone Bay Seven. Unlike majority of the founding families, the Foxes don't flash their money or titles. Not since Delilah's grandparents, Zachariah and Amelia Fox, opted for a different way of life. Between the shop and all the properties the Fox family owns, they have more money than they let on.

Though I don't know the full story as to why Zachariah and Amelia decided to raise their children with a different set of values, I love the entire Fox clan for their big and generous hearts.

Goose bumps paint my skin as frigid air gusts from the open door. Rubbing my arms, I shiver and snuggle into Travis's side as he and Lawrence discuss saving for the future.

Delilah sucks in a sharp breath as her body tenses on my right. My eyes flit to hers, Skylar and Oliver also locking onto her pale face. I follow her gaze to the pickup counter and spot a woman with fiery auburn locks.

Phoebe Graves.

The most *in your face*, snippy person in town. The youngest Graves in Stone Bay—another of the founding families. And the woman my dear best friend, Delilah, has crushed on for a decade. Why? I have no fucking clue. It sure as hell isn't for her personality.

Releasing Travis, I give my weight to Delilah. On her right, Oliver mimics the action.

"You alright, Dee Dee?" I ask in a hushed tone.

Eyes locked on Phoebe as she carries a large paper bag and heads for the door, Delilah twists her lips and nods. When Phoebe disappears from view, Delilah's body turns to mush.

Oliver grabs Delilah's head, one hand under her chin and the other on her crown, and places a loud, sloppy kiss on her cheek.

Delilah flails her arms in his direction and tries to pull away. "Ew, Ollie!" She clutches his face, the same as he's doing to her, and shoves. "Get off me, weirdo."

Laughter erupts around the table as Oliver refuses to let go and Delilah tries to free herself. This lasts far longer than necessary, but ends the second Sandi sets plates on the table. Conversations cease as we eat and moan over our meals.

And it is in this moment, as I stare around the table at my closest friends and sexy as hell boyfriend, that gratitude washes over me for all I have. There is nothing good about what happened to my father. Losing him was tragic and is forever tattooed on my soul.

But if Mom had never uprooted us from Smoky Creek to Stone Bay, I wouldn't know a single person at this table. My found family. The most incredible friends I could ever ask for.

I miss Dad like hell. But the love I get from everyone here… it envelops me with constant warmth and heals my tender heart.

"I don't want chicken tenders," a young voice complains from a nearby table.

Every set of eyes at our table shifts to the table closest to the kitchen, where a young boy with dark curls plays a game and not looking at Ray—also known as Tré or Raymond George Calhoun III. The Calhouns aren't a founding family, but the Calhoun and Kemp families garner almost the same level of respect as the Stone Bay Seven.

"Well, what *do* you want? Papa RJ gets upset when we waste food," Ray says with a sigh, shoulders slumping forward.

The boy slams the game down, his entire face tightening as he looks up at Ray. "Fine, *Dad*. I'll eat the stupid chicken."

"You're welcome, Tucker." Ray does some royalty hand flourish, then hinges at the hips and bows. "So happy I pleased his highness." And then he disappears into the kitchen.

Skylar leans across the table and cups her mouth. "Can't believe Ray's ex abandoned their kid," she whispers. "Ray Sr. says the whole family has been trying to undo all the shit his mom did to him." She sits back, loads her fork with home fries, and slathers them with sausage gravy. "Sad." She nods. "Hope he heals soon."

The whole table hums in agreement.

Though we all haven't found happy endings yet, I sense a shift on the horizon. Something else brewing in this affluent small town.

Question is... which of my friends will get their happily ever after next?

# BONUS CONTENT

## TRAVIS

*August—Four Years Later*

"Think there's enough food?" Kirsten slides a zucchini chunk on the end of the skewer, then sets it on the mountain of vegetable kebabs ready for the grill.

My eyes scan the kitchen counters, not an inch of free space to be found. Platters and large bowls piled high with a rainbow of fresh fruit, raw veggies and several dips, chips with salsa and guacamole, caprese pasta salad, and a sweet Asian coleslaw. Sheet pans loaded with grill-ready food—burgers, mojo chicken, jerk shrimp kebabs, vegetable kebabs, and foil-wrapped corn cobs slathered in oil, herbs, and spices. Smoked Arctic Char, Muktuk, and Bannock on a small pan to be warmed in the oven.

And let's not forget the drink bar near the pool.

When we sent out invites for the party, we asked everyone to bring a dish, something small, and we'd provide the rest. Obviously, none of us understand small.

Rubbing the back of my neck, I chuckle. "Yeah, sunshine, there's plenty." I pick up the pan of meat for the grill and tip my head toward the sliding glass doors. "Let's join everyone." Sliding the door open, I point to the pan in front of her. "Bring that with you."

Ten feet out the door, Tucker whizzes past us, launches into the air as he reaches the edge of the pool, tucks his knees to his chest, and cannonballs into the pool. The second he surfaces, Ray reads him the riot act about barreling through people. Tucker rolls his eyes and gives the goofiest apology. But I expect nothing less from a preteen.

"Go." I kiss her temple after she sets the pan on the outdoor kitchen counter. "Mingle. Get a drink, park on a lounger, and soak up the sun."

Kirsten sticks out her bottom lip in the cutest fucking pout. "Don't want my help, oh mighty grill master?"

I close the distance between us, snake my arms around her waist, and suck her bottom lip between mine. "Nah, baby." Chest to chest, my hands drift down and cup her ass. Releasing her lip, I inch back. "Don't want the food to burn." I swat her ass, then dive from her reach.

"Ha ha." She doesn't attempt to chase me. Instead, she waves me off. "Fine. I'll go where people value my presence."

Firestorm that my woman is, she sashays across the deck, peeks over her shoulder, and blows me a kiss. Tied at her hip, the sheer red sarong does nothing to hide the supple curves of her ass. I all but drool as she fills a cup with sangria. If I were insecure in our relationship, I would have begged Kirsten not to wear her new crimson bikini—a cage, backless top and thong bottom.

But I'm a lucky son of a bitch.

I love Kirsten with the fire of a hundred suns and, without a doubt, she loves me just as fiercely.

So instead of giving her a hard time for flaunting so much skin while we have company, I stare after her with a devilish smile on my face. Kirsten Sparks is mine, and not a damn thing will change that fact. Only reason she put on the sarong today is because our parents and siblings will be here in an hour.

"Need a hand?" Ray sidles up to me at the grill as I add the chicken and corn cobs.

I point tongs at his chest. "For the umpteenth time, I'm not making seductive food videos with you," I tease.

A loud snort-laugh rips from his chest. "Pssh. As if you could replace Fin."

On a fake gasp, I press a hand to my chest. "That hurts, man." A second later, laughter bursts from us both. "Jokes aside, I appreciate your kitchen expertise."

Black hair secured in a braid down her back, Kaya joins us. Her arctic blue two-piece bathing suit is modest, covering yet accentuating her curvy body. The bright color pops against her light brown skin.

She snakes an arm around Ray's waist, his arm wrapping around her shoulders and hauling her closer. "We can warm the Char, Muktuk, and Bannock on the grill. Just wrap it in foil and set it on the top shelf, away from the flame."

"Wasn't sure," I say. "It's one thing to burn someone's burger. But messing up cultural dishes…" I tip my head to Ray. "I'll let him run that show."

Ray bends at the knees, his expression serious as he holds Kaya's gaze. "Have I ruined any of your family's recipes?"

"Never," she says with a bright smile. Ray opens his mouth, probably to gloat, but Kaya holds up a hand and cuts him off. "But that's probably because *I* do most of the work."

Laughter rips from my chest as I flip the chicken and corn over and add the burgers.

Kaya pats his chest, kisses his shoulder, and slinks out of his embrace. "Be right back."

I focus on the chicken and burgers while Ray grabs a second set of tongs and helps with the rest.

Music and chatter and laughter marry together as we soak up the August sunshine. Smoky and sweet drift through the air, the occasional *How much longer?* asked as we remove food from the grill. Oliver threatens to toss Delilah and Phoebe in the pool, while Levi promises he will rescue them. Maddox whispers something in Emery's ear while they recline on the double lounger beneath a canopy, a wicked smile on his face, while she covers her mouth with a hand and shakes her head.

As I open my mouth to tell everyone it is time to eat, my family and Kirsten's wander out onto the deck. After a round of greetings and hugs, everyone files into the kitchen, grabs a plate, and loads up.

With the end of summer right around the corner, I used it as an excuse to have this get-together. Not that we wouldn't be able to coordinate something when the school year begins and some of our friends are busier. If we want to have everyone over, we make it happen.

But I have an ulterior motive for this party. And several in attendance are fully aware.

Seated around the lengthy live edge banquet table on the deck, we talk about summer trips and the town quieting down once school starts up. Phoebe sparks heated conversation when she mentions taking over the Stone Bay Gazette in the next few years as her father takes a step back and semi-retires.

As the sun edges closer to the horizon and our plates empty, I take a moment to breathe and gather my thoughts.

*This is it, Emerson. The moment you've been counting down to for months.*

As if my father senses the shift in my demeanor, he nudges my foot beneath the table. I shift my gaze to his and find a subtle smile on his lips. *"Proud of you,"* he mouths, then imperceptibly nods.

Three words. Simple to so many, but impactful to me, especially from Roger Emerson.

The first time I heard those words from him, I swore I misheard him. But since the bunker incident, Dad has been more forthcoming with affection and declarations.

Hearing them never gets old.

The backs of my eyes sting as I smile and give a single nod. *"Thanks, Dad,"* I mouth back.

Running a hand over the pocket of my board shorts, I take a deep breath, scoot my chair back, and rise.

Kirsten stops talking to Skylar and looks up at me, brows slightly pinched. "Everything okay?"

Perspiration dampening my skin, I nod then turn my attention to everyone at the table. "Excuse me, everyone. May I have your attention for a moment."

The few unaware of what is about to happen look at me with confusion or curiosity. Everyone else bites back a smile or takes a drink.

"Wanted to thank you all for coming out today and enjoying the last bit of summer." I shove my hands in my pockets, my pulse soaring in my veins as my fingers wrap around the engagement ring in my right pocket. "But summer was just an excuse to gather our friends and family today."

"What?" Kirsten mutters, confusion evident in her tone, as she sets her fork down.

At the opposite end of the table, Ben smiles and lifts his chin in my direction, his wife, Dylan, curling into his side. Odd as it felt to receive their wedding invitation last year, the moment Kirsten and I saw them together at their engagement party, I knew Ben had found his person.

Peering down at Kirsten, I chuckle. "Sunshine, you didn't

find it odd that I wanted to have a pool party in the middle of August?"

Her lips twist as her brows scrunch impossibly closer. "No?" she answers questioningly. "We have a great pool. And it's summer."

At this, everyone laughs.

"We do, and it is." I bend and kiss her crown. Then, I push my chair back farther, pull the ring from my pocket, and squat down beside her, presenting the ring. "This," I say, "is the reason for the party."

Kirsten gasps as her hand covers her mouth.

Nestled between two rose gold bands, a radiant cut, two-carat canary diamond appears to float in the setting. Embellishing both bands front to back are four dozen canary diamond chips. The moment I laid eyes on the ring, I knew it belonged on Kirsten's finger. And when I saw the way it sparkled in the sunlight... I'd never handed my card faster to a clerk in my life.

"Not a day goes by I'm not grateful for you. Your infectious smile and flirty words give me life and keep me on my toes."

Skylar snort-laughs.

"For a long time, I had difficulty trusting people. I feared being vulnerable. I refused to accept that not everyone was out to hurt me. But seeing your smile every morning as I took my seat at the counter gave me new life. And somehow, over the years, you'd wiggled your way in, latched onto my heart, and showed me what love really was."

Tears rim her eyes as she sniffles into her hand.

"I love you, Kirsten Kaylee Sparks. So damn much. And I'd be honored to call you my wife, if you'll have me." The last words get knocked out of me as Kirsten falls from her chair and tackles me to the ground.

"Yes!" she shrieks as I band my arms around her. "Hell yes!"

Cheers sound around us as I hug the air from her lungs and she smothers me in kisses. I sit us up, frame her face with my hands, and break the kiss, laughing when she pushes out her bottom lip.

Inching back, I reach for her left hand and slide the ring on her finger. And like her, it radiates brighter than the sun.

Eyes locked on hers, I tuck a lock of hair behind her ear. "Love you, sunshine."

"Love you too, Trav."

And then she kisses me as if no one is watching.

# EMERSON
## family tree

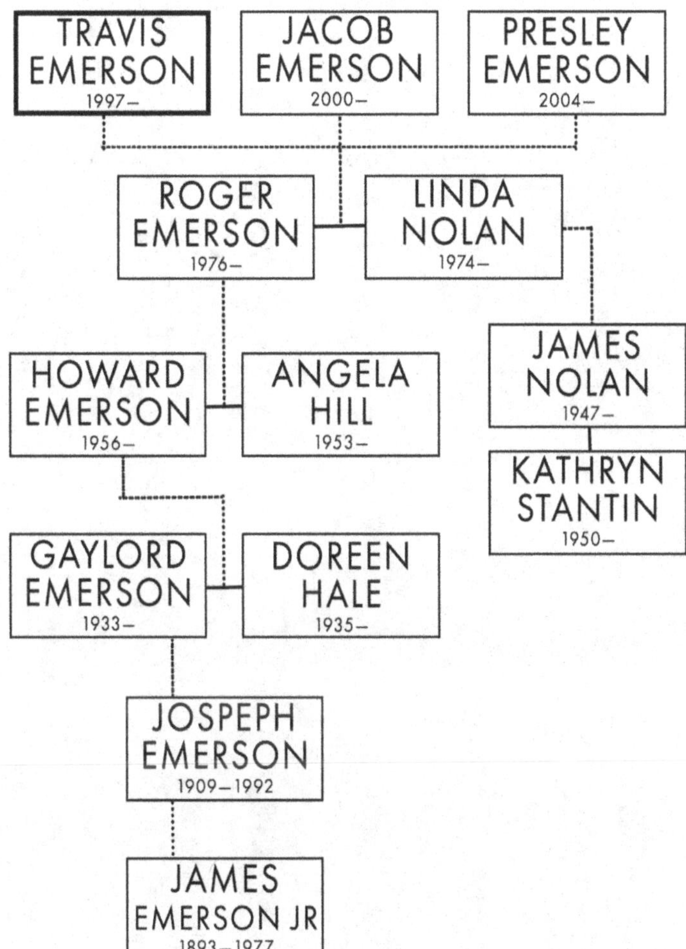

### Broken Sky

Their eyes meet across the bar, but she looks away first. Does her best to give him zero attention. But when he crowds her on the dancefloor, she can't deny the instant chemistry. After one night together, he marks her as his. Unfortunately, another woman thinks he belongs to her.

### Depths Awakened

A small town romance which captivates you from the start. Mags and Geoff are two broken souls who have sworn off love. Vowed to never lose anyone else. But their undeniable attraction brings them together and refuses to let go.

### One Night Forsaken

One night. No names. No romance. Just fun. Nothing more—at least, that's what she tells herself. Until he appears in her coffee shop months later with that addictive smile. She swore off commitment. He vows to never love again. But the more they fight it, the more life brings them together.

### Every Thought Taken

As young children, an unshakable friendship brought them together. As teens, they discovered an undeniable love. Then life pulled them in different directions—into darkness and light—and slowly ripped them apart. Years later, he returns home in the hopes of a second chance with his first love and to conquer the demons of his past.

### Distorted Devotion

Free-spirited Sarah lives life to the fullest. When a new love interest enters her life, she starts receiving strange gifts and letters. She doesn't want to relinquish her freedom or new love, but fears the consequences.

## Undying Devotion

A long-term couple with a secret life. Their friends envy the bond they share, but remain oblivious to their lifestyle and how deep the bond lies. A turn of events has her wanting to spill every secret.

## Darkest Devotion

At an underground rave, the last thing either plans is a hook up. When he takes her home the next day, an unexpected confrontation threatens to keep them apart.

## Transcendental

A musician in search of his muse and a woman grieving the loss of her husband. Two weeks at an exclusive retreat and their connection rivals all others. Until she leaves early without notice. But he refuses to give up until he finds her again.

## The Click Duet

High school sweethearts torn apart. When fate gives them a second chance, one doesn't trust they won't be hurt again. Through the Lens (Click Duet #1) and Time Exposure (Click Duet #2) is an angsty, second chance, friends to lovers romance with all the feels.

## The Inked Duet

A man with a broken heart and a woman scared to put herself out there. Love is never easy. Sometimes love rips you apart. Fine Line (Inked Duet #1) and Love Buzz (Inked Duet #2) is a second chance at love, single parent romance with a pinch of angst and dash of suspense.

## The Insomniac Duet

He was her high school bully. She was the outcast that secretly crushed on him. More than ten years later, he's her boss, completely oblivious to their shared past, and wants no one but her. More importantly, he doesn't understand her animosity toward him.

## The Artist Duet

A tortured hero with the biggest heart and a charismatic heroine with the patience of a saint. Previous heartache has him fighting his desire to be more than friends with her. But she is everywhere, and he can't help but give in. The Artist Duet is an angsty, friends to lovers slow burn.

# PLAYLIST

Here are some of the songs from the **Shattered Sun** playlist.
You can find and listen to the entire playlist on Spotify!

Boyfriend | Dove Cameron
Love In The Dark | Leroy Sanchez
War Of Hearts | Ruelle
Hands | ORKID
Lost My Mind | Alice Kristiansen
Him | Isak Danielson
Hide and Seek | Klergy, Mindy Jones

# CONNECT WITH PERSEPHONE

**<u>Connect with Persephone</u>**
www.persephoneautumn.com

**<u>Subscribe to Persephone's newsletter</u>**
www.persephoneautumn.com/newsletter

**<u>Join Persephone's reader's group</u>**
Persephone's Playground

**<u>Follow Persephone online</u>**

instagram.com/persephoneautumn
facebook.com/persephoneautumnwrites
tiktok.com/@persephoneautumn
bookbub.com/authors/persephone-autumn
goodreads.com/persephoneautumn
amazon.com/author/persephoneautumn
pinterest.com/persephoneautumn

## ACKNOWLEDGMENTS

To my family... The way you continue to stand on the sidelines and cheer me on... it's the best feeling ever. You put up with my crazy ideas and obsessive love for all things books. I love you!

Ellie at My Brother's Editor! Let's just say we made it to the other side of this one alive. I'm still sending a million hugs.

Abi of Pink Elephant Designs! You continue to astound me with the covers you deliver, especially when I have no clue what I want 😂 🤷

Danah Logan! Thank you for helping me with the German translations. You were the perfect example of why no one should just take stuff off the internet 😂

To everyone that picks up my books, I love you! Whether Shattered Sun is your first Persephone Autumn book or your 20+ book, I never take a single one of you for granted.

# ABOUT THE AUTHOR

*USA Today* Bestselling Author Persephone Autumn lives in Florida with her wife and psycho cat. A proud mom with a cuckoo grandpup. An ethnic food enthusiast who has fun discovering ways to vegan-ize her favorite non-vegan foods. Most days, you'll find her with a tea latte or fruity concoction in her hand. If given the opportunity, she would intentionally get lost in nature.

For years, Persephone did some form of writing; mostly journaling or poetry. After pairing her poetry with images and posting them online, she began the journey of writing her first novel.

She mainly writes romance and poetry, but on occasion dips her toes in other works. Look for her non-romance publications under P. Autumn.